Gray Paree

Garrett Hutson

Warfleigh Publishing first edition October 2020
This book copyright © 2020 by Garrett B. Hutson
All rights reserved, including the right of reproduction in whole or in part in any form.

Cover design by Stuart Bache

For more information, or to book an event, please contact the author at www.garretthutson.com

Gray Paree, Published in the United States
ISBN 978-1-953846-01-3 (hardcover)
ISBN 978-1-953846-02-0 (paperback)
ISBN 978-1-953846-00-6 (eBook)

Part I

1

April 6, 1940

Oliver saw her through the blue haze of cigarette smoke that hung thick in the air of the dimly-lit lounge, and she looked so much like Lisette that he had to look twice. She glided behind the farthest row of tables, following a middle-aged barrel of a man in a three-piece suit. It looked just like her, but in stylish clothes. She wore a dark dress with white polka-dots, and a wide-brimmed hat set at a high angle. *It couldn't be Lisette; she would never dress so bourgeois.*

He stared a few seconds too long, and she caught his eye. He looked away, but not before that spark of recognition hit. It was her, and on the arm of some boor.

He almost missed the cue for his solo, but recovered from his distraction in the nick of time. He put his trumpet to his lips and wailed out several riffs, his fingers flying on the valves. He channeled his hurt and anger into the music, and the jazz benefited. In the audience, toes tapped and heads bobbed.

They often did. The band here at *Le Chien Errant*—The Stray Dog—played the best American hot jazz in Paris.

Terrance, the band leader and pianist, gave Oliver a toothy grin as he crescendoed into the solo's climax. Applause rose from the crowd, and Terrance nodded in appreciation. "Yeah! Yeah!" he shouted in English.

1

Oliver raised his arm to acknowledge the applause, then put his trumpet back to his lips and joined the rest of the band in the chorus. He kept his eyes focused on Terrance.

The song finished with ad libbed flares. The crowd roared its applause, and Terrance beamed. "That's it!" he shouted to his band, then turned to the crowd and bowed.

"*Merci! Merci beaucoup, mes chers amis,*" he said. Though most of the jazz aficionados in this city spoke English, it was always best to address the crowd in their own language, so he continued in French. "We've got something special for you all next. This is the first time we've played this number. I wrote it one snowy night a month ago while I was walking home from my woman's place. I call it 'After Glow.'"

Oliver did his best not to glance Lisette's way while they played the next three numbers, but it was hard not to. From time to time his eyes drifted that direction. Usually, she was smiling and watching Terrance at the piano, but inevitably she looked at him, and their eyes locked. He could feel the heat that used to smolder for him behind those dark eyes, and he could almost imagine it was still there. Then he cursed himself for being so stupid. *She doesn't love you anymore, fool*!

His palms began to sweat as they concluded the last number in the set, and he felt his stomach jump when Terrance announced they were taking a break, and would be back in fifteen minutes. He didn't look up as he gathered his sheet music and slipped backstage. Most of the guys headed for the back door, lighting cigarettes.

Oliver held back, tempted to peek around the curtain. Would she be holding hands with that boor? Would he be nuzzling the side of her neck with his pasty face? Or would his hand be slipping up her thigh and under the hem of her skirt...

His hands fisted at the imagined scene, and he trembled for a moment before shaking his head and storming out the backstage door.

"Hey Oliver, what's eatin' you?" Jerry, the alto saxophonist, asked in English. He was a big, round-faced black man from Chicago, and his voice was deep and resonant.

"Why you ask?"

"Your face, man, it's red as a tomato. And just look at you—your shoulders are all hunched up. What's got to you?"

"Nothing, don't worry about it." Oliver looked down the alley toward the little circle of dim light where the alley met Boulevard de Rochechouart. The glass panes of the street lamp had been painted black in nominal compliance with the blackout that had been in place since war was declared.

'The Phony War,' as the newspapers called it, since no major action had occurred in seven months. Just a few skirmishes and a handful of naval engagements.

"You better shake it off before the next set, brother. We got ourselves a hot crowd in there tonight. Don't be messin' us up now, you hear?"

Oliver looked at the gathered musicians. Their faces were turned toward him, waiting, while cigarette smoke curled around their heads in the chill night air.

"I'll be alright," Oliver said, and looked back down the alley. He took a few deep breaths of cool air, then turned around and went through the door. He walked to the men's room, relieved to find it empty. He bent over the sink and splashed cold water onto his face, then looked up at the mirror.

On the outside he looked put together—shiny silver suit with a narrow black necktie, light brown hair neatly combed and parted on the side—but tonight he didn't feel put together.

"Don't be so damn pathetic," he mumbled to his reflection. He grabbed a towel and dabbed his face before exiting.

He stopped in his tracks in the door, and her big brown eyes looked right into his. He was surprised by the smell of Chanel; she never used to wear perfume.

"Oliver," she said.

He used to love the way she said his name, Oh-lee-vere. It wasn't that anyone else in France pronounced it any differently; it was just the way it seemed to lilt off her tongue.

"Hello Lisette." A thousand times he'd imagined what he would say if he ever ran into her again, and now he couldn't think of a damn word of it.

"How are you?" she asked.

"I'm well enough."

She seemed to sense his awkwardness. Perhaps she was fighting it herself. Either way, she straightened her posture and narrowed her eyes, and her words came hard and fast.

"I didn't mean to come here tonight. It was Jean-Louis's idea. He wanted to come, not me. I tried to suggest other places, but he insisted. He's always wanted to come here, he said, and tonight he wouldn't be dissuaded."

"I understand," Oliver said, even though he didn't.

"I wouldn't have come if I could have helped it," she added in a hurry, redundant.

Oliver stiffened. "I didn't realize you disliked *Le Chien Errant* that much. I always thought you enjoyed coming here." *When we were together*.

"I did—I do enjoy it. I just…" she let her voice trail off.

"Of course. Enjoy the rest of the show." He turned his back on her and marched backstage.

**

A cold wind howled down the street after the club closed at four AM, and Oliver turned up the collar of his jacket and pushed his hands deep into his pockets.

Early April in Paris did not feel like spring time, at least not at night.

He walked down the Boulevard de Rochechouart with the wind at his back, toward the Metro station at the Place Pigalle. The neon lights shone faintly through a thin layer of black paint; he missed their bright gaudiness, and the way they used to shine off the heavy cloud cover, making the cold gray sky glow a deceptively warm yellow.

He couldn't get the image of Lisette next to that man out of his head. His fingers wiggled with nervous energy in his pockets. He knew he'd never be able to sleep tonight. He needed a distraction, a soft and warm distraction. He knew *that* would get his mind off Lisette.

But it was too late to call up Hélène. And besides, her husband would probably answer the phone. He thought of some of the girls in his building, but they would all be fast asleep by now. The Pigalle district was notorious for its cat houses, but the thought of fucking some whore didn't satisfy him. That wasn't what he wanted, a quick rut between the sheets and then a cold walk to the Metro.

The train was nearly empty at this hour as it barreled through the dark tunnels toward the Left Bank. He got off at the Sorbonne station in the 5th Arrondissement, and mounted the stairs to street level two at a time. The street was deserted, and even the wide Boulevard St. Germain was quiet. He turned two corners and went another half-block to his building, a grimy six-story stone façade much like countless others in this part of Paris.

The hallway was unheated, and he rubbed his hands together before taking the stairs two at a time, up four flights to the fourth floor, and down the hall to his apartment—number 17. He inserted the key into the lock, but paused and glanced back at the stairs.

He could go up one more flight to the top floor. Marcel would be asleep, but he would never complain about being awakened. Not if it meant a warm body in his bed. That wasn't what Oliver wanted tonight, it wasn't his preference—but it wasn't a bad thing, and it might be better than lying in his bed alone stewing about Lisette and that fat swell in the expensive suit.

He hesitated a moment. He'd never not enjoyed it. It could do the trick. *No*, he reasoned. *That's not what I want, not tonight.*

What he wanted was a long, slow lovemaking, with tender kisses and nuzzling his nose into the soft, fragrant skin of a slender neck, followed with falling asleep in each other's arms. Turning the key, he got angry all over again as he realized the neck he was imagining nuzzling, and the arms he imagined around him, were Lisette's.

It's been six fucking months, get over it already.

2

Oliver slept until one o'clock on Sundays, if the chimes of Notre Dame didn't wake him sooner. This Sunday he slept hard, once he finally drifted off sometime around six AM.

He yawned and stretched and scratched his chest. His silver suit lay draped across the back of the chair where he'd left it last night—this morning.

He poured water from the pitcher on the dresser into a bowl and splashed it on his face and neck, then dried with the faded yellow towel. He dressed in brown corduroy pants and a dingy white shirt, a long-sleeved coarse cotton pullover. He looked in the mirror long enough to run a comb through his hair a couple of times, until he looked presentable.

The sun was out this afternoon, providing a break from *le grisaille*, the usual gray Parisian weather. Puffy white clouds dotted the blue sky. He walked next-door to the bistro Chez Marius.

It was warm inside, and the windows were slightly fogged, though he could see through to the sidewalk. He spied his friend Sébastien Bonnet sitting with a book at a table near the back, facing the door. It was a peculiarity of French cafes and bistros that everyone sat facing the door, or toward the street if at a sidewalk table, even when reading. The idea was always to see and be seen.

Sébastien nodded, and Oliver took that as his cue to join the young artist. Sébastien stood, and they kissed each other's cheeks, right then left. On the table sat an apple core, eaten down to its most skeletal remnants.

"*Salut*," Sébastien said, giving the informal French greeting. "Just waking up?"

Oliver confirmed, and ordered a coffee and a *Croque Monsieur*.

"Marcel's not working today?" he asked, nodding toward the departing waiter, an older man who was poorly shaven with unkempt brown hair.

"His day off this week." Sébastien returned his attention to his book.

So he and Marcel could have enjoyed a lazy Sunday in bed, Oliver mused.

"I saw Lisette last night."

Sébastien put his book down on the table, upside down to hold the page; he wore a concerned expression. "*Ouai*?" Yeah?

"It was a little bizarre," Oliver said. "I didn't know what to say. She was there with some rich fellow."

"Did you speak with her?"

Oliver nodded. "She came to see me between sets. Apologized for being there, said it wasn't her decision. The rich guy wanted to try the club."

"What did you say to her?"

Oliver shook his head. "I don't remember," he lied. "Nothing important."

Sébastien nodded. "You've moved on." It wasn't a question. Not expecting an answer, he picked up his book.

"She was dressed very chic," Oliver said. "Nice dress, silk stockings, stylish hat and shoes. Not the Lisette we know."

Sébastien made a grunt, but didn't glance away from his book.

Oliver contemplated Lisette's new look. She'd looked nice, he had to admit. And something in her eyes said she was happy—no, content. Yes, that's what she'd seemed, content. Perhaps her new life suited her better than the old one.

And how could that be? She was happy here in the 5th, with all our friends. We *were happy.*

"Where is everyone?"

Sébastien looked up with a shrug. "Around."

"Usually they're here."

Sébastien stared at him in silence for several seconds with his intense dark eyes. Oliver sometimes wondered what went on behind those dark pools that never revealed anything.

"Adrienne has an audition today at the Theatre over in the 6th. Madeleine is sitting for someone who needed a model at the last minute. I don't know who." He added that last with a dismissive wave of the hand. Some *unknown* artist, therefore not worth his consideration. "Marcel I have not seen today, nor Serge." He returned his attention once again to his book.

"Thanks." The *Croque Monsieur* arrived, and Oliver ate in silence, allowing Sébastien to read without interruption.

After four years in Paris, he was used to this sort of behavior. It was no wonder Anglo-Saxons thought of Parisians as cold and rude, but Oliver had come to see that they lived their lives without the curiosity about others' business that was considered normal to the rest of the world. And they were baffled that anyone should ask such impertinent questions.

He usually found it refreshing. Nosy busybodies had always driven him crazy back home in Indiana. But there were still times he missed that neighborly feeling of knowing what everyone was up to. There was a comforting certainty to that.

Bof. No sense getting sentimental about Indiana when he was sitting in the middle of the greatest city on the planet.

He finished his sandwich and laid a five-franc coin on the table. Bidding Sébastien good bye, he stepped out into the sunshine.

He needed to clear his head. He could go home and get drunk, but a better idea struck him. He walked a few blocks to the Cathedral de Notre Dame de Paris. The church would be devoid of worshipers by now, Mass having ended a couple of hours ago. He could still find a quiet corner to sit.

He looked up at the massive façade, with its great rose window and solid twin towers. Crowds milled around the square in front of the cathedral as he made his way to the doors.

It took a minute for his eyes to adjust to the dim light, and he paused; he stood for several minutes, taking in the grandeur and multi-colored beauty of the sunlight streaming through countless stained glass windows rising a hundred feet on either side of him.

This was the most beautiful man-made place on Earth.

He took a seat near the front. A couple of old ladies kneeled together a few rows in front of him, ticking off beads on their rosaries, but otherwise this section was empty.

Lisette was Catholic, more or less. That had been a sticking point with his parents when he'd written about her. They'd had a hard enough time understanding why he would quit college to be a musician, and run off to New York, then Paris; then to fall in love with "some Catholic French girl"—they had not been as happy for him as he would have liked.

"She'll ask you to convert," his father wrote in response to their engagement. "They're very stringent on that. The priest will insist, in any case."

I'm not going to become Catholic, Dad. He didn't want to be anything anymore, not even Presbyterian. His father was a Presbyterian minister, and Oliver's most enduring act of rebellion was a steadfast refusal to set foot inside a church—present circumstances excepted. An occasional visit to Notre Dame was *de rigueur* to any expatriate living in Paris. Hardly the same thing.

He shifted in the pew, and his mind drifted to their last fight. She'd been nagging him again about the future. He'd never understood the impetus for her sudden nagging last summer. What was wrong with the way things were? They were happy—why couldn't they continue as they were, only married? What more did she want?

He was still baffled by her assertion that he didn't know her at all. How could she say that? He'd spent almost every day with her for two-and-a-half years.

They used to laugh a lot. He also remembered quiet evenings, him reading a book, she with a notebook and a pen writing poetry, and after a while he would slip behind her and nibble her ear until she put her pen down and kissed him. Then they would make love, and collapse into each other's arms. They'd been happy, why couldn't that be good enough?

Maybe she'd been right after all—he didn't understand her.

Hélène, on the other hand—it was easy to know exactly what *she* wanted. There was nothing mysterious about that.

He pushed that from his mind. He hadn't come here to think about his current paramour, enjoyable though she was. He'd come to work out why he couldn't get Lisette from his mind.

Because after six months, he still didn't understand why she left him.

3

Tuesday, April 9

It was oddly comforting to look out his window that morning and see that the overcast sky had returned. The streets of Paris always looked better in gray. He needed that sense of normalcy.

Oliver walked to the bakery down the street for his croissants. Something felt different, but he had no idea what. An older lady walked her little dog on the other side of the street. A couple of men stood talking next to an automobile. A pair of housewives walked together carrying their groceries, their heads leaned close in quiet conversation.

It took Oliver a moment to register that they all seemed a little agitated for some reason. There was something in their expressions, their postures, that said something wasn't right.

When he entered the bakery, there was no one behind the counter. He could hear the muffled sound of a radio broadcast coming from the kitchen. He rang the bell, and the baker's wife hurried out.

"I am sorry, sir. We were listening to the news. There were no customers, so…" she let her voice trail off with an apologetic shrug.

Oliver cocked his head. "What news?"

"You have not heard? The Germans invaded Denmark and Norway this morning. Denmark has already surrendered. In Norway they are fighting, but the broadcast says that the *Boche* have taken all the ports, and the capital Oslo. The Norwegian government has fled to the north."

"Oh!" Oliver counted the months in his head—seven months since the Germans invaded Poland, which was six months after they invaded Czechoslovakia. The pattern was clear. "What is France doing?" Last time, France and Britain declared war—not that much had come of it.

The woman made a grand shrug. "Who knows? The British are landing troops in central Norway. But France?" Another shrug.

Oliver nodded. He supposed the British had more to fear if the Germans got control of airfields in Denmark and Norway.

**

The feeling was the same on the Metro train that afternoon when Oliver went to *Le Chien Errant* for rehearsal. Hushed conversations, tense expressions. He remembered this same feeling last September after the declaration of war.

He wondered if that was why Lisette had become so quarrelsome. It was during that tense time that she'd flung her engagement ring at him and stormed off, never to return.

The band seemed unaffected. All but one of them were Americans, and the lone Frenchman put on a brave face. Terrance might well have been unaware of the news, considering he behaved as he did at any rehearsal. And so they played.

Terrance added some new songs he'd written, and they concentrated on those for most of the afternoon. It took Oliver a while to get his fingers around the complicated riffs, but by five o'clock he'd played it perfectly.

"Yeah! That's the way I want it," Terrance said, beaming. "You fellas ready to add that one to the show?"

"You gonna let us practice it again tomorrow, ain't ya?" the bassist asked.

"Sure, if you play it for me like you just did."

Jerry the saxophonist asked, "Boss, what we gonna do if them Nazis attack France like they did them other countries today?"

Oliver was glad Jerry voiced what everyone was thinking.

Terrance made a face. "Shit, that ain't gonna happen. They got all them fortresses on the border, the Germans be crazy to try and attack the Maginot Line. You fellas concentrate on your jobs, and give the folks a good show, ya hear?"

**

After rehearsal, Oliver went to Shakespeare and Company, the Left Bank's English-language bookstore, owned and operated by the famous—or notorious, depending upon whom you asked—Sylvia Beach. He entered the store and was greeted with a warm smile by the rail-thin proprietress.

"Bonjour, Monsieur Carmichael," the fifty-ish American woman said.

"Bonjour, Mademoiselle Beach," Oliver replied. It was their habit to greet one another in French, though their conversations inevitably switched to English. "How are things?"

"Quiet today."

Oliver nodded. It had been quiet ever since most of the thirty-thousand Americans living in Paris departed in September, on Ambassador Bullitt's advice after the declaration of war. Oliver never considered leaving—he was still engaged to marry Lisette then, and where else would he want to go? Where else but Paris could you be poor and still have the world of art and letters at your doorstep?

"I finished *The Grapes of Wrath*," Oliver said, handing the hardback volume to Miss Beach.

In addition to selling books, Shakespeare and Company loaned them like a library to anyone who paid a small subscription fee. Unlike the matrons at the American Library across the Seine on the Right Bank, Miss Beach didn't censor her collection on moral grounds. This was popular with the students from the nearby Sorbonne. Oliver had been a subscriber for four years.

"And what did you think of Mr. Steinbeck's latest?" she asked with a gleam in her eyes.

"So sad! Very moving, though—I couldn't put it down."

Miss Beach nodded with a satisfied smile. "I knew you'd enjoy it. Will you be taking out something new today?"

"Of course. You wouldn't happen to have anything new by Hemingway, would you?"

"Nothing you haven't already read. I got a letter from Mr. Hemingway a couple of weeks ago, always so nice of him to remember me, and he indicated his next book should come out in the fall. But we have other new titles. Mrs. Christie's new whodunit is here, *And Then There Were None*. I guarantee you won't figure that one out! It was published in the States in January, but I just received it last week."

"I'll give it a try," he said with a shrug. Her books usually made him angry at himself for being caught off guard by the solutions.

"Her best one yet. You'll enjoy it."

As Miss Beach noted the check-out in the ledger, Oliver looked over to the open area where, two years earlier, he'd sat in the audience and listened to Ernest Hemingway give a drunken reading of his short story "Fathers and Sons." It was the first time in his life he had been close to someone world-famous, and Oliver had been a regular at Miss Beach's events ever since.

The books here stirred nostalgia for America, but also reinforced his expatriate snobbery. It annoyed him that so many Americans preferred films to books, including all of his brother Paul's friends— basketball jocks, the lot of them, who had never once cracked a book by Hemingway, Steinbeck, or Faulkner, but who could name every role ever played by Gary Cooper or John Wayne.

The front bell clinked, and he looked over to see Serge Faucheux entering, with Sébastien in tow. They nodded to Oliver's wave, and proceeded to the literary journals section. Serge addressed Miss Beach in French.

"Have you the current edition of *The American Mercury*?"

"Yes sir, it was returned yesterday," Miss Beach replied in flawless French, and showed him the location of H.S. Mencken's journal.

Serge was a young writer with a taste for the *avant garde*, not exactly Oliver's preference. A cultural refugee from a small town far to the south—Montélimar he'd once said—Serge was a strange-looking fellow; tall and rail-thin, his shoulders always slouched; a rat-faced boy with large ears, deep-set closely-spaced hazel eyes, a weak chin, and a huge hooked nose that dominated his otherwise long and narrow face, framed by stringy dark brown hair.

The nose was disturbingly long, and Oliver had heard that same description applied to another part of Serge's anatomy. Lisette once said that Adrienne had told her about it. That explained why most of their friends—Adrienne, Madeleine, Collette, Marie-France, even Sébastien and Marcel—had spent long evenings alone with Serge in his tiny unheated garret. Oliver often saw them emerging from Serge's building—where none of them lived—in the morning as he returned from a night at *Le Chien Errant*. Serge's penchant for intellectual conversation over cheap cognac by itself couldn't explain such long stays into the dead of night.

Sébastien approached. "Many of us are meeting for dinner tonight at Chez Marius, at eight. Will you join us?"

"Yes, of course," Oliver said.

"Good." Sébastien hesitated, seemingly unsure if he wanted to say more.

"Yes?" Oliver asked, eyebrows arched.

Sébastien suddenly smiled, that crooked smile he had that made him look even more boyish than usual, with the right side of his mouth turned up. "It is nothing. See you at dinner."

4

The interior of Chez Marius glowed with warm light, and rang with laughter. Wisps of cigarette smoke rose from the tables, and collected at the ceiling in a blue-gray haze. It was not crowded; Oliver and six friends around the large table in the back were half the clientele that evening.

They were a bit of a rag-tag group, four young women and three young men, their clothes generally faded and worn, and of the young men in attendance Oliver was the only one who seemed familiar with the use of a comb. Serge's fingernails were permanently stained black at the ends by the ink he worked with at a printing shop.

They were a picture in contrasts. Madeleine's flaming red hair contrasted with Collette's blond and everyone else's brunette. Collette was curvy and busty, in sharp distinction to Madeleine's androgynous frame. Adrienne was petite and dark; Oliver tall and fair. Sébastien was handsome and boyish; Serge anything but.

The only things they seemed to have in common were their youth and apparent poverty. Dinner for all of them consisted of two shared baguettes, a large cheese plate, a bowl of endive salad, and two bottles of cheap red wine.

Marcel stood beside the kitchen door in his uniform of black clothes and white apron. The curly-haired young man appeared to ignore them, though Oliver knew he hung on their every word.

They debated the relative merits of Sartre vs. de Beauvoir. Oliver had read both of them, but only in English; he'd never been brave enough to tackle existentialist thought in French. And while he had opinions, he didn't get as passionate about them as Serge.

"A toast to Serge," Sébastien said, raising his glass. "He has found someone crazy enough to publish that novella he's been working on for two years."

"To Serge!" they echoed, clinking their glasses. Oliver grinned at his rat-faced friend.

"How did you do it?" Marie-France asked.

Serge gave a big shrug of false modesty. "I met the publisher at *Les Deux Magots* last week, and convinced him to read my manuscript."

"As simple as that?"

Adrienne nudged Marie-France with an elbow and gave the group a conspiratorial smile. "He heard the man frequents *Les Deux Magots*, and so he went there to write every day for two weeks until he could get a table next to his. Then he stepped on the man's foot for an excuse to talk to him!"

They laughed. Serge shrugged again, and took a long drag on his cigarette.

"And to me also!" Adrienne said, raising her glass and her chin, a proud smile spreading across her lips. "Today I was cast as a lead dancer in *Les Follies*. It pays better than the chorus, so I can finally quit that horrible cleaning job at the Hotel Trémont."

"To Adrienne!" Sébastien said, and they clinked their glasses again and drank. "Just don't let the success go to your heads, either of you."

Adrienne waved her hand dismissively. "*Bof*! The pay is not *that* much better. I won't forget where I have been. And besides, I am not like Lisette, wanting the fancy new wardrobe with a different dress for every day of the week, as if she were more than a shop-girl selling wine. And all of those hats, my God!"

Oliver's attention snapped her way. "You've seen Lisette?"

For a few seconds Adrienne looked sheepish. But then Gallic defiance set in, her mouth set into a firm line, and she squared her shoulders and raised her chin.

"Yes. We are still friends. She bought me lunch last week. I see her regularly."

"Regularly?" His brow furrowed in irritation.

Sébastien interrupted. "Do you all remember my friend Franz, the Swiss artist who stayed with me for a few months three years ago?" Oliver scowled at his blatant change of subject.

Collette's blue eyes lit up. "Of course! We haven't seen him in at least a year."

Sébastien gave her a crooked grin.

"I don't believe I've met him," Oliver said.

"No, I believe you haven't," Sébastien agreed. "The last time he was here for a holiday, you were spending all your time with Lisette."

Oliver's stomach clenched for a second. "You're probably right."

"I received a telegram from him today. He wants to come for a holiday this month. I think a welcome celebration is in order. We can host it at my studio."

The conversation drifted to politics.

"Reynaud is no better than Daladier," Serge said, referencing the Prime Minister and his predecessor, who was now Minister of Defense. "They won't cooperate, and so nothing will ever happen. The idiots!"

Murmurs of agreement met his pronouncement. Oliver said nothing. He had few opinions about French politics.

Sébastien shook his head. "Daladier's only fault was his passivity, his willingness to appease Hitler for peace. Reynaud is the idiot. He was in power only a few days before he eliminated the forty-hour work week."

"*All* of the men who run France are idiots because they oppose women's suffrage!" Adrienne declared. This received hearty agreement from Collette, Madeleine, and Marie-France.

Serge ignored them, and continued to argue with Sébastien. "Eliminating the forty-hour week was a travesty—but you cannot say that Daladier was a friend to the workers. The last true friend the workers had in the government was Blum."

Oliver chuckled. He'd heard Serge and Sébastien debate these points before. Serge was a Socialist, like former Prime Minster Leon Blum. Blum was replaced two years ago by Edouard Daladier, of the center-left *Parti Radical*—the name a legacy of the 19th century when liberalism was radical—the party to which Sébastien belonged.

It amused Oliver that the Radicals and Socialists were coalition partners, yet they never seemed to agree on anything. *So very French.*

*

As the others put on their coats and moved toward the door, Collette hopped into the chair next to Oliver. She put her hand on his thigh, and he felt the warmth radiate up his leg. She leaned in, and her bust brushed his arm. Her voice was soft and low, her breath warm against his ear.

"I know it has been difficult for you these past months. I'm still available to talk any time you'd like. Or, we don't have to talk." She gave his thigh a squeeze before withdrawing her hand and sitting back up.

Oliver looked into her eyes. "We can talk here."

She smiled and shrugged. "Yes, we can. Then, who knows?"

"You seemed excited about this Franz fellow from Switzerland coming to visit."

She twirled a lock of her blonde hair around a finger. "Why wouldn't I be? *Oh la la*! Franz is a dear. And a wonderful lover." She glanced at Marcel within ear-shot, then leaned close and continued in a lower voice. "The night I spent with him and Sébastien together—my God! The most incredible night. Franz is very talented. And so attentive—to both of us, I'm sure you guessed."

Oliver shrugged, not surprised.

A sly gleam came to her eye. "I invited you to join me and Sébastien once, but you declined. Too soon after Lisette? It couldn't have been because of Sébastien—we all know about you and Marcel."

Oliver's stomach dropped. He forced a smile. Of course they knew—Collette's garret shared a wall with Marcel's, and Sébastien was a regular visitor of hers. If they hadn't seen him entering or leaving Marcel's room at one time or another, they had heard things through the wall.

But Marcel's body was so androgynous that Oliver could almost ignore that he was not female. It had been their fourth encounter before Oliver could bring himself to reach around and touch the young man's penis. Sébastien, on the other hand, was not androgynous. But how could he explain that?

"I don't really like the *ménage a trois*," he lied.

"*Bof*!" Collette waved her hand dismissively. "We both know that is not true. You've had more than one woman in your bed at the same time. But that was before Lisette."

"Yes, it was before Lisette."

"That is not what I'm proposing now." She put her hand back on his thigh.

He smiled in spite of himself, and his eyes rested on her large breasts. He couldn't deny the twitch between his legs. Then he looked up into her eyes with an apologetic expression. "I already have a new lover."

She didn't remove her hand. "So I surmised. There are nights that you don't come home until daylight. For many months."

"Yes." He had to give her credit for being observant. He knew he shouldn't be surprised—while none of them broadcast their romantic liaisons, there were no real secrets.

"I am not proposing to replace your lover, Oliver." She leaned in even closer, and her breasts pressed fully against his arm. "But an occasional visit would be lovely, would it not?"

He swallowed hard, and he leaned forward and pressed his thighs closer together in a vain attempt to hide his growing erection. "Yes, it would." The words croaked, his throat had gone dry.

"We could stay at your place, if you're worried that Marcel might get jealous," she whispered, and her breath made a tingle run up the side of his neck.

He took another look into her blue eyes, so intense with yearning, and had to resist the temptation to kiss her then and there.

What the hell did it matter, anyway? This was Paris, damn it! He put his hand on top of hers. "Let's go."

*

Oliver walked Collette up the four flights to his floor, when she suddenly leaned in and kissed him on the mouth—soft, her lips parted slightly, briefly, a hint—and then she pulled away with a smile and turned back to the stairs, her hips swaying as she climbed the last flight.

"I'll be down in fifteen minutes," she said over her shoulder.

Oliver jammed the key into the lock, nearly tripping over his feet in his haste to get inside.

A telegram lay on the floor, where it had slid under the door. It was posted from the 16th Arrondissement, and he could guess what it said before he read it.

MY DEAR OLIVER, STOP
I WILL BE ALONE TOMORROW EVENING. STOP
I WOULD ENJOY YOUR COMPANY. STOP
AFFECTIONATELY, H.C.

Her husband would be staying with his mistress, so Hélène wanted him to come. And he always did.

But he wouldn't think about that tonight. He hid the telegram in a drawer and hurried to tidy up before Collette arrived.

He rushed around, taking the dirty coffee cups and bread plates from the sink and hiding them in a cabinet with the clean ones. He straightened the pile of discarded newspapers in the corner of the main room. He wiped the crumbs off the tabletop into the palm of his hand, and threw them into the trashcan. Taking a quick glance around the room, he nodded. *Good enough.*

He rushed into the bedroom, tugging off his shirt. He shoved it in the dresser, followed by his pants. His shoes and socks soon found their way under the bed, and he stood in his boxer shorts. He yanked his bathrobe off the hook on the back of his bedroom door, replacing it with his silver suit from the back of the chair. He slipped the robe on and tied it around the waist, hurrying back into the main room to light the pair of candles on the table.

He had just a moment to stand still and catch his breath before she knocked on the door.

She stood in the hallway wearing a coat, but he noticed her legs were bare. He motioned for her to come in.

"Ooo, it's warm in here," she said, rubbing her hands together. She slipped out of her shoes and pushed them together with her toe. She seemed short in her bare feet.

He offered her a glass of wine, and she agreed with a smile, so he excused himself to pour some. He uncorked a half-empty bottle of a cheap red *vin de pays* from his cupboard, and poured two glasses.

When he returned from the little kitchen with the glasses, she was standing in the middle of his living room with her coat open to reveal her naked form underneath. She slipped it off her shoulders.

Her body was soft and curvy and white, Rubenesque, with wide hips and large breasts. He stared.

Collette took a few steps toward him and he gave her a glass. She sipped, then set it down on the table. She untied the front of his bathrobe and slipped inside, pressing her body against his and turning her face up to reach his lips.

They kissed for a long time, soft and slow at first, with barely parted lips; then more urgently, with open mouths and entwining tongues. She pushed his robe off his shoulders, and slipped her hand down the front of his boxer shorts and took hold of his erect penis, murmuring appreciation.

He pulled away from her embrace long enough to tug down his shorts, then buried his face between her breasts, inhaling the scent of her soft skin. Her head fell back and she moaned as he squeezed her breasts, then gasped when his tongue began to play with a nipple.

She took his hand and led him to the bedroom, then guided his hand between her legs as she lay back on the bed. She gasped at the movements of his fingers, and took hold of his penis again.

For a second, images of Lisette crossed his mind. He banished them, and rolled on top of Collette.

5

Wednesday, April 10

Oliver rang the doorbell of the enormous townhouse, and through the cut glass in the door he recognized Hélène's figure descending the stairs. She smiled when she opened the door.

"My dear Oliver, so good of you to join me this evening." She kissed his cheeks and took his coat. She looked stunning in a green evening gown, long and elegant, with a slit up one side and a moderately low back. Her hair, nearly as much gray as dark brown, was shiny and curled. "Dinner is ready for us in the dining room. I hope you won't mind the every-day china."

Oliver smiled and shook his head. Hélène was always the impeccable hostess.

She guided him into the large dining room, with its long table of dark cherry, big enough for ten, but set for two. The lights in the chandelier had been dimmed, and two long white candles burned, framing the two place settings. She removed the covers from the plates, and steam rose.

"Please have a seat," she said, taking the chair at the head of the table. Oliver took the seat next to hers, and she took his napkin and laid it in his lap, letting her eyes linger on his as she did. Then she returned to hostess mode and reached for the uncorked bottle of wine, a '36 Bordeaux, and poured his glass first before pouring her own.

"*Salut*, my dear," she said, raising her glass to him. He raised his in return, and they drank. "I believe you like veal, do you not?"

"Yes, of course," Oliver said.

They chatted amiably while they ate, and she poured him more wine the moment his glass was empty. She asked about his performances at *Le Chien Errant*, and listened attentively as he described the latest music Terrance had given them. With Hélène, he felt that his life and his music were the most interesting topics in the world.

He needed that.

They lingered long after the plates were empty, even after the wine was empty, and lounged in their chairs.

He asked if she and her husband—Jacques Chastain, a government bureaucrat of some type—planned to visit *Le Chien Errant* again in the near future. That was where they met last fall, during an intermission when Oliver went to the bar for a drink, and she sidled up to him. Her husband had stepped outside to discuss business with some industrialists they'd come with, and Hélène sought Oliver out. The conversation ended ten minutes later with her address slipped into his pocket, and an invitation to call on her the following Wednesday night.

She didn't answer, just stared into his eyes. He arched an eyebrow at her, and she started as if awakened from a dream.

"I'm sorry my dear, what were you saying?" Her hand went to his knee.

He looked down, his eyes following her hand as it slid slowly up his thigh. "Nothing."

She held his eyes, and her smile grew until she finally nodded her head in the direction of the door and took his hand. She led him upstairs.

Thursday, April 11

Lisette sat at the edge of her bed and buttoned her blouse. Behind her, Jean-Louis stood on the other side of the bed, tugging up his trousers and tucking in his shirt.

"I would like to take you to the Opéra on Saturday," he said, pulling his suspenders over his shoulders. "You enjoyed it last time, did you not?"

"Yes, I did." She replied, turning to face him as he sat next to her.

"Excellent! We'll go to the Opéra at eight, and then supper at the Bistro Bofinger at ten-thirty. Then I can stay overnight with you here." He put a hand on her shoulder. "I should buy you something special that you can wear to the performance. Some new earrings, perhaps? Diamond earrings. Would you like that, my love?"

She smiled at him. "That is very kind of you, Jean-Louis, but it is really not necessary. I can wear the pearls you bought me last month, and the earrings that go with them."

"Nonsense! You wore those the last time we went out. The Opéra always calls for something new. Diamonds are just the thing— earrings and a matching pendant."

"What if we see someone you know?"

"What if we do? They would never be so tactless as to approach us. Some of them will no doubt be with *their* mistresses."

Lisette nodded. "I wish you could stay tonight."

"So do I. But I have a dinner party to attend, at the home of an important business associate. Many important people will be there. I cannot send my regrets. And I must take my wife with me. You understand."

"Yes, of course."

He smiled and patted her cheek. "You will miss me. Fear not, I will be with you again in two days." He leaned down and kissed her, then put on his suit coat and walked from the room.

She followed him out of the bedroom, and waited as he put on his overcoat and picked up his hat. At the door, he turned and kissed her one more time, wished her a good evening, and left.

Lisette walked into the little kitchen and poured herself a glass of wine. She stood for a moment staring at the wall, then picked up the glass and downed the contents.

What a fool she'd been! Oliver may have been unambitious, but he had been completely devoted to her without other—entanglements.

She scolded herself. It wasn't her fault Oliver refused to grow up. Her father had even offered him a job—a good job, that would support a family—but he wouldn't take it. He chose his trumpet and that damn club over a secure future. *Their* future. He could be so damned stubborn! No, she did what she had to.

She poured herself another glass of wine, and carried it into the living room. She sat on the couch and pulled her feet up under her. She opened the book she'd been reading, but couldn't concentrate. A few minutes later she set it down and leaned back, sipping her wine and letting her thoughts wander.

Adrienne told her she was selling out to bourgeois standards that were artificial, frivolous, and stupid. Lisette smiled to herself. She could always count on Adrienne's honesty. She admired and appreciated that, how Adrienne wouldn't hold back her honest opinion of everything and everyone. Adrienne didn't mean to be brutal, she was just direct. Deep down, Adrienne cared deeply—otherwise she and Lisette wouldn't have stayed friends after Lisette moved away from their neighborhood. And Adrienne never held back her feelings regarding Lisette's relationship with Jean-Louis.

"You know I do not judge you for sleeping with a married man," she told Lisette at their most recent lunch—as if Lisette would've ever thought such a thing. "God knows I have slept with several married women, and a few married men. But that is not for you, Lisette. You know this is true. You want to marry and have children, and you can never have this with that bourgeois pig."

Lisette hadn't meant for it to happen. She'd known Jean-Louis as a customer at the store for a long time. He had flirted with her shamelessly, and she flirted back from time to time—but that was harmless. After she broke off with Oliver, Jean-Louis must have sensed her sadness and vulnerability, and he asked her to lunch. She refused at first, but he insisted. He took her to a nice bistro on the Champs-Elysee, and afterward took her to a hotel. She still wasn't sure how he talked her into it. He was so nice to her, and so complimentary of her beauty—and the next thing she knew they were in bed together.

She told herself it would only be the one time, but he kept coming to the store and flirting with her, and then he asked her to dinner. She refused, and the next time he came to the store he brought her a little box of chocolates. She let him take her to dinner, and they ended up in the same hotel. It just went from there.

She asked him once if he worried his wife would find out.

"She knows," he said. "She always knows."

"Always?"

He chuckled. "Yes, always. You are not the first, dear. I tell her that I am not going to be home, and she knows what it means. But of course, she has her own lover. She's been seeing the husband of her friend Elise for two years."

"Does that bother you?"

"Why should it? We are not going to have any more children, and she is a good wife. I provide for her and the children, so what is she to complain about? She is happy, I am happy, we are good friends when we are together—what is there to bother anyone?"

Lisette knew it wasn't an uncommon arrangement. Still, it was not one she had considered for herself. She had taken casual lovers when she was at the university—that was normal. She even experimented once with Adrienne. But when she was seeing someone regularly she did not stray, and expected the same from him. She and Oliver had been—

Stop comparing this to Oliver! *It is not the same thing.*

She needed to get out of the apartment. The thing she disliked most about the evenings when Jean-Louis came over for an hour or two was then she had the rest of the night by herself. She had friends, but she didn't make plans with them when she knew Jean-Louis would be coming over.

She got up from the couch and marched to the bureau in the corner. She removed a phone directory from the drawer and flipped through it until she found the listing. She picked up the receiver of her telephone—Jean-Louis had insisted she have a telephone, so that he could reach her when he wanted—and dialed the number.

"*Cinema.*"

"Yes, what is the film you are playing this evening?"

**

Oliver was surprised by the knock on his door. It was quarter to one in the morning. He'd been home a short while—the club closed at midnight on Thursdays—and was reading a book with a glass of wine to wind down.

He opened the door to find Marcel standing at the threshold. "I thought you might be lonely," the young man said, his brown eyes staring intently at Oliver.

"I was reading before bed."

"You haven't come to see me in a while."

"It hasn't been that long," Oliver said. "I came up on Easter Monday, remember? It rained that night, and we listened to the water rushing in the gutters beside your window."

"That was more than two weeks ago."

Oliver counted back in his head. Yes, it had been seventeen days. He didn't have a reason he hadn't been up to Marcel's garret since then—he just hadn't.

"May I come in?"

Oliver stared at Marcel. His youthful face was expressionless, and his intense gaze gave away nothing—but he had never asked to come in before. Oliver always went up to him.

"Yes, of course," he finally said, stepping aside and letting Marcel in. "I just got home from work a few minutes ago."

"I know." Marcel continued to stare at him with that unreadable expression.

"Would you like some wine?"

"No, thank you."

Oliver wondered what was going on behind those deep brown eyes. The nineteen-year-old was a man of few words. Even when Oliver paid him a visit, they usually got right to business with little said, and it was Oliver who did most of the talking afterward.

If that's what he'd come for, because Oliver hadn't given that to him in seventeen days, well—the boy was just so *loud*, Oliver was reluctant to do it in his own apartment. Surely Marcel had others, why would he have come here? "Would you like to sit?"

"No."

Oliver's eyebrows pinched in frustration. "Marcel, what do you want?"

The boy took two steps, staring into Oliver's eyes. He took Oliver's right hand and placed it on his buttock without a word. It was firm, small but round, and it fit perfectly in the palm of Oliver's hand. The image of it rushed to mind, and he felt the familiar twitch between his legs. "You want me to come up tonight?"

"If that is what you want."

Oliver nodded.

"Then come up." Marcel turned away and let himself out the door.

Oliver waited a few minutes before following. Not that anyone cared who he fucked, but discretion was expected.

He climbed the stairs and entered the narrow hallway on the top floor—barely two feet across, narrower than the hallways on the lower floors. He went to the third door on the right, coincidentally the same garret where he'd lived for two years after he first came to Paris, and knocked.

"Who is it?" Marcel's voice asked through the door.

As if it would be anyone else. He put his face to the doorframe, aware that Collette's door was only a few feet away. "It's Oliver" he whispered.

"Come in."

He opened the door and entered the dim space, lit by three candles, their light dancing on the steeply pitched ceiling and the age-blackened beams of the walls. It was a small room, eighteen feet long and twelve feet across, with a single dormer window on the far wall covered by a tattered curtain. In this space were crammed a chair next to a dresser beside the window, a standing wardrobe on the other side of the window, and a narrow bed next to a chimney, its bricks radiating the only heat available during the colder months.

Marcel stepped from the shadows next to the bed, already naked. He stood an inch taller than Oliver, but at least thirty pounds skinnier. He was waifishly thin, his body hairless except for the single dark mass of curls above his penis. Aside from the penis, his body was androgynous.

Without a word he pressed his full lips against Oliver's. His hands unfastened Oliver's belt and unbuttoned his pants, then he broke the kiss and dropped to his knees.

Oliver threw his head back and gasped. No one was better at that.

He leaned against the door and enjoyed Marcel's ministrations for several minutes, then the young man abruptly stood and kissed him again. His mouth tasted different now, and Oliver pulled away. Marcel accepted this without a word, and glanced down as he unbuttoned Oliver's shirt and pushed it down his shoulders.

The coolness of the air gave Oliver goose bumps.

Marcel took a step back and waited as Oliver removed his shoes and trousers, then he took Oliver's hand and led him to the bed.

He took hold of Oliver and stroked him. Then Oliver turned him around and bent him over the bed. Marcel let out a loud moan as Oliver entered him, and as usual Oliver had the momentary impulse to clap a hand over his mouth. But as he began a slow rhythm, the boy's cries became exciting. He moved faster, and Marcel grew even louder.

"Touch me," Marcel said, breathy, and Oliver obliged, reaching his hand around. It only took a few strokes before Marcel's body began to shudder, and his cries crescendoed into shouts that Oliver imagined could be heard a block away.

He collapsed onto Marcel's sweat-soaked back, hugging him tightly to his chest for a moment while he waited for his breathing to return to normal.

Moments later, Oliver lay on his back in bed, with Marcel's body wrapped around his, the boy's head on his chest. Marcel's mass of curly black hair warmed Oliver's throat, and the thin cotton blankets were tugged up around them to protect their bare skin from the chill air of the unheated room.

Oliver stroked the back of Marcel's neck, and sighed.

6

Friday, April 26

The weather turned mild at the end of April, and when Oliver went to Chez Marius for lunch, he found Adrienne and Marie-France sitting at an outside table. He kissed them on the cheeks, and took a seat at the table next to theirs.

Marcel was working, and Oliver ordered a *croque monsieur*.

"Will we see you at the holiday tonight?" Marie-France asked.

Oliver shook his head. "I'll be at the club. I'll have to miss it."

"That's a shame. Sébastien has invited everyone we know. It will be a big holiday. His friend Franz is very popular."

"Sébastien will be disappointed," Adrienne said.

"I'll give him my regrets when I see him."

"He won't be here today," Marie-France said. "Franz is supposed to arrive by noon, and Sébastien and Dolph are going to have lunch with him at Brasserie Lipp."

"Wow, it *must* be a special occasion, then!" Brasserie Lipp, an Alsatian eatery and beer-hall on the Boulevard Saint Germain, was famously inexpensive for large portions, but it was still a treat for someone on Sébastien's budget.

Adrienne shrugged. "Franz and Sébastien shared an apartment for several months a few years ago. They were good friends. I know Sébastien was excited for his visit."

Oliver nodded. It was just like Sébastien to keep his excitement inside.

37

Marcel brought his sandwich, and Oliver asked if he were going to the party that evening.

"Yes, of course."

"Have you met this Franz person, the one visiting from Switzerland?"

"No."

Oliver smiled. "Good, then I'm not the only one."

"You should go meet him after lunch," Marie-France insisted. "They will be at Sébastien and Dolph's studio all afternoon, preparing for the holiday."

**

Sébastien's art studio occupied the ground floor of a building near the Seine, a couple of blocks east. He shared the space with Dolph Hansen, an expatriate German who had been in Paris for six years, one of several thousand anti-Nazis in exile.

The studio had a high ceiling with exposed pipes, and large windows that let in a lot of daylight. It was a large space—fifteen feet wide and twenty feet deep. Half-painted canvases stood on easels or leaned in stacks against the wall in the front half of the room, while blocks of stone in various shades of white and gray stood in the back half, some partially carved, and others rough. A fine white dust covered that half of the studio.

Sébastien and Dolph stood in the middle of the room, a shorter dark-haired young man between them wearing brown corduroy pants, a dingy white shirt, and a flat brown newsboy-style cap.

Sébastien smiled when Oliver entered, and came forward to greet him. They kissed each other's cheeks, and Oliver gave Dolph's hand one firm shake.

Dolph was tall—six feet four inches—and muscular. His shoulders were nearly as wide as the other two young men combined, and his arms were as big as some men's thighs. He had light blond hair kept short and neatly combed in the Teutonic style, deep blue eyes beneath a prominent brow, a strong jaw line coming to a dimpled chin; a long face made handsome by square cheekbones. Everything about his appearance oozed masculinity, with the exception of full, almost feminine lips. His grip was strong, just short of painful.

The tan-faced young man between them stepped forward with a broad smile that dimpled his cheeks, which already wore a five o'clock shadow at one-thirty in the afternoon. He extended his hand.

"Oliver, this is Franz Lemiel, from Basel," Sébastien said, hurrying to make the introduction before Franz introduced himself. This made Oliver smile—manners were important to the French, and Sébastien would be mortified if he were made remiss. "Franz, this is our American friend Oliver Carmichael."

"A pleasure," Franz said, still wearing that broad smile. "I have heard much about you. I understand you are quite an accomplished musician. Jazz, no?"

"Yes, jazz. I play the trumpet at a club in the *Quartier Pigalle* called *Le Chien Errant*."

"Excellent, I will have to go there one evening while I am here." Franz's golden brown eyes were warm, but the intensity with which Franz held Oliver's gaze made him uncomfortable, and he looked away.

Oliver's eyes fell on a large sculpture along the back wall, away from the windows, hidden from the sidewalk by a portable privacy screen. Larger by far than any other in the room, it was a well-muscled youth, naked in the classical Greek style, lounging against the body of an older bald man, also naked, whose hand rested low on the youth's belly, just above the groin.

Oliver wondered aloud who would purchase such a sculpture.

"A man I know who has a townhouse in the Marais, a *viscomte*, commissioned that," Dolph explained. "He purchased the stone in advance, and was very specific. I have made other sculptures for him, much smaller. He likes the pastoral youths, but usually standing. He has a room in his basement dedicated to such artwork. I have been to parties there. He is fond of hosting young men like us while his family is at their chateau."

He didn't elaborate, but Oliver got the picture. As much as it didn't seem to fit his masculine appearance, Dolph Hansen was strictly male-oriented.

When Oliver first arrived, it had come as a bit of a shock to learn that everyone he knew in the neighborhood was bisexual. It wasn't that this bothered him—he'd worked in New York City in the music business, he'd met a few homosexuals. But it was still a culture shock that everyone seemed to sleep with everyone else, without regard to gender. It was their devil-may-care attitude that soon endeared this group of artists, writers, and actors to him.

At first it seemed that he and Lisette—and Dolph Hansen—were the *only* ones he knew who weren't bisexual. Then one night he'd said as much to Lisette, who looked at him in surprise and said that she had assumed he knew. Knew what? That she had experimented with girls a couple of times as a student at the Sorbonne.

There had been suggestions from friends that he give it a try, but Oliver resisted.

"You can't say you don't like it if you never try it," Sébastien said.

"Everyone is bisexual," Serge asserted. "If they are honest."

Oliver doubted that, but alone at night, he couldn't deny a bit of curiosity.

After Lisette called off their engagement, one night after too much wine, he stumbled down the hall to the bath, forgot to knock, and found Marcel in the tub. The curly-haired young man waved off his apologies and told him to stay, he was finished. He'd stood, his smooth androgynous body dripping, turned his back, and dried himself. Oliver was certain that Marcel's backside brushed his hand on purpose, and he thought, *what the hell*. He was surprised at how much he enjoyed it. And so the occasional night with Marcel worked itself into his routine.

Oliver looked back from the sculpture to Sébastien. "I won't be able to attend tonight. I have to play at the club."

"I understand."

"Perhaps we can visit his club tomorrow night," Franz Lemiel suggested to Sébastien, who shrugged.

"If you like jazz, I suppose," Sébastien said.

"Yes, let's do," Franz said, then turned back to Oliver with another broad grin. "Is it Swing jazz?"

"No, not Swing. It's hot jazz." Like Terrance, Oliver preferred the rapid syncopation and fast rhythm of the music that had been popular in Harlem a decade before, to the watered-down jazz coming from larger Swing orchestras these days. But Swing was easy to dance to, and it had become popular in the last few years.

"Ah, yes," Franz said, a twinkle in his warm brown eyes. "We don't hear that often. I will look forward to it."

Oliver nodded, bid them a good festivity that night, and took his leave.

What a strange fellow, he thought as he walked home. He wasn't sure whether to like Franz Lemiel, or to be slightly uncomfortable around him.

**

They came to the club the next night. Oliver was certain that none of them—Sébastien, Serge, Adrienne, Dolph—had ever been to *Le Chien Errant* before. Four years he'd played here. He supposed he could thank Franz for their visit.

He saw them enter during the first set. The club was full—Saturday nights usually were—and they stood in a bunch near the end of the bar and drank *kirs*.

He went to see them during the first break.

"Thank you for coming," he said, kissing cheeks all around and shaking Franz's hand.

"Our pleasure," Franz said with a big grin. "The music is quite good. You must be proud."

"Thank you. We work hard to put on a good show, I'm glad you've enjoyed it." Oliver looked toward Sébastien, Serge, and Adrienne. "How do you like the club?"

"It is very busy," Adrienne observed.

"The bartender makes a good *kir*," Serge added, and took a drag on his cigarette.

Sébastien shrugged. "It is not my favorite music. It was Franz's choice."

Franz patted him on the shoulder. "Sébastien is being a good host, allowing his guest to choose. And besides, this can be his birthday gift to me."

"It's your birthday?" Oliver asked.

"Last week."

"Happy birthday anyway. How old are you?"

Franz gave him an amused smile. "I am twenty-three years, like Sébastien."

Oliver waved over the maître'd. "Clément, these are my friends. Would you please see that they get the next available table?"

Clément cast an imperious look at their clothes. The men were not wearing neckties, and Adrienne was in a housedress. He looked back to Oliver with his nose elevated. "There is a long wait for a table tonight."

Oliver felt the blood rush to his cheeks. He refused to be embarrassed in front of his friends, but he also knew that arguing with a Frenchman after he has made up his mind was a waste of time.

"I'll speak to Terrance about it," he said, and started to walk away.

"I will do what I can," Clément said.

Oliver grinned. "Thank you, Clément." He turned to his friends and added, "Enjoy the rest of the show."

**

The waiter brought another round of *kirs* to their table before the next set of music. They stopped talking for a moment, resuming their quiet conversation after he stepped away.

"I have been inside the Reich," Franz told them. "It's not only jazz clubs such as this that are banned as 'degenerate.' Theaters have been closed for showing 'immoral' plays. Abstract and Surrealist art has been confiscated and destroyed, countless canvases. And book burnings are a main form of entertainment. The Nazis are grave enemies of all art and culture."

"That is why so many German artists and writers have come to Paris," Serge said, nodding toward Dolph. "Paris welcomes them with open arms, and takes them to her bosom."

Franz nodded. "Indeed. But if the Nazis attack France, that will end. We must be prepared to maintain communication. It is only a matter of time, you must realize this. The British and French expeditionary forces are losing the fight in Norway. This will give Hitler air and naval bases, plus stores of iron ore."

"The Germans can't attack France again," Sébastien said. "They could never get through the Maginot Line."

Franz didn't look convinced. "Let us hope you are right."

Serge folded his arms and cocked his head. "Why do you bring this up?"

"I think that Germany *will* attack France, and the Wehrmacht will be able to blitz deep into the country before they are stopped. Everyone was amazed at how fast they blitzed across Poland. Large parts of France could be under Nazi rule for some time."

They all gave him dubious looks, except for Serge. "And then?" he asked.

Franz looked around and leaned far over the table. When he spoke, his voice was just above a whisper.

"I have friends inside the Reich who are working to establish a network of underground groups. Mostly their work is cultural, but one friend in Heidelberg has organized a group of eagle eyes, who can observe troop movements and report to me. I can arrange to relay the information to similar groups inside France, should the need arise."

Sébastien and Adrienne scoffed, but Serge nodded. "If that day comes, you can count on me. How do we do it?"

The stage lights came up, a spotlight switched on and shined on Terrance and his band, and loud music began.

"We'll talk later," Franz shouted over the music.

7

Friday, May 10

The sounds of sirens and shouting in the street roused Oliver from his sleep after only a few hours. He sat up long enough to close the window, and flopped back onto the bed and put his pillow over his head.

He felt like he'd just gotten back to sleep when someone began pounding on his door, over and over. Boom, boom, boom...Boom, boom, boom...Boom, boom. boom...

"Oliver! Oliver!"

He groaned and hugged his pillow tighter to his ears, but Sébastien's voice continued to shout through the door. "Oliver! Wake up! Oliver!"

He hauled himself out of bed, stumbled to the bedroom door to grab his bathrobe, and struggled to slip his arms through the sleeves as he made his way to the front door.

Sebastian stood in the hall, his face flushed and his dark eyes wild. "The Germans have invaded!" he blurted.

"What?" Oliver struggled to wake up his brain.

"The Germans have invaded France!"

It took a few seconds for his mind to grasp this, but it still seemed fuzzy. "But the Maginot Line—"

"They invaded Luxembourg and Belgium at dawn, and the Netherlands, too. They entered France a short time ago through the

45

Ardennes. I heard it on the radio. Everyone is listening to the broadcast."

"Where is everyone?"

"At my studio. Get dressed and join us." Sébastien sprinted back toward the stairs.

Oliver rarely wished he had a radio in his apartment, but this was one of those times. He got dressed and rushed downstairs. It was a couple of blocks to the art studio, and on the way he stopped to buy a newspaper.

The morning editions had obviously been printed before the news broke, but when Oliver reached the Boulevard Saint Germain he saw newsboys hawking late editions. Crowds of people shoved to get one, and Oliver had to push and elbow his way through the crowd, giving the boy a franc coin in exchange for the newspaper.

There was the confirmation, splashed across the front page in big bold letters: ***BOCHE INVADES!***

Oliver stood aside for a moment and read, trying to wrap his mind around the massive assault Germany was launching.

So much for the 'Phony War.'

He made his way down the boulevard, aware that the sidewalks were more packed than usual. He crossed to the building where Sébastien and Dolph rented space.

Several of his friends had already gathered around the radio in the back of the room, their faces grim as the broadcaster announced French army units moving north to support the front.

"Reynaud has already called a general mobilization," Serge said, scowling, when Oliver approached.

"What does that mean?"

"It means conscription notices are coming," Sébastien said.

"What will you do?" Collette asked, her eyes on Sébastien.

The young artist shrugged. "I'll go where they tell me."

"Not me!" Serge declared, thumping his chest. "I will not fight for those corrupt bastards. They are not concerned about France; they are only concerned about their own power."

"How can you say that when France needs you?" Madeleine asked, looking aghast.

"I am not refusing to fight for France. I am refusing to fight for a corrupt government. That is different."

"So you will let the Nazi pigs take over more countries?" Adrienne demanded. "Have they not taken enough? Was it not you who said that France must fight to protect Czechoslovakia?"

"Of course."

"And you were furious when France did not, when France abandoned the Czechs to the Nazi aggressors! You, who wanted to take to the streets because France didn't fight then, will not fight the fascist pigs now?"

"It is not the same!" Serge insisted. "France swore to protect Czechoslovakia, and Daladier broke our pledge. For that, we should have taken to the streets to call for the government's removal. Generations of Frenchmen have taken to the streets of Paris to remove unjust governments—but not this generation. No, this generation will not build barricades or throw stones, no matter how corrupt our bureaucracy. So, now that France has passed every opportunity to take a stand—a real stand, not that pathetic attempt in Norway—now the Nazi bulldozer has come to France herself."

"So you would let the Nazi pigs take over the Low Countries, just as they did Denmark and Norway, and Poland and Czechoslovakia?" Adrienne's dark eyes blazed with fury.

Serge shook his head. "The people do not want another bloodbath in the trenches. Too many died for nothing in the last war, and the people do not want to march into another pointless death trap. Not for those corrupt bastards who dare to call themselves our leaders."

Adrienne's hand slapped across Serge's face with a loud crack. Everyone stared at her in stunned silence.

"You are a selfish little boy, Serge Faucheux!"

He stared at her angry face for several seconds before storming out without a word.

The radio announcer's voice continued to crackle from the radio and echo from the bare walls.

"When will you be called up?" Oliver finally asked, looking at Sébastien.

The young man shrugged. "A few days, probably. No more than a week."

"What will you do?"

"I'll report for duty."

"I meant what will you do after you go?"

Sébastien gave Oliver one of those looks that Parisians were so good at, a look that combined incredulity, amusement, and pity all in one. Oliver had had the effrontery to ask a stupid question.

"I'll fight for France."

Collette put a hand on Sébastien's shoulder, and Oliver noticed her eyes were wet.

**

A telegram lay on the floor of his apartment a few hours later. The moment he stooped to pick it up he noticed it was posted from Indianapolis, Ind.

He glanced at his watch. It was a few minutes past two o'clock—just after seven AM in Indiana. His father must have called in the telegram the moment he saw the headlines.

He almost didn't need to read it, but he tore it open anyway.

DEAR OLIVER, STOP
SAW THE NEWS FROM FRANCE. STOP

CALL HOME AS SOON AS POSSIBLE. REVERSE
CHARGES. STOP
        LOVE, DAD.

Reverse the charges! That was unexpected. He'd assumed his
parents wanted word that he was alright, but by reply telegram. They
only spoke on the telephone once a year—on Christmas night.

He walked to the corner where a payphone stood. He waited
while the older woman inside finished her conversation, then entered
the booth, picked up the receiver, and asked for the international
operator.

The international operator spoke English, and he gave her the
telephone number and asked to reverse the charges.

God, I'd hate to know what this is going to cost Dad, he thought
as the line rang.

"Hello?"

"Mother, it's Oliver."

"Oh Oliver, thank God you called. We've been worried ever since
your father saw the headline in the morning paper."

"I'm fine, Mother."

He could hear his father's voice in the background, and then his
mother saying "He says he's fine, Walter." More of his father's
muffled voice, then his mother said "Oliver? Hold the line, honey.
Your father wants to speak to you."

"Oliver, we think you should come home right away," his father
announced without preamble.

Oliver took a deep breath. "There's no need for me to come
home, Dad, things are fine here."

"You'll be safer outside of the war zone, son."

"I'm not in the war zone, Dad. This is Paris. The fighting is up at
the Belgian border, hundreds of miles from here."

"That's where the fighting started in 1914, too. Didn't stay there."

"You don't have to worry about me. I'm perfectly safe."

"Haven't you been there long enough? It seems to me you've had enough time to 'find yourself' over there, or whatever it is you young people call it. It's time to come home."

So that was it. Oliver took another deep breath. "My life is here, Dad. I don't want to go back to Indiana."

"Oliver, you're twenty-seven years old. It's time to grow up, son, get a real job. Now that you're not marrying that French girl, you can pick up your life and bring it back with you."

Oliver's hand fisted. He controlled his tone with effort.

"It's not that easy, Dad. I have a lot of things here that I don't want to leave."

"If it's money you're concerned about, your mother and I will pay for your passage. And your train ticket from New York, too."

Oliver sighed, not hiding his frustration. "It's not about money. I'm doing fine. I don't want to leave, that's all. Why can't you accept that?"

The line was silent for a few seconds. When his father spoke again, his voice was gruff. "Well, see that you don't get trapped there if the war goes like the last one. Your mother will be worried. Good bye now. Take care, son."

The line clicked off.

**

Sébastien got his notice to report the next day.

A notice also arrived at Serge's garret, but no one was there to receive it.

Collette cried when Sébastien left for the front a few days later. Everyone came out to see him off—except Serge, who seemed to have disappeared. The girls all embraced and kissed him, but Collette wept openly.

50

Oliver wondered how he had never noticed before that Collette was in love with Sébastien. He took for granted that they were close, that they spent a lot of time together, but he'd never looked deeper than that. He wondered if Sébastien were also in love with her.

Marcel also received a conscription notice, but when he reported for his physical they sent him home. He was relieved of duty without explanation. He appeared unfazed by the experience.

For Oliver, his routine continued. He kept playing at the club, Terrance continued to write new music for them, and Hélène continued to summon him for a visit once a week.

There were fewer young men on the streets, and workmen added another coat of black paint to street lamps, but otherwise Paris seemed the same. It hardly felt like a city at war. Aside from the dramatic headlines and battle photographs splashed across the front pages of newspapers, there was almost no evidence of it.

It seemed to Oliver that his father couldn't have been more wrong.

52

8

Friday, May 24

Frank Dryden couldn't have been more excited to learn his assignment in Paris was extended "due to the uncertain circumstances." The understatement made him smile, even while others were more inclined to panic.

Excitement was not exactly the feeling in the room that morning at the Embassy.

Colonel Horace Fuller, the U.S. Military Attaché, was grim-faced as he reported to the senior staff meeting. "The German 10th Panzer Division has reached the English Channel, and began attacking the port of Calais this morning. The British landed reinforcements last night from the 3rd Royal Tank Regiment, but the French and British forces in the city are still gravely outnumbered."

He pushed a round brown piece of metal from the coast of England to the French port of Calais, lining it up beside a blue piece and a red piece.

Several men stood around a long table, with a large map of the Low Countries and northern France spread before them. Three men in military uniforms—Colonel Fuller, his assistant, and Naval Attaché Commander Roscoe Hillenkoetter—stood on one side of the table, while five men in civilian suits spread around the other sides. All watched as Colonel Fuller pointed to or moved metal pieces across the map.

"And what's the latest in Belgium?" Ambassador William Bullitt asked.

"No improvement. The Germans control ninety percent of the country, and continue to bombard the remaining defenses along the coast. The Belgians continue to fight, along with the French and British Expeditionary Forces, but it's hopeless."

Numerous red pieces representing German military units stretched in a long line across northern France below the Belgian border, following the Somme River—now reaching all the way to the coast at Abbeville, facing blue pieces representing French military units.

A second arc of red pieces stretched from the coast between Calais and Dunkirk in France, around to the Belgian coast near the Dutch border. Several blue pieces, along with numerous brown pieces representing British units, sat trapped between the red circle and the English Channel.

Ambassador Bullitt's face was grim as he pointed toward the entrapped brown and blue pieces. "So the British Expeditionary Forces, along with the entire French First Army, are going to end up with their backs to the Channel somewhere around here—Dunkirk, or maybe Neuport or Ostend in Belgium. Is that your assessment, Colonel?"

"It is, sir." Colonel Fuller's face looked pained.

"Can they possibly hold out?"

"No sir," Colonel Fuller said. "Not with the Luftwaffe in control of the skies. And with all of these Panzer units closing in, the Germans have more fire-power on the ground as well."

The ambassador's face looked as if he'd been punched in the gut. "How many men would you say the Allies would lose if they were forced to surrender?"

"Nearly four hundred thousand."

"Damn!" Bullitt's voice boomed, and everyone else in the room was silent. The ambassador paced for a moment before turning back to the table. "Two weeks! They've advanced this far in just two weeks! Did anyone foresee this?"

Colonel Fuller shook his head. "No, sir. Speed and mobility have always been attributes the German military strived for, but this is unheard of."

"What about our people in Berlin?"

"Our military attachés in Berlin, most recently Colonel Peyton, have been granted more access to the German military than almost any other nation, and they have reported extensively to MID on Germany's advances in armor and mechanization. I've read many of the reports. What was not foreseen was the tactical way in which the Germans would use air power to support armored units on the ground. That is unprecedented."

The ambassador looked the military attaché hard in the eyes. "Will the Germans end up in Paris?"

Colonel Fuller was silent a moment before answering. "I pray not, sir—but I don't see how they can be stopped."

Ambassador Bullitt turned toward his civilian staff. He looked at Frank Dryden. "We have about five thousand Americans still in Paris, is that correct?"

Dryden nodded. "Yes, it is."

"Damn," the ambassador muttered, looking down. Then he looked back at his staff. "The president is going to ask us to do everything we can to assist U.S. citizens during this crisis, and to ensure their safety to the best of our ability. I'll need you all to work together to come up with a plan of action. We may not have much time."

**

Dryden's normal two year rotation at the embassy was ending, but he was glad to be staying in Paris. It was his favorite assignment so far. Geneva had better natural scenery and nicer people, but there was something magical about Paris that suited him.

And Ambassador Bullitt was the best head of mission he'd ever worked for.

It also helped that he enjoyed his job here. Information Officer suited him. It allowed him to interact with French and foreign diplomats—often in entertaining ways—and also use his analytical skills to understand and communicate both the big picture and the minutiae. He had never been happier.

Now he set all of those skills into action as he helped to compile the most recent known addresses of American expatriates in Paris, and analyze the data to determine who was most likely to stay in the city. Those who owned property were naturally more likely to remain, while the smaller number with children were most likely to flee—that part was simple.

The more intriguing questions surrounded the less attached. How long had they been here? Were they married to a French national? And most interesting of all, in Dryden's opinion—did they have any past activities that would make them dangerous to the Nazis?

More than a few had fought in Spain against the Nationalists— what would these men do? Would they flee for fear of the Gestapo? Or would they stay and fight tyranny as they had in Spain?

And then there were the intellectuals. What of them? Such people were difficult to predict. And into that same category fell writers and artists. A pretty left-leaning crowd, most of the time. What would they do?

Already his mind was working ahead, after the Germans arrived. Colonel Fuller seemed certain they would, that the French army would collapse—and no one would know better than he. So Paris would be occupied, like Prague, Warsaw and Krakow, Copenhagen and Oslo, Amsterdam and Brussels.

The chatter from the British intelligence community hinted at active resistance in Poland and Czechoslovakia. Dryden had seen some intercepted communiqués, and while they were vague, it was not hard to read between the lines.

Would the same happen in Paris? Dryden assumed it would—eventually.

He read back over the list, along with his hand-written notes about various individuals. Which of these Americans was most likely to not only stay in the city, but to also know French nationals who would be likely to form a resistance movement?

That was what he needed to determine, that was his primary job—and that was the reason his assignment in Paris had been extended indefinitely.

9

Wednesday, June 12

Oliver's heart leapt into his throat when he read the headline:

PARIS DECLARED OPEN CITY.

The English-language Paris Herald Tribune was the only newspaper still published that day. All other papers had shut down yesterday, their publishers and editors fleeing the capital.

The French government had fled south to Tours on Monday, and Oliver had received a telegram from Hélène saying she and her children were leaving with her husband. The army had collapsed, and what was left of it would not make a stand to defend Paris.

The Boulevard Saint Germain was packed with refugees from the north, many of them driving carts pulled by donkeys, loaded with whatever belongings they could gather before the Germans reached their villages. Cattle, sheep, goats, and chickens further clogged the thoroughfare, adding their noises to the shouts and curses of their owners.

Parisians in automobiles bellowed in frustration, also eager to flee the city ahead of the advancing Wehrmacht, but unable to move in the mass of humanity. Drivers uselessly blared their car horns, further panicking the livestock and fraying the nerves of the peasants.

Oliver fought his way through the crowds. It took a lot of effort, but by his own street it was less crowded, and he was able to hurry home.

He ran into Adrienne, carrying a suitcase.

"Adrienne! You too?"

"I am going to my parents' house in Tours," she said, barely pausing as she reached him. "My mother telegraphed that the trains are still running, and they are taking everyone they can cram on board. I'm going to try to get to Tours before nightfall."

Oliver knew Marie-France and Madeleine had left yesterday. "What about your apartment?"

"Help yourself to the food in the icebox," she said, walking away. "I'd rather you ate it than the Germans." She hurried down the street and disappeared.

Oliver had always thought of Adrienne as fearless. She was the last of his friends that he expected to see fleeing the city. It disturbed him, gave him a gnawing dread in his gut like a cold, heavy lump.

He glanced upward, wondering if Collette and Marcel were still in residence in the garrets, or if they, too, had taken their leave. Would he face this alone?

He climbed past his own floor to the top of the stairs, and knocked on Marcel's door. The curly-haired young man answered a few seconds later.

Oliver breathed a sigh of relief. "I thought you might have left."

"Left where?"

"Fleeing to the south like everyone else."

Marcel shrugged. "Where would I go?"

"Adrienne just left."

Marcel grunted. His expression was unreadable.

"Is Collette still here?" Oliver asked.

"I don't know."

"Let's check on her." Oliver motioned for Marcel to come with him, and the young man followed without a word.

Oliver walked to the next door and rapped on it. He breathed another sigh of relief as he heard footsteps inside, and then Collette answered the door.

"Oliver, Marcel," she said.

"Are you staying? Or are you planning to leave like everyone else?" Oliver asked.

Collette shrugged theatrically. "Where would I go?"

"I don't know. To your parents' house?"

Collette shook her head, and her eyes filled with sorrow. "No. My parents live to the north, in Ailly-sur-Somme in Picardy. The Germans have been there for three weeks."

Oliver felt suddenly embarrassed. "Oh, I didn't realize. I'm sorry." Should he have known that? He felt like he should have. But she'd not said a word.

An awkward silence fell over them. Oliver shifted his feet. Collette looked at Oliver expectantly, and he finally broke the silence. "I just wanted to check on both of you, to see if you were staying or leaving. I wanted to be sure you were both alright."

Collette gave him a weak smile. "Yes, I am fine. Thank you."

He hesitated, and they both stared at him. "Would either of you like to join me in my apartment for a while?"

Collette looked from Oliver to Marcel and back again. "I suppose. What are we going to do? It's the middle of the day, and we can't go anywhere because the streets are full of refugees."

"I don't know," Oliver said, feeling suddenly stupid. He hadn't thought it through. It was one thing to sit alone in your own apartment, bored; it was infinitely more uncomfortable to be bored in a group.

"Are you going to the club tonight?" Marcel asked.

"Yes—well, I assume so. It's Wednesday night. I guess I don't know if Terrance will have the club open or not. I suppose I should at least go there and see."

"Then perhaps we can keep each other company later," Marcel suggested.

Collette seemed to like this idea, so Oliver nodded in acquiescence and walked downstairs to his apartment.

The telegram from his parents still lay on the table where he'd left it yesterday. They asked if he was leaving Paris, and begged him to let them know he had gotten out safely.

He'd ignored it. He had no desire to explain why he was staying, and no energy for the argument with his father that would ensue. Maybe if they got no reply, they would assume he'd left before their telegram could be delivered.

Adrienne's departure rattled him. People had been leaving steadily for two days, but she was the most surprising.

He'd been mildly surprised two days ago to see Dolph Hansen outside of the art studio he shared with Sébastien, directing laborers who were loading all of his sculptures into a delivery truck. Oliver had stopped to ask him about it.

"I must leave. I will be arrested by the Gestapo if I stay. My friend the viscomte has agreed to store all of my sculptures in his basement in the Marais, and I may have them back after all of this madness is over."

"Why would you be arrested? You haven't done anything wrong, and you're a German citizen."

Dolph looked him in the eyes for a few seconds before he answered, his deep blue eyes intense with a mixture of determination and sorrow. "I had to flee Hamburg six years ago, when they suppressed the homosexual clubs. Many of my friends were arrested in the purge, and shipped to Breitenau concentration camp—as I would have been if I hadn't left in the middle of the night. To the Nazis, I am a traitor to the Fatherland. And they do not forget. When they get here, everyone will have to register; my name will be on a list, and the Gestapo will find out that I fled to escape arrest. I might be shot without question. I *must* leave."

Oliver had felt foolish, wondering if he should have known all of that. "I'm sorry," he said quietly.

He'd wished Dolph luck, and started to walk away, but the big German grabbed his arm.

"When Sébastien returns from the fighting, tell him that I will be back once the Germans have left Paris." He hesitated before continuing. "And if the unthinkable happens, and the Germans win the war and stay in Paris, tell Sébastien that I will be in contact."

Oliver had promised. "Can I tell him where you've gone?"

"Lyon," Dolph replied. "If the Germans make it that far south, then I will go on to Marseille. I will get word to Sébastien somehow."

Oliver wished him luck again, and left.

Now, sitting at his table staring at the unanswered telegram from his parents, Oliver wondered for the first time if this really was as dangerous as everyone seemed to believe. He had always assumed that Paris was the safest place to be, that nothing would happen. Now, for the first time, he had doubts.

He pushed those doubts away and scolded himself for worrying. He went to the cupboard and poured himself a glass of wine.

**

Oliver left for work early. It took a while to fight his way through the crowd to the Metro station, but the trains were running on time, and less crowded than usual.

The club was open, and Terrance was dressed in his flashy orange and brown suit, acting as if it were a normal Wednesday night. Only half of the staff showed up, and only two other musicians besides

Oliver. Terrance mentioned quite casually that the absent Americans in the band had taken the train to Bordeaux this morning, planning to catch a ride on the last steamship leaving for New York.

"And good luck to them," Terrance said with a big toothy grin. "It's gonna be one *hell* of a madhouse trying to get on that ship."

"You're not planning to leave, Terrance?" Oliver asked.

"Hell no! How could I leave my club? I *own* this place, damn it, and I worked too damn hard to get my own place just to leave it to the Nazis!" He pronounced Nazi with a short "a".

"It might not make a difference," Oliver said. "They say the Nazis don't like jazz. And, well..." He left the rest unspoken, embarrassed to say it out-loud.

Terrance grinned again. "You mean they don't much care for Colored folks like me, neither? Hell boy, I know that. You think I don't know how to deal with racist bastards? I been doin' it my whole life."

They had to improvise the arrangements that night, with only one trumpet, an alto saxophone and a string bass. They did the best they could, but Oliver knew it sounded weak.

They had a really sparse crowd, tiny even by midweek standards. Oliver counted only eleven patrons all night, but at least these seemed to be drinking enough for everyone else. By the time they closed at Midnight, he wondered if Terrance had broken even.

"Are we gonna be open tomorrow, boss?" Jerry the alto saxophonist asked.

"Hell yeah we're gonna be open tomorrow!" Terrance said with a bravado that seemed forced. "And I expect all of you to show up and play your fucking hearts out. If the Germans show up, they can come on in and enjoy the show."

Oliver and Jerry exchanged a look, but said nothing.

Oliver lingered after the others left, knocked on the half-open office door, and stuck his head in.

Terrance leaned back in his chair with his feet on his desk, a tumbler of bourbon in front of him. His arms were folded across his chest, and his expression was more somber than he'd shown them earlier. He looked up at the knock, and motioned Oliver in.

"Can I be honest, boss?"

Terrance chuckled without humor, staring at his feet on the desktop. "Of course you can, but I already know what you're gonna say. You think it's a mistake to open tomorrow."

Oliver nodded. "I think it could be dangerous for all of us to venture out onto the street, that's all. And I don't think we'll have any customers, anyway."

"Yeah, I bet you're right about that," Terrance admitted with a heavy sigh. "It was pretty pathetic tonight. Receipts barely cover what I gots to pay y'all."

"Why don't you send word to Jerry and Rufus to stay home tomorrow," Oliver said. "And you stay home yourself. There's no sense in provoking these people. Lord knows what's gonna happen tomorrow night."

Terrance snorted, his expression bitter. Oliver wondered what was going on inside his head. They sat in silence for a moment, then Terrance sat up and turned to face Oliver. "You a bourbon man, Oliver?"

Oliver shook his head. "Gin."

Terrance nodded. "That's right, I knew that. Have a drink with me. On the house."

He stood and walked to a cabinet on the far wall, removed a bottle and another tumbler, filled it with ice from a bucket and poured gin to the top. He walked back and handed the drink to Oliver. He retook his seat and raised his own glass. "Cheers, my friend."

"Cheers." Oliver clinked his glass against Terrance's and took a drink.

Terrance leaned back again and put his feet back on his desk. "You know, I went down to the American Embassy this morning. Read in the paper how they're giving out these red certificates you can put in your window to show this is a home or business owned by Americans. It said under international law, our belongings can't be touched by the Germans, and the red certificates is what's gonna tell them to leave our places alone.

"So I go on down to get one for the club, and they asked me to take a seat. I sat for three hours, while plenty of white folks came after me and didn't have to wait much more'n twenty, thirty minutes. They'd go on in to Mr. Thompson's office, and come out a few minutes later with a red certificate.

"After they kept me waitin' all that time, Mr. Thompson comes out and says they have no more, so I'm gonna have to do the best I can on my own. I says 'Thank you,' and I go on out.

"I sat at the cafe down the street for a while and had me a cup of coffee before I had to come back here and open—and you know I saw at least a half-dozen other white folks come out of the embassy with red certificates in their hands."

He took a long drink of bourbon, his dark eyes narrow and hard. "My own government," he muttered.

Oliver's mouth hung open in incredulity, and then outrage set in. "How can they do that? You're an American citizen! They can't refuse to help you."

Terrance chuckled again and shook his head. "Boy, that's what I like about you—always the idealist. I saw that in you the first time I met you. Oh, you was street-wise, I saw that right off, too—but there was an innocence to you. I see it every time you smile. But this is the way of the world, son, and there ain't no way you can change it by yourself."

"I can go to the embassy with you tomorrow, and demand that they let you have a certificate for the club."

Terrance shook his head. "It wouldn't do no good. I'm still an old Colored man, no matter who I take in there with me. And besides, I don't need you to fight my battles for me. I ain't never needed *nobody* to fight my battles, I always done that myself."

Oliver sat in silence, knowing what Terrance said was true. A terrible sense of helplessness settled into the pit of his stomach, and he took a long swallow of gin to try to dull it. But the feeling remained.

Then an idea popped into his head. He tossed back the rest of the gin, and smiled at Terrance.

"Don't you worry boss, I think I know what to do about it."

10

Thursday, June 13

Captain Robert Allard strode into the Police prefecture on Rue Domat early, as usual, in spite of the crowds still clogging the streets and sidewalks. He straightened his brown three-piece suit and removed his brown bowler hat the moment he stepped in the door, the picture of calm in a sea of chaos.

"Any looters arrested overnight, Sergeant?" he asked the gendarme at the front desk.

"Nine, Captain."

"They are safely locked up?"

"Yes, Captain."

"And the belongings returned from whence they were taken?"

"Yes, Captain."

"Excellent. Good work, sergeant. Did every gendarme report for duty last night?"

"Yes, Captain, every one."

"Very good. You will let me know immediately if anyone fails to report for duty this morning."

"As you wish, Captain."

Allard was already walking toward his office in the rear of the prefecture.

When the government declared Paris an open city the day before, they named the American Ambassador as acting mayor until the Wehrmacht arrived; one of Ambassador Bullitt's conditions was that all police and firemen remain on duty. And so Roger Langeron, the Paris Prefect of Police, had issued the order that all gendarmes were to remain at their posts.

Captain Allard was determined that Langeron's order would not be disobeyed in this prefecture.

He set himself to reviewing the reports from the overnight shift, and signing authorizations. When eight o'clock arrived, he waited impatiently for word that all of the day-shift gendarmes were on duty.

The sergeant brought him that news a few moments later, and Allard immediately called the office of the Prefect of Police, identified himself and asked to speak with Prefect Langeron.

He had to wait a few moments before the call was transferred.

"Yes, Allard?" the Prefect's gruff voice said, sounding rushed.

"I am pleased to report to you, sir, that all gendarmes have reported for duty, both last night and this morning. Nine arrests were made last night for looting, and all are in custody. There were no looters that escaped arrest. We have things under control in this part of the 5th Arrondissement."

"Good. Is that all?"

"That is all for now, Prefect."

"Thank you, Allard." The line clicked off.

Allard took the prefect's impatience in stride. Certainly Langeron was very busy today, with the city in chaos and the Wehrmacht less than twenty kilometers away. It was understandable that he did not have time to listen to a detailed report.

And perhaps other prefectures had not kept their districts as well under control as Allard's had. He nodded in satisfaction and returned to his paperwork.

**

Oliver awoke earlier than usual and took the Metro to the Place de la Concorde. Few passengers rode the train that morning. He climbed the stairs to the famous square that had been home to the Paris guillotine during Robespierre's Reign of Terror in 1793 and '94. A giant obelisk now occupied the spot where the guillotine had beheaded more than two thousand Parisians, and Oliver noticed that the obelisk was surrounded by piles of sandbags.

Curious, he thought as he crossed the square, and wondered what on Earth the sandbags could be for.

The Place de la Concorde was nearly deserted, only a handful of pedestrians hurrying about. No leisurely strolls today.

The thought crossed his mind that the embassy might have closed, but he was relieved to see its front door open, and an elderly black man standing guard. He asked if it was still possible to get a red certificate.

"Yes sir, you got to see Mr. Tyler Thompson, Third Secretary. He's on the third floor, sir."

Oliver didn't see many people milling around as he made his way upstairs, and when he found Mr. Thompson's office there was no wait.

"You should have been here yesterday," Thompson said when Oliver commented on the lack of a line. "It was a zoo." He flipped through several pages until he located Oliver's name. "There you are—Carmichael, Oliver. Do you still live at number 13 Rue de Lagrange?"

"Yes."

"Any family members living in Paris?"

"No."

Mr. Thompson made a quick note, then produced a large red certificate of stiff paper. "Put this in your window, and it will protect your property when the Germans get here. Just so you're aware, the last trains left this morning, and German forces are starting to encircle the city, so we don't recommend trying to leave at this point."

"When do you expect them to get here?"

"Probably some time tonight. Tomorrow morning at the latest. We recommend you stay in tonight."

Oliver thanked him and left.

He hurried back to the Metro station, and took the train to the Place Pigalle. From there it was only a couple of blocks to the club, which he found locked. He checked his watch and saw that it was nearly noon, so he pounded on the door and called Terrance's name.

A moment later he heard the deadbolt open before the lock turned, and then Terrance cracked the door and poked his head out.

"What are you doing out, boy?" he asked, grabbing Oliver's arm and dragging him inside.

Oliver noticed that the liquor bottles were conspicuously absent from the shelves behind the bar. Otherwise, the main room of the club appeared as usual when it was closed, with chairs turned upside down on tables and most of the lights out.

"I brought you something," he said, and grinned as he produced the red certificate.

"Where'd you get that?"

Oliver told Terrance about his visit to Mr. Thompson at the embassy.

"So you let them believe this was for your apartment?"

Oliver nodded. "The certificates aren't specific, so you could put it in the window here and no one would ever know you didn't get it from the embassy yourself."

"And what about your apartment?"

"What have I got to steal? My couch has got holes in it, my table is scratched and my dishes are chipped. The Germans would be nuts to want any of my stuff."

Terrance's face broke into a grin. "You got that right, boy." He slapped Oliver on the back, and then the grin faded and his expression grew serious. "Thank you, brother. Now get your ass on home before it's too late. Go on now!"

He pushed Oliver toward the door. Oliver laughed and allowed himself to be pushed along. Out on the street he turned back briefly and told Terrance, "I'll see you in a couple of days."

"You better."

The sound of the deadbolt sliding closed rang in the near-empty street.

**

Frank Dryden looked over the updated list Tyler Thompson provided him that afternoon. Their best estimate was that 2,500 Americans remained in Paris—about half the total that had lived here five weeks before.

It was more than Dryden had expected. But when he analyzed the list, he smiled to himself as he realized he'd accurately predicted the patterns.

When the time came, he'd learn if his other predictions also held true.

11

The street lay in deep shadow as Sébastien trudged the final block toward home. His khaki clothes were filthy and tattered, his face streaked with dirt. Dusk was falling, and the sky was bathed in a beautiful rose color, but Sébastien barely noticed, and no one else was out to see it.

He'd been walking for a week, sleeping in barns for a few hours each night, and then continuing down the country roads of northern France. Alone and on foot, he found himself moving faster than the flood of refugees with heavily-loaded carts and flocks of livestock. Like them, he dove into a ditch every time Luftwaffe fighters roared overhead. A couple of times a Stuka dive-bomber peppered the road with machine gun fire, killing civilians and livestock, but mostly the planes roared off to the south to drop bombs on bridges and factories.

He'd finally reached the northern suburbs of Paris shortly after midnight that morning. It had taken him the whole day to make it on foot to the Left Bank. He had no idea if the Metro was running or not, but either way he had no coins in his pocket to pay the fare.

In his pocket he still held the SACM Modele 1935-A, the semi-automatic pistol he'd taken off the body of a dead officer nine days ago. That was the day the Germans broke through the main lines, and his unit seemed to fall apart before his eyes. Everyone scattered. Some talked of rejoining the army as it retreated southward, and hopefully making a last stand north of the capital—but Sébastien was finished with the fighting. He knew it was hopeless, and he joined the throngs of refugees heading south.

The Germans blitzed west through Normandy, so Sébastien and the other refugees hadn't been overtaken.

Now home stood before him. He entered the building, which sat eerily silent, and trudged up the stairs to his apartment on the 4th floor. He fished the key out of his pocket, but looked down the hall and wondered if Oliver had stayed in the city. He turned away from his door and shuffled to Oliver's.

**

The rapping at the door startled them all, and the three of them stared at one another for a few seconds before Oliver stood and walked to the door. Collette and Marcel stayed on the couch, watching. Collette pulled her legs up and hugged her knees.

Oliver cracked the door open and peeked outside, then let out a cry of surprise when he saw Sébastien standing in the hall. He flung the door open and embraced him.

Oliver brought Sébastien inside by the arm, and Collette leapt from her seat. She ran to Sébastien and threw her arms around his neck, kissing his cheeks and crying.

Marcel stood by the couch and watched. His lips spread in a slight smile, which was about as expressive as his face ever got.

Collette took Sébastien by the hand, beaming, and walked him to the couch. She sat next to him, slipping her arm through his.

Oliver poured a glass of wine, which Sébastien accepted gratefully.

"We thought you might have been the Germans when you knocked," Oliver said.

Sébastien gave him a weak smile. "You'll know when the Germans arrive. You'll hear them shouting all the way up the stairs. And they won't knock."

"We've been so worried about you since you left," Collette said. "You might have been killed, or captured. How did you escape? The Germans could have caught you."

"By the end, I wasn't far ahead of them."

"Tell us all about it," Oliver said.

Sébastien recounted the first weeks sitting along the defensive lines on the south banks of the Somme, building fortifications, far from the action as the Germans raced westward toward the sea, rather than southward toward Paris as they did in the last war. Then when the full assault had finally come on June 4th, it had barely lasted three hours before the lines broke and everyone scattered.

Collette listened with eyes wide. "Were you frightened?"

"Yes." He sat in silence for a few seconds before continuing. "I was frightened at first, but then I became angry. There was no will to fight in our army. No one wanted to be there, no one wanted a war. It was no wonder everyone broke and ran the moment the Panzers tore through our fortifications."

There was real contempt in his voice, cold and bitter.

"What did you do?" Collette asked.

"I decided to come home."

"And you made it just in time," Oliver said. "We're the only ones left. Everyone else—Adrienne, Marie-France, Madeleine, your friend Dolph—they all left over the last three days, gone south."

"It might have been safer to stay," Sébastien said.

Oliver watched him for a moment, wondering what he had seen on the road.

Collette touched Sébastien's cheek. He turned to face her, and they stared into each other's eyes for a moment. Then he kissed her, and she laid her head on his shoulder. He put his arm around her and hugged her to him, staring into the distance.

It was touching, and Oliver suddenly thought of Lisette and felt pangs of loneliness. Had she fled the city with everyone else? Had she left with her new boyfriend, her sugar daddy?

He scolded himself for thinking that. Of course she hadn't left with *him*, he was probably married. No doubt he'd fled, but with his wife and children, leaving Lisette to fend for herself—

Oliver leapt from his seat and ran for the door.

"Where are you going?" Marcel asked as Oliver reached for the doorknob.

"I've got to check on someone. All of you stay here." And he ran out the door.

*

Marcel looked down the hall and watched Oliver disappear down the stairs. His heart sank into the pit of his stomach.

**

The streets were deserted, and Oliver sprinted toward the Metro station. He was half-surprised to find the trains still running, though no one else stood on the platform, and when he boarded the train it was empty. Still, it pulled away toward the Right Bank, and Oliver silently congratulated himself on taking the time to check, rather than running off on foot.

He got off at the Place de la Madeleine. He ran up the stairs to find the square as deserted as the streets in the *Quartier Latin*.

He ran up the Rue de Seze, then turned onto Rue de l'Arcade. The distant boom of artillery shells was the only sound, besides the softer thud of his footsteps. He sprinted past the Hotel de l'Arcade, which sat in complete darkness, toward Lisette's apartment building half a block down.

He knew where she lived because he'd followed her there twice after she moved out of her apartment in the 5th last October, a few weeks after she broke off their engagement. He waited outside the wine shop where she worked in the 8th, and followed her home. He followed her again the next night to be sure she went to the same place. He was sure she didn't know he had followed her, but he wanted to be certain she was going home and not to a friend's place. He'd watched from around the corner until he saw her shape in one of the windows, drawing the curtains closed.

He'd often imagined going to her apartment, where she would embrace him and kiss him and tell him how much she'd missed him, how wrong she'd been to ever leave him. He'd never been brave enough to call on her. Until now.

He ran inside the building and tore up the stairs. Her apartment was on the third floor, and he was winded by the time he reached it. He banged on the door and shouted. "Lisette! Lisette! Are you there? Please answer. Lisette!"

**

Lisette sat on her couch with her feet tucked under her, a pad of paper on her knees, writing poem after poem. The emotions pouring through her were too many to count, and she knew from experience that the best way to sort them out was on the page, letting the words flow from her hand, from some unknown part of her brain that always seemed to surprise her with what it put down.

All of it came out on the pages in front of her—anger, abandonment, fear, loneliness—tumbling forth in lyric form. Page after page filled up before her eyes.

She lost track of the time, and when she heard pounding footsteps on the stairwell down the hall, she looked up in shock at the clock on the wall. Her heart leapt into her throat.

The Germans were here already, and it wasn't even eleven o'clock yet.

Then came the pounding on her door—why *her* door, and not the neighbors closest to the stairs? But then the sound of a familiar voice—familiar, but out of context—shouted her name, and she was confused. Was she dreaming? It sounded like Oliver, but how could that be? He didn't know where she lived. And how could he have known that she would still be in Paris?

He continued to bang on her door and call her name, so she set the paper and pen down on the coffee table and hurried to the door. She leaned her face close to the door jam. "Oliver? Is that you?"

"Lisette! You're home, oh thank God," Oliver's voice replied. "Yes, it's me. Please open up."

She kept the door closed. "Why are you here?"

"I had to make sure you're alright."

"I'm fine."

"I'm glad. Please open up, and let me talk to you."

She hesitated a few more seconds, but then unlocked the door and opened it. From the other side of the threshold, Oliver stared at her. She waited for him to say something, and finally he spoke.

"Lisette." His voice sounded relieved, and the relief shone from his eyes. For a second her heart melted. Then she stiffened her resolve.

"What do you want, Oliver?"

"I had to see if you were still here, if you were alright. And you are. I'm glad. I was worried."

"As you can see, I am alright."

"You shouldn't be alone, not with the Germans just outside the city."

She had no ready argument against that, so in true Parisian style she simply turned her back and ended the discussion. She walked to the couch and sat.

She heard Oliver enter and close the door. She didn't look back at him. He hesitated a moment, but then walked to the couch and sat down next to her.

"How did you know where I live?" she demanded, still looking away from him.

"Adrienne told me."

"That's a lie. She would never do such a thing."

"She told me before she fled the city. She was worried about you, and knew I would be too."

Lisette turned her face toward him and glared. "Do not treat me like a fool, Oliver. I know Adrienne would never tell you where I live."

"These are extraordinary circumstances." The look in his eyes said he knew he wouldn't convince her, and his voice sounded flat with lack of effort.

"It is not important," she said with a flippant wave of the hand, looking away again.

"Lisette, please." He reached out to take her hand, but she pulled away in a flash and slapped him across the face.

Stunned at her own actions, her eyes widened, her hand in the air near her face as if she didn't know what to do with it.

Oliver said nothing, but put his own hand against his reddened cheek.

"Oh Oliver, I'm sorry," she said, her voice barely above a whisper. "I don't know what got into me. I'm sorry."

He looked away from her. "I just came here to help you," he said quietly.

Seeing the hurt look on his face, her heart felt like it was breaking all over again. "I know. It was sweet of you to look in on me. I should have been more appreciative. I'm sorry."

He kept looking straight ahead, so she reached out and took his right hand in both of hers. "It is good for you to be here. It will be safer, for both of us. Have you eaten?"

He shook his head, and she got up and walked into the kitchen. She cut some sausages, thick ribbons of fat marbling the meat, and then sliced up some cheese and put it all on a plate. She poured him a glass of red wine, and carried the plate and the wine into the living room.

"Here, eat with me," she said, sitting on the couch next to him.

He nodded and reached for a slice of sausage. They sat side-by-side and ate in silence for a few minutes.

"Thank you for checking on me," she said after a while, her voice soft and low.

"You're welcome." He hesitated a second, then added, "I thought you might be all alone."

*

They continued to eat in silence for a moment, but then Oliver turned toward her and took her hands in his. He stared into her eyes and spoke from his heart.

"Lisette, all I've ever wanted was to take care of you. I don't know what happened between us before, but I'd like to show you tonight that I can protect you, keep you safe. Will you let me? Please?"

She looked down at her hands, but didn't pull them away. "We're not the same, you and I. We don't want the same thing. You want us the way we were, living in those tiny apartments in the 5th, eating bread and cheese because we can't afford meat, spending hours with our old friends talking about philosophy and politics, staying up late and sleeping half the day. I don't want that anymore. I want what my parents have."

"We were happy."

She nodded, a faint smile on her lips. "Yes, we *were*."

Oliver felt the pain stabbing into his heart, but it quickly changed to anger.

"So what, then? Do you want to pretend it didn't mean anything? That we didn't love each other? That that wasn't enough?" He could hear the anger in his voice, though he fought to control it.

She ignored his tone, and her voice stayed low as she replied. "No. It meant everything, once."

"Once," he repeated, bitterly.

She gazed at him sadly for a moment, then looked away. She pulled her hands away and folded them in her lap.

"Please don't. It does no good to rehash this. It was lovely of you to come here and check on me. Let's leave it at that. You said you wanted to keep me safe from the Germans, so stay with me and wait for them to come. I would like to have a friendly face with me when they arrive. We are good friends, you and I, after all."

"Friends," he repeated, but his voice lacked the bitterness he had expected. He surprised himself at how resigned he felt. *Friends*. That was something, wasn't it?

He looked up, and saw her staring at him in expectation. He nodded. "Yes, friends."

**

He didn't know how long he'd been asleep when the rumble of a motorcycle engine awakened him as it went by.

He was still sitting on the couch, and his neck ached from the awkward angle at which his head had hung. Lisette's head rested on his shoulder, and her breathing told him she was sound asleep. Both of the lamps in the room were still on. He glanced up at the clock on the wall. It was nearly four.

He may have been only half-awake, but it didn't take him long to realize that motorcycles running on the street meant German soldiers.

He sat still and listened, but the unnatural silence resumed. Even the distant artillery was now silent.

That motorcycle must have been a vanguard, he thought. More would arrive soon.

He looked down at Lisette's face, peaceful in its slumber. Her dark brown hair, thick and wavy, cascaded over her shoulder. He reached up and gently stroked it. She stirred, and he stopped for a moment, resuming after he convinced himself that she was still asleep. He dropped his face down to the top of her head, and inhaled the rich smell of her hair.

In the stillness of this Paris night, with their world teetering, staring down the precipice at disaster—in this moment at least, she was his again.

He closed his eyes and rested his head against hers, and drifted back to sleep.

**

The growing rumble of mechanized vehicles roused them both three and a half hours later. Morning light streamed through the windows, and Lisette seemed embarrassed that she'd been leaning against him, her head on his shoulder. She got up to turn off the lamps.

Oliver went to the window and parted the curtains just enough to look out. Lisette joined him a moment later, her hand on his arm, and they stared down in silence.

A column of German military trucks rumbled down the Rue de l'Arcade, dozens of them in a row, flanked by motorcycles driven by helmeted soldiers in gray.

After a while, Oliver heard her whisper, "It is not possible." Then no more words, only the rumble of the German trucks and motorcycles.

**

The telephone worked, and Lisette dialed her parents' number.

"They didn't leave?" Oliver asked.

Lisette shrugged. "Papa said that the Germans would never reach Paris, that it would be like 1914, when taxis drove volunteers to the front to shore up the defenses because there were so many of them. But Maman said that they would take the last trains from the *Gare de Lyon* yesterday morning."

"Why didn't you go there?"

"Because I wanted to stay here."

Oliver understood. This was her space, her furniture, her books; if she had to stay in Paris she wanted to be here. She didn't want the Germans to take it while she was gone.

Lisette hung up the receiver with a sigh. "I suppose they caught one of the trains after all."

Oliver came up behind her and put his hands on her shoulders. "I'm sure they're alright. Don't worry about them."

"I'm not worried about them. They got out."

He turned her around and lifted her chin with his finger. "And don't worry about us, either. We'll be fine. I haven't heard any shots fired. No one's screaming, so it may not be as bad as we feared."

"It's just begun."

He couldn't argue with that, and said nothing.

**

They heard the loudspeaker around noon. A deep, commanding voice, in clipped German, broadcast from a loudspeaker atop a military truck.

Oliver didn't speak a word of German. "Can you understand it?" he asked Lisette.

She nodded. "They will have a victory parade this afternoon, down the Champs-Elysee and through the Place de la Concorde. All citizens of Paris are ordered to come out and witness their 'military might.'" Her tone grew bitter on those last two words.

The loudspeaker continued, moving slowly down the street, but Lisette said he was just repeating himself.

Oliver wondered if Sébastien would obey the order to watch the Germans' parade. He suspected not. He wondered how many Parisians would.

**

The number of people lining the sidewalks of the Champs-Elysee truly shocked him. He had no idea there were that many people left in Paris, let alone willing to come out and watch their enemy parading down their streets in full victorious strut.

Some stood with slumped shoulders and weary faces; others stood rigid and stiff-backed, their faces set in stony disapproval. All of them stood in silence.

It was the most unnatural spectacle Oliver had ever witnessed.

Thousands of German soldiers goose-stepped down the grand avenue from the direction of the *Arc de Triumphe*, toward the obelisk in the Place de la Concorde. Their leather jackboots smacked against the pavement in perfect unison, like a staccato drum beat that reverberated deep inside Oliver's chest. He felt his heart sink a little further with each beat.

To his right he heard a soft sob, and turned his head to see a middle-aged woman holding a handkerchief to her mouth, tears flowing. The man next to her, probably a veteran of the last war, looked as if he might join her in tears—his mouth turned in a deep frown, his lips trembled, and he seemed to fight back the emotion with tremendous effort.

An unexpected lump caught in Oliver's throat, and he turned back toward the parade of soldiers.

Lisette slipped her arm through his and leaned against him. He could feel her trembling. Whether she was trembling with rage or sorrow, he couldn't be certain. Her face gave away nothing.

On and on they marched, thousands of them in a seemingly endless column of gray.

Incongruously, a garbage man shuffled past them, sweeping cigarette butts into a dustpan and emptying it into a trash bag. He seemed oblivious to the German soldiers marching just feet from him, and Oliver stared at him for a moment. The man's eyes focused on the gutter and the debris there, never wavering, taking in neither the soldiers to his right, nor the crowd to his left. He shuffled on at a steady pace, sweeping.

Doing his job.

Oliver scanned the crowd on the opposite side of the Champs-Elysee. Police gendarmes stood at regular intervals, their hands behind their backs, staring ahead at the passing soldiers. They were on duty to control the crowd, but they watched in silence like everyone else.

The ground vibrated continuously from the trucks, motorcycles, and tanks that rumbled past, but then Oliver felt a different vibration rising up through the sidewalk, this one coming from below. Several seconds later, it died away.

The Metro trains were still running, as if this were a normal Friday.

It was as if all of Paris had fallen down the rabbit hole.

Part II

12

Thursday, July 25, 1940

Oliver had come to dread this part of the night.

It was stifling inside the club, and even hotter on the stage under the lights. Beads of sweat poured down his cheeks. Ceiling fans succeeded in circulating the cigarette smoke without bringing any relief from the stuffiness. And the heat started to fray tempers.

A long night of heavy drinking contributed. The German officers spent a lot of money on drinks, and while a Frenchman would savor a glass of wine, it had become apparent to Oliver that Germans drank much faster.

With the nine o'clock curfew in place, they didn't have many French patrons these days—only the girls who came in on the arms of German officers, and they were certainly not going to be arrested for being out past curfew. The officers started out well-mannered, polite to a fault, but as the night progressed they always became louder and more demanding. By the time eleven o'clock rolled around, they had typically become insufferable.

And they were armed.

Oliver didn't know how Terrance put up with it. There had initially been a question about whether or not *Le Chien Errant* would be allowed to reopen. The military commanders and their men wanted entertainment, but the Nazi civilian administrators who followed on the heels of the occupying army were rigid and disapproving. Jazz was degenerate music in the Nazi worldview. And they didn't want their good German soldiers listening to degenerate music performed by *a Negro*.

Apparently less ideological minds prevailed, for Terrance got word from the local police after a week that the club would be allowed to reopen—under restrictions. No risqué lyrics on the nights that Terrance sang. The employees were given employment cards that allowed them to stay out until midnight. This meant the club had to close at eleven-thirty—far earlier than four AM, as they used to.

None of them had been pleased at the new restrictions, but what could they do? The new authorities could shut them down permanently if they failed to comply. So they complied with the new rules, and they put up with the drunken Germans who patronized the club.

Now the song was interrupted by angry shouts from one of the tables near the back. Then the clatter of falling chairs caused Terrance to stop playing and rush to the table where the commotion arose.

A tall, big-muscled German 2nd Lieutenant, held one of the French waiters by the collar, his huge right arm pulled back ready to punch. He shouted angry German words that none of them could understand.

Terrance planted himself next to the German, but carefully avoided physical contact, and spoke to him in French, asking what the problem was.

"He insult me, this one," the big blond German said in heavily-accented French.

Terrance glanced at Oliver and motioned with his head toward the bar. Oliver hurried to the bartender and asked for a refill of what the German was drinking.

Meanwhile Terrance looked to his waiter, whose face was etched in a deep disapproving scowl. "Did you insult him?"

"He was rough with the *lady*," the waiter said with biting sarcasm, "and she did not like what he was doing. He would not stop, and he slapped her. I told him what I thought of his behavior." He looked away with a disapproving sniff.

Terrance looked at the young woman sitting at the table, her pale face redder on one side than the other, and her long red hair disheveled. "Are you alright, Miss?"

"Yes, I'm fine," she said, but her eyes stayed down.

Terrance looked up at the angry German. "Then I apologize for my employee, *mein herr*. Please accept a complimentary drink for your trouble." Seeing the German's confused expression, he added, "Free."

The German understood that word, and he released the waiter's collar and nodded. "*Danke.*"

Oliver arrived at that moment with a tall glass of schnapps and handed it to the officer, who accepted it with a curt nod. He took a long drink, then threw his arm around the red-haired young lady. "Play!" he ordered Terrance. "Play! Play!"

They resumed playing, and the club returned to raucous gaiety.

Everything seemed to have returned to normal, and the band concluded its final number minutes before eleven-thirty. Terrance thanked the audience, and announced they were closing.

Oliver gathered his music, packed up his trumpet, said goodnight to the other musicians, and was on his way out when he spied the waiter standing in the back, having a heated argument with the red-haired young French woman. Oliver distinctly heard the words "traitor" and "whore" in his diatribe.

She shot back furious retorts, but her words tumbled forth so fast that Oliver couldn't understand most of it.

Then from the corner of his eye Oliver spied the big blond German exiting the men's room and coming back into the lounge, his gait weaving and his eyes glassy. But a few seconds later his ice-blue eyes focused squarely on the angry waiter berating his woman, and he tore through the lounge without regard to tables or chairs, sending everything tumbling away in his wake.

His big fist pummeled into the side of the waiter's head before Oliver had a chance to react. He shouted Terrance's name and hurried toward the fight, but in the few seconds it took him to reach them the waiter had hit the ground, the big German landing punch after punch on his face.

Oliver grabbed at the German's upper arm, in a futile attempt to stop the punches.

In a flash, Terrance was at their side, kneeling down and putting himself between the furious German and the bloodied Frenchman.

"Please sir, please! We don't want trouble, please!" he pleaded in French.

The German hesitated a moment, then turned and landed one punch square on Terrance's jaw, sending the lanky black man sprawling.

Oliver lunged toward the drunk German, but felt big strong hands on his shoulders holding him back.

"Let it go, man," Jerry whispered near his ear. "Terrance be alright. Don't get yourself punched out, too."

Other employees dragged the waiter behind the bar, barely conscious. Blood stained the floor where his head had laid.

The big German gave all of them a smug and satisfied look, and with a final nod he took hold of the red-haired French girl's arm and marched her out the door.

Terrance climbed to his feet, wiping a bit of blood from the corner of his mouth. "I'm alright," he assured his employees, who encircled him with concerned expressions. His voice sounded as if his tongue had grown to twice its former size, which Oliver figured it might well do given how hard the German had decked him.

"I'm alright!" Terrence insisted to their offers of help. Jerry and Oliver began to pick up chairs, and he put up his hands to stop them. "I'll get all that. Y'all get on home, before you miss the curfew. Go on now."

Oliver and Jerry exchanged a reluctant look, but Terrance insisted they go.

"It's already quarter 'til, y'all best hurry yourselves."

Oliver did hurry to the Metro station at the Place Pigalle, managing to catch the last train.

The clock tower at Saint Sulpice was chiming midnight as he sprinted up the stairs. The boulevard was empty, and he hurried across toward his neighborhood.

He had a decision to make—take the short route home, which went past the police prefecture, or go around the block and waste precious minutes. He opted to take the long way.

It turned out to be a moot point. As he hurried past his normal turn, he spotted a pair of gendarmes a half-block ahead, and they shouted for him to stop.

"Shit," he cursed under his breath, knowing they would have spotted him even if he'd turned where he normally did.

"What are you doing out at this hour?" one of them demanded.

"Coming home from work."

"Papers, please."

Oliver handed over his passport and his employment card. The gendarme glanced at the employment card, and then opened the passport.

"American? You think you don't have to comply with the curfew because you are not French?" the gendarme demanded.

Oliver gave them his best apologetic and conciliatory look and tone. "No, I understand the curfew. I was just coming home from work."

"Your employment only allows you to stay out until midnight," the second gendarme said with a haughty look. "It is three minutes past midnight."

Oliver nodded. "I know, and I apologize. There was an incident at work, and I left a bit later than I normally do—"

"We do not wish to hear your excuses," the first one interrupted. "Come with us."

He took Oliver by the shoulder and marched him toward the prefecture.

**

Oliver felt like he'd been in the interrogation room for hours.

How many times could they ask him the same questions? Why are you in Paris? How long have you been in France? What are you doing in France? Who do you work for? Where do you live? And if he didn't answer quickly enough, they smacked him on the back of the head.

Then they would leave him alone for long stretches, with nothing to look at but the portrait of Marshall Pétain on the wall. Under his image in bold letters was the new national motto *"Travaille, Famille, Patrie"*—Work, Family, Fatherland—adopted at Vichy a couple of weeks ago to replace *'Liberté, Egalité, Fraternité'* when the National Assembly voted to abolish the Republic and grant emergency powers to Marshall Pétain.

When the gendarmes came back, the litany of questions began all over again.

Eventually his frustration snapped. "Listen to me! I've answered all of these things already, many times."

This earned him a hard smack across the face from the nearest gendarme, then back again. His left cheek stung from the initial smack, but his right cheekbone felt bruised from the backhanding.

He was not cowed. "I haven't done anything wrong."

"You were out past the curfew."

"Am I under arrest, then?"

The gendarme didn't reply, but walked from the room, leaving him alone again.

A few minutes later they opened the door and told him he could leave. "Your passport is not fake."

Of course it's not fake, you bastards. He took his passport and marched from the prefecture. It was only a block to his apartment, and he plopped on the couch in relief.

He sat and seethed. It was an outrage, and he was determined to do something about it.

13

Friday, July 26

"I'm afraid there's nothing that can be done in the way of redress, Mr. Carmichael," a U.S. consular employee told him the next day. "American citizens in France have to obey the law the same as anyone else, and that includes the curfew. If you disobey French law, you're subject to arrest and prosecution."

"But they got physical with me," Oliver insisted. "Isn't it against the law for them to do that?"

The consular employee gave him a weak smile. "It was. Now that Vichy makes the rules, it's less clear. Either way, you disobey the curfew at your peril. There's nothing the U.S. government can do to help you."

"Don't I have *any* rights as an American?"

"From the German occupation authorities, certainly. Your property is protected under international law, as a citizen of a neutral country. And Americans are given more generous rations than the French, as I'm sure you're aware. But the French police answer to Vichy, and Vichy is officially in charge, even in the Occupied Zone. You are residing in France voluntarily, and you're subject to their laws."

Oliver resisted the impulse to ask the man what good he was to anyone, and instead thanked him for his time. He stood to leave, but the man stopped him.

"Wait just a moment please, Mr. Carmichael. Given your circumstances and your recent interaction with the police, Mr. Dryden would appreciate an opportunity to speak with you."

A minute later, Oliver was ushered into a larger office. A tall thin young man with thick blond hair, neatly parted, stood behind a desk and smiled at him as he entered. He was nearly as tall as Oliver, and walked around the desk to shake Oliver's hand. Behind him on the wall hung a framed degree from Columbia University, 1932.

"Mr. Carmichael, welcome. Have a seat please, make yourself comfortable. Frank Dryden. May I call you Oliver?"

"Yes."

"Would you like some water, Oliver?"

"Yes, thank you."

Dryden smiled at him again as he handed him the glass of water. "There you go, spring water from Vichy. The new regime sent us cases of it a few weeks ago." He sat on the corner of the desk and folded his hands across one knee. "I understand you had quite an ordeal with the police last night."

Oliver summarized the incident again, but assumed Dryden had already heard the highlights.

"Yes, it's troubling when civil liberties are violated like that," Dryden said, putting on a suitably sympathetic expression. "I am sorry to hear that happened to you."

He stood and walked around the desk to his chair, taking a seat and picking up a file. He opened it and read for a moment.

"Ah! I see you have a birthday coming up in a few days. Twenty-eight years old? That makes you about my age, then—I turned thirty a few weeks ago."

Oliver thought Dryden didn't look a day over twenty-one. He had no crinkles around the eyes or creases around the mouth, and his smile seemed boyish.

"You're from Indiana—that makes us practically neighbors. I'm from Michigan myself. Looks like you've been in France a while, over four years. You must be right at home here, eh?"

He looked up and smiled again, and Oliver nodded. Dryden set the file back down on the desk. "You must have made a lot of friends in Paris over the last four years."

Oliver nodded. "Yeah, a few I guess."

"Musicians such as yourself?"

"No—well, I mean, other than the guys I work with."

"No?"

"Most of my French friends are artists, writers, dancers—things like that."

"I see. Creative types, though, all of them?"

"Yeah, I suppose so."

"Men? Women?"

"Both."

"Have any of your French friends expressed opinions about the new regime in Vichy, or about the German occupation?"

Oliver shrugged. "Not really. I think it's a pretty safe bet they don't like either very much, though."

Dryden chuckled. "Indeed. But you wouldn't describe any of them as agitators?"

Oliver instantly thought of Serge. The young writer had mysteriously reappeared two weeks after the Germans marched in, with no explanation, and refused to say where he'd been. Over the five weeks since then, Oliver had noticed him flash hostile looks in the direction of German soldiers whenever they'd pass, looks that vanished after a few seconds.

"I don't think so," he answered, keeping his thoughts to himself.

"Have any of them been harassed by the police since the Occupation began? Any difficulties?"

"Not that I'm aware of," Oliver said, his eyebrow arching in curiosity. What was this fellow getting at?

Dryden gave him a disarming smile. "We're interested in hearing about any civil liberties abuses. The political situation here is so uncertain—Vichy officially in control, but all of the authority really lying with the German occupation, at least here in the north—it could easily lead to abuse."

Oliver nodded, but said nothing.

"We'd appreciate it if you kept your eyes and ears open, and let us know about any abuses you or your friends should happen to witness, or hear of. Would you do that for us?"

Oliver shrugged. "Sure, I suppose."

"Thank you, Oliver." Dryden stood and extended his hand. "It was a pleasure meeting you, and I hope you have no further difficulties with the police."

Oliver thanked him and left.

As he exited the embassy, he reflected back on the strange conversation. Frank Dryden hadn't taken any notes, but he seemed to file everything Oliver said in his memory. He had a big, easy smile, but it never seemed to extend to his eyes. He'd been friendly and disarming, but there was something about his manner that told Oliver there was more going on. It made him uncomfortable, but he couldn't say why.

**

"More wine, my dear?" Frank Dryden asked the woman seated across from him in the restaurant of the Hotel Bristol, the official American diplomatic residency since the beginning of the Occupation.

"You should not be trying to get me drunk, darling," she replied, but held out her glass anyway. "A little. That's all."

"What time do you perform tonight?"

"Nine o'clock. As usual."

Cécile Fournier was one of the most popular *chanteuses* in Paris. She had a sultry voice, and sang in a rich alto. Her style ranged from the traditional French folk songs, to soft jazz anthems. At thirty-nine years of age, she had been performing on the Parisian nightclub scene for twenty years, and had earned quite a following.

"Will you come to hear me tonight, then?" she asked with a batting of the eyelashes, and looked down as she took a sip of wine. "Or will you only come to see me after I am home?" She glanced back up, a hint of smile on her lips.

"I would love to hear you sing tonight, darling," Frank said.

"And will you also accompany me home after my show? To protect me, of course."

"Of course."

She smiled at him, a twinkle in her green eyes.

Dryden snapped his fingers and widened his eyes in a convincing show of surprise. "I almost forgot—I spoke with a jazz musician yesterday, a trumpet player who performs at a club called *Le Chien Errant* in the *Quartier Pigalle*. I believe that's not far from your club, darling—are you familiar with it?"

"Of course," Cécile said. "On the Boulevard de Rochechouart at the Villa Dancourt. It is not my style of music, but it is said that the band there is quite good, and I have heard that their leader composes some of the songs. It was quite popular, before the curfews."

Dryden knew perfectly well that *Le Chien Errant* was only five blocks south of the club in Montmartre where Cécile sang, and perhaps six blocks from her apartment. "It seems there are several Americans there. Including the owner."

"Yes." Cécile inclined her head slightly and regarded him with a curious expression. "What is it that you want me to do? That is why you brought up the subject, is it not?"

Dryden's face broke into a wide grin. "Oh, I just adore you, my dear! I can never get anything past you, can I?"

She shook her head and smiled, but waited in silence for him to explain.

"Would you pretend to like that type of jazz for me? Go sit in the crowd on your nights off, pay attention to the German officers in attendance, and let me know what they say?"

Her smile widened. "What I used to do for my own government, before the invasion? You want me to resume that, but for you?"

"I hope that's not an imposition on you. You did it so well for French intelligence, I am hoping you'll do it for me—considering how much you mean to me."

"Yes, of course." Cécile's smile remained in place, but no longer extended to her eyes. She was under no illusions. Their relationship was quite satisfying—he was young and vigorous, this American diplomat, and so handsome—but she knew he wasn't in love with her, any more than she was in love with him, even after more than a year. She knew he had approached her because he'd somehow learned of her arrangement with the French intelligence bureau, and he wanted a piece of the pie.

The fact that he got more than just her professional cooperation was an unexpected bonus for both of them.

For two years she had been called upon to spy on the expatriate Germans in Paris, surreptitiously listen to their conversations, and report back to the intelligence bureau. She was one of several such operatives, all fluent in German, that *Deuxieme Bureau* employed in the late 1930s to keep an eye on the forty thousand-strong German community in Paris.

She spoke German as fluently as French. Her father was Parisian, but her mother was born in Alsace in 1870—months before the Prussian victory gave the German-speaking province to the new

German Reich in January 1871. The peace treaty had given Alsatians twenty-one months to decide whether to stay and become German citizens, or migrate to France and remain French citizens. Cécile's maternal grandparents waited until the last minute before moving from Strasbourg to Paris in late September 1872. They were among 100,000 Alsatians—five percent of the population—that chose French identity over German language and ethnicity.

Even now, seventy years later, that dichotomy persisted. Cécile's mother, elderly now, still spoke French with a slight Germanic accent, and preferred to converse with her children in the Alsatian German dialect as often as not. But she considered herself French through and through.

It was this loyalty that had caused French intelligence to use Parisians of Alsatian heritage to spy on the newly enlarged expatriate German community in the city during the 1930s. Most of the new arrivals were political refugees, fleeing Nazi rule, but French intelligence was certain there were spies in their midst.

And they had been correct.

Cécile had overheard many quiet conversations in restaurants and clubs—in particular the two largest Alsatian restaurants, the Bistro Bofinger on the Right Bank, and the Brasserie Lipp on the Left Bank—between visiting Wehrmacht officers in civilian clothes and expatriate Germans who were presumably on the Abwehr payroll.

And Cécile had filed away the details in her sharp mind, reporting back to the *Deuxieme Bureau* in perfect accuracy. She became a highly prized asset to the intelligence bureau—and she presumed that was how she came to the attention of Frank Dryden, the handsome boy diplomat who played at being an Information Officer.

Her handlers at the *Deuxieme Bureau* agreed to allow her to share some of what she learned with Dryden, always vetting it before agreeing on what could be shared. And in that way she earned Dryden's trust.

His physical ministrations were an unexpected pleasure, and a reward she wanted to maintain more than money. When the Occupation began seven weeks ago, the job ended and the money dried up—but the incorrigible Frank Dryden remained a frequent nighttime guest at her apartment. And at that, he was far from amateur.

And so now she smiled at Dryden and agreed to do her part.

14

August 2nd began as most Fridays, with Oliver sleeping until mid-morning; but when he awoke and went to the bakery on the corner, he treated himself to something special for breakfast—*croissant au chocolat* instead of the regular croissant.

It was said that chocolate wouldn't be available much longer, with the British naval blockade preventing import of cocoa. The bakery had raised the price since the beginning of the Occupation, but Oliver thought, *What the hell, my birthday only comes once a year.*

He bought a Herald Tribune on his way back to his apartment, and sat at his table and read while he ate his *croissant au chocolat* and drank his coffee. He still drank coffee every morning in spite of the rationing and the sharp increase in price.

Even though it was an American paper, it was obvious that the Paris Herald Tribune was subject to the same censorship as the French newspapers. All of the war news emphasized the prowess of the German military over the British. And while there had been considerable speculation on the streets over the last month concerning whether Switzerland or Britain would be invaded next, the newspapers never ventured an opinion on that matter.

There was a knock at his door, and Oliver opened it to find a deliveryman in the uniform of Bon Marché department store, holding a small gift-wrapped package. He asked Oliver to sign for it, and handed over the package.

Oliver carried it to the table and read the card.

My dear Oliver,
Happy birthday, my love
Hélène

He opened the package and found an expensive gold watch inside. It was already set to the correct time, and it ticked to the movement of the second hand. He tried it on, and was only momentarily surprised that it already fit. Of course it did, Hélène would have seen to that.

He took it off his wrist, and as he put it back in the box he noticed an engraving on the back. His name, and today's date written French style: 2-8-1940.

He would be sure to wear it every time he went to meet Hélène.

**

Oliver had taken the night off from the club so that he could have dinner with his friends, all of whom had returned after the armistice. Every worker in France was still guaranteed at least two weeks of paid vacation every year, which was something the new regime in Vichy hadn't reversed—at least, not yet.

Many things had changed, and not just the curfew and the rationing. Oliver had received two letters from his mother since the Occupation began, and both times the enveloped was torn open and taped closed. It irritated him, but he knew there was nothing he could do. He wondered if his letters back to his parents arrived in the States in the same condition.

On the street, no one complained about the invasion of privacy, but people did quietly grumble that mail now took twice as long to be delivered—because the censors opened and read every letter.

Shortly before noon he left home, dressed in dark slacks and a nice button-down shirt, and walked west down the Boulevard Saint

Germain into the 6th Arrondissement. It was a bright clear day, and the sidewalks were crowded with people enjoying the summer weather. Summer was Oliver's favorite time of year in Paris. There was a break for a few months from the *grisaille*, and it wasn't usually as oppressively hot and humid as the summers back home in Indiana.

At the Place Saint Germain-des-Pres, a tower of directional signs printed in German reminded passersby of who was in charge now, but aside from a few German soldiers patrolling the sidewalks in their gray Wehrmacht uniforms and the lack of cars in the street, Paris looked much as it always had.

As he approached *Les Deux Magots*, Oliver spied Pablo Picasso sitting alone at an outside table, drawing furiously in a sketch pad, his brow furrowed in concentration. Oliver smiled to himself. He never grew tired of spying world-famous artists and writers sitting at sidewalk cafes in this part of Paris.

He saw Lisette sitting in the far corner, facing the Rue Bonaparte. He waved, and she smiled as he sat down.

"Happy birthday, Oliver."

He grinned. "Thank you! And thank you for agreeing to meet me for lunch. It wouldn't be my birthday without lunch at *Les Deux Magots*."

He and Lisette had taken lunch at the famous cafe in the *Quartier Saint Germain-des-Pres* for his last two birthdays, and it seemed a shame not to continue the tradition for his twenty-eighth. Especially now that they were speaking again. He'd still wondered if she would agree, and was ecstatic when she did.

They engaged in small talk for a little while before they ordered food and a half-bottle of red wine in a carafe. Then he reminisced with her about previous birthday lunches here, and they smiled at the pleasant memories.

Eventually the conversation lulled, and she looked out onto the square and took a sip of wine.

Oliver was surprised to find that he had no idea what else to talk about. An uncomfortable silence fell as they both avoided looking at each other, pretending to people-watch instead.

It dawned on Oliver that it wasn't that he didn't know what to say—it was that he was afraid to ask what he was really wondering. *Don't be stupid. You and Lisette are friends now; you should be able to ask her anything you want.*

"How is your, um, friend?" he stumbled over it, not sure what word to use for the man Lisette was seeing.

She looked at him, her brown eyes momentarily widening in surprise that he should ask that.

"Jean-Louis is well." She hesitated a moment before adding, "He is very busy these days. He is in upper management at a factory in Aubervilliers. They sustained some damage in the bombardment, and now they have several new contracts with the Wehrmacht. So they are rebuilding, and also building trucks for the Germans. It is a busy time for him."

Oliver leaned in and whispered with a sly smile. "Lisette! You're seeing a collaborator? What will people think?"

She scowled. "It's just business."

He leaned back, the sly smile still in place. "Of course, just business."

Her scowl deepened, and she folded her arms across her chest. "I didn't realize you invited me to lunch to mock me."

"No, Lisette please, don't feel that way. I'm sorry. I shouldn't make fun of you. Please accept my apology."

She considered a moment, then gave him a slight nod and unfolded her arms. She took a sip of wine and looked out onto the street.

Their food arrived, and they ate mostly in silence, punctuated by occasional small talk. After they finished eating and drinking, Oliver removed some cash and ration coupons from his pocket and paid the bill.

He walked her across the Place Saint Germain-des-Pres to the Metro station. She thanked him for lunch, he thanked her again for coming, they kissed each other on the cheeks and parted company.

**

Lisette sat on the underground train with her arms crossed, her legs crossed, shaking her foot. Why had Oliver asked about Jean-Louis? What horrible manners! And so typically American. It was not seemly.

But she knew what really irritated her wasn't that he'd asked. Why had she mentioned the Wehrmacht contracts Jean-Louis's company had won? It was none of Oliver's business. She should have kept that to herself.

She hadn't been entirely comfortable when Jean-Louis told her about them five weeks ago, but she'd hidden her discomfort. And after a few days she came to hold the same attitude that Jean-Louis did—it was business. After all, life had to go on, people had to continue to make a living, and companies had to conduct business. It was just a fact of life that the business to be conducted these days was with Germans.

German soldiers came to buy wine at the store where she worked, and the store didn't refuse to sell to them. Why would it? The soldiers were polite, and they had money. Lisette didn't smile at them as she did her regular customers, but she was polite in return. It was just business.

So why did it bother her so much that Oliver insinuated that Jean-Louis was a collaborator? Why should she care what Oliver thought?

Because deep in the recesses of her mind, she had thought the same thing.

**

Oliver walked back along the Boulevard Saint Germain to the 5th Arrondissement at a much faster pace than usual. He ignored the crowds around him, not caring to people-watch right now.

Once inside his apartment he couldn't sit still. He got up from the couch and washed some dishes in the kitchen sink. He sat back down and tried to read, but couldn't concentrate. He got up and paced the room.

Damn her! Why did it have to be so tense?

He left his apartment and climbed the stairs two at a time. He knocked on Marcel's door, certain that the young man wasn't working this afternoon.

Marcel answered the door, and Oliver barged in without a word, pushed him against the wall and kissed him. He kicked the door shut with his foot.

**

Oliver ordered multiple plates at Chez Marius that night. First came the cheese plate and the fruit plate, followed by the charcuterie, and finally a large bowl of salad—all for sharing with Marcel, Sébastien, Adrienne, Marie-France, Serge, and Madeleine. It was a simple meal, certainly, but to his friends it was a feast.

It was earlier than they would have normally eaten—only seven o'clock—but the nine o'clock curfew had necessitated a change in their dinner habits.

Serge was the first to notice the gold watch. "That is very expensive. Too expensive for a musician, I think."

"It was a gift, from a lady friend," Oliver explained.

Adrienne gave him a knowing look. Marcel looked away.

Serge's expression registered disapproval. "It is Swiss, is it not? Difficult to find these days."

Oliver shrugged. "I hadn't thought of it, but I suppose so."

"Your lady friend must know someone important," Serge said, his words clipped.

Oliver ignored that. "Where's Collette?" he asked as the first plates arrived.

"Collette got a part in a movie," Adrienne said. "They are still filming."

"A movie? That's fantastic!" Oliver said.

"Of course *she* was chosen for a film role," Marie-France said. "She's blonde. That's what they want now, blondes. And she has blue eyes."

Oliver detected a note of bitterness from Marie-France, whose hair was brown and eyes were green. She was also an actress, but to his knowledge she had never worked in film. "Is it a large role?"

Marie-France sniffed. "I don't know."

Adrienne gave Marie-France a scowl. "She told me that she has more than fifty lines."

"I've been helping her with her lines," Madeleine said. "She's not bad."

Marie-France sniffed again.

"Perhaps she can join us later?" Oliver suggested.

Adrienne shrugged. "She told me this morning that they would be filming quite late. She will need to be careful about the curfew—unless of course she has someplace to stay." She cast a sideways glance at Sébastien.

Sébastien studiously ignored her.

"Well, it's too bad she can't be here," Oliver said.

"Especially since you are buying dinner!" Serge said with a wide grin, bringing laughter from everyone.

Sébastien raised his glass of wine. "To our dear friend Oliver, on his twenty-eighth birthday—may your glass never be empty, may your pocketbook never be empty, may your head never be empty, and may your bed never be empty. *Salut!*"

"*Salut!*" they all said, as they clinked their glasses and drank.

Oliver ordered an extra bottle of the house red, and by the time dinner was finished he was nearly drunk. His friends were in the same condition, however, so he didn't give it a second thought.

It was only a few minutes before nine o'clock, but none of them lived far. Adrienne, Madeleine, and Marie-France lived in the building above *Chez Marius*, and had only to step outside of the bistro to find the front door of the building. Serge lived in the building across the street, and he stumbled across the cobblestones, stopping midway to turn around and give Oliver one last poetic toast, before stumbling back toward his front door.

Sébastien put his arm around Oliver's shoulder, and Marcel walked beside them as they made their way to their own building on the corner. They supported each other up the stairs until they reached the fourth floor, and stopped in the hallway in front of Sébastien's door.

"I have an unopened bottle of Burgundy in my cupboard," Sébastien said. "Why don't you fellows come in and we'll continue this holiday?"

Marcel nodded and looked to Oliver, who shrugged and said "Why not?"

Oliver plopped down on Sébastien's large cushiony couch and stretched his legs out, taking a quaff of the wine rather than a sip. "Excellent Burgundy!"

Sébastien grinned. "I've had this in the cupboard since the day before I left for the army. I was going to save it for a victory celebration, but now that is not possible—so instead I have saved it for you, my friend, and your birthday. *Salut!*"

Oliver took another drink, and then set the glass down on the coffee table. "Speaking of wine," he began, following his own stream of association. "I had lunch today with Lisette at *Les Deux Magots*. She told me her lover is a collaborator."

Sébastien looked stunned. "I didn't know you were seeing Lisette."

Oliver shook his head. "No, just for lunch, for my birthday." Clearly Sébastien had missed the point. "But she said that her lover's company is making equipment for the Germans—he's a *collaborator*." He stressed the word heavily this time, to make sure Sébastien and Marcel got the point.

Sébastien looked troubled, but then his face took on an almost pitying expression that took Oliver by surprise. "I wish you wouldn't torture yourself, my friend."

"What do you mean?"

"I wish you wouldn't delude yourself with Lisette."

Oliver scowled. "I'm not deluding myself. Lisette and I are good friends, that's all. I only wanted to have lunch with her for my birthday. Nothing delusional about that."

Sébastien smiled, that charming easy smile of his that made him look so boyish. "Of course not. I'm glad that you are friends. It's good to see you happy again."

"I *am* happy," Oliver insisted.

Marcel stared at him, and Oliver couldn't decipher his expression. He wondered what was going on behind those intense dark eyes.

Sébastien topped off their glasses, and set the empty bottle on the coffee table. Then he kicked off his shoes and put his bare feet up next to the bottle.

Oliver smacked his thigh as an idea struck him. "We should see if Collette is home yet! I have a bottle of wine in my apartment that I can fetch, and she can join us!"

A brief scowl flitted across Sébastien's face, and Oliver noticed. "Is something wrong?"

"Why should Collette join us? We are having an amusing time without her."

"Yes, but we missed her at dinner," Oliver said. "Let's see if she's home."

He started to get up from the couch, but Marcel placed a hand on his shoulder. Oliver looked at him, and the young man shook his head almost imperceptibly.

"She is probably not home, anyway," Sébastien said, looking away and taking a drink.

Oliver's inebriated mind struggled to make sense of this. "Am I missing something?"

Sébastien looked him in the eye. "Collette owes me an apology, and I do not wish to see her until she gives me that apology. I certainly don't want her in my apartment."

Now it was Oliver's turn to give Sébastien a concerned look. "What happened?"

Sébastien shrugged. "We had a fight last weekend," he said, as if it were nothing.

"What about?" Oliver ignored Marcel's warning look.

Sébastien's scowl deepened, and his face flushed red. "She brought a German officer to my studio on Saturday. She met him when she auditioned for that film. He said he wanted to buy one of my paintings. *Bof*!" Sébastien waved his hand dismissively.

"Did you sell to him?"

Sébastien looked at Oliver as if he were missing the point. "I tried to dissuade him, but he insisted. So I charged him more than the painting was worth, and took his money. It wasn't one of my favorites anyway."

Another dismissive wave of the hand.

"I asked Collette to stay and have a word while the German took the painting to his car. I demanded to know why she would bring one of the *Boche* into my studio. She said he was Austrian, as if that were somehow better. 'Austrians love art,' she said. *Bof*! They have embraced the Nazis just like all the other Germans. We fought. There was shouting. We called each other names, and she stormed out. I told her not to come back."

Sébastien shrugged, and took a long drink of wine.

Oliver stared at him with open mouth for a moment, then reached across Marcel to pat Sébastien's knee.

"That's difficult," he agreed. "I understand now why you don't want to see her. I'm sorry that I mentioned her."

Sébastien gave Oliver a half-hearted grin. "Don't apologize. How could you know? And let's not dwell on unpleasant things. This is your birthday, and I asked you back here so that we can continue the holiday. So drink, please! *Salut*!"

"*Salut*!" Marcel and Oliver echoed, and drank.

"Ah, women—we can't live with them, we can't live without them," Oliver said, using a literal translation of the American expression. This received blank stares from the two Frenchmen.

Oliver tried to explain what that meant, but gave up after a moment and took another long quaff of wine. "I should go get that bottle from my apartment."

"Nonsense, I have more wine," Sébastien said, rising from the couch and walking toward the kitchen. "It is a *vin de pays*, but it is not bad." He reappeared a moment later with the uncorked bottle.

Oliver drained his glass, and held it out. After Sébastien refilled his and Marcel's glasses, Oliver raised his in a toast.

"Here's to a night with the boys," Oliver said, again literally translating an American idiom. His toast was met with bemused smiles from his companions, but they drank to it without question.

Two bottles of wine later, it occurred fleetingly to Oliver that he had never cabled his parents that day. But then, neither had he received the usual telegram from them with their birthday wishes.

Oh well, too late now, he thought as he took another gulp of wine. He briefly considered finding a phone and calling them—it wasn't yet midnight, and with the time difference it would be before dinner back home—but the thought of talking to them completely drunk, and his father's certain disapproval, made him laugh out-loud.

Marcel and Sébastien laughed too, as others do when they are also drunk, though they had no idea what he'd found so funny. He laughed harder at them, which caused them to laugh harder.

"My parents never touch the stuff!" Oliver said between laughs, pointing at his wine glass, and soon they were all doubled over with fits of hysteria.

More wine, and his vision began to blur. He was vaguely aware of soft wet lips on his, and not sure if they were Marcel's or Sébastien's. It took him a moment to realize that it was actually both of them. His mind briefly protested, but it never formulated into an actual thought, and before he realized it he was kissing them back; both of them, at the same time. Two sets of hands rubbed all over him, sliding under his shirt, unbuttoning the front of his pants.

Oliver's own hands wandered, and he hardly thought about it.

And then, somehow they were all on the floor, naked, arms and legs entwined, bodies pressed together. In the euphoric buzz that enveloped him, inhibitions slipped away.

And it was fantastic.

15

Collette awoke to Karl Gruder brushing her cheek with his fingertips. Her eyes fluttered open, and she slowly smiled at him. The handsome Wehrmacht captain, with his short blond hair and pale blue eyes, looked almost shy now.

"I didn't mean to wake you," he said, staring at her while his fingers stroked her hair.

"It's alright." Her voice sounded sleepy. This was the most luxurious bed she'd ever slept in, and it lulled her. She stretched, and the sheet slipped below her breasts. She saw his eyes drift toward them.

He'd looked at her breasts the first time she'd met him, on the set of a French film that the thirty-year-old was overseeing as representative of the Office of Culture. She'd made eyes at him, of course, and then noticed he would find excuses to be on-set whenever she was filming, and to talk with her between scenes. It was awkward small-talk at first, but she touched his arm often, and enjoyed the rapturous looks that crossed his face. He started talking her about his childhood in Salzburg, his father the police inspector, and his mother who sang in the choir at St. Agnes Church. He spoke of his days at University in Vienna, and beamed when he described his victories as a member of the rowing crew, and his love of art.

When he'd invited her to accompany him to the Louvre last week, she'd been delighted, and agreed at once. He'd been there as a student, ten years ago, he said, and babbled on in excitement while explaining the great works of art they passed. So she told Karl that her friend Sébastien Bonnet was a painter, and asked if he'd like to see his work.

That was when Sébastien embarrassed her by being cold and rude, even after Karl asked to buy one of his paintings. She chastised Sébastien after Karl took the painting to his car, and they fought. When she rejoined Karl at his car, he took one look at her face and threatened to go back inside and confront the "insolent artist," but when she begged him not to, he nodded.

Then tonight the filming had gone quite late, nearly to midnight, and he offered her a ride home in his black Citroën. He drove them to the Left Bank, but instead of taking her to her home in the 5th Arrondissement, he turned off the Boulevard St. Germain early and drove to the Hotel Lutetia.

He touched her breasts before he'd even shut off the engine, slipping his hand down the front of her blouse to squeeze one and play with the nipple. Then he took her hand and led her upstairs to his suite without a word…

And it had been wonderful. She'd fallen asleep in his arms afterward. Now he watched her, so tender and affectionate.

"You can stay." He hesitated, then added, "I'd like for you to stay."

"I'd like that," she said, reaching out to stroke his thigh.

He slipped down beside her, put his arm around her and hugged her to him. She kissed his chest, and he ran his hands through her hair. She moved her hand across his chest, down his belly, and then between his legs. She began to stroke him, and brought him back to arousal.

"You are not ready for sleep, my dear," she said.

He didn't answer, but placed his mouth on hers and moved his body on top of her.

**

Collette awoke to the smell of coffee. She rubbed her eyes and sat up, looking around the suite. She was alone, but the door was partly open and she could hear Gruder moving around in the other room. The clock on the table indicated half past seven, and she smiled to herself. Military men really did wake up early, even after a late night.

"Good morning," she called out.

He came through the door a moment later, carrying two steaming cups on saucers.

"Good morning." He set a cup and saucer on the bedside table next to her.

"Thank you." She took a sip of the coffee and smiled at him. He returned the smile half-heartedly.

"What's wrong?"

He looked away. He sat in a chair with his cup in his right hand and the saucer in the other, and sipped his coffee in brooding silence.

She threw off the sheets and walked naked toward him, sitting in the other chair and pulling it up close to him, close enough that their knees touched. She placed her hand on his thigh and looked into his eyes. "What is troubling you, my dear?"

He was silent for several seconds, staring into his coffee cup. "I have not been honest with you," he said at last, still not looking at her.

"Oh?" She pulled her hand back from his thigh, her stomach clenching in fear.

"I am married. My wife Greta and I have three children back home in Salzburg. I didn't want you to know."

She breathed a small sigh of relief. She wasn't sure what she had been afraid he would say, but this wasn't as bad as she'd feared. She put her hand on his forearm and gave it a gentle squeeze.

"I understand, my dear," she said, her tone soft and soothing.

He gave her a surprised look. "You are not angry?"

"No, I am not angry."

He looked away again, embarrassed. "I should have told you before."

She shook her head. "It is alright. It would not have changed anything."

He stiffened, and pushed her hand off of his arm. "Get dressed!" He bolted from the chair and stormed out of the room.

Stung, Collette felt her heart sink into her stomach. Then her eyes flashed with anger, and her cheeks flushed red. She stomped to the bed, picked up her clothes off the floor, and began to dress. The front of her blouse was torn, so she removed it again and flounced from the bedroom with her bra exposed, holding out her blouse clenched in her fist.

"Who is going to replace my blouse that you tore?"

He stared at the blouse for a second in confusion before he seemed to remember what happened. He took the garment from her and held it out to examine the torn fabric.

"I apologize for your blouse. I'll have a new one delivered within the hour." He gave her a polite nod. "I'll have some breakfast sent up as well. I would be honored if you would stay and eat with me."

She shrugged and tossed her hair in indignation. She flounced back into the bedroom and took a seat on the end of the bed. In truth, she had nothing better to do on a Saturday morning, and she could hardly afford to turn down a free breakfast.

But she'd be damned if she'd wait in the same room.

*

He walked into the bedroom a few minutes later. She glared at him, and crossed her arms. He took a few steps, and stopped in front of her. He held out his hand and waited.

Collette stared at his hand for a moment, then looked up at his face. His eyes—soft and full of regret—said more than any words he could utter. She looked back at his hand and placed her own in it.

He pulled her up, lifted her chin with his other hand, and kissed her—softly, slowly. Then he pulled away and stared into her eyes.

She thought she understood. He felt guilty about his wife, and hadn't understood when she didn't. It was understandable—he was not Parisian. She leaned her head against his shoulder, and he held her tight until their breakfast arrived.

**

Frank Dryden sat across from the bearded man, who ate his lunch of pork chops and *choucroute*—French for sauerkraut—with gusto.

At forty-six years old, Grigori Aleksandrovich Trusnik was a throwback to the years when Czar Nikolas II still ruled Russia. His beard was more gray than brown these days, but it was still thick and long, hanging nearly to the middle of his chest. The professor of Russian literature had toured all over Europe in the past twenty years, lecturing at universities from Krakow to Oxford, and yet his style had not updated in all that time.

They spoke at length about Tolstoy—Dryden was not a fan of *War and Peace*—before getting to the heart of the meeting.

"So, Mr. Dryden," the professor began, lowering his voice, and folding his hands on the table in front of him. "I was referred to you by Dr. Jackson. I believe you know him?"

"Yes." Dryden nodded.

Dr. Sumner Jackson was the head physician at the American Hospital in Neuilly, in the western suburbs of Paris. Starting the day after the Occupation, on June 15th, Dr. Jackson had reported back to the embassy on the position, size and condition of German POW camps in France. He also ensured that any French or British POWs who were transferred to the American Hospital did not return to the camps when they recovered. He somehow managed to arrange escape routes by which they could make their way to Great Britain.

Few knew the details of Dr. Jackson's escape routes. Frank Dryden of the U.S. Embassy was one of those few.

"Dr. Jackson mentioned to me that you were interested in resistance movements," Professor Trusnik continued. He spoke excellent French—all educated Russians of his generation learned French as their second language, and then German as their third, but rarely English.

Dryden nodded again. "I understand you are familiar with the subject?"

"Yes, yes. Unfortunately, most of my acquaintances in Krakow and Prague were eliminated not long after the Nazis occupied their cities—intellectuals are prime targets of the Gestapo. I am happy that Paris—so far—has escaped that fate."

"How is it that you have become familiar with this particular area of interest?" Dryden pressed.

"Oh, just because the Gestapo eliminated the intellectual class early, does not mean that they eliminated the intellectual basis for nationalist resistance. It is sadly true that most of my acquaintances in Poland and Czechoslovakia were murdered last year, but that is not to say that I know no one else in those countries. I was feted on my speaking tours over the years, and I met a great many people. And like you, Mr. Dryden, I am a citizen of a 'neutral' country, which affords me certain liberties."

"Understood."

"So, what would you like to know, Mr. Dryden?"

"How is it that these movements get started? And why did they start in Czechoslovakia and Poland almost immediately, but not yet in France?"

"To answer the first part of your question, they grow from the will of the people. Nothing more, nothing less. Individuals talk, networks form—it can happen quickly, even with the need for secrecy.

"So then, what is different about France? Many things. For one, the Occupation here has not been as brutal—at least, not yet. For another, there is the sense among the French that they still have their own government, even if in truth it is only a puppet regime. But the figurehead speaks with a French accent and has unquestionable patriotism, and so for now the French listen."

Dryden grew impatient. "Yes, I know that much. What I'm curious about is where to look for the nascent signs of a network."

Professor Trusnik smiled indulgently. "I would tell you to look at the people who are most likely to be targeted by the Occupation's policies—the Jews, the labor unions, intellectuals of course, the bohemian set of writers and artists. They will chafe at the censorship. Ordinarily I would say look to the Communists, but for now at least the Politburo in Moscow is keeping the local Reds on a tight leash. That may not always be the case."

Dryden nodded. "I believe you know such people, Professor? Jews, intellectuals and bohemians, anyway."

Professor Trusnik smiled again, his pale blue eyes twinkling. "Yes, I know many such people, Mr. Dryden."

"And have you seen signs of a gathering resistance?"

Professor Trusnik shrugged in a noncommittal way. "There are signs."

"But?"

"Just signs, Mr. Dryden. Nothing concrete. Yet."

"And if things should become more concrete?"

Professor Trusnik nodded. "You will know it, Mr. Dryden. I will see that you know it."

16

It had been a while since Oliver had come to the swank Passy neighborhood in the daylight.

At one time, that was Hélène's preferred time for him to visit. Her husband was at his government office on the Champs-Elysee, her children were in school, and she could send the maid on a long errand. But eventually they'd shifted to mostly evening visits, when her husband was with his mistress, and she could send the children to friends' houses.

He got off the Metro at the Place Victor Hugo, and strolled down the wide avenue of the same name for several blocks before turning left towards the Seine. The streets were lined with elegant townhouses, three and four stories tall. He came to the familiar one with its green mansard roof, and walked up the steps to ring the bell.

The lady herself answered the door, smiled, and took his wrist to pull him inside. The less time he stood on the doorstep, the less likely to be noticed by nosy neighbors, he knew. Hélène was not ashamed— but she also refused to be the subject of gossip.

"Oliver, so good of you to come," she said. "Let me fix you a drink. Make yourself comfortable."

She led him into a parlor and sat him on the couch, a formal piece with curved wooden legs and tight mauve upholstery.

"Scotch?"

He nodded. "Thank you."

She stepped over to the credenza in the far corner where several crystal decanters stood, carrying liquids of various colors. His eyes followed her swaying backside as she walked, and as she leaned forward over the credenza. She wore a black skirt today that stopped at her knees, and a white blouse with a high frilly collar. She took two glasses and poured scotch, then set them on green marble coasters on the mahogany coffee table in front of the couch.

"You can make yourself more comfortable than that," she said, and loosened his necktie before unfastening the top three buttons of his shirt and spreading his collar open. "Much better," she pronounced, leaning back with a satisfied look.

They chatted amiably for a while, sipping their drinks and exchanging news. She asked about his birthday, and he thanked her for the watch. She looked at his wrist and told him how handsome it looked there.

She told him about her weekend. "We spent a lovely Sunday in the Bois de Boulogne. Jacques had to show his pass at the checkpoint—his permit to drive, as a government official—and we were able to pass through. Many of our neighbors do not have that luxury anymore." Her proud smile showed a certain amusement at her neighbors' jealousy.

Most French in the Occupied Zone were not allowed to drive cars, though certain exceptions were made. Government bureaucrats such as Jacques Chastain, as well as doctors, police, and important collaborators, were given special permits, which they had to show at German military checkpoints.

Oliver wasn't surprised that Hélène was proud of her husband's special privilege.

"Does his permit allow you to drive?" he asked.

"No, unfortunately," she said, her tone a bit more clipped. "But I'm sure that in time this can be rectified." She leaned forward and played with his loosened necktie. "Have you seen our car, Oliver?"

*

It had been years since Oliver had made love in the back seat of a car, but it made his blood pump. The sight of her leaned back against the door, her skirt hiked up to her waist, her blouse open to reveal a lacy brassiere and an elegant pearl necklace, her mouth open to let out cries of pleasure, was as surreal as it was thrilling.

The girls he had seduced in college were not of her caliber, and yet here she was in the back seat of this 1939 Citroën Traction Avant, not even all the way undressed, panting and moaning like a young girl.

Her thighs, slightly plump though not unshapely, squeezed his sides, pulling at the tail of his shirt. He, too, had not bothered to disrobe. His pants and his underwear bunched around his ankles, but he still wore his shirt, and the end of his loosened necktie dangled between her lace-covered breasts.

She reached behind him and placed her hands squarely on his buttocks, pushing him into her. She cried out and turned her face to the side, her breath steaming the glass even on this warm day.

Afterward, they lay there for a moment, catching their breath.

"It's too bad you can't take the car," Oliver said. "We could do that more often."

She smiled and stroked his cheek. "You enjoyed that, my love? Yes? I'm glad."

She sat up, tugging her skirt back down over her thighs and straightening the fabric, then buttoned up her blouse. She patted down her hair, and reached for her purse in the front seat. She removed a cigarette holder and cigarette, and handed him a pack of matches. He struck a match and she leaned forward to light the end of the cigarette.

Her dark brown eyes lingered on his as she inhaled, then blew a long stream of gray smoke toward the front of the car.

"It is a pity you don't have a permit to drive, my dear," she said. "I would let you drive this car. On a beautiful day like today, we could drive into the Bois de Boulogne, and make love under the trees. That would be lovely, no?"

"That would be lovely."

"You do know how to drive, do you not?"

"Yes, of course." Oliver hadn't driven in several years, but that was beside the point.

She leaned back and sighed, took another long inhale and slowly exhaled the smoke. "Then it is such a shame that neither of us is permitted."

Oliver thought he saw a flicker of resentment cross her dark eyes, but it disappeared as quickly as it had come, and she smiled at him.

"Come, put your pants back on and join me for another drink, yes?"

Oliver had nearly forgotten that his pants were still around his ankles, and he tugged them up and exited the car.

"Perhaps I could drive the car, and tell the soldiers at the checkpoint that I'm Jacques Chastain," Oliver suggested when they were seated once again in her parlor with another glass of scotch apiece.

"That would not be possible. The permit bears his photograph. And thankfully, my dear, you do not look anything like Mr. Jacques Chastain." She touched his chin and gave him a playful smile.

Oliver shrugged in exaggerated fashion. "Then I suppose we'll never be able to take a trip to the Bois de Boulogne."

They chatted and sipped their drinks for another half-hour, and then she said that it was time for him to leave. "The maid will be back soon." She walked him to the front door and gave him one long kiss, then opened the door and shoved him out.

**

Jacques Chastain greeted his wife in the front hall that evening with a kiss on each cheek. He wore a gray silk suit with a black silk necktie and a matching handkerchief in the front pocket. The cuffs of his blue silk shirt were held by gold cufflinks.

"Good evening, dear," she said after they'd kissed cheeks. "How was your day?"

"It was fine," he said, but his tone sounded distracted.

"Oh?"

Jacques didn't answer as he walked into the parlor and poured himself a full glass of scotch. Hélène followed, but stopped in the entrance to the parlor and watched him, waiting. He would tell her what was on his mind, if she didn't pry too hard. He always told her.

He took a long drink of the scotch before he turned back toward her. "The Germans want to reduce the rations, starting in September."

"Oh? For whom?"

"For everyone."

Hélène's mouth opened in surprise, but she recovered her composure quickly. "Everyone? That is not possible."

"I'm afraid it is. Everyone except for themselves, of course."

Of course. "Even government officials, such as you?"

He sighed, a long and heavy exhale. "Yes, even government officials like me." He took another long drink.

"How can that be?"

"It's simple economics," he replied, his voice gruff. He poured himself another measure of scotch. "The Germans take twenty percent of our agricultural production as reparations for the war, from both the Occupied and Unoccupied zones. They use some of that to feed their soldiers in the Occupied Zone, and the rest is shipped to Germany for

131

their domestic consumption. Given our current level of rationing, there will not be enough left to feed their soldiers to their satisfaction. Therefore, they reduce the rations for all of the French in the Occupied Zone, and continue to feed their soldiers as normal."

"Incredible," she said, more to herself than to Jacques, looking off at nothing in particular.

"We will still have a more generous portion than most, but it will be less than what we are accustomed to," he said.

She looked back at him. "How much?"

He took another drink and was silent for a moment. "A bit less bread, a bit less milk and cheese, much less meat. In the end it will amount to 1,600 calories per day for each of us."

Her mouth dropped open again, and this time she didn't bother to close it right away. "How can we live on that?"

"It is more than enough food to survive," he snapped, his voice sharper than she had heard it in a long time. "Civilians in Poland and Czechoslovakia already get by on 1,100 calories per day, and they've been doing that for almost a year. And most of our countrymen will live on 1,300 calories—so you see my dear, we are still better off than most."

She glanced at his midsection. At forty-four years of age, he was not as thin as he once was, his torso squarer than in his youth. She was also slightly plumper than when they had married twenty-one years before.

"I suppose we shall all lose some weight, then," she said, faking a smile.

He nodded. "We will indeed."

"When does this start?"

"In September. We will also be on more strict rations of coffee and tea. It's difficult to import through the British naval blockade, so there is little to go around. The Occupation authorities want to keep most of it for themselves. Most French will have to do without coffee and tea altogether—so once again, we are given a more generous portion, my dear. Be grateful that I work for the government."

She thought of her conversation with Oliver earlier. "And the car? Will you still be permitted to drive it?"

"Yes, of course. Our gasoline rations will remain the same, for now." He set his glass on the top of the credenza and strode toward her. He put his hands on the sides of her shoulders and gave her a quick kiss.

"We should go on a weekend trip into the country, take the children to see Chartres Cathedral, or the chateaux of the Loire, before the fall term begins. Would you like that, my dear?"

She faked a smile again. "Yes, that would be lovely."

17

September 1940

It didn't take Collette long to pack. Only a few outfits hanging inside the standing wardrobe, plus the contents of her dresser drawers, and a few little personal odds and ends. The rest she wouldn't need. She packed up the bed linens and blankets anyway; she had room inside the second box.

The two Frenchmen who showed up to carry the two boxes—wearing dingy, slightly ragged clothes, and with dirt dusted on their faces—flashed her ill-concealed looks of hatred. She ignored them, and walked out the door with her head high. She stood in the hall and waited as they exited with her boxes, then went back to the doorway and looked around.

She would not be sorry to be away from this tiny, unheated garret. Especially not with autumn on the way. It was only mid-September, and already the *grisaille* was taking hold of the Parisian sky.

What she would miss were the people she knew here. At least, she would miss the way they were, before.

Before Karl.

She took one last look around, and turned away. They were jealous, she told herself. She had found a nice man who would take care of her, who appreciated her, and who was young and handsome to boot. She was sure they resented her recent success with the studio, especially Marie-France.

She descended one floor, and walked down the hall to knock on Oliver's door. She could hear him moving inside before he answered.

"Collette," he said, seeming surprised to see her.

"Hello Oliver."

He stood aside and offered for her to come in, but she shook her head with a sad smile and said that she only had a moment.

"You haven't been around much," Oliver said.

"No. It's been—awkward."

Oliver nodded. He was the only one of their friends who was still speaking with her. "You've been, well—busy."

She smiled. "Yes, I have. Very busy." She paused for a second, staring at him with a sad smile. "Oliver, I've come to say goodbye."

"Goodbye?"

"Yes, I'm leaving."

He seemed genuinely stunned. "Where are you going?"

"Not far. To the Hotel Lutetia, on the Boulevard Raspail over in the 6th." It was one of the big grand hotels that the Germans had requisitioned for themselves.

"I know it."

"It is close to *Les Deux Magots*," Collette added. "Perhaps we could meet there for lunch one day."

"I would like that," Oliver said.

They stood there for a moment, staring at each other, neither knowing what more to say. Then suddenly Collette leaned forward and kissed him on the cheek, and her lips lingered for several seconds.

"It was lovely, Oliver," she said, her voice low and husky. "Always so very lovely. Thank you, my dear."

She kissed his cheek again, quickly this time, then spun away and hurried down the hall to the stairs.

*

He stood in his doorway and watched her go with a curious mix of sadness and pity. And maybe a little bit of regret.

**

Out on the sidewalk, Karl Gruder waited beside the black Citroën sedan. He opened the passenger door the moment he saw Collette emerge from the building.

"We've been waiting for you, my dear."

She smiled at him and placed her hand on his cheek. "I'm sorry. I wanted to say goodbye to someone who has been a good friend."

Gruder nodded toward the two workmen who stood on the sidewalk near the rear of the car. "These men say that you have no more things to move. Is that true? They only brought out two boxes."

"Yes, that's all." She noticed that they looked at her now with blank expressions, and none of the hostility they had shown her inside.

Gruder handed each of them a coin worth one Reichsmark—the equivalent of twenty francs under the artificial exchange rate in effect since June—and they scurried away. He put his hand on Collette's back as she got into the car, and closed her door. Then he walked around to the driver's side.

Before he entered the car, Collette looked up at the building next to hers, and found the window to the apartment Adrienne shared with Marie-France and Madeleine on the first floor. The curtains were parted, and she saw both Adrienne and Marie-France staring down at the car with sullen expressions. She met their gaze, and a second later they disappeared, and the curtains fell back into place.

Karl started the car, placed his hand on her knee and smiled at her before taking the gear shift and pulling away from the curb.

Collette watched in the mirror as the neighborhood she'd known as home slipped away.

138

18

Captain Allard stared at the poster on his desk with a deep frown. It was an image of Marshal Pétain, a copy of the official portrait that hung in every government office and schoolroom in France, but with the word "TYRANT" printed across it in red capital letters.

"How many were there?" he asked the gendarme who stood across from him.

"Ten, sir. They were all over the Metro station Sorbonne."

"Only this one station?"

"We do not know, sir."

"Have you contacted other prefectures, to find out if they have also encountered these outrageous posters?" Allard did not try to disguise the irritation and impatience in his voice.

"No sir."

Allard exhaled loudly. He placed his hands flat on the desk in front of him, and stood slowly.

"Then may I suggest, corporal, that you contact all of the neighboring prefectures immediately, and find out if any more of these illegal and seditious posters are out there? If Prefect of Police Bousquet sees one of these, he will be livid. And if any other government official should happen to see one of these, it is certain that heads will roll. I can assure you that my head will not be one of those, do you understand, corporal?"

The gendarme blanched and swallowed hard, but he gave Allard a crisp salute. "Yes sir!"

Allard sat back down, and returned his attention to the poster. Though his face was the picture of calm professionalism, he seethed with anger on the inside.

Marshall Pétain is a hero! He saved France from further bloodshed and humiliation. And he has restored order. The illegal poster in front of him seemed to belie that last point, but Allard ignored that minor detail.

Robert Allard had always been an unapologetic traditionalist. Family and the Catholic Church were the bedrock of his life—should be the bedrock of every French citizen's life. That had always been the weakness of democracy, that liberals could disestablish the church from public life, repeal morality laws, and reduce penalties for criminal acts. This was why French society had become weak—and that was precisely why it had fallen so easily when the Germans invaded this time. Twenty years of debauchery had doomed the Republic.

Well, perhaps after sixty-nine years it was time for the Republic to end. He would not have said so before—he was just a policeman, after all—but it was time for stronger leadership in France, more than democracy could provide. What France needed was the kind of strong leadership that old Marshal Pétain now provided her.

In France's hour of need, in her darkest days, Pétain had saved her.

And it infuriated Allard that ungrateful hooligans—in his own jurisdiction, no less—would dare to insult that noble leader in such a public and outrageous way. He would find them, and he would see them punished for their seditious libel. He swore it.

He opened a drawer and removed his magnifying glass. He spent several minutes poring over the poster, looking for the tiniest details, imperfections in the lettering, any pattern that could be traced to a particular printing press.

And then he found it.

A tiny squiggle that ran through the first "T" that was darker red and ever so slightly raised, wasn't duplicated in the second "T." It was a tiny detail, easily missed, but it told him that the block letter that had printed that "T" bore a tiny crack, just big enough for more of the red ink to seep inside.

And they should be able to match the size and shape of that squiggle to the crack in the original block letter.

He stood, a look of satisfaction on his mustachioed face. He pressed a button on the intercom and asked the corporal to come to his office.

"Have you found out if there are any more of these out there, corporal?"

"None of the neighboring prefectures have seen anything, sir. To be certain, they are canvassing their areas in search of more."

"Excellent. Now bring me a list of all the print shops operating in this prefecture. I want to see it on my desk in ten minutes."

**

Serge heard the commotion at the front of the print shop as he set letters for a wedding announcement. He paused and went to the doorway to have a look.

The shop owner, M. Beauxdoin, stood at the desk opposite several police gendarmes, an official-looking paper in his hand. Behind the gendarmes stood a short mustachioed man in a brown suit, holding a derby hat in his hands, staring at M. Beauxdoin. One of the gendarmes held up a poster of Marshall Pétain that bore the word "TYRANT" in red capital letters.

"Of course not! I have never seen such a thing. I can assure you that it did not come from this shop."

Serge slipped away from the door, made his way quietly to the back of the shop. He looked through the block letters on the racks, quickly searching for any sign of red ink. He removed several that had traces of dried red, stuffed them in his pockets, and slipped out the back door.

**

Captain Allard followed his gendarmes and M. Beauxdoin into the print rooms, and stood with the proprietor as the gendarmes searched everywhere.

"How many workers do you employ, sir?"

"Besides myself and my wife, plus our son, there are only two."

"How old is your son?"

"He's fourteen, sir."

"A childish prank, perhaps?" Allard suggested.

"Certainly not! Alain would never do such a thing, he is a good boy. And he never works the presses alone, he is always supervised."

"Oh yes?" Allard's eyebrows rose. "By you? Or by your employees?"

"Sometimes me, sometimes Serge or Andreas."

"And your wife works the front of the store?"

"Yes, of course."

The two men stood in silence for several minutes while the gendarmes searched everything in sight. Captain Allard stood perfectly still, while Beauxdoin fidgeted.

**

Serge returned through the back door, and the gendarmes were still inside searching. One of them ordered him to stop and identify himself.

"Serge Faucheux. I work here."

The gendarme ordered him to stand next to M. Beauxdoin and Captain Allard.

Captain Allard looked closely at Serge, his green eyes narrowed, then addressed himself to Beauxdoin. "This is one of your employees, sir?"

"Yes. Serge Faucheux, he has worked here for five years."

Captain Allard continued to regard Serge with suspicious eyes. "Where were you just now, young man?"

"I was on my break."

Allard glanced at Beauxdoin, but the proprietor said nothing.

The gendarmes had stopped searching, and the corporal motioned for Captain Allard to join him in the back.

"There is nothing, sir."

"And red ink?"

"Yes sir, they have ink of many colors, including red."

Allard marched toward the racks of letters, noting immediately that they were sorted by size. His eyes found the correct size, and narrowed.

He spun around and called for Beauxdoin and Serge to join him. He took the poster from one of his men.

"There are several letters missing in this size, sir," Allard said, his words clipped. He picked up several capital letters and held them up to the poster. "This is the size that was used by the criminals we seek. We have in your rack here many letters—D, E, I, W, etc.—that are six each of the capitals, and many more of the lower case. But you have only four capital T's, and only five capitals Y, R, A, and N. Does that seem odd to you, sir?"

Beauxdoin's mouth hung open for a second before he stiffened his posture and stared back at Captain Allard. "It is a mistake. The letters you seek must have been misplaced."

"Exactly the letters that spell out T-Y-R-A-N-T?" Allard tapped each letter on the poster as he said it. "How truly bizarre."

"It is a mistake," Beauxdoin repeated.

Allard looked at Serge. "And where exactly do you live, young man?"

"At number 8 Rue des Anglais."

"I believe that is between two metro stations—Cluny-La Sorbonne, and Maubert—is it not?"

"That is so."

"Two metro stations where these seditious posters were found this morning," Allard said, staring hard at Serge.

Serge stared back with a blank expression, then shrugged.

"You will come with us," Allard ordered, and motioned for his gendarmes.

Two of them took position on either side of Serge, took him by the arms, and marched him out.

"Who is your other employee, sir?" Allard asked Beauxdoin.

"His name is Andreas Horvath."

"He is not French, then?"

"No. I believe that he is Hungarian."

"Does he also live close by?"

"I believe so. I do not know where exactly."

"But you have his address in your records, I presume?"

Beauxdoin was certain that he did.

"You will provide me with his address, then. We shall have a word with him as well. And after I speak with your employees, sir, I may also like to speak with your son. Please provide your address as well."

"Yes, of course."

As Allard left the print shop a few moments later, he smiled to himself in smug satisfaction.

19

"No one has seen Serge since yesterday morning," Sébastien told Oliver the next afternoon.

"He has disappeared before," Oliver said.

Sébastien shrugged, but looked skeptical.

"I'm on my way to Shakespeare and Company. I have a book to return. Would you like to join me?" Oliver asked.

Sébastien agreed, and the two of them set off for the bookstore.

"I wouldn't worry about Serge," Oliver said as they walked. "He's very clever."

Sébastien's expression was unreadable.

******

A few hours later, Oliver and Sébastien sat at an outside table in front of Chez Marius, reading the books they'd borrowed from Miss Beach at Shakespeare and Company. In front of each of them sat a cup of ersatz coffee made from chicory. A sketch pad also sat in front of Sébastien, and from time to time he set down the book and drew something for a while, before closing the sketchbook and resuming reading.

One of the times Sébastien looked up, he nudged Oliver and pointed, a deeply concerned look on his face.

Oliver saw Serge walking slowly down the sidewalk on the other side of the street, shuffling his feet and holding his side. His shoulders were stooped, and he stared at the ground in front of him.

Oliver got up immediately, fished in his pocket for enough franc coins to pay for both ersatz coffees, and laid them on the table. "Come on," he said to Sébastien.

They reached the front of Serge's building at the same time he did. As he looked up at them, they noticed his lip was swollen, and dried blood crusted at the corner of his mouth.

"Serge! What happened?" Oliver asked, reaching out to touch his shoulder.

Serge winced at the contact, and pulled away. "It was nothing."

"We need to get you inside," Oliver said, and put his hand on the skinny young writer's back to push him toward the door. He noticed the sharp intake of breath when he touched Serge's back, but still nudged him to the door.

Serge winced again as he took a step up the staircase, and a groan escaped through his tightly clenched mouth.

"Give us your arms," Sébastien told him.

Serge shook his head, and took another step, wincing again. And so he continued, one step at a time, slowly upward.

"How many flights up is your room?" Oliver asked Serge.

"It's on the fifth floor," Sébastien answered for him.

Shit, five flights. This was going to take a long time. Oliver looked behind Serge at Sébastien. "Do you think we can carry him?"

"No!" Serge said, his voice sharp and loud.

"It might be less painful," Oliver said.

Serge shook his head emphatically, and took another pained step up.

It took them more than five minutes to make it up five flights of stairs, and then another minute to get him down the hallway and into his room.

Serge lived in one of the small unheated garret rooms found on the top floor of nearly every apartment building in the 5th

Arrondissement. His small bed sat under the dormer window, and they helped him to it and eased him down into a seated position.

Sébastien took the pitcher from the top of Serge's rickety dresser, and drained it into the wooden cup sitting on the table on the other side of the room. It didn't quite fill the glass, but he handed it to Serge anyway.

Sébastien pointed to the washbowl on top of the dresser, and the ragged towel sitting next to it, and looked to Oliver. "Go get cold water, and wet the towel." He turned back to Serge and began to help him pull his shirt over his head, an action that brought a cry of pain from Serge.

Oliver hesitated, seeing the large purple and black bruises on Serge's side and back, wanting to stay and help.

"Go!" Sébastien ordered, giving him a scowl.

Oliver took the pitcher and towel and hurried down the stairs to the fourth floor. He found the bathroom at the end of the long hall, thankful it was empty. He filled the pitcher with cold water, and then held the towel under the faucet until it was soaked through before wringing it out.

Returning to the garret, he saw Serge still seated on the side of the bed, wearing only his boxer shorts, his trousers pushed down around his ankles. Sébastien crouched in front of him, removing his shoes and then tugging off the trousers. Oliver walked to the dresser and filled the washbowl.

"Lie face-down," Sébastien instructed Serge, who complied, moving slowly and wincing as he did.

"Give me the towel," Sébastien said to Oliver. "Hold the bowl for me."

As Serge lay face-down on his bed, Oliver saw for the first time the extent of his injuries, and gasped. His entire back was discolored with bruises, many of them quite dark and angry-looking, and there were also several small cuts and gashes along his shoulder blades, and on his elbows. His arms and legs were bruised as well, though not as horribly as his back.

Sébastien took the wet towel and dabbed at the cuts. Serge took in a sharp breath, but didn't complain. Sébastien dipped the towel in the washbowl, wrung it out, and repeated the process.

Oliver noticed a small amount of red swirling in the cold water.

Sébastien continued the gentle washing of the cuts for several minutes, and when finished he took the cool wet towel and draped it across Serge's back. He pulled up a chair next to the bed and sat.

"Who did this to you?"

Serge was quiet, but turned his head to look at them.

"There is no one else here but Oliver. You can speak safely."

"It was the fucking police," Serge said.

Oliver crouched down next to the bed. "The police? What for?"

"They wanted to know if I was responsible for some posters in the Metro station."

"What posters?"

"Posters calling Marshall Pétain a tyrant."

Oliver glanced at Sébastien, who was looking at Serge with an unreadable expression.

"What did you tell them?" Oliver asked.

"As little as possible."

Sébastien nodded. "That's good."

Oliver chose his words carefully. "Why did they think you might be responsible?"

"They came to the shop, snooping." Serge started to sit up, but cried out and lay back down, clutching his side.

"Let us help you," Sébastien said, and motioned for Oliver.

They helped Serge to sit up on the side of the bed; he grimaced the whole time, and clutched at his side. Oliver noticed tears in his eyes.

"You must have broken a rib or two," he said. "My God, Serge—what did they do to you?"

"They tried to get me to confess. I wouldn't."

"You should see a doctor."

"No!"

Serge's vehement response took Oliver by surprise. "You need to be checked out. Your ribs need attention."

"No doctors."

"I can pay for it," Oliver offered, and instantly regretted it.

Serge said nothing, but the look he gave Oliver made him feel like a child who had no idea what was going on.

"I will see if we can find one we can trust," Sébastien said, his voice quiet, his eyes staring at Serge with an intensity that Oliver didn't comprehend.

Serge shook his head, but kept silent.

Sébastien stood, put his hand on Oliver's shoulder, and guided him toward the door. "I'll stay with him, and help him get around. There's nothing more you can do, Oliver. You should go home."

Oliver started to protest, but decided against it. He nodded and turned to leave.

Sébastien's hand came back to his shoulder, and he turned back. "Keep this to yourself, Oliver."

Sébastien's dark eyes stared into his own, and he knew better than to ask any questions.

**

Serge walked into the print shop a few days later, expecting to collect his wages and leave. He was certain M. Beauxdoin would fire him for what he had done, and putting the shop in danger.

Instead, the printer asked Serge to join him in the alley behind the shop.

Serge followed him out the back door. Beauxdoin pointed a finger at him, and said, "You are a foolish young man. Very foolish indeed. You were lucky this time."

Serge hardly considered the beating he'd received lucky, but he supposed they could have locked him up indefinitely.

Beauxdoin stared at him for several seconds, and Serge felt as if the printer were weighing his character. Finally, he spoke. "Keep your mouth shut, keep your head down, do your work—and when told, you will have a special assignment."

The look in the printer's eyes told Serge what the nature of the "assignment" would likely be, and he relished the thought.

**

"Thank you for contacting me, Oliver," Frank Dryden said as they took their seats at a corner table in the Brasserie Lipp.

"You said you wanted to know about civil liberties violations, police harassment, that sort of thing," Oliver said. "I know people who've been arrested, or at least held by the police and harassed because they expressed an opinion the authorities didn't like."

"That's exactly the sort of thing we want to keep track of," Dryden said with a nod. "Tell me more."

"Last week my friend Serge was detained for a whole day while they questioned him about some posters in the Metro station that called Marshall Pétain a tyrant. They couldn't prove anything, but they kept him anyway. And they beat him, too. When they finally let him go, he was bruised up pretty bad, had some cuts, maybe broken ribs. We don't know for sure, he won't go to the doctor."

Dryden leaned closer and lowered his voice. "Did he make those posters? The ones calling Pétain a tyrant?"

"I don't know, he wouldn't say."

"Hmm." Dryden sat back and waited for Oliver to continue.

"One of his friends, someone who works with him at the Beauxdoin print shop, was also detained. His name's Andreas Horvath, and I heard the police turned him over to the Hungarian embassy. I don't know if he was beaten or not."

"Hmm, that's very interesting." Frank Dryden seemed lost in thought for a moment, but then he looked back at Oliver with a smile. "This is very helpful, Oliver. Please continue."

"Then a couple of days ago several of my friends and I went to the cinema, and there were some German soldiers there. The cinema was crowded, and the Germans sat in the row in front of us. They all had French girls with them. Adrienne said something to Marie-France about them, and one of their girls overheard. I don't know exactly what happened, I was sitting several seats away, but Adrienne argued with them—the French girls with the soldiers, I mean—and then the Germans turned around and started threatening. We tried to calm them down, but one of them called for the gendarmes. They took Adrienne into custody, and wouldn't release her until the next day. They made her pay a fine for insulting the soldiers and their girlfriends."

Dryden gave him a suitably sympathetic look. "Unfortunately, there is no freedom of speech in France any longer. Vichy saw to that right away."

The waiter came to their table, and Dryden ordered the *choucroute* and sausage plate, with the house beer. Oliver ordered the same.

When the waiter left, Dryden asked him, "How have your friends reacted to these events?"

"Serge has been quiet, not saying much. Adrienne was furious."

"And your other friends?"

"Concerned of course. It seems like everyone is quieter now, always careful what they say in public. It feels strange." Oliver decided to ask the question that had been on his mind since he first met Dryden. "Why are you interested in these things? What are you going to do with all of this?"

Dryden smiled, and folded his hands on the table in front of him. "No more beating around the bush, is that it? Alright—the answer to your first question is that it's my job to be interested in these things. I'm an Information Officer for the embassy. And as for what we're going to do with the information, well, nothing for now."

Oliver regarded Dryden with curiosity for a few seconds. "Information Officer—is that a fancy word for spy?"

Dryden smiled again, but it was clearly not a friendly smile this time. "I wouldn't use that word. In fact, I'll ask that you not use that word, either."

Oliver nodded, but his stomach seemed to fill with butterflies. "Alright."

The waiter brought their beers, large one-liter mugs, deep amber in hue.

"Drink up," Dryden said, a friendly smile returning to his lips. "With the grain shortages, there won't be any good beer soon."

Oliver took a long drink—it was good beer, rich and slightly sweet—and set the mug back down and looked Dryden in the eyes. "You said 'for now.' What did you mean by that?"

Dryden glanced around, then leaned in and motioned for Oliver to do the same. When he spoke again, it was just above a whisper.

"It's no secret that the United States is not happy with the German occupation of so many countries. The president himself has had harsh things to say in his speeches about the 'march of Hitlerism' across Europe, and that it must ultimately be stopped. Reversed, even. It's not exactly a secret the United States favors the British in this war."

He paused for a second, considering his words carefully. "We're also interested in the national resistance movements against the occupying German garrisons. That's the purpose of my questions. I need to see if a cohesive resistance is forming."

Oliver stared at Dryden for a long moment. "You think *my friends* are going to start a resistance movement?" It seemed so preposterous.

"They're as good candidates as any others."

Oliver tried to wrap his head around that, but couldn't. "Why do you think so?"

Dryden just smiled. "What were their politics before the war?"

Oliver shrugged. "Different parties. Serge was in the SFIO, and Sébastien in the PR. Adrienne just wanted women's suffrage. The others I don't know, really."

"But all left of center, it seems."

Oliver said nothing.

Dryden nodded. "And now the country is run by far-right elements, who are eliminating the civil liberties that the left has struggled to earn for a hundred and fifty years. Oliver, your friends are the *perfect* candidates for a resistance movement."

Oliver thought back to that afternoon in Serge's garret, when Sébastien seemed to know more than he would say. Was something already going on?

The thought strangely bothered him. If something were going on, why would they not tell him? Why would him in the dark? Did they not trust him? Or deep down, did they not consider him one of them? After almost five years in Paris, did he still not really belong?

Dryden saw the consternation on his face. "Does that bother you?"

"I don't know."

"Hmm."

Oliver wondered what that meant.

He didn't get the chance to ask. The waiter arrived with their food—large plates with fat Alsatian sausages on top of mounds of sauerkraut. He wished them *"Bon appétit,"* and left with a polite bow of the head.

They ate for a while in silence, Dryden eating his lunch with enthusiasm, while Oliver picked at his. After a while, Dryden paused, wiped his mouth, and leaned forward to talk.

"Oliver, you have the opportunity to be of great service to your country."

"What do you mean?"

"I mean, you can find out what your friends are doing, any anti-German or anti-Vichy activities they might participate in, and pass that along to me."

Oliver felt his stomach drop. "How would I do that?"

"Simple really, you gain their trust—which shouldn't be difficult, they're your friends after all—and when they let you in on their activities, you find a way to let me know. We can make arrangements for a suitable communication method."

"So you want me to betray their confidence?" Oliver's words came out clipped, irritated.

"I wouldn't put it quite like that."

"Then how would you put it?"

"You would be doing us all a favor—them as well as us."

"How so?"

"Well," Dryden searched for the right words. "Not now, of course, but in the future, when the time is right, the United States will be prepared to assist any well-organized resistance movement. As long as we have a good working knowledge of their activities, and have an inside track to their operatives—that would be you—we could be a powerful ally to them."

Oliver mulled that for a moment. His father always spoke of good and evil as if they were easily determinable opposites, but this didn't seem to fit that dichotomy at all. What should he do? How could he know he was doing the right thing? Could he trust Frank Dryden?

Then again, could he trust his friends if they were keeping secrets from him?

"Is it dangerous?" he asked.

"That depends. As the citizen of a neutral nation, you have certain liberties that most Parisians do not. The Germans are not keen on alienating the United States, so they're not likely to mistreat our citizens. On the other hand, if you were caught actually taking part in an illegal activity, by either the French police or the Gestapo, we would of course be powerless to prevent any repercussions."

Oliver nodded. His voice was deadly serious as he continued. "But, if I were caught in an illegal activity, I would be doing it with my friends. So if I didn't get involved, they would still be caught, and I would still lose my friends, isn't that right?"

Dryden's expression was serious, but there was a glimmer of admiration in his blue eyes. "Yes, probably so."

Oliver sat in silence for several seconds. What if he could help? Wouldn't it be better to do what he could, than to do nothing while his friends struggled?

"Alright, Mr. Dryden—what would you like me to do?"

156

20

Thursday, October 10

Le Chien Errant was crowded that night, full of German soldiers and officers with their French girlfriends. It was a chilly night, and Cécile Fournier wore a fur wrap. She handed it to the maître'd, and his eyes lit up in recognition.

"Miss Fournier, welcome to *Le Chien Errant*! You are indeed an honored guest. I will find you a table right away, near the band—unless you would prefer something in the rear? No? Alright, a front table it will be. Just a moment, please."

He hung her wrap in the cloak room and handed her a number, then scurried away. He returned a moment later with a big smile. "This way please, Miss Fournier."

Cécile was used to being recognized. Her face adorned posters all over Montmartre, and she was a popular performer.

She waited as the maître'd pulled out a chair for her, and sat at a small table in front of the stage. He handed her a menu, but she waved it away. "Just drinks this evening, thank you."

"They are on the house, Miss Fournier," the maître'd said. "I have told Mr. Washington that you are in attendance, and he insists."

"Thank him for his hospitality, and tell him I look forward to the show."

The maître'd bowed, clearly pleased, and disappeared.

The next table was occupied by a paunchy and balding German in the uniform of a Wehrmacht colonel. He had a narrow face and a long narrow nose that protruded quite a ways in profile. Surrounding him were younger German officers with the insignias of lieutenants, their hair short and neatly combed—one blond, one medium brown. These two were more handsome than their colonel, and they seemed to be listening to him quite closely, but without much enjoyment.

Apparently they were too busy to have yet noticed the attractive and elegantly-dressed woman who sat alone at the table next to them. She crossed her legs to allow them a better view.

The waiter arrived and she ordered a Cointreau. She looked toward the empty stage, but listened to the conversation between the colonel and his underlings. The colonel was holding forth about procedures which had not been properly adhered by the men under their command, and how best to rectify the behavior.

Nothing interesting, but she wasn't prepared to give up on this group. She continued to eavesdrop after the waiter returned with her drink, and she sipped and listened closely.

She almost didn't notice the musicians filing onto the stage, and then the spotlight came on and illuminated them. A tall black man with graying hair turned to face the crowd and bowed.

The applause was merely polite, and Cécile knew it was because the Germans were loath to applaud a Negro, at least until they'd had more to drink.

The music began, and it was too loud to eavesdrop. Cécile doubted she'd have been able to hear anyone talking at her own table. This was not the sort of establishment that patrons came to for long or important conversations, she suspected.

The music was good, even if it wasn't a style that Cécile usually listened to. It wasn't that she disliked jazz—quite the contrary, she'd sung many songs with jazz rhythms—it was that she was not accustomed to such loud and complicated syncopations. And yet, the music still stirred something inside her, and she found herself wagging her foot in time with the beat. She could understand why this "Hot Jazz" had once been all the rage.

She wondered which one of the musicians Frank Dryden knew. A couple of them were black men like Terrance Washington, and she surmised it was not one of them. Americans tended to be more sensitive about race than the French. That left three white musicians for her consideration. Two of them looked too French to be Americans, with their cool Gallic expressions.

The young one was probably an American, though. Something about his look didn't seem French. He was also far more expressive in his musical style than either of the other two, so he must be American.

She glanced over at one point toward the next table, and caught the eye of one of the young lieutenants, the blond. He looked away quickly, and she smiled to herself.

She turned back toward the band, but continued to cast glances his direction every couple of minutes. More often than not, she caught him looking at her. At first he always looked away quickly, but by the fourth or fifth time he didn't look away immediately. She smiled at him before lowering her eyes and glancing down at her drink.

If there was one thing French women knew better than anyone else in the world, it was how to flirt.

Terrance Washington turned toward the crowd at the end of the next song, and announced that the band was taking a break, but would be back in twenty minutes.

She looked back at the handsome young lieutenant, but the colonel resumed his oration where he had left off. She sighed and looked around the room.

She could read lips fairly well, and she practiced on several of the tables nearby. Most of these men were trying to impress their French girlfriends, speaking in mostly French, and she soon determined that there would be nothing useful from them.

She looked up to see Terrance Washington approaching her table, a broad grin spread across his face. "Miss Fournier, it is an honor!" he said, taking her hand in both of his. "What brings you to *Le Chien Errant* this evening?"

"I have a much overdue night off, and I have heard that the jazz here is second to none. I have not been disappointed."

"Oh, you flatter us, Miss Fournier!" Terrance beamed. "I had the pleasure to hear you sing once, about five years ago, before I opened this club. I'm afraid I've not had the time to take in one of your shows since then. The downside of being the proprietor is that I never get to visit other clubs."

She smiled. "I am glad you enjoyed my show, Mr. Washington. Perhaps someday you will have more time, and you can come hear me sing again. I would be delighted to return your hospitality." She lifted her nearly empty glass of Cointreau in a silent toast.

"I would like that as well, Miss Fournier. And I will see that you get another glass right away." He hurried off toward the bar. Less than a minute later, her waiter hurried over with a new glass of Cointreau, a harried look on his face, and apologized profusely for making her wait. She waved him off with a gracious smile and finished her first glass.

She caught the eye of the young lieutenant as she set down the empty glass, and smiled at him. A faint smile crossed his lips for a second before he returned his attention to his colonel, who was still preaching discipline.

The maître'd approached a moment later with a small envelope, and handed it to Cécile with a smile.

"You seem to have an admirer, Miss Fournier."

She thanked him and took the envelope. It was sealed, and her name was handwritten on the front, in a man's handwriting. She opened it, and removed the small card, which bore the emblem of *Le*

Chien Errant on the cover. She opened the card and read the short message, in the same masculine script:

"After the next set, in the ladies' room."

She returned the card to its envelope, and placed it in her small handbag.

A moment later the stage lights came back on. As the first notes began, she glanced over to the next table, and caught the eye of the blond lieutenant. He didn't look away, but stared at her with deep blue eyes that reflected the lights from the stage. She smiled and glanced away, looking back a few seconds later to find him still staring.

The card had had an effect; she just wasn't sure if it was jealousy, or something more. Probably jealousy, but she knew she couldn't be too careful.

This second set was longer than the first, and she grew restless as it went along. It wasn't that she wasn't enjoying the music—it was still quite good, each song unique—it was that she could feel the nerves building in the pit of her stomach every time she glanced over and saw the German lieutenant staring at her with those big blue unreadable eyes.

The waiter brought her a third glass of Cointreau, but she barely sipped it.

When Terrance Washington announced the last number of the set, she nearly slumped back in relief. She listened for a couple of minutes, and then discreetly got up and slipped along the side wall to the hallway near the entrance that led back to the restrooms and the stage door.

The door to the ladies' room was first on the left, with the men's room several feet beyond, and the stage door on the right opposite the men's room. She found the ladies' room empty, slipped inside, and locked the door.

The knock came before the music ended. She leaned close to the door frame. "Who is it?"

"Miss Fournier?" the young man's voice asked in an American accent.

She breathed a sigh of relief and opened the door as the band on the stage was playing the final climactic notes of the last song. It was only then that she realized there was no trumpet sound. The trumpet player stood in front of her.

She took a quick glance down the hall as the sound of applause and cheers filled the club. The hall was still empty. But that would only last a few seconds.

"Quickly," she said, motioning him in and locking the door behind him.

"This was from you?" she asked in English, removing the little envelope from her handbag and holding it up.

He seemed surprised that she spoke his language. "Yes. Mr. Dryden told me you would be here sometime this week. I knew it was you when I saw you during the first song."

"And he told you my name." She was mildly irritated—Dryden had told this young man who would be meeting him, but he hadn't given her the same information. She'd had to guess.

"Yes." He hesitated a moment, his face unsure, then added, "I'm Oliver."

A faint smile crossed her lips. An even playing field, more or less; at least, a token of good faith.

Someone pulled at the handle of the locked door, and they heard a muttered curse of "*Merde*" when it didn't open.

"You didn't finish the song."

He shook his head. "Terrance and I arranged it. I knew I needed to get out here before any customers. Mr. Dryden knows."

Terrance Washington was privy to their clandestine meeting. More secrets that Dryden hadn't divulged to her. If he knew himself.

"That was very clever, Oliver. Now we should arrange another meeting, at a time and place that we can spend more time. Tomorrow?"

"Alright. I live in the 5th, between the Boulevard Saint-Germain and the Quai."

She shook her head. "It should be somewhere neutral, not near our usual places. Do you know the Bistro Bofinger?"

"I've heard of it."

"That would be an excellent place. There are many secluded tables, more conducive to private conversations."

There was a loud knock on the door. "We should leave," he said, and started to reach for the lock.

"Wait," she said, and motioned for him to come close. She stood on her tip toes and reached her mouth up to his face, placing a kiss on his cheek beside his mouth and let it linger a few seconds, then placed another on his lips.

He started to say something as she pulled away, but she placed a finger on his lips and placed another kiss on the side of his neck. Then she took her finger and lightly smeared all three lipstick smudges, and did the same to her own lips.

She gave him a wink and a smile, and then reached for the door lock. "Tomorrow for lunch, one o'clock. The reservation will be under my name."

She exited the ladies' room with a proud smile, ignoring the young women waiting there, and strutted toward the lounge.

**

Oliver knew he was in over his head the moment she stopped to put her lipstick on him. He would've never thought of that, but as he followed her out of the ladies' room door, he saw the four French girls

163

lined up for it looking at him with wide-eyed surprise, followed by sultry appreciation.

Thank God she knows what she's doing, he thought as he slipped back through the stage door. That was reassuring, but he still felt apprehensive. He wasn't exactly sure what he'd gotten himself into.

**

The blond lieutenant was not seated at his table when Cécile returned to the lounge, but she saw him standing at the bar, and sauntered toward him. He noticed her half-way, and she smiled at him.

"Good evening," she said in French when she was next to him. Time to find out if he spoke her language, or only German. If he didn't speak French, she would give him a regretful smile and disengage—best not to let on that she understood German.

He returned the greeting in heavily-accented French, paused as if unsure what else to do, and then asked if she was enjoying the show.

She gave him a dazzling smile. At least he could converse. "Yes, very much. And you?"

He nodded, an enthusiastic look on his face. "Yes, very much as well." He paused again, eyes up as if he were trying to formulate the words. "There is no jazz in Bremen. No jazz in Germany."

She gave him a sympathetic look. "Oh, that is a shame. Is this the first time you've heard music like this?"

"No, but, uh, uh, only in Paris."

"You speak good French," she lied.

He lit up. "Thank you. I studied in school, but, uh, many years since."

"Ah, not so many years ago, I think," she said with a wink.

She wondered if it would be worth the trouble to try to find out what branch of the Occupation forces he was in, and their role. His language skills might not be sufficient. She decided to give it a try.

She held out her hand, palm down. "I am Cécile, Cécile Fournier."

"Alfred Hillenmaier," he replied, taking her hand and giving it one firm Germanic shake.

She suppressed the urge to scowl. German manners were different than French manners. "Enchanted, Mr. Hillenmaier." She flashed him a brilliant smile.

"I know your picture," Lt. Hillenmaier said.

"Yes, there are many pictures of me in this area," she said. "I sing at a club, much like this club—only not as loud."

"Sing?" He looked confused, but then understanding dawned on him. "Oh, sing! I understand. Jazz?"

"Sometimes. Not jazz like this, though."

He seemed to be struggling to come up with words, and he made a walking motion with his fingers.

"Walk?" she suggested.

He shook his head, and held his hands far apart, then brought them closer together.

"Is the place where I sing nearby?" she prompted.

"Yes, near," he repeated.

"Yes, it is near." She was ready to give up on the conversation, but thought she'd give it one last try. "So, Mr. Hillenmaier, what is it that you do?"

He looked confused again, and her hopes faded. "Do?"

"Yes, what work do you do? In the army, that is." She nodded toward the insignia on the shoulder of his uniform.

"I am lieutenant," he said, beaming.

She decided to give up. "Good night, Mr. Hillenmaier. Perhaps I will see you at one of my performances." She gave him a polite nod and walked away, trying not to be bothered by the obvious crestfallen look on his face.

She retook her seat, and lit a cigarette. The colonel at the next table was in the process of paying his tab, so her opportunity to learn anything from him was ending. She took a deep inhale and blew out the smoke hard in frustration.

A moment later, the colonel and the brown-haired lieutenant got up from the table and left the club. She glanced back at the bar and saw the blond lieutenant still standing there with a half-full glass, looking her direction with a sad puppy-dog sort of expression.

Sometimes she hated this business.

Then she was angry at herself for feeling sympathy. He was the enemy, it was as simple as that. He was enslaving her country. He was part of the problem, and she had to be part of the solution. And to do that, she couldn't let herself humanize him.

The lights went down in the lounge as the lights went up on stage, and the band began to play again. She stubbed out her half-smoked cigarette, stood, and strode toward the door. She handed her number to the maître'd, though she hardly needed to—he knew who she was, and he retrieved her wrap without bothering to look at the token.

She pulled the wrap around her shoulders and stepped out into the cold night.

Her breath was visible as she walked down the boulevard. She turned left at the next corner, and walked half a block. She crossed the deserted street and opened the passenger door of a green Renault coupe parked at the curb.

"You met him?" Frank Dryden asked in English from the driver's seat.

"Yes. We made arrangements to meet for lunch tomorrow, Bistro Bofinger."

"Very good. Thank you, darling." He leaned over and kissed her cheek.

"You did not tell me his name."

He looked surprised. "Would you have expected me to?"

"You told him my name."

He smiled, as one would smile at a child. "My dear, your face is recognizable to anyone in the entertainment business. He would have known who you were the moment he met you."

She looked away. If the argument was lost, never admit it, just disengage. That was the Parisian way.

"Any information from the Germans tonight?"

She shook her head. "Nothing tonight."

He shrugged and started the engine. Most nights were like that.

"Your place or mine tonight, darling?" he asked as he pulled away from the curb.

She looked back at him with a faint look of resentment, but then the expression melted into a smile. He was such a lovely boy, her Frank. "*Chez moi.*"

21

The three figures moving through the trees were hardly visible in their black clothing, stopping behind the trunks and looking around before moving on to the next tree.

It was past curfew, and they would be arrested if caught.

Serge followed the stranger in front of him, always staying one tree behind. They made their way quietly through the *Jardin des Plantes*, on the Quai Saint-Bernard across from the Seine. The trees were thick here, and there were still enough leaves in the branches to block the moonlight, keeping the ground cloaked in darkness.

Serge kept his eyes on M. Beauxdoin, until his boss arrived at the greenhouse door. He stood with his back to the glass, facing out, and reached back to rap on the door.

Today a crate of print supplies had arrived at the shop, larger than usual. Serge didn't recognize the delivery driver—not one of the regulars—but he didn't think much about it. When he got the crowbar to open the crate in the shop, M. Beauxdoin told him to bring it to his office instead, and to close the door.

When they opened it, at first it looked like a regular shipment of inks, pads, and a few replacement letters. But then Beauxdoin removed these things and there was a smaller crate inside, surrounded by dry hay. He had Serge pry that crate open, and inside were two dozen Colt .45 handguns.

"Where did these come from?" Serge had asked, foolishly expecting an answer. Beauxdoin claimed not to know, and Serge opted to believe him. It didn't matter anyway.

Tonight he had shown up at the shop as directed, just before curfew and wearing all black. One other man showed up, a tall, big-framed, dark-complected man of about thirty with a slight scruff of beard. Beauxdoin introduced him only as Laurent. They divided the guns between them, hiding them in coat pockets, and slipped out into the night.

It was several blocks to the relative safety of the *Jardin des Plantes*, but they made it there without seeing anyone. And now they waited outside of a greenhouse.

The door opened a moment later, just a little, and Beauxdoin disappeared inside. The door closed immediately. Serge could see the glimmer of a lamp through the frosted glass, and the figures of two men talking. Then the unknown figure walked away, leaving the lamp with Beauxdoin, who opened the door, looked around, and motioned for them to join him.

Serge looked around also, saw no one, and dashed for the door. Laurent slipped through right before him.

Beauxdoin placed the lantern behind a work desk, dulling its light to the outside, while still illuminating the interior. He handed them each a shovel, and took one himself. He directed them to follow him to a freshly-turned bed on the far side of the greenhouse, and they began digging holes a half-meter deep.

They wrapped the guns in rags and placed them inside cardboard boxes, which they put at the bottom of the holes. They covered them with the dirt, took a moment to spread the mounds level with the surrounding soil, and finally took the sharp ends of the shovels and made it all look freshly-turned, like before.

"Remember where these are, but do not write it down," Beauxdoin instructed them. "Do not ever write anything down, do you understand?"

They agreed, and he took the shovels from them and put them back in their place.

Serge noticed several beds appeared recently turned, and wondered how many pistols were hidden here.

Beauxdoin motioned for them to go to the door, and told them to wait there while he extinguished the lantern.

He joined them, and whistled once before opening the door and ushering them out.

As they began to dash back to the safety of the trees, they could hear the greenhouse door lock behind them.

They hurried away, going separate directions.

172

22

Oliver arrived at one o'clock the next day, and was glad he'd dressed in the suit he normally reserved for the club. A grand staircase stood in front of him under a gigantic crystal chandelier. He went upstairs to the first floor, found Bistro Bofinger, and gave Miss Fournier's name to the maître'd.

She was seated at a semi-private table in its own alcove, separated by half-walls from the tables on either side. She smiled when she saw him, and stood to greet him, kissing his cheeks. The maître'd held her chair, and Oliver took the seat across from her.

"You have not been here before?" she asked in English.

"No." He decided not to mention that it was probably beyond his budget, judging by the decor. All of the mirrors and crystal chandeliers told him the meal would probably be expensive.

"Just relax," she said. "As long as we don't talk too loudly, no one will overhear."

"I'm not really sure what we're supposed to talk about anyway," he confessed.

"What did Mr. Dryden tell you?"

Not much. "He told me you work with him, and that I should meet with you to help me get started. He wants me to let him know if I see or hear about any resistance activity. I'm not really sure what I'm supposed to be doing, though. I guess that's where you're supposed to help."

She smiled and reached her hand across the table. "First, hold my hand. And smile, act as though you were excited to see me. Anyone observing will think we are lovers out for a lunch date."

He did as she said, and took her hand. And he forced himself to smile.

"Now lean forward a little. Remember, you are happy to see me. And look into my eyes, always into my eyes. That's it, that's good."

"So how can you help me?"

"It all comes from attention. You must constantly pay attention, to everyone and everything around you. Do not be lost in your own head; you will miss things, important things. So lesson number one is to always pay attention. That's good?"

"But won't it make me seem nosy?" He felt confused—the French heartily disliked nosiness.

"You must pay attention without staring long, without looking around from side to side. Keep your face forward, and move only your eyes. Even then, you do not move too much. The French are very good at this—better, I think, than you Americans, no?"

"Maybe." That might explain the way his friends always seemed to know things, even though they didn't ask the "nosy" questions he often asked.

"You must learn to be subtle," she said, and leaned back as the waiter brought a bottle of white wine—an Alsatian Riesling.

The waiter poured a little bit into the glass in front of Oliver, took a step back and waited.

Oliver froze. They didn't do that at Chez Marius. He looked at Cécile, who made a subtle circular motion underneath her nose.

"It is to check the bottle, to make sure that the wine has not gone bad. If it smells good, and not like vinegar, you set the glass down and nod to him."

Oliver sniffed as instructed, his forehead starting to bead with sweat. The waiter filled Cécile's glass, and then Oliver's before setting the bottle down and disappearing.

"I'm sorry," Oliver said, dabbing his forehead with his napkin.

"It is not a problem, my dear," she said, and wiggled her fingers on the table. Remembrance dawned on him, and he took her hand back in his and held it.

"That's good. And relax, you are having a good time."

He nodded and took a deep breath, lowering his tense shoulders.

"Let us practice. Tell me what you see from where you sit."

He looked away from her face, and she scolded "Tut, tut, tut! Keep your face toward me. That's good. And remember, don't move your eyes much. Take your time, see everything."

Oliver did as she instructed, and tried to focus on his peripheral vision. It was difficult, and inevitably his eyes veered off to the sides. A quick "Tut!" from her, and he brought his eyes back toward her.

"You can look at my ears or my neck if that helps. You need not always stare at my eyes only. No one else but me will notice."

That did help, and he found that he could see things to the side more clearly than before.

A moment later, she repeated, "Now, tell me what you see."

He described the patrons at other tables, and as he spoke in general terms she interrupted with specific questions. What is he wearing? What type of suit is it? What color is the suit? What color is his tie? Does he wear a watch? On the left or right wrist?

It was difficult, and Oliver felt the beginnings of a headache from the concentration.

"You are not smiling. Remember, we are lovers on a date, and you are very happy. Smile!"

It was too much to remember, and Oliver's mind rebelled. He wanted to scream, to tell her it was too difficult, that he was not cut out for this type of thing. But he kept silent, and continued to try, though it made his head hurt.

They were interrupted by the arrival of their lunch. "I ordered us pork chops with *choucroute*. It is the speciality of the house."

Oliver was relieved, and dug into his food.

"Continue to look at me," she reminded. "A man does not ignore his lover when the food arrives. His wife, perhaps, but never his lover."

That made Oliver smile, and he relaxed.

They chatted, about the clubs where she had sung, the people she knew in the Paris entertainment scene. She asked him about *Le Chien Errant*, how long he had played there, what he had done before coming to Paris. He told her a little about his friends, but mentioned first names only. He left out Serge's beating, and the fact that Collette was seeing a German officer. He also never mentioned Lisette.

"It sounds like you have an interesting life," she said. "Your friends sound very carefree. They must hate the new restrictions on their freedom."

He shrugged, pulling back a little from the friendly conversation. "I suppose so."

She seemed to sense his wariness and left it alone. "I enjoyed the show last night. You are obviously a dedicated and passionate musician."

He relaxed a bit again, but didn't totally drop his guard. "Thank you."

"Oliver, I have been performing a long time. Yes, a very long time. I know people who could help your career—important people, very influential—if you ever decide that you want more from show business than to play in someone else's band."

He tensed again, reminded of Lisette and her constant urging for him to get a "real" job. Why did everyone think he needed anything more than to play his trumpet?

He thanked her and said he'd keep that in mind.

She again seemed to sense his discomfort and changed the subject.

The waiter returned a while later and cleared their dishes. Cécile reached her hand across the table, and Oliver took the cue and held her hand again. She leaned far forward this time, and he followed suit.

She put her cheek next to his and whispered in his ear. "Now that you have practiced observing with your eyes, I want you to listen closely and tell me what you hear. Pretend you are whispering romantic things in my ear, but listen to the people around us."

He listened carefully for a moment, until she whispered to him, "Now tell me what you heard."

"The lady to my left is talking about her dog. He's been misbehaving, digging in her flower pots. The other ladies are giving her advice, telling her to put pepper around the edges of the pot."

"Very good," Cécile said, her tone showing her approval.

"The gentlemen to my right are discussing finance, but I don't really understand what they're saying."

"Anything else?"

Oliver hadn't had time to try listening to any other conversations but the two closest, and wondered how she could possibly think he could have heard anything else; but he only said "No."

She leaned back and smiled. "That was a good start."

The waiter returned and set the check in front of Oliver with a bow, and left without a word.

Oliver blanched when he saw the amount. Then he felt Cécile's hand on his knee, and it made him jump. She let go of his hand on the table, and glanced at his other arm.

It took him a second to realize what she meant, and he moved his hand to meet hers on his knee. A quick movement of her fingers, and a wad of cash was in his hand.

He counted out the bills under the table, and realized it was enough for the check, with ration coupons. He laid the stack on top of the bill, and within two seconds the waiter seemed to appear out of thin air and took it.

Cécile smiled at him again, and stood. He followed her to the front, where she handed a token to the maître'd, who returned a moment later with her fur wrap. He placed it around her shoulders, and bid them good day.

As they descended the grand staircase, Cécile told him he had done a good job.

"Now your task is to continue to practice what you have learned. Practice all the time. You are a performer, you know how important practice is. Before you know it, you will be as observant as a police inspector."

She stopped at the door, and he opened it for her. On the sidewalk, she leaned in to kiss his cheek. "I hope that we have the pleasure of meeting again. I will tell Mr. Dryden that you are ready. Good luck, my dear."

She wiped the lipstick off of his cheek and walked away, her high heels clicking on the sidewalk.

Oliver watched her for a few seconds, the way her hips swayed, and the way she glided down the sidewalk without bobbing her head. A real lady.

And a spy.

It seemed so incongruous, and he wondered if he would ever get used to it. He doubted it.

23

Monday, October 21

Sébastien had suspected for a while.

He knew Serge had created those posters calling Pétain a tyrant. That was obvious, though Serge never admitted it. Sébastien had known for some time that Serge was writing criticisms of the Vichy regime in his room at night, and printing clandestine leaflets to leave on the train, or a park bench. Serge had been doing that since August, and Sébastien agreed to help him surreptitiously leave them around the arrondissement. It was a low-risk way of speaking the truth, in a time when that was not permitted.

But he had suspected there was more. And now it was confirmed.

He looked his friend in the eyes, and without a sliver of doubt told him, "Yes, I'll do it."

A slight smile crossed Serge's mouth. "I knew you would. You may not be a good Socialist, but I knew I could count on you." There was a teasing twinkle in his eyes.

"What do we do?"

"We wait. When there is a mission, my commander will tell me and my partner, then I will tell you and one other that I will choose. You will only know me and that one other."

"Who is it?"

Serge was cryptic. "I have someone in mind. You will know when it is certain."

"How long do we wait?"

Serge shrugged. "I do not know. But whenever we are given a mission, we will have to act quickly."

"And weapons?"

"That is already arranged."

Sébastien nodded. He'd suspected as much. "Will we get to kill Germans, then?"

"Yes, that is the plan."

A satisfied look came to Sébastien's face. "Good. I have one in mind."

Serge scowled and shook his head. "No, you cannot do anything that would jeopardize the security of the group. You must never act alone. We will not pick the targets; they will be given to us. If you cannot obey orders, then you cannot do this work."

Sébastien suppressed his disappointment. He understood. "Agreed. I am in."

Wednesday, October 23

Marcel looked out the window of Chez Marius. Business had been slow since the new rations took effect, but it was particularly slow that day, and he was bored. He stood near the door and watched the few pedestrians who passed at two o'clock in the afternoon.

He saw Oliver walk by, dressed in a nice suit, clean white shirt and necktie. His hair was neatly combed, and he was wearing that fancy Swiss watch.

And it was his day off.

Marcel's heart sank. He knew what that meant. Oliver was on his way to see his mistress, the rich lady who'd bought him the watch. That would mean no visit to Marcel for a while.

It had already been a while.

His heart ached. His body ached, too. Sometimes, sitting alone in his garret, Marcel thought he couldn't take it anymore. When that happened, he would lie on his bed and remember the last time Oliver had come calling. He would imagine Oliver's touch so vividly, it almost seemed real. That would take the edge off the longing.

Lately, however, it had gotten harder. The longing stayed.

He was released from work an hour later, and walked next-door. He climbed the five flights, and let himself into his room. He looked around the little space, imagining another evening alone.

He walked to the dormer window and stared out over the rooftops of Paris. There was a teeming city full of opportunities, he knew. One just had to know where to go.

He knew where. If it were still open.

He got out his bath towel, wash cloth and soap, and a change of clothes. He marched downstairs to the 4th floor bathroom, and as he'd suspected it was empty this time of day. He closed the door and started the water in the tub.

It was cold, of course. With the coal shortages, the building only had hot water for a couple of hours a day. He only filled the tub a little bit before he shut off the tap, took off his clothes, and stepped in. An instant chill ran up his legs and into his core as his feet hit the frigid water. He braced himself and sat down.

He gritted his teeth, and dampened his washcloth. He squeezed water from the cloth over his head and shoulders, shivering. He ran the bar of soap over the cloth, and scrubbed his body as fast as he could. Then he rinsed out the cloth and held it over his head to squeeze water from it, over and over.

The cold water felt like needles pricking his skin as it ran down, and he couldn't help but cry out softly at the pain, but he kept at it until he'd rinsed off all the soap.

He released the drain and bolted from the tub, grabbed his towel, and dried as fast as he could. Then he stood in the middle of the bathroom, holding his towel in front of him, shaking.

He felt as if he would never be warm again.

His hands trembled as he tugged on a clean pair of boxer shorts, and then his trousers. He pulled a clean white shirt over his head, then hugged his arms around himself and tried to get warm.

It was only October. He knew it would get much worse. And for a long time.

His teeth began to chatter as he tugged on his stockings and shoes. He sprinted up the stairs and into his garret. He tugged on his coat and wrapped a scarf around his neck, then jumped under his bed clothes for a few minutes, until he stopped shaking.

Twenty minutes later he descended the stairs to the Metro station.

He changed lines and got off at the *La Forche* stop.

A mile north-west of the *Quartier Pigalle*, in the 17th Arrondissement, the Avenue Clichy split in two—the fork in the road. From the Metro station La Forche, he ascended the stairs to the Avenue Clichy, and stood at the heart of the infamous *Quartier La Forche*.

He stood aside for a moment, watching the crowds heading home from work. This was a gritty working-class neighborhood, not a bad area per se, but definitely not *bourgeois*.

He waited a while and watched the housewives going home from the grocer, dingy coats over house dresses, scarves on their heads, carrying the evening's meal in a bag on their arms. Working men in dirty coveralls ascended from the subway in groups, bidding each other good evening in a variety of accents upon reaching the street, and parting ways.

From time to time he spotted a middle-aged, well-dressed *haute-bourgeois* businessman in his fancy suit and tie, conspicuous in his finery, hurrying toward a shadowy alley.

So the clubs were still open. It hadn't been a foregone conclusion, with all of the morality laws the Vichy regime kept enacting.

He had come here several times a couple of years ago. For a young homosexual new to Paris, with no friends, and no other outlet, this was the place to come.

While the *Quartier Pigalle* was notorious for its strip clubs and brothels, the *Quartier La Forche* was infamous for its underground sex clubs catering to any fetish; and as such it was frequented by high-powered businessmen who came to be humiliated by a working-class dominatrix. There were dark rooms off back alleys where a man could be paddled or whipped—or worse—by a leather-clad madam who was only too happy to oblige his masochism.

The neighborhood catered to other clandestine desires as well. That was why it was the after-dark destination of choice for those seeking an anonymous encounter with a member—or members—of the same sex.

Marcel walked in the gathering dusk toward an arch off the Avenue Clichy a half-block north-west of the fork—a dark archway alley underneath a tenement building. Midway down the covered alley, there was a wooden door recessed in the stone wall. Marcel pulled the cord, and heard the old-fashioned bell ring.

A narrow window in the door slid open, and a high-pitched voice asked what he wanted.

"Anything goes," he said.

The door opened a crack, and he slipped inside.

A large, exceedingly muscular man stood in front of him, tall and bald-headed, and asked him in a ridiculously high voice for his identification. Marcel knew the drill; he gave his name—"Marcel Thibeaux"—and showed his identification papers.

The huge man held his papers in the light, scrutinized his face, and then handed them back with the question, "Well?"

Marcel opened his fly and pulled out his penis—standard proof that he was not an undercover policeman.

"Go on down."

Marcel buttoned his fly, and descended the dimly-lit stairwell, where he encountered the coat-check lady behind a counter, standing beneath a single electric light bulb. Elderly and silver-haired—at least sixty in Marcel's estimation—she was probably also the concierge of the tenement building.

"One franc, please," she said.

Marcel was relieved the price had not increased. He handed her a franc note, and she handed him an open-topped cardboard box. "Number twenty-seven," she said, echoing the number painted in black on the front of the small box.

He opened the heavy wooden door to the right, and descended into the dark cellar.

He paused a moment to allow his eyes to adjust to the dim light. The cellar had never been retrofitted for electricity, so the only light came from a handful of kerosene lamps scattered around, their warm glow casting circles in the darkness, with shadow beyond. Through the shadow moved vague shapes, and he waited as his eyes dilated and the shapes came into better focus.

A large room spread before him, smelling of mildew, musk, kerosene, and semen. An alcove stood to his left where boxes sat along a wall, and a dark hallway beyond. There were sounds of men moaning in pleasure. From time to time a man's voice cried out in ecstasy.

Marcel walked to a corner of the alcove, and set his box on the ground. He removed his shoes and stockings, then his shirt, and finally his trousers, placing them inside the box.

He turned to face the room wearing only his boxer shorts.

His eyes had adjusted enough to see numerous men moving around. Some were clad in boxer shorts, like he was; others wore frilly women's panties and corsets, or stockings with garters; still others walked about completely naked, some with erections. At least one wore a sequined carnival mask with brightly colored feathers, and nothing else.

Marcel moved slowly toward the side of the room closest to the dark hallway. A group of five clustered in the far corner, hands and mouths exploring more than one partner apiece. He paused and watched for a moment, mesmerized, before turning away.

He walked down the hallway, which was lit by candles on the wall, spaced a couple of meters apart. Doorways to private rooms appeared as dark portals to his right and left, each lit by a single candle on a simple wood table. Many of the rooms were occupied, judging by the sounds emanating from within. He allowed himself a few moments of voyeurism, looking through open doors at pairs and threesomes engaged in every imaginable activity.

At the end of the hall was another open space, not as large as the first room.

A short, dark man approached from the shadows, completely naked, with a short-cropped black beard and hairy chest. He groped Marcel through the front of his boxer shorts.

"You are a very pretty one," the man said in a gruff whisper, his accent Greek or Italian.

Marcel reached out and felt the stranger's body, which was hard and wiry from manual labor; attractive, arousing even, but the overwhelming smell of garlic turned him off. He lingered for only a moment before moving on, the man disappearing in the darkness.

He gravitated toward the light of a kerosene lamp on the wall, and as he did he saw the tall and lithe form of an athletic man in fishnet stockings sashaying toward him. The sight seemed so incongruous— the body was muscular and masculine, but clad only in four-inch stiletto heels and mid-thigh fishnet stockings held by a garter belt. An enormous erection jutted forth before him.

As he came into the light, Marcel saw his handsome face—long, with a handsome cleft in the chin, and full pink lips. He was blond, with short neatly-combed hair and wire-rimmed glasses.

His lithe body and blond hair called to mind Father Jerome in the sacristy—Marcel pushed the image from his mind.

"Hello handsome," he said to Marcel in thickly-accented French, then dropped to his knees and tugged down Marcel's shorts.

Marcel enjoyed the oral ministrations, letting the stranger continue as long as he liked. He was very good at it. Oliver never did this. Then the stranger disengaged, but stayed kneeled and looked up at him with hungry eyes. "Smack me in the face with it."

Marcel complied, and the stranger expressed his appreciation. "*Ja, Ja, Ja!*"

Marcel recognized the accent then, and pulled away. "You are German. I don't associate with Germans."

"But I'm a pilot," the young man said, voice pleading. "I have a two-day furlough in Paris, and then I have to go back. I could be killed on Friday. Please, use me."

Marcel started to walk away, but the pilot grabbed his hand. "Please, this could be my last chance before I die."

Marcel hesitated. "You are not a good partner for a French man."

"No, I am bad. Very, *very* bad," the pilot said. "You should punish me. I've bombed English cities. I'm a very bad man. I deserve your punishment. Punish me! If I die on Friday, I can die with a clean conscience if you punish me."

Marcel shrugged. "What punishment is sufficient for how bad you've been?"

"Hit me," the German said, his voice husky and deep. "Hit me in the face."

Marcel smacked him hard, and the German pilot moaned. "*Ja!* Hit me again."

Marcel smacked him harder, and the German moaned louder. "Again! I have been very bad."

Marcel wasn't into this sort of thing, but he found himself hitting the pilot ever harder, his hatred of the Occupation and the humiliation at his country's defeat coming to the surface. No matter how hard he hit him, the German begged for more.

"*Ja, Ja*! Do what you want to me, I'm your bitch," the pilot said, his husky voice incongruous with the youthful handsome face.

Marcel found himself doing things that he would never ordinarily do. It was not like him, yet it felt cathartic. His sexual frustrations, his loneliness, his childhood inadequacies, all of it came out against this Luftwaffe pilot.

He preferred to receive, but it seemed natural to penetrate this German and use him, until he was satisfied.

"That was incredible," the pilot said when they collapsed side-by-side on the cold concrete floor, panting in exhaustion. "*Danke*."

Marcel didn't respond. He rose to his elbows, looked down at the pilot, and smacked him again, hard enough that his glasses went skipping across the floor. "*Boche*!" he said, and spit on the pilot's face.

"*Ja*!"

Marcel stood and grabbed his underwear from the floor. He marched through the dark hall to the main room, and turned into the alcove. He found his box in the corner, and began to dress.

He'd just finished dressing, when he heard a commotion behind the door, scuffling feet and muffled shouting. A red light bulb began to flash next to the door—a light he hadn't known was there—and men began to scramble toward the alcove, grabbing clothes from boxes.

The Luftwaffe pilot appeared next to him. "Is there another exit?"

Marcel looked at him. "What?" He appeared suddenly shorter, and then Marcel realized he had lost the stilettoes.

"I can't be caught here!" the pilot said, his eyes wide and shining in the light from the nearby kerosene lamp. "Is there another exit?"

Marcel grabbed him by the wrist. "Come with me." He started to pull him down the hall.

"Wait! My clothes." The pilot grabbed his uniform and shoes from a box, held the bundle in front of his crotch, and followed Marcel.

Marcel remembered there was a connection to the coal room from the back of the cellar, and he felt along the wall until he found the opening. Others had the same idea, and they formed a small crowd.

The furnace was dark—a result of the coal shortages, no doubt—and he stumbled over the low pile of coal on the floor. He could hear the Luftwaffe pilot's breath behind him. "Do you have a lighter, *Boche*?"

He could hear the German fumbling with his clothes, and a moment later his cigarette lighter illuminated the small space.

Three wooden steps next to the furnace ascended toward a set of metal cellar doors. A padlock held them closed from the inside. One man shook the lock in frustration, then turned away. The others followed him.

"Hold this," the pilot instructed, handing Marcel the lighter.

He fished in his clothes again and removed a Walther pistol from the belt of his trousers. He aimed it at the padlock, and fired.

Marcel thought his ears would explode.

The padlock flew away, and the pilot pushed the heavy metal doors out. Cold night air rushed in, and he bounded up the stairs. Marcel followed behind his bare buttocks.

They found themselves at the edge of a planted garden, surrounded by six-story tenement buildings. A young woman in black clothing, pushing a baby stroller and holding the hand of a small child, stopped in front of them, her mouth open, gawking at the tall blond man wearing only fishnet stockings, holding his clothes in front of his nakedness.

The pilot shouted at her in German, his voice suddenly harsh and commanding, and she scurried away with her children.

"Come!" the pilot said, and Marcel was happy to follow him.

Shouts in French to their left, down the covered alley, told them the police were in control of the entrance to the club. They ran the opposite direction along the side of the square, keeping to the shadows, and slipped down another long alley toward the Rue Lemercier.

Here they stopped, and the pilot tugged on his pants. Marcel stole a look at his buttocks before they disappeared beneath the blue fabric. The German finished dressing in his white shirt and blue coat, and transformed into the image of a masculine Luftwaffe pilot.

No one would have guessed he wore fishnet stockings under that uniform. The corner of Marcel's mouth turned up in amusement.

He noted the name tag pinned above his left breast pocket said "Lt. Burmeister."

They hurried down the street a quarter mile until they came to the Boulevard des Batignolles. A Wehrmacht squad on patrol had just marched past, moving into the Place Clichy.

"Thank you," the pilot said to Marcel when they stopped at the corner, breathless. "If they had arrested me, the Gestapo would send me to Buchenwald."

Marcel wasn't exactly sure what that meant, but he surmised the gist of it.

Then in the light of the rising moon, his eyes saw for the first time what his subconscious must have already perceived—the resemblance between this Luftwaffe pilot and Oliver. Aside from the blond hair and the glasses, they could have been brothers.

Marcel followed him down the boulevard and across the Place Clichy to the Metro station.

"I don't know your name," the pilot said when they were on the train, two empty seats between them.

Marcel hesitated for a moment. "My name is Marcel; that is all you need to know."

"I'm Jan."

Marcel grunted. For all he knew, it was a fake name.

"I'm staying at the Hotel Majestic. I'm here for two days."

Marcel ignored him, looking away.

Burmeister exited the train a few stops later, looking back longingly before disappearing.

A jumble of conflicting emotions poured through Marcel as he continued home.

24

Saturday, November 2

Collette enjoyed getting dressed up. The sleeveless silver dress was exquisitely cut, the matching hat bore stylish pheasant feathers, and the long white gloves made her feel like a *Grande Dame*. And the mink stole she'd worn over it all was the most luxurious thing she had ever felt. That was the most recent gift in a seemingly endless stream of new luxuries, and she felt proud to hand it off to the coat check when they arrived.

It was easy for Captain Gruder to lavish her with gifts when he paid for them in Reichsmarks, thanks to the artificial exchange rate the Occupation Authority enforced.

She smiled as Gruder held her chair for her before taking the seat across from her.

She had gotten quite used to eating at fancy restaurants, and she looked over the menu with anticipation. Her eyes lit up when she saw the escargot. She had come to adore the dish.

The Wehrmacht colonel seated to her right ordered onion soup for all of them, and she tried not to show her disappointment. It wasn't that she disliked onion soup—on the contrary, she found it quite tasty—it was just that she loved the escargot, swimming in garlic butter, and the thought of having something else broke her heart.

Collette glanced at Gruder, and saw from his sympathetic expression that he knew how she felt.

191

"Colonel, might I suggest an order of the escargot as well? The flavors will compliment, I think."

That was what she loved most, how he seemed to always know how she felt, and took pains to make her happy. She was overjoyed when the colonel agreed. She turned to the French girl seated to her left, across from the colonel—a pale girl with a pretty heart-shaped face, bright red lipstick, and well-coifed brown curls piled on top of her head—and inquired if she enjoyed escargot.

"Oh yes, very much," the girl said.

The conversation was mostly in French, for the benefit of the ladies, but from time to time the two officers would say something to one another in German, and at those moments Collette turned to the colonel's girlfriend.

"What work do you do, Annick?"

"I am Colonel Von der Saar's secretary. And you?"

"I am a film actress," Collette said. She enjoyed the looks on people's faces when she said 'film.' People no longer turned up their noses when she said she was an actress. "You'll see me in the film 'Charlemagne' next month. I play Lady Hildegard."

"I look forward to it," Annick said, suitably impressed.

"How long have you worked for Colonel Von der Saar?" Collette asked.

"Since the beginning of July. He has been good to me."

Collette smiled. Annick was pretty—thin, but large chested—and no doubt the colonel had taken a shine to her from the first day she showed up to work. Like Collette, she was also wearing stylish clothing—far too expensive for a girl to buy herself on a secretary's wages.

"Do you enjoy working at the Culture office?"

"Yes, very much. Albert—Colonel Von der Saar—has been able to get us seats to many shows. We've been to the Opera, the ballet, the symphony, and many cabarets. Last week we went to see Cécile Fournier, and between acts she came out and had a drink with us. She sat right next to me!" The smile lit up Annick's face.

Collette smiled back, the enthusiasm contagious. "I hear she is an amazing performer."

"Yes, she is amazing. You must go with us to see her sometime. I'll ask Alb—Colonel von der Saar—to invite Captain Gruder and you to join us the next time."

"Thank you, that's very kind," Collette said, pleased. She'd always hated being too poor to afford tickets to see the big names in the entertainment business, and Cécile Fournier was near the top of that list. "Have you seen others that you enjoyed?"

Annick nodded. "Yes, I enjoyed Edith Piaf, the young singer at the One Two Two Club. She sings ballads. She is our age, I think, but she sings with such depth of emotion, you would think she were much older. Beautiful songs. But she did not come out to meet anyone after her show." Annick added this last with a note of reproach.

"The One Two Two Club—that's a German officers' club?" Collette asked.

"That's right."

Collette wrinkled her nose. "Humph. If a star such as Cécile Fournier can come out and meet the new fans, and she sings in a regular cabaret, it seems bad manners for Miss Piaf to not extend the same courtesy when working in an officers' club."

"They say she received permission to have her photograph taken with French prisoners of war," Annick said. "She could not have gotten that permission without charming someone in authority. Perhaps she is just selective." Annick's tone suggested that her colonel should have made the cut.

*

Meanwhile, the two officers discussed official business in German. Neither of their girlfriends understood German, and they relied on the assumption that few other French men and women in attendance did, either.

"It seems the directive on minimal interference with the French film industry is bearing fruit," the colonel said.

Gruder agreed. "The guidelines we instituted have had a persuasive effect. Our presence alone has given us results. It was Monsieur Defresne who suggested Charlemagne as the subject for a film, not us. When it is released next month, it will remind the people of the last time that the French and the Germans cooperated, and what a great Reich that was."

"The greatest ever. There has been nothing since to compare to it—until now, of course." The colonel smiled with great pride. "It took eleven and a half centuries, but a German Reich is once again inclusive of France and the Low Countries."

Gruder continued. "I have been pleased with the level of cooperation we have received. Even the few times we have taken direct action, there has been little, if any, negative reaction. The removal of the Jewish elements, for example, was not met with resistance."

Colonel Von der Saar snorted. "I am sure the remaining directors and executives understand the corrupting influence the Jews wielded in their industry. They can see as plainly as anyone how their removal has improved things."

"Of course you're right, Colonel," Gruder said. "But it also helps that they no longer have to compete with Jews."

"Indeed. No one is immune to their own self-interest."

"Most of the Jews in the film industry emigrated to the United States," Gruder said.

The colonel snorted again. "Let the Americans have them. Everyone knows the Jews run Hollywood as it is."

He gave the matter a dismissive wave of the hand. "The ministry has noticed the fine work you have done. They are pleased with the progress our office has made, and they are handing out quite a few Christmas furloughs. I have decided that you should receive one. How would you like to spend a week at home in Salzburg, Captain?"

Gruder glanced at Collette, who was busy chatting with Annick, and looked back at the Colonel. "I would like that very much, sir. Thank you."

"You deserve it, Captain." The colonel wore a big smile, Saint Nicholas dispensing brightly colored presents. "You may leave on December 23rd. You should arrive in Salzburg in plenty of time to spend Christmas Eve with your family. I will expect you back at work on the following Monday, the 30th. How does that suit you, Captain?"

Gruder forced a smile. "That will do nicely, sir, thank you.'

The escargot arrived, along with four bowls of onion soup with melted Gruyere, and the colonel clapped his hands together with pleasure and returned the conversation to French.

25

Monday, November 11

The sound of police sirens caught Oliver's attention, sitting at a table in Chez Marius on Monday, reading a book after lunch. It wasn't unusual to hear police sirens these days; what struck him was the volume, and that they seemed to be coming from every direction.

He set the book down and cocked his head to listen. The sirens all seemed to be moving in northerly or westerly directions.

He saw Sébastien running up the street toward the Boulevard Saint Germain. Oliver rushed to the door and called his name, and Sébastien hurried back.

"What's the matter?" Oliver asked.

"There is a march on the Champs Elysee!" Sébastien said, breathless.

Oliver wondered what was so unusual about that—the Germans paraded down the grand boulevard through the cultural and financial heart of the city two or three times a week, disrupting normal life.

Sébastien must have noticed the look on his face, and clarified. "A protest march! Hundreds of students from the Sorbonne, protesting German repressions."

"Are you joining them?" Oliver asked, suddenly concerned for his friend's safety. Not to mention his sanity.

"No. The police are moving. I'm going to see what is happening, before it's over. Are you coming?" Sébastien's body language, turned away, muscles tense, indicated his impatience to get moving.

197

"Why not?" Oliver hurried back to the table, laid a few coins and ration coupons next to the empty plate, retrieved his book, and came out to see Sébastien already sprinting toward the boulevard. "Hey! Wait for me!"

They took the Metro to the Place de la Concorde, and hurried upstairs to find the sidewalks jammed with people craning to look up the Champs Elysee in the direction of the Arc de Triumphe. Murmurs rippled through the crowd, mingling with the sounds of police sirens.

Oliver could hear shouts in the distance—angry young male voices—but couldn't make out the words. Sébastien motioned for Oliver to follow him, and they weaved through the crowd, up the boulevard to get closer.

The shouting grew angrier as they neared, and Oliver saw police gendarmes and young men scuffling in the street, the police wielding batons while the students swung protest signs. Nearby, hundreds of German soldiers in Wehrmacht gray stood and watched, some smoking cigarettes, as if this were entertainment.

Oliver took Sébastien's arm to stop him from going any farther. "I don't think we should get any closer. We might get caught in the melee."

Sébastien gave him one of those looks the French reserve for stupid foreigners, who could never be expected to understand anything.

"You can stay where you are, then." He turned and disappeared in the crowd.

Oliver felt as if his feet were encased in concrete boots, unable to move. Should he hurry after Sébastien, keep him out of trouble? Or should he worry about his own safety and get the hell out of there? His doubt kept him rooted in place.

A few minutes later, a gendarme strode past on the boulevard, ordering the crowd to disperse and return to their business. Most of the civilians around Oliver complied, but he noticed several who took their time, taking tiny steps and keeping their eyes on the commotion.

Even that seemed to be winding down, with few students still visible. The police had control over the boulevard, and the German soldiers seemed to be turning their attention elsewhere.

Oliver stayed where he was for a few minutes, standing on his tip toes and looking around for any sign of Sébastien. His friend seemed to have vanished, and Oliver hoped he hadn't gotten into trouble.

He finally turned toward the Place de la Concorde, and walked back the way they had come. Passing the U.S. Embassy, he glanced up, wondering what their reactions were. He saw Frank Dryden staring down at the sidewalk from a third-floor window.

Their eyes met, and Dryden nodded. Then he looked back up the boulevard. Oliver turned toward the square and pushed through the crowd toward the Metro station.

**

Sébastien hurried up the alley, occasionally casting a glance backward to see if they were being followed.

The student beside him held a blood-soaked handkerchief to the side of his head. His nose was already purple and swollen, no doubt broken. *Pity. He was so adorable.* The youth couldn't be more than eighteen years old.

Sébastien had only been able to rescue one. There wasn't enough time for more. He'd seen this young man near the curb at the entrance to an alley, bent over and shielding his bloody face with both arms while a rat-faced gendarme with a black mustache cracked his baton against the youth's back. Sébastien's knee to the gendarme's groin had been swift and unanticipated, and the man had doubled over and fallen sideways to the street, hands clutching his crotch and face contorted in agony. Sébastien grabbed the student's arm and tugged him away.

They ran the length of the alley, taking the first turn they found and ran again until they found another turn that led further away from the Champs Elysee.

"Do you know this area?" Sébastien asked.

The student shook his head, and Sébastien silently cursed the luck. The last thing he wanted was to get lost in the 8th Arrondissement.

At the next turn he stopped, and the student looked at him in expectation. Sébastien stood for a moment and thought. Then an idea hit him. "Come with me."

**

Lisette was helping a customer when the bell on the door caught her attention, and she looked over to see Sébastien. Her eyebrows shot up in surprise, but Sébastien shook his head and pretended to look at their collection of Rhône reds. Lisette turned back to the middle-aged woman with the shopping bag hanging from her arm.

It was several minutes before she'd finished, and she strode toward Sébastien, who had ensconced himself in a corner of the store.

"Good day, Sébastien," she said, giving him the formal greeting. It had been a long time since she'd seen him, long enough to make the informal *Salut* inappropriate. "What brings you here?"

Sébastien's gaze was intense, direct. "When is your break?"

"Not for another hour."

"Take your break now."

Her mouth opened, but it took a moment to form the protest. "I can't—"

"Take your break *now*." Sébastien's stare seemed to burn into her.

This confounded her. What was wrong? Was Oliver in trouble, or hurt? She nodded, and walked to the office. She told the manager she had an upset stomach, and needed to take her break early. She had some peppermint at home, she wouldn't be gone long.

The lie worked, and when she went back with her coat, Sébastien was nowhere to be seen. She found him outside, leaning against the wall near the street corner. He didn't look at her as she approached, but turned away when she was a few steps from him, and began walking ahead.

"We need your help," he muttered over his shoulder as she followed a step behind. "Do you have bandages at your home? Rubbing alcohol?"

"Yes." She noticed he hadn't said who the other half of 'we' was. "Is it Oliver? Is he hurt?"

"No."

They walked in silence for a moment, and when they reached an alley Sébastien turned and strode toward a collection of trash cans along a filthy brick wall.

Behind the last can sat a young man, practically still a boy, with his legs pulled into his chest to hide him from view. His nose was broken, and his left temple was scabbed with blood, which also caked his hair.

Sébastien motioned with his head, and the young man scrambled to his feet. Sébastien turned to Lisette. "Lead us to your home, and take as many back alleys as possible."

Lisette understood, and nodded without a word.

She wasn't sure what route to take, not being used to traveling by back alleys, but she led them on a winding journey, moving more-or-less in the direction of home. After a while she recognized the back of the Hotel de l'Arcade, and knew where they were.

"We're almost there." She glanced at the boy striding along next to Sébastien. "What is your name?"

"Xavier." His voice was surprisingly deep for one so young, with such a boyish face.

She looked at Sébastien. "A good friend of yours?"

Sébastien shrugged. "A wounded patriot, which makes him my friend and yours."

"I see."

They reached the corner across from her building, and she held up her hand while she peered around. There were a few people on the street, at the far end of the block near the entrance to the Hotel de l'Arcade. She motioned for them to follow her, and they hurried across the street.

Once inside her apartment, she directed the injured young man to the sink in her bathroom, and closed the door for him to clean up in privacy. Then she spun and marched to where Sébastien stood in her living room.

"What is the meaning of this?" she demanded, livid.

Sébastien seemed unphased at her outrage, and shrugged. "I rescued him, and I didn't know anyone else to call on."

"And from whom are you hiding him? The police? The Gestapo?"

"We have no desire to encounter either."

She held up a finger, wagging it at his face. "If either of them comes calling at my door, I will not protect you, understand? I will help you this time, but I will not be part of your intrigue."

She spun around without waiting for his reply, and marched back to the bathroom. She knocked once on the door and opened it without waiting for an answer.

The young man turned toward her, startled. He'd removed his shirt, and his back was covered with black and blue welts. Lisette grabbed a hand-towel and held it under the faucet, soaking it with cold water. She wrung it out and placed it on the bruises.

"Hold this in place."

She opened the cabinet beneath the sink and removed a bottle of rubbing alcohol, a roll of bandages, and adhesive tape. She searched in vain for cotton balls, and silently cursed Sébastien at the thought of getting blood on her towels. She'd use a rag from the kitchen before she'd stain one of her nice towels. She excused herself long enough to retrieve one that she used for washing dishes, deciding the alcohol would be sufficient to sanitize it.

Back in the bathroom, she applied the rubbing alcohol to the gash along the boy's left temple, causing him to grimace. He didn't utter a word of complaint, though, and she continued to clean the wound with a less than gentle touch.

"I don't want to know anything about how you got this, do you understand? And you will forget coming here."

He nodded and kept silent, enduring the sting of the alcohol and the brush of the wet rag against his cut.

When she'd finished, she tore off a length of bandage, folded it twice, and held it against the cut. Then she tore off strips of the adhesive tape with her teeth and slapped them onto the edges of the bandage, her anger at Sébastien taken out on this stranger.

"There, it's finished. Put your shirt on and leave before the police come looking for you."

"No one will come here looking for me," the boy replied, not disguising the resentment in his voice, or in his eyes. "Thank you for your help."

Sébastien also thanked her before they left. She gave him only a curt nod in reply, and slammed the door.

**

As they exited the building, Xavier looked at Sébastien and thanked him for rescuing him from the gendarme. "Why did you help me?"

"I wanted to help. I would have saved more if I had arrived sooner." Sébastien paused for a moment as they passed a woman and her two small children. "I will take you home, and make sure that you

203

are not molested by the police on the way. You live at the Sorbonne, no? When we get there, we will have a word in private, and I will explain how you can repay me."

26

Oliver was not surprised by the lunch invitation from Frank Dryden.

It arrived on Tuesday, the day after the protest, on plain stationery, slipped under his door; a politely-worded invitation to a friendly lunch at Brasserie Lipp on Friday "to catch up." There was no RSVP requested.

Oliver found Sébastien at Chez Marius, eating an apple and drinking a cup of ersatz coffee while reading a book. Marcel stood watch beside the kitchen door in a white dress shirt and black necktie, a clean white apron around his waist. There were few other people inside the bistro—rationing had cut down on restaurant business over the last two months.

Oliver took the seat next to Sébastien, also facing the front windows. Sébastien looked up from his book long enough to exchange greeting and kisses on the cheeks, and went back to reading.

"I knocked on your door last night, around seven," Oliver said, quietly enough that no one would overhear. "I wanted to make sure you hadn't gotten hurt yesterday."

Sébastien looked at him, his expression unreadable. "I did not."

"I'm glad. I was worried about you."

Sébastien said nothing, but continued to look at Oliver with the same unreadable expression.

Oliver wondered how far he could push the inquiry. He knew from experience that the French didn't like to be pressed for information if they didn't offer it themselves. He considered his words carefully.

"I heard that the police arrested most of the protesters."

Sébastien's only response was a low grunt and a slight nod.

Judging by the way Serge had looked after his arrest a few weeks ago, Oliver decided it was unlikely that Sébastien had been arrested. Then where had he been last night?

"Marie-France told me that the students were outraged because a popular professor was fired. She said that she knew him, had taken one of his classes a few years ago. Did you know him as well?"

Sébastien nodded. "Yes, I knew him at University."

"Marie-France said he was fired for criticizing the cancelation of Armistice Day observances by the Germans. So the students held an Armistice Day parade for him, to protest the Occupation."

Sébastien nodded again, but said nothing, and continued to stare at Oliver with that unreadable expression.

Oliver felt the frustration welling up, and opted to abandon this line of questioning. The French could be so damned infuriating sometimes.

Marcel brought him a Croque-monsieur. He didn't need to order anymore; Marcel knew to bring his regular lunch.

"I noticed that the Germans didn't interfere with the protest yesterday," Oliver said after taking a few bites of his sandwich. "It was the French police who broke it up."

Sébastien looked back up from his book. "Yes, that's true."

"I was a little bit surprised, that's all. I'm sure many of the gendarmes were veterans of the last war, so they should have been more outraged than anyone that the Armistice Day parade was cancelled."

"The police take their orders from the *Boche*." Sébastien's dark eyes had narrowed, and his black eyebrows bunched together.

Oliver detected a note of bitterness in Sébastien's tone. The first crack in the facade. "I suppose you're right. The students were very brave. If only the war veterans on the police force had been as brave, things might have gone differently."

He saw Sébastien's eyes narrow further, and his friend scrutinized him with an intense stare for several seconds. "The Germans are not the only fascists in this country." Sébastien's voice was barely above a whisper, and he continued to stare at Oliver.

Oliver took the plunge. "So who will be brave enough to challenge their fascism?"

Anger flashed across Sébastien's face. He hissed at Oliver through tightly clenched teeth. "Shut up, you fool!"

Stung, Oliver looked away and muttered an apology.

"You do not know what you are saying," Sébastien whispered, and raised his book to his face.

"But I think you do know, my friend," Oliver whispered.

Sébastien said nothing, his nose buried in the book held close to his face. But Oliver noticed a quick sideways glance of his friend's eye.

"We'll talk more in private," Oliver said, and turned his attention back to his lunch.

Friday, November 15

Frank Dryden waited at a corner table when Oliver arrived at Brasserie Lipp at one o'clock. He stood and greeted Oliver with a smile and a handshake.

The days had seemed to drag since the invitation arrived, as Oliver anticipated their conversation. He hoped the anxiety he felt in the pit of his stomach didn't show on his face when he took a seat.

"Have we eaten here before?" Dryden asked, his tone pleasant and friendly.

"Yes. It's been a while, though."

"Then I'm sure you remember their food, some of the best sauerkraut in Paris. And of course their famous home-made beer. Shall we order a couple of mugs?" He motioned for the waiter, and rattled off the order in French.

It hadn't escaped Oliver's notice that these people liked to meet in Alsatian brasseries. The irony of the German-style food bewildered him a little.

"I'm sure you noticed the little 'disturbance' on the Champs-Elysee on Monday," Dryden continued in English after the waiter departed.

"You know I did," Oliver replied, irritated. "You saw me through the window."

"Ah yes, that's right. I did see you briefly as the crowd was breaking up." Dryden's expression gave away nothing.

Oliver's irritation grew. "I'm sure that's the reason you asked me to lunch."

Dryden gave him a disarming smile and spread his hands. "It had been too long since our last chat; I wanted to catch up on how things are going."

Oliver glanced around—every table in the restaurant was occupied, a few of them by Wehrmacht soldiers in gray uniforms, others by men in expensive suits speaking German, plus the usual contingent of well-dressed French businessmen lunching with their mistresses. Did Mr. Dryden really want to discuss their business *here*? *Now*? If Oliver was supposed to speak in some kind of code, he hadn't the faintest clue how.

Dryden noticed Oliver's hesitancy. "Are things going well?" His blue eyes seemed to bore into Oliver.

"Yes, quite well," Oliver replied, assuming they would speak of it in benign generalities.

"Excellent! Very glad to hear that. Any news I'd be interested in?"

"Yes, I'm sure you would be," Oliver said, unsure what to say in this public venue. He could feel a trickle of sweat running down his side under his shirt.

"Then I look forward to hearing all about it," Dryden said with another smile. "Where would you like to begin?"

A chill ran up Oliver's spine. He had no earthly idea. How could he possibly convey what he'd learned, here, around all of these people? Who knew how many of them were secretly eavesdropping the way Miss Fournier had taught him to do?

"I don't know anything for certain," Oliver whispered, leaning in close.

Dryden did not lean forward, but remained sitting with his back straight. He smiled, that smile that never seemed to reach his eyes.

"There are so few certainties these days," he said. "We must learn to live with the uncertainty, and find our way as best we can. There are always clues."

Oliver nodded. "Yes, there are." He glanced at a table of Germans some distance away, and nodded toward them.

Dryden smiled again. "I spoke with a mutual friend of ours the other day. You remember Cécile Fournier?"

Oliver nodded.

"She spoke highly of you. She said you have tremendous potential. She told me you are very capable, and might even run your own business someday. I told her I had never heard you play."

Oliver caught his meaning. So this was how they were going to do it. Oliver feared the conversation could drag out all afternoon this way.

"You've never come to the club."

Dryden's smile tightened. "No, I haven't, you're right. I still hope to hear your music, though." His face seemed to light up at a sudden thought. "Are you free after lunch? Would that be a good time?"

Oliver wondered if Mr. Dryden had done theater. "I have to be at work by four."

"Plenty of time, then," Dryden said as their beers arrived. He raised his mug toward Oliver in a silent toast before taking a long drink.

"You might enjoy working with Cécile," Dryden continued. "She usually sings to piano accompaniment, but I'm sure a trumpet arrangement can be written that wouldn't overpower her voice. Perhaps you could write the arrangement."

Oliver wondered if Mr. Dryden were still using double-meanings. He suspected so. "I would have to get to know her voice first, her style, before I'd know what kind of arrangement would sound best."

Dryden's grin broadened. "Of course. You musicians have your own ways, but I suspect you and Cécile would make a good team. That's a performance I would pay good money to see." He stared hard into Oliver's eyes.

Oliver understood perfectly.

"I would love to work with Mademoiselle Fournier," he said. "I wish I knew her well enough to approach her. She's famous, and I'm no one to her."

"Don't underestimate yourself, Oliver," Dryden said. "Cécile was impressed with you after your previous meetings. I'm certain she would jump at the chance to work with you. Like any true artist, she's always looking to add variety to her art. I'll give her a call, suggest the idea to her. Would you like that?"

Oliver smiled in spite of himself. "Yes, thank you."

"Excellent. Let's order some lunch, eh?"

**

After lunch they took a walk toward the *Jardin de Luxembourg*. There was a chill wind at their backs blowing from the northwest, and they turned their coat collars up and walked with their hands stuffed in their pockets.

Once they reached the sculpted park and its wide open spaces, Dryden looked at Oliver.

"Perhaps it was too soon to ask you to have a business conversation in a restaurant. Speaking in code is a skill you'll learn with practice. One thing you'll learn is there is nothing obviously suspicious about two people meeting for lunch."

He removed one hand from his pocket and motioned around the park. There were a few people strolling the gardens—lovers holding hands, young mothers pushing baby strollers—but no other pairs such as themselves.

"Here, we can be sure that no one will overhear us; but we can't be certain that no one is watching. In fact, the Gestapo probably are."

Oliver felt the hair stand up on the back of his neck. "The Gestapo? But why would they watch us?"

Dryden's face was grim, and he stared at the concrete in front of them. "They have eyes all over Paris. The local police do most of the dirty work, but make no mistake, the Gestapo are gathering information all the time."

Oliver felt a lump drop into the pit of his stomach. "What do we do, then?"

"Just act natural, and don't look around too much. You'll be a lot less interesting if they think you have no idea they're there." After a moment, he added, "And for Heaven's sake, tell me what you've learned before I have to drag it out of you."

"I've noticed that my friend Sébastien goes out after curfew about once a week. He lives across the hall from me, and though he's quiet I can still hear his door and his footsteps. I've watched at my window after he leaves, and I've seen him cross the street and join our friend Serge."

"The one who was beaten by the police a few weeks ago."

"That's right."

"That's very interesting, Oliver. Any idea what they're up to?"

"Not for certain. Probably distributing protest leaflets. I find them around sometimes, on the train or on the floor of the Metro station."

"That stands to reason," Dryden said. "You've mentioned that Serge is a writer, and he works for a print shop. What else?"

"When I went to see the protest on Monday, Sébastien was with me, but when we saw the fighting in the street he left me to get closer. He didn't come home until late; I don't know what time, but he wasn't arrested."

"How do you know he wasn't arrested?"

"He wasn't beaten-up like Serge."

Dryden nodded. "So what was he doing all afternoon and evening?"

Oliver shook his head. "I don't know. I asked him the next day, and he wouldn't say. It was something, though—he told me to shut up."

"Hmm."

Oliver wondered what that meant.

They walked in silence for a moment.

"Oliver, I think it's pretty certain that your friends Sébastien and Serge are involved in more than just the distribution of protest leaflets. The question is what. Can you find out?"

Oliver considered Sébastien's reaction to his questions earlier in the week. "I don't know."

"Then you need to do more to earn their trust. See what you can do."

It irritated Oliver that Mr. Dryden didn't seem satisfied.

"When you know more, send me a message at the embassy that you want to meet. You choose the location."

Dryden held out his hand, and when Oliver shook it, he felt hard paper slip into his hand. He put his hand in his coat pocket and turned toward the 5th Arrondissement. Dryden went back the way they had come.

After Oliver left the park and passed through the neighborhood of stately townhouses that bordered it—several with large red and black swastika flags draped from the roofs—he crossed the wide Boulevard Saint Michel into the 5th.

Only then did he take his hand out of his pocket and look at the money folded in it. He counted five crisp new ten-dollar bills, neatly folded in half.

Fifty dollars! They must really want my help. He wondered why it was so important.

**

Collette finished lighting the candles on the table in their hotel suite when Karl entered. He looked at her in surprise, and then a smile spread across his face.

"What is all this?" he asked, motioning toward the table, laid out formally for two.

"I ordered dinner in tonight," she said, removing the covers from the plates, sending steam into the air. "I know how much you adore veal, so I ordered the veal chops with *haricots* and potatoes. And chocolate cake for dessert."

"It is lovely my dear, how thoughtful." He touched her cheek and stared into her eyes for a moment, then kissed her. "Shall we eat, then?" He held out her chair.

"Just a moment," she said, and went into the bedroom. She came back out with an ice bucket holding a bottle of chilled champagne, a

Maison Perrier-Jouët. "I thought this would be nice to drink with the veal."

He looked startled, and she became afraid that she'd made a mistake. Perhaps champagne didn't go with veal. In the weeks since she'd been living here, she'd learned many things, but she was far from expert at matching wines with fancy meals.

"You do not mind that I ordered the champagne, do you, my love?" It was expensive, and of course she had charged it to their— Karl's—account. Was that why he didn't seem delighted? Was it too expensive?

He seemed to recover. "No, of course not my dear—it is just that champagne is usually reserved for celebrations, not for romantic dinners."

She gave him her most dazzling smile, and put her arms around him.

"It is a celebration, my love. I have news."

He put his arms around her as well. "Oh?"

"Yes, and I hope you are as happy as I am." She hesitated. "I saw a doctor today, over in the 8th. I was referred to him by the studio. He told me that I am going to have a baby—your baby."

He looked stunned; his arms dropped from around her, and he took a step back. "Oh, I see." He stood there for a moment, looking downward, then turned away.

Her heart sank. She had also been stunned at first. Her immediate reaction was panic—much as she had felt the first time she was pregnant, years ago as a seventeen-year-old girl in Picardy. The abortion was what initially brought her to Paris, where she stayed to pursue a career in the theater. Since then she'd been careful—until this relationship. Karl did not wear condoms. And she'd never insisted.

Her panic this morning was aggravated by the realization that the Germans had outlawed abortions. Or was it the reactionaries in Vichy who had outlawed it? Either way, they were no longer easy to find.

But then she began to think about her life with Karl, and how for the first time she wanted no one else; how she'd begun to think of them being together forever. Wouldn't a child solidify that? The child would be a bond they would share forever, make them a family.

She forced a smile. "It will be in June."

He turned toward her, put his hands on her shoulders, and looked her straight in the eyes. She tried to read his expression, but couldn't.

"Are you happy, my dear?"

Her eyes grew moist, and all she could do was nod.

A slight smile spread across his lips, and his eyes softened. "Then I am happy, too." A moment later, his grin widened, and the twinkle returned to his eyes.

He kissed her, softly at first, and then passionately. When he pulled away, he placed his hand on her belly. His grin spread even wider, and he laughed. "Yes! We will be a happy family."

She laughed with him, and he took her face in his hands and kissed her again, quickly this time.

"This calls for a toast," he said. "Pour the glasses, darling."

She poured the champagne and handed him his glass. He raised it.

"To my darling Collette, who has made me the happiest man in Paris tonight. And to our child—*our* child!—who is loved already more than he knows. *Salut*!"

They drank, and the bubbles tickled her sinus, making her giggle.

**

Professor Trusnik sat alone in a four-person booth in a dark corner of the club, a half-empty glass of vodka on the rocks in front of him. The overhead lights had already been turned off in preparation for the show, and the tables were dimly-lit by small lamps with dark

215

shades; the light was further dampened by the thick blue haze of cigarette smoke.

The cigarette girl almost didn't see him as she passed. He had to snap his finger to get her attention.

"Do you have cigars, or only cigarettes?"

"Yes sir, we have cigars. Ten francs, please."

"Ten francs! My God," he muttered, more to himself than to the girl. Inflation had become a huge problem in Paris, but tobacco was outrageous.

He counted ten franc notes and handed them to her, along with a fifty-centime coin for a tip, and a tobacco ration coupon.

She snipped off the end of the cigar for him, and held out a lighter.

He puffed at his cigar as she walked away, and admired the wiggle of her buttocks.

A tall thin figure slipped into the booth beside him.

"Good evening, Mr. Dryden," Trusnik said.

"Good evening, Professor," Dryden said. "It seems we are both fans of Miss Cécile Fournier."

Trusnik smiled. "You are not here to discuss singers."

"No. I'd like to continue our conversation from a few months ago. It seems things have changed in Paris since we last spoke. That demonstration on Monday was evidence of that."

"The most obvious evidence, certainly—but not the only signs. Have you noticed them, Mr. Dryden?"

"If you're talking about the general sense of discontent this autumn, then yes, I have noticed. The demonstration on Monday took everyone by surprise, though."

Trusnik chuckled. "Not everyone."

Dryden's expression was unreadable. "I thought you might have known about it."

"Not in any great detail—but yes."

"I'm sure some of your students were involved."

Trusnik nodded. "Indeed." He took a long drag on his cigar, and exhaled the smoke slowly. "The Germans were in an impossible position. There was no possible way that they could allow the celebration of their defeat in the last war; they *had* to cancel Armistice Day. But in so doing, there was no way to avoid patriotic outrage among the French, even if most of them said nothing—publicly, that is.

"But inevitably, someone would be brave enough to criticize the decision in public. It was not surprising that such a person would be a professor at the Sorbonne, and not surprising that he would get his students impassioned. Of course, he had to be fired—the Germans had to insist upon that. What choice did they have? To have not punished the dissident would be to encourage more dissent. And naturally that enraged the students. At that age, the passions run strong. So you see the inevitable outcome."

Dryden nodded, his expression thoughtful. "It seems there are nascent resistance activities beginning in Paris. It took a while, but there are beginnings."

Trusnik chuckled. "Yes, of course. Are you surprised? This summer it was as if nothing had changed—the Germans paraded their might down the Champs Elysee every few days, and there are all of those horrible swastika flags everywhere, and signs in German—but daily life continued as always. Then came September, and the stricter rations. And then the Vichy regime began to crack down on everything in October. Everyone is hungry, and the working class have seen all of their gains swept away in legislative fiat. Of course there are stirrings of resistance."

Dryden gave Trusnik a knowing look. "And last week it resulted in violence."

Trusnik watched him, waiting.

Dryden continued. "The Germans arrested a man last week—Jacques Bonsergent—for attacking a German soldier. It seems there was a fight between a group of young Frenchmen and a group of soldiers, and all but Bonsergent got away."

Trusnik stubbed out his cigar. "I am surprised that you know of that, Mr. Dryden. It was not reported in the newspapers."

Dryden smiled broadly. "Reporters make good informants, even when they aren't permitted to print what they know. Clearly you also knew, Professor."

"Yes."

"Were the others—the ones who were not caught—students of yours?"

Trusnik shrugged. "Not current students, no."

"But you have been in communication with them?"

"Perhaps."

"Did they say anything I'd be interested in knowing?" Dryden asked, slipping a hundred-franc note across the table to Trusnik's hand.

Trusnik swept the money off the table in one swift move.

"Probably not. I have learned that these individuals are involved in other activities against the Germans—small acts of sabotage, underground protest newspapers. Nothing significant yet."

"But you expect the scope of their activities to increase?"

Trusnik nodded. "I would bet on it."

The waitress came by, wearing a short skirt and a tight short-sleeved blouse. Dryden ordered bourbon, and another vodka for Trusnik.

He watched the waitress leave before returning his attention to the professor.

"My source told me that the Germans are holding Bonsergent themselves. They haven't turned him over to the French police."

"Yes. The Germans will try him and convict him themselves, and then they will broadcast it in the newspapers. Good propaganda to report on the punishment of dissidents. A demonstration of their strength."

"And how do you know that? Intuition only, or do you have information?"

Trusnik chuckled. "I have sources."

"What sources?"

"Good sources."

"How good?"

Trusnik leaned back. "I really can't say."

"Then how am I supposed to know they are good sources?" Dryden's tone was irritated.

Trusnik's expression grew cold. "Betrayal is punished most harshly by these people, Mr. Dryden. I would not think of crossing them."

Dryden scowled. "Understood. Just tell me how they would be in a position to know what the Germans are going to do? And how do you know they aren't feeding you false information?"

"They are not friends of the Germans, Mr. Dryden. Of that you can be certain. But circumstances have made relations—cordial. *Non-aggressive*, you might say."

Dryden nodded and gave the professor an appreciative look. "Understood."

**

He should have guessed that Trusnik was working for the Soviets. The professor wasn't a communist, but neither was he a White Russian exile. And rumor had it the NKVD liked to use Russian ex-pats.

219

The waitress arrived with their drinks as the stage lights came up. Dryden paid her, and took a long drink of his whiskey.

**

A tall man in a black tuxedo came out from behind the red curtain, took a bow to acknowledge the applause, and sat at the piano. He wiggled his fingers above the keys.

A moment later the spot light came on, shining at the center of the curtain, and Cécile Fournier slipped between the curtains and seemed to materialize on stage. She wore a shimmering silver dress that swept the floor, with a long slit up the side that reached half-way up her thigh.

The applause rose, and she smiled and bowed. Then she nodded to the pianist, who began to play. After the introduction, her silky alto voice filled the room.

Trusnik looked to his left a moment later, and saw the booth empty save for him. Dryden had slipped out unnoticed.

27

Saturday, December 14

Snow fell softly as Oliver left *Le Chien Errant* shortly after eleven-thirty. Nearly an inch covered the ground, hiding the pavement.

It had turned suddenly cold a couple of weeks before, and blustery with wintery winds whipping down off of the English Channel; but tonight it was still and silent.

Oliver loved the snow. It made the city look clean and bright for a change.

Stepping out of the Sorbonne Metro station in the 5th Arrondissement, he opted to take the long way home, up the Rue Saint-Jacques. He had fifteen minutes until his midnight curfew, and he wanted to enjoy the peace of this snowy night. He took his time, strolling and looking around.

His hat kept the snow off his head and face, and without wind it didn't seem all that cold. Besides, his apartment wouldn't be much warmer than outside.

He passed the Church of Saint Severin, pausing for a moment to admire the nativity scene. With snow falling over the wooden frame of the miniature stable, glowing in the light from the candles burning behind the Virgin Mary and Joseph, it finally seemed like Christmas.

By the time he strolled the remaining two blocks to his building, the church bells were beginning their midnight chime.

As he rounded the corner, he saw two figures dressed in black creeping along the edges of the building across the street. The building where Serge lived. Oliver might not have noticed them if it weren't for the contrast they made with the fresh snowfall.

The moment he stepped around the corner, they froze in place, flattening against the wall in the shadow of an awning.

Oliver kept walking the remaining few yards to his entrance, but he couldn't help staring at the figures trying in vain to hide in the shadows. Nights were usually dark in Paris these days, thanks to the black-out meant to hide the city from RAF bombers; but tonight what little light there was reflected off the snow.

He paused in the doorway. The figures looked familiar. When he looked closely at them, only twenty feet away, he noticed the stack of papers under their arms, and the black of newsprint.

Serge and Sébastien, of course. Those papers were too big to be leaflets; it looked more like newspapers. He should've known that Serge would print clandestine opposition newspapers. Ever the Socialist agitator. He probably wrote them himself, printed them at M. Beauxdoin's shop, and distributed them at night.

He hesitated for a second, then looked up and down the street; there was no one out. He glanced up at the windows across the narrow street, but saw no blackout curtains out of place. He took a deep fortifying breath, and jogged across the street.

He recognized his friends' faces when he was halfway to them.

"Oliver! Go, get inside," Serge whispered as he approached.

"Can I help?"

"No, you should not be involved."

"But I want to help."

Sébastien shook his head. "It is dangerous enough for two, leaving tracks in the snow."

Serge nodded in agreement. "The more tracks we leave, the more likely the police will see and follow."

Oliver held his hands out and raised them toward the falling snow. "Then why are you out at all?"

"We have an obligation," Serge said. "The snow is unfortunate, but we must fulfill our duty. You are not involved; it would be pointless for you to take on the danger."

Sébastien stared at Oliver. When he spoke, his voice was softer than Serge's commanding tone. "If you want to help us, Oliver, the best thing you can do is go home now, get in bed, and forget that you saw us."

Oliver met Sébastien's gaze and held it. After a few seconds, he replied, "Alright, I'll go home—under one condition. Sébastien, you come and see me the moment you return. We'll talk then."

Sébastien looked at him in silence.

"Agree, or I'll follow you wherever you're going."

Sébastien continued to look at him without a word.

Serge glanced sideways at Sébastien. "It's too dangerous to involve him," he muttered.

Oliver continued to look Sébastien directly in the eye, challenging him.

At length, Sébastien nodded. "Fine. When I return home, I will knock on your door three times, pause two seconds, then knock two times more. I will wait only a moment, and if you do not answer I will go home and we will never speak of this."

"Agreed." Oliver extended his hand, and Sébastien shook it, staring hard at Oliver.

Oliver extended his hand to Serge, who turned away and walked without a word toward the entrance of the nearby alley.

Sébastien nodded at Oliver before following Serge and disappearing into the shadows of the alley.

**

Sébastien followed Serge in silence through the labyrinthine alleys of the 5th Arrondissement south of the Boulevard Saint-Germain. He had no idea where they were going, or for what purpose—only that it was a mission assigned to them from up the chain of command.

They had delivered their outlaw papers to all of the usual places—dropping them inside boxes or empty trash cans from which others would retrieve them before dawn—and it had taken an hour. Ordinarily they would sneak home now; but this night they had an additional assignment, about which Serge had only hinted.

Sébastien trusted his friend, and did not ask questions.

They reached the edge of the *Jardin des Plantes*, and Serge raised his hand to order a stop. He looked around, then put his fingers to his mouth and whistled, once.

From across the street inside the botanical garden, two whistles in rapid succession were the answer. Serge motioned forward, and he and Sébastien sprinted across the street and hid behind the tree trunks.

A short distance away, a figure in black emerged from behind another tree, and crept quickly toward them. The figure was small, feminine, and moved with cat-like stealth.

As she neared, Sébastien was only slightly surprised to recognize Adrienne.

"You are certain you were not followed?" Serge whispered.

"I am certain," Adrienne said, also in a whisper.

"Come," Serge said.

They moved from tree to tree until they reached the greenhouses at the north end of the *Jardin*. Serge held up his hand for them to wait where they were hidden, while he crept to the wall of the greenhouse, his back to the glass, and knocked on the door in a complicated sequence.

A moment later the door opened half-way, and Serge motioned for them to follow him.

The air inside the greenhouse was warm and heavy, and the glass was so fogged with condensation that rivulets ran down as though it were raining inside.

A middle-aged man dressed all in black stood before them, and shut the door quietly. At the other end of the room stood three men whom Sébastien did not recognize, also dressed in black. A single candle illuminated the space, glistening off the condensation and casting deep shadows in the corners.

They gathered in the middle of the greenhouse, where the middle aged man addressed them.

"Most of you do not know me. It must stay that way. For tonight, you will know me as Alpha. Only these two know my identity," he motioned toward Serge and a tall dark man. "Most of you know only one of these men. Tonight, you will address them as Beta"—he nodded to Serge—"and Gamma"—he nodded to the tall dark man. "This way, if anyone is captured, he will not be able to identify more than two others. Those two will be sent into hiding immediately."

The middle aged man picked up a black bag, and began removing guns—Colt .45's—and handing them out. When he reached Sébastien, he began speaking again. "You will be known as Delta. You, young woman, you will be Epsilon." He continued with the other two unknown men, going down the Greek alphabet—"You are Zeta, you are Eta."

When he finished handing out guns, he turned back to the center and addressed the group. "You will obey orders without question. I am in command, and Beta and Gamma are next in command. We will travel secretly by automobile, hiding under blankets in the trunk or on the floor of the back seat. The man driving the car you will address simply as Doctor. For security, you will not know our mission until we arrive. For now, know that what we do tonight is for the benefit of the French people. Are there any questions?"

Sébastien held up his pistol. "Are we going to kill Germans tonight?"

The middle aged man looked him hard in the face. "Only if necessary. The guns are for defense. We do not want to draw their attention if we do not need to. Is that clear?"

Sébastien nodded, mildly disappointed.

The middle aged man consulted his wrist watch. "We leave in five minutes."

Serge motioned for Adrienne and Sébastien to huddle with him. "Alpha is in charge of the operation, but absent orders from him you will take orders from me. Gamma will give orders to the other two. You understand?"

Sébastien and Adrienne nodded.

"And you are not to call each other by name, or call me by name. To maintain security, we use only our code names."

"Understood," Sébastien said. Adrienne nodded in agreement, her face drawn.

A few minutes later, they crept toward a large automobile idling at the curb on the Rue Cuvier, along the side of the *Jardin*. Thick black smoke belched from the tail-pipe, staining the fresh snow— exhaust from the charcoal converter that Frenchmen lucky enough to have a driver's permit had been forced to install, because the Germans reserved all of the gasoline for themselves. The headlight beams were dimmed by slitted black-out covers.

A bearded man in his fifties, dressed in a dark brown overcoat and matching hat, stood next to the driver's door, looking impatient.

The trunk was open, and Gamma bade his two companions to get inside before following them in. How they all three fit, Sébastien had no idea. Alpha covered them completely with two dark blankets and closed the trunk.

Serge opened the back door and motioned for Adrienne and Sébastien to get inside. A black medical bag and a pair of boxes sat on the seat. The interior of the car reeked of charcoal smoke.

"Get on the floor, pull your knees to your chest," Serge whispered. They complied. He climbed in after them and squeezed against them, his shoulder pushing against Sébastien's feet, which caused Sébastien's knees to bang his chin. He bit his tongue and grimaced, but kept silent. He tasted blood.

Alpha threw a dark blanket over them and closed the door.

From beneath the blanket, Sébastien heard the front doors close, and then the gear shift cranked, the engine rumbled, and the car pulled away into the night.

The car made several turns, and Sébastien soon lost track of where they were. This continued for some time, until he felt the car slow suddenly, and heard the brakes grind beneath him.

The car came to a stop, and he heard the squeak of the window being rolled down.

A voice demanded something in German. Sébastien tensed.

The Doctor replied in French that he was on a run to deliver a baby in Gournay-sur-Marne.

"Who is he?" the soldier asked, switching to French with a thick German accent.

"The father," Doctor replied.

"And what is in the boxes?"

"Chloroform."

The German soldier demanded to see their identity papers and the doctor's driving permit.

Sébastien heard the faint sound of papers being exchanged, and then silence for several seconds.

He held his breath.

After what felt like an eternity, he heard the rustle of papers, and the German soldier said in crisp, clipped syllables, "You may proceed."

The gear-shift cranked, and the car lurched forward.

They cruised for some time without stopping or turning. After a while, they slowed for one turn, and then another. Sébastien heard the crunch of gravel under the tires, and felt the bumpiness of an unpaved road.

Several minutes later the car came to a stop, and the engine died.

Doors opened, the blanket pulled away, and cold night air assaulted them.

"Come. Quickly, quickly!" Alpha whispered.

They scrambled out of the car.

Sébastien's legs were stiff and his side sore from the awkward position he'd held, but he kept it to himself and stayed close to Serge.

It was almost completely dark, the only hint of light being a soft glow in the clouds where the moon would be.

Three beams of electric light appeared, searched the ground until they settled on a set of train tracks some thirty meters away, and then quickly switched off.

"Come, quickly!" a whispered voice said.

They ran for a moment, Sébastien listening to the sounds of footsteps in front of him to find his way in the dark. When those steps slowed, so did he.

He heard a clicking sound, and then the small flame from a cigarette lighter illuminated Serge's face a few feet away. Alpha and Gamma also lit cigarette lighters a short distance away, and Sébastien saw the faces of the rest of the group with them.

Serge had one of the boxes on the ground at his feet, and he crouched down next to it.

"Tear it open," he ordered.

Sébastien ripped open the top of the box, and saw bottles of chloroform. Under them he found an assortment of paper-wrapped bars in pairs, connected by wires at the top and bottom. The Nazi eagle and swastika was stamped on each bar, along with a few words of German over the name "Amatol 41."

Explosives.

"Lay them along the rails, two meters apart," Serge whispered. He tapped Sébastien on the shoulder and said, "You lay them out to the left, on both rails." Then he tapped Adrienne's shoulder and instructed her to do the same to the right.

Sébastien did as instructed, pacing off approximate meters with his feet.

Serge came along a few moments later with his cigarette lighter, and held it out to Sébastien. "Shine the light for me. Not too close."

Sébastien hardly needed the warning.

He held the lighter a half-meter from the explosives as Serge connected each to a main wire. Serge took light steps, barely crunching the gravel under his feet, and Sébastien found himself doing the same.

While Serge worked, moving quickly from one set of explosive to another, they heard the sound of the car starting behind them, and then saw the dimmed beams of the headlights through the slitted covers.

After Serge had finished his work, he whispered to Sébastien and Adrienne, "Get back to the car. Go!"

They hurried toward the idling car, and found the rest of the group there, other than Serge and Gamma. They all stood in silence for a moment, staring toward the railroad tracks hidden in the darkness somewhere beyond the dimmed headlight beams.

"Come on, hurry!" Alpha muttered under his breath.

A moment later there was a spark to their left, and another a few seconds later to their right. They heard the crunch of gravel beneath running feet as the sparks snaked through the darkness.

"Run! That way!" Alpha said, no longer whispering.

The doctor threw the car into reverse and spun the tires in his haste to put distance between the car and the tracks. They all ran after him.

The ground was frozen hard and lumpy. Sébastien stumbled in the darkness and nearly fell.

A loud boom shook the ground, and a ball of fire lit the landscape behind them. Turning his head, Sébastien saw railroad cars illuminated some fifty meters to his right. He also saw the running figures of Serge and Gamma.

More explosions followed in rapid succession. The doctor slammed on the brakes, and the tires skidded in the snow before coming to a stop.

Alpha spun around. "Zeta, Eta—in the trunk, now! Delta, Epsilon, on the floor!"

Car doors opened and people scrambled, a mass of controlled chaos. Bodies crammed themselves into tight spaces, and a blanket blocked the light of the explosions. Within a minute, car doors slammed shut and the car began moving again, spinning a quick 180 degrees and accelerating quickly, the engine whining under the strain.

Sébastien's heart raced as he pictured German soldiers racing after them. He heard no gunshots, but that didn't stop his imagination from conjuring up the image of a hundred pursuers hot on their trail.

**

They stopped at a military check-point some time later—probably not the same one, Sébastien supposed, since the soldier's voice was different—and papers were shown. This time, Doctor said, "This man has broken his arm, a compound fracture that I cannot set by myself, and I am taking him to the hospital in Neuilly."

Sébastien wondered how Alpha and the doctor had faked a compound arm fracture.

The explanation worked, and they drove away a moment later.

Sébastien knew they were back in the city when they began to make frequent turns. Once again he grew disoriented, but didn't try to figure out where they might be. Eventually the car came to a stop, the engine died, and car doors opened. The blanket flew off, and cold air again assaulted them.

They were back at the edge of the *Jardin des Plantes*.

Alpha demanded the pistols back, and Sébastien removed his from his belt and handed it over. Then he, Serge, and Adrienne crept back through the alleys of the 5th Arrondissement toward home.

None of them spoke until they reached the Rue Lagrange. As Serge poked his head out of the alley to look up and down the street, Sébastien asked the question that had been on his mind since arriving at their mission.

"Where did you learn how to use explosives?"

Serge turned back and looked at first him, then Adrienne. Both stared at him. "In Switzerland."

"Switzerland? When were you in Switzerland?"

"In May."

"When you disappeared after the invasion," Adrienne said.

Serge said nothing.

Sébastien's eyes narrowed, and he stared at Serge for several seconds. "Who taught you about explosives in Switzerland?"

Serge hesitated, then said "Franz Lemiel."

Sébastien's mouth opened and his eyes widened. Then he laughed.

Adrienne shushed him. "Sébastien, quiet! Have you lost your mind?" she whispered.

He continued to laugh. He looked at Serge with genuine mirth. "Franz is a busy man," he said. "I have a story to tell you."

**

Oliver lounged on his couch, huddled under a thick blanket with his legs pulled in to his chest, dozing. He woke to the sound of knocking at his door—three times, then a pause and two more knocks.

He glanced at the clock on the wall as he scrambled from beneath the blanket. It was quarter past four in the morning. His breath crystalized in front of his face as he hurried to his door.

Sébastien stood in the hallway, still dressed all in black.

"Come in," Oliver offered, and stepped aside.

"I came here as soon as I returned, as you instructed," Sébastien said, his voice flat. He stared Oliver directly in the eyes and stood with his hands clasped in front of him, waiting.

"You were doing more than delivering outlaw newspapers," Oliver said.

Sébastien didn't respond.

"That wouldn't take four hours."

Sébastien continued to stare at him in silence.

Oliver lost patience. "Sébastien, I want you to tell me what is going on."

"No."

"I can help you."

"You shouldn't involve yourself."

"But I can help you!" Oliver repeated, more emphatically.

"It is not your fight."

The time had come to play his hand. Oliver saw no way around it. "I have connections."

Sébastien cocked his head, and a glimmer of interest came to his eyes, though he said nothing.

Oliver responded to the unspoken question. "The United States wants to see the Germans defeated, and the Occupation ended. I have connections who can assist the resistance—" he paused, and then added slowly, "If I knew someone in the resistance."

Sébastien's breath seemed to quicken, and though he did not move and said nothing for some time, Oliver could almost see him weighing the options in his mind.

"Have you been spying on us?" he finally asked.

Oliver shook his head. "No. But I've been asked to let my connections know if I learn of any resistance activities. I know that you and Serge are involved—and in more than just writing opposition newspapers."

Sébastien was silent again for a moment. Oliver watched his face closely, and it seemed that his friend was struggling with indecision.

"I am not permitted to say anything to anyone," Sébastien finally said.

"Is Serge in charge?"

A tiny smile flickered at the corner of Sébastien's mouth. "I am not permitted to say anything to anyone," he repeated, though this time his voice was softer and warmer.

Oliver nodded. "I understand. I'll talk to Serge tomorrow. Tell him to come see me here, at eleven o'clock."

Sébastien started toward the door, but hesitated and turned back. "What if he tells you nothing? What will you say to your connections?"

Oliver took a deep breath. He hated this.

"I'll have to tell them what I've observed, and what I've concluded from my observations."

The distance returned to Sébastien's eyes. "I will tell Serge to come see you at eleven, here in your apartment. Goodnight."

He spun on his heels and walked out.

28

Serge knocked at precisely eleven o'clock. When Oliver opened the door to let him in, he wasn't surprised to see Sébastien standing behind him.

"You are asking too many questions," Serge said without preamble, shoving past Oliver. Sébastien followed him in without a word, nodding to Oliver as he passed.

"I don't understand why you are so reluctant to accept help," Oliver said.

Serge stared at him for a long time. Oliver waited.

"Who are these 'connections' of yours that you told Sébastien about? The ones who want to know about the resistance, who are they?"

"Someone from the U.S. embassy," Oliver said.

Serge's hazel eyes narrowed. "Why are they interested in the resistance? The United States is neutral."

"Officially neutral, yes—but not neutral in spirit."

Serge continued to stare at him for several seconds. "Why do you trust them?"

Oliver didn't have a good answer. Why did he trust Frank Dryden? Was it only because he was from the American embassy?

He thought of Cécile Fournier, and how Dryden had arranged for him to meet her and learn. She'd treated him above board, and something about her told Oliver that she could be trusted without question.

"My connection at the embassy has a French agent, someone with experience, and he put me in contact with her. She has been most helpful, and I trust her completely."

Serge stared at him again for several seconds. When he finally spoke, his words were slow and deliberate. "You must remember something, Oliver—governments are never to be completely trusted. They will sacrifice ideals for expediency and compromise, and there are no pure alliances."

Oliver nodded to concede the point. "Understood."

"Do not think for a moment that I do not trust you, Oliver. But the American government—" Serge paused and shrugged—"who can be sure?"

Oliver felt relief that his friends trusted him. He'd started to wonder otherwise. But although Serge had professed trust, they still hadn't let him in. "I know that the American government wants to see the Germans defeated, and they are willing to help in any way they can."

Serge snorted. "But not enough to risk the Germans finding out, I am certain. They won't risk their official neutrality for us—not much, anyway. The British, though, they have more interest in our success, and they take risks to help us."

Oliver's eyebrows rose. This surprised him, though he wasn't sure why. It made perfect sense. "Tell me more." When Serge hesitated, Oliver added, "Please trust me. You have to know that I would never do anything to put you in danger. Come, both of you, sit with me and let's talk—as friends."

He sat on the couch, and after a few seconds more hesitation, Serge nodded and joined him. Sébastien followed, sitting between them.

Oliver turned sideways so that he could face them both. He pulled his legs up and sat cross-legged, or "Indian style" as they called it back home.

Serge looked him in the eye. "Sébastien and I also have connections, Oliver, which no one knows. If we share this information, you must keep it to yourself."

Oliver nodded. "I won't betray your confidence." A thrill rushed through him—that his friends trusted him with secret information, and also at the nature of what they were doing.

"Do you remember the day after the invasion, when I left Paris?" Serge asked.

"Yes."

"I went to Switzerland. I crossed the mountains, snuck across the border, and went to Basel to see our friend Franz Lemiel. You met him in April when he came to visit."

"I remember him."

"Like all the men in Switzerland, Franz is a reservist in the army. For three weeks he taught me things, about different guns, and also how to wire explosives. And he promised to be in touch.

"When I returned to France in June, the French Army had collapsed. The Germans were sweeping through Normandy toward the Atlantic, and advancing toward Paris. I knew it was hopeless, but I did what I could. I went north into Lorraine, even as the refugees clogged the roads heading south. I met soldiers who had become separated from their units, and I gathered a few together. We scavenged for weapons. When we got close to the lines, we blew up a few bridges to slow the *Boche*. We kept moving, always staying ten or twenty kilometers ahead of the Germans."

Oliver listened in amazement. He looked at Sébastien, whose expression remained passive.

Serge continued. "We did not join with the Fourth Army fighting in Alsace, knowing that would only get us killed or captured, and agreeing amongst ourselves that we would have more impact with guerilla tactics. The Maginot Line collapsed on June 15th, and we knew we had been right. That was the day after Paris fell, though we did not hear that news for several days. When the Germans trapped the Fourth army in the Vosges Mountains on the 17th, coming at them from the east and west, we slipped south toward the Juras. They are taller than the Vosges, and offered us places to hide.

"For the next seven days we hid in the mountains, shooting at German columns from cover when we could, and blowing up railroad tracks and German trucks at night. We didn't stop until the cease-fire on the 24th.

"That was the day we found the British pilot. His plane had been shot down, and he parachuted into the woods. Local villagers hid him, and when they heard we were partisans, they brought him to us. He told us he was a colonel, and his name was Baxter. He asked us to help him find a two-way radio. We stole one from a German camp, and he sent a message to London. He asked for a reply at the same hour the next day."

Oliver could barely breathe, and his skin tingled.

"So, the next day we tuned in, and a message came. He was to get to Geneva, dressed as a civilian, and go to the British consulate. That's when we knew he was more than a pilot. We agreed to help him get to Geneva *if* he would tell us the truth about who he was, and if he would promise to get us help to continue the fight. He agreed.

"He said his mission was not bombing targets or shooting down German planes, but aerial observation. That is why he was so far from the fighting—he was observing German supply lines. He had film he needed to get back to England. He agreed to find a way to get guns and explosives to us by airdrop."

Oliver shook his head in amazement. "Did he keep his word?"

"Eventually," Serge said. "He couldn't get anything sent to France until late November. But we did not know that for many weeks."

"What did you do?"

"We got him civilian clothes from a farmer, and took him along forest paths in the high ridges toward the border near Geneva. He told us to carefully guard the two-way radio, and he would contact us on that frequency. We made a code.

"After he crossed the border, we couldn't agree what to do. Some of us wanted to go home and wait. Others wanted to continue the fight in the mountains as guerillas." Serge shrugged. "I argued that there was little good we could do that way now. The cease-fire had come, and the government was meeting in Vichy to dissolve the Republic.

"In the end, we agreed that each would decide for himself what to do, but we would exchange contact information. Then five of us went home—to Paris, Reims, Troyes, Epinal, and Besançon—and the other four stayed in the mountains to shoot Germans."

"So then what?" Oliver asked, almost breathless.

Serge shrugged. "I came home, and I waited. By the end of July we had heard that there could be no air drops while the Luftwaffe was bombing Britain."

"Were you angry?"

"No, it was understandable."

"And that's when you decided to act on your own, to print opposition leaflets?"

"No, I decided before then." Serge's lips pursed, and his voice grew bitter. "Everyone in Paris was relieved that the fighting was finished, and everyone praised Marshall Pétain for saving us from further bloodshed. No one saw that the counterrevolutionaries in

Vichy were eliminating every freedom our forebears fought for during the Revolution. I resolved to remind them."

"I agreed to help him," Sébastien said.

"When?" Oliver asked. He had to know how long this had been going on under his nose.

"In August. Before he was detained for those foolish posters in the Metro station." Sébastien's tone hinted that he had voiced disapproval of Serge's posters before.

"That was how I came to the attention of my local commander," Serge said, as much to Sébastien as to Oliver.

That piqued Oliver's interest. "Tell me about that. What do you do? And what did you do last night?"

Serge exchanged a look with Sébastien.

"I will not tell you who my local commander is," Serge said. "Do not be offended—even Sébastien does not know. This is for security. I do not know who is above my commander in the chain, or who else he works with. I know one other person that he recruited, and only his first name. I recruited Sébastien, but even my commander does not know Sébastien's name, or anything about him."

Oliver was amazed at the precautions. "What do you do?"

Serge hesitated a moment. "Last night was our first operation. Until now, we have only stockpiled guns. I cannot tell you where we keep them. I do not know where they came from. I'm not certain if my commander knows. Perhaps, perhaps not. But it is not important."

He hesitated again, and it seemed to Oliver that he was struggling with what to tell.

"And then last night?" he prompted.

"I will tell you, but only because you are likely to hear it on the street, and you will figure out that it was probably us. The Germans will keep it out of the newspapers, but word will spread. Best for you not to pass on rumors to your person at the American embassy."

"Thank you."

"We blew up several lengths of track east of Paris—tracks that the Germans use to ship weapons and food to Germany."

Oliver whistled. "They'll try to come after whoever did that."

Serge shrugged. "I don't think they will be able to. We took many precautions."

"How long will it take for them to repair the tracks?"

"I do not know," Serge said with another shrug. "Days, weeks. But until they do they are unable to move supplies."

"What next?" Oliver asked.

"We will not know until it is time for the next job," Serge said.

Oliver supposed that was another security measure.

"My commander here knows little about my other connections, just as I know nothing of his. He knows only that I have access to explosives through my connections outside of Paris. That is all. Only Sébastien knows the whole truth—and now you."

"Thank you for trusting me," Oliver said. "I won't tell anyone about your connections. I'll only tell my contact at the embassy about the railroad tracks tonight."

"I suppose you have to tell him something," Serge said. "Just remember your promise, and keep our contacts secret."

That reminded Oliver, and he looked at Sébastien. "Serge said you both have contacts. Will you tell me about yours?"

"I got a telegram from Lyon at the beginning of July," he said. "He only used his initials—DH—but I knew it was from Dolph. He said he found a small studio in Lyon and would continue sculpting. He said he had spoken with our mutual friend in Switzerland, and would send word soon. Of course I knew he meant Franz Lemiel."

Oliver felt a little confused. "Is Dolph involved in the resistance?"

Sébastien gave him a look of exasperation.

Oliver's face flushed, but he wasn't sure why he felt embarrassed. "I don't understand."

"He is working with Franz," Sébastien said, as if that made it obvious. "He is part of an underground operation to get wanted dissidents into Switzerland, up the Rhône River. They also bring in literature that has been banned by Vichy's censors."

A foggy picture was forming in Oliver's mind, but he still wasn't clear what the connection to Sébastien was. "How are you involved?"

Sébastien stared at him for a few seconds, and Oliver wondered—as he often did—what he was thinking behind those dark eyes. He imagined Gallic condescension at his inability to put the puzzle together. The thought irritated him. He stared back.

"I am a courier on the underground escape route out of Paris," he said. "That is all you need to know."

Oliver nodded. "I understand. Thank you for telling me all of this." He paused a second, then added, "I knew something was going on, and it bothered me that you wouldn't let me in. I wondered if you didn't think I was a good enough friend."

Sébastien seemed genuinely surprised. "No, that is not it at all. Why would you think that? It was for your *safety* that we did not include you. We would not want to endanger you, Oliver. You must know that."

That brought a smile to Oliver's lips. "I know you're right." He rose from the couch. "Thank you for this. I'm sure we can find a way that I can help. I'll do anything I can for you."

Serge stood and shook Oliver's hand. "We know you would. But please be cautious about whom you trust. Others' loyalties are not as pure as yours."

"I'll be careful."

**

When they were in the hall, Sébastien nodded for Serge to join him inside his apartment.

"Why did you tell Oliver that you and I are the only ones who know about Franz and Dolph, and the partisans in the Juras?"

Serge smiled. "I do not trust the American government, my friend. We may learn that we are pawns in their chess game with the Germans. They may turn us in someday if it gives them some advantage. If so, they will not get Adrienne."

244

29

Saturday, December 21

Cécile arrived at eight-thirty to find the party already in full-swing. Laughter and conversation could be heard halfway down the street. The door was opened by a liveried butler, who took her invitation and her fur coat with a bow, and directed her to the dining room for hors d'oeuvres.

At least fifty people filled the large dining room, which was lit by a heavy crystal chandelier. Waiters in tuxedo jackets circulated with trays of small bites or champagne flutes. Dried apples and Christmas ribbons decorated the mantle.

A middle-aged woman with platinum blond hair and pencil-thin dark eyebrows approached her with a big smile, and took Cécile's hands in both of hers. "Miss Fournier, we are so honored that you could come. It is always a privilege to see you."

"Thank you for the invitation, Mrs. De Forêt," Cécile replied, and accepted the hostess's kisses on her cheeks.

"Champagne?" the hostess asked, taking a glass from the tray of a passing waiter, and handing it to Cécile without waiting for an answer.

"Thank you," Cécile said with a wry smile.

"Allow me to introduce you to some people, won't you?" Mrs. De Forêt took Cécile by the elbow and led her into the parlor, where they approached a stylish group standing in front of the piano. One of the men wore a black, red, and white Nazi armband around the left sleeve of his gray suit coat, and spoke with a barely-detectible German accent.

A strikingly handsome man in a navy blue suit looked directly into Cécile's eyes and held them as Mrs. De Forêt interrupted their conversation. He was a few years younger than she, Cécile judged, with dark hair and chiseled chin and nose, and he exuded an air of confidence.

Mrs. De Forêt stood next to this man as she inserted herself and Cécile into the circle. "My apologies, but I would like to introduce Miss Cécile Fournier, the well-known singer. Miss Fournier, allow me the honor of introducing Mr. Christian-Jaque, the film director."

"Enchanted," the handsome Christian-Jaque said, his eyes never leaving Cécile's as he kissed her hand.

Mrs. De Forêt continued with the introductions. "And Miss Fournier, this is Mr. Alfred Greven, head of Continental Films." She indicated the man with the Nazi armband, who also kissed Cécile's hand.

"I have been to hear you sing, Miss Fournier," Greven said. "You have a most beautiful voice. We should find you a role in Christian-Jaque's next film."

Cécile laughed. "I'm afraid I cannot act, Mr. Greven. My talents are better suited to the cabarets of Paris than to the silver screen."

"You are being too modest, Miss Fournier. You should consider it—shouldn't she, Christian?"

"Yes indeed," the handsome Christian-Jaque said. "You might find, Miss Fournier, that you have more talents than you are aware of."

"I will take that into consideration," Cécile replied with a coy smile.

Mrs. De Forêt beamed.

"You have begun production then?" Cécile asked.

"Soon, after the first of the year," Christian-Jaque said.

Greven puffed out his chest. "Now that so many of France's great film actors and actresses have returned to Paris to sign with Continental Films, we can resume the work of French cinema to the levels that the French people knew before the war."

"Congratulations, Mr. Greven," Cécile said. He acknowledged her accolade with a nod.

She turned back to Christian-Jaque. "Who has recently returned?"

"Danielle Darrieux, for one, is in the next room." He pointed to a tall blond laughing and talking with a circle of admirers near the dining room table, and Cécile recognized her immediately. She was one of the biggest movie stars in France. She'd also done work for UFA in Berlin before the war.

"Her husband is Henri Decoin, another film director at Continental. He is around somewhere. I'll introduce you if we find him."

"That would be lovely, thank you," Cécile said.

Mrs. De Forêt continued to stand watch, beaming.

"Anyone else I would know of?" Cécile asked Christian-Jaque. From the corner of her eye she noticed the irritated look coming to Alfred Greven's face at the amount of attention she was giving his underling.

"Young Louis Jourdan has recently returned to Paris, though he is not in attendance tonight," Christian-Jaque said. "I had lunch with him recently, and he is eager to get back to work. I have heard that Fernandel is in Paris, though I have not seen him; and many others." He waved his hand in the air.

Mrs. De Forêt apologized, and said that she needed to greet other guests. She smiled at Cécile as she departed.

I'm sure she'd love nothing better than to tell all of her friends that she helped Cécile Fournier get a part in Christian-Jaque's next film, Cécile thought, more amused than irritated.

She turned her attention back to Alfred Greven, who still seemed irritated at not being the object of her attention. "Tell me, Mr. Greven—what sort of films will Continental make?"

*

Jean-Louis was immediately on-stage the moment they walked through the door, Lisette noticed.

He'd invited her to accompany him to the party barely an hour before, because his wife had fallen ill and wouldn't be able to attend.

"I need a companion for the party," he'd said over the telephone. "There will be important people there, I cannot show up alone."

"Is your wife terribly ill?"

Jean-Louis had snorted. "Not terribly. A sniffle and a headache, just a cold. It might even be an excuse to go see her lover tonight."

Lisette had quickly put on her nicest cocktail dress. She was irritated to find a run in the last pair of silk stockings she owned, and so she had braved the cold bare-legged.

She felt underdressed the moment she entered the fancy townhouse in the 16th Arrondissement. The butler took her nice white trench-coat, and she watched as he hung it next to luxuriant fur coats. She looked around; other ladies wore long, elegant evening gowns; her cocktail dress only reached her knees. The sparkle of diamonds glittered on the hands and necks of most of the ladies in the room; she'd opted for the pearl necklace and matching earrings.

She took Jean-Louis' arm and followed him around the room as he glad-handed numerous men in three-piece suits. He introduced them to her, but eventually the names flew right through her ears. Businessmen and industrialists with whom he had worked over the years. They were all polite, kissing her hand as though she were a lady, but then they turned back to Jean-Louis and focused on commerce.

At one point she had to stifle a yawn.

She looked around the room, admiring the mirth with which other groups of people enjoyed the party. Then she was startled to recognize first the voice, and then the face, of Danielle Darrieux, the movie star.

A moment later she recognized another face, that of the singer Cécile Fournier. She stood next to a handsome and well-dressed man with striking features, who stared at her the entire time she spoke to various people in their circle.

Jean-Louis nudged her with his elbow. She looked at him, and his expression told her that he was irritated with her lack of attention to their conversation.

"Lisette Rousseau, allow me to introduce our hostess, Mrs. Pierre De Forêt."

Lisette looked at the woman standing next to her. She stood two inches shorter than Lisette, and was probably around forty-five years old, with hair dyed an unnaturally pale blond.

"Delighted to meet you, Miss Rousseau," Mrs. De Forêt said, though her smile seemed forced.

"Her husband, Pierre De Forêt, is one of the other directors at *Fabrique Monnaie*," Jean-Louis explained.

"Ah, I see," Lisette said. Their host was one of Jean-Louis' equals at the factory. That explained the look in Mrs. De Forêt's eyes. No doubt she had met Jean-Louis' wife at other functions, and viewed Lisette as some young tart.

Paris had changed; the reactionaries in charge nowadays didn't turn a blind eye.

"Are you enjoying yourself, dear?" Mrs. De Forêt said, smiling through her condescension.

Lisette forced herself to smile back. "I'm afraid I don't know much about what the gentlemen are discussing."

Mrs. De Forêt's smile spread a little. She seemed to take a cold pleasure in Lisette's discomfort. "Well, of course. Their talk of commerce is not the place for a lady, my dear."

"I'm afraid you're right, Mrs. De Forêt," Lisette said. "Would you mind introducing me to some of the ladies?"

She took pleasure in the fleeting pained look that crossed their hostess' eyes. "Of course, dear. Come with me."

*

Cécile managed to break away from the Continental Film circle with the excuse that she needed to visit the powder room. It wasn't that she was not enjoying the conversation—quite the contrary, actually—but she had work to do.

The dining room was filled with party guests, including dozens of high-ranking industrialists—a veritable "Who's Who" of Paris collaborators. She had already deduced from their serious expressions that much business was being discussed in the corners, while the wives socialized separately.

She paid a visit to the restroom so that it wouldn't be obvious that she'd ditched the others, and took a moment to gather her thoughts. She recognized several of the men in the dining room—former members of the French-German Friendship Committee—having eavesdropped on their conversations at parties before the war. French Intelligence had been suspicious of the motivations of the French-German Friendship Committee—and rightly so.

She exited the restroom a few minutes later, and returned to the dining room. She took a moment to look around, trying to appear that she was searching for someone.

A tall, stocky man with slicked-back hair approached her. "Miss Fournier? I thought it was you that I saw earlier. We met about a year ago, at a reception for Roman Peltier."

Cécile knew perfectly well who he was—he was one of her targets for the evening—but she pretended otherwise. She faked a lack of recognition and made an apologetic shrug.

"I regret, sir—but I met so many people at that reception, and I don't recall."

He frowned for a second, and then smiled and waved it off. "Of course, how silly of me. Jean-Louis DuBois."

"A pleasure to renew your acquaintance, sir."

"We spoke at length about Giancarlo Fauci, do you remember?"

Cécile faked confusion. "I'm sorry, but…" she let her voice trail off, and shrugged again.

"Oh, but you must remember!" Jean-Louis said, his face flushing. "You were standing next to Isabel Peltier, and she had entertained us with stories of their recent tour of Italy, and gave us an amusing anecdote about meeting Mussolini after one of her husband's performances. You remember that, do you not?"

"I remember that conversation. Mussolini had confused Gaetano Andreozzi with Gaetano Donizetti, and everyone was afraid to correct him, and then Roman shouted 'For Heaven's sake, that was Donizetti!'" Cécile laughed. "Isabel tells the story so well. 'Mussolini took his leave then'—that's how she always ends it."

They shared a chuckle at the recollection.

"There were so many people gathered, listening to Isabel tell the story; I didn't realize you were among them, Mr. DuBois."

His eyes widened. "But don't you remember? It was right after Isabel Peltier finished her story about Mussolini that we spoke about Fauci. I said 'I saw Giancarlo Fauci direct his *Giorno del Leone* at l'Opéra last weekend, and it was fantastic,' and you replied that you had not seen it."

Cécile faked sudden remembrance. "Yes, of course! I remember." She didn't say that she wouldn't be caught dead attending that Fascist propaganda. Instead she gave him an admiring look and a flirtatious smile. "I hardly recognized you, Mr. DuBois. You have lost some weight, no?"

He smiled and touched his belly. "A bit, I suppose. But haven't we all?"

It was true, everyone in Paris had lost weight since September's reduction in rations—everyone except the Germans, of course, and their mistresses.

"It looks good on you, sir."

"Thank you, Miss Fournier. And if I may say, it looks good on you as well. And you may call me Jean-Louis."

"And I am Cécile."

A young woman approached, and slipped her arm through Jean-Louis'.

"Ah, there you are, my dear," Jean-Louis said, looking sheepish. "Miss Fournier, allow me to introduce my companion, Miss Lisette Rousseau. Lisette, this is Cécile Fournier, the famous singer."

"Jean-Louis and I have been to several of your performances, Miss Fournier," Lisette said, casting a glance sideways at him.

"Ah, I hope you enjoyed them," Cécile said with her most charming smile.

Lisette seemed to relax, and smiled. "Yes, very much."

The conversation slipped into small talk, and after a while Cécile excused herself. "I must talk with Henri Decoin about something. Do come see me again at the club, won't you?"

"Yes, of course!" Jean-Louis beamed.

Cécile smiled and moved on.

*

"Mrs. De Forêt doesn't like me," Lisette said quietly after Cécile departed, leaving her alone with Jean-Louis.

"Nonsense! I saw her take you around the room and introduce you. She is an excellent hostess."

Lisette almost described their hostess' subtle hostility, but decided it would be pointless. Jean-Louis had already made up his mind. She just nodded. "Yes, that's true."

He turned toward her, his chest puffed out with pride. "How do you like coming to a party with me and meeting famous people like Cécile Fournier?" he asked.

She smiled up at him. "It is fantastic. Thank you, Jean-Louis."

Even though she was famous, Cécile had acted less stuffy than the wives of Jean-Louis' business associates. And much more approachable.

He stretched his neck to look over the room in the direction Cécile had gone. "Perhaps she can introduce us to some of the other famous people here. We should make a point of seeking her out again later."

A man in a three-piece suit approached and took Jean-Louis by the arm. He said something about business that Lisette didn't understand, and Jean-Louis turned to her. "I'm sorry my dear, I must go conduct a bit of business. You'll mingle, won't you?"

He walked away without waiting for her answer.

*

Cécile managed to arrange for the ladies she was with to be near the corner where the industrialists stood discussing production figures and deadlines. She took up position on the side of her circle closest in proximity to theirs.

Of course these conservative businessmen were universal chauvinists, and they didn't bother lowering their voices when the

253

only people in earshot were women who couldn't possibly be expected to understand the intricacies of industrial production.

Cécile took mental notes of their details. Two thousand tank shells per week, shipped every Saturday at two AM on an east-bound train to Germany. Five hundred plastic cockpit covers for Luftwaffe fighters, due by January 2nd. Ten thousand rifles a month for the Occupation forces, delivered to General Von Stupnagel no later than the 5th of each month. And so on.

She filed away each of the details to report to Frank Dryden.

And all the while she managed to follow the conversation of the ladies around her.

"It will be quite nice to have *French* movies to see again," one of the ladies said. "I probably shouldn't say this, but I *am* getting a bit tired of reading the subtitles at the German films playing at the cinemas these days."

"It's true," another lady agreed. "All that's ever playing is some German melodrama, or a re-release of an old French film that everyone's seen many times."

Mrs. De Forêt raised a finger in reprimand. "It is not the fault of the French studios that most of our film stars have spent the last six months basking in the sun at Cannes. And the cinemas are simply attempting to appeal to everyone in Paris these days."

One of the ladies turned to Cécile. "You have sung for German officers at your performances, have you not, Miss Fournier?"

"Yes, of course," Cécile said. "There are always Germans at every performance, usually more than half the audience."

Mrs. De Forêt's expression grew haughty. "It is the duty of Parisians to share culture with our neighbors. It is France's unique burden to spread civilization among the nations."

A chorus of agreement greeted this pronouncement, and Cécile smiled in amusement. The others took her smile as agreement.

Cécile noticed that the businessmen behind her had dispersed, and she excused herself from these ladies and mingled.

*

"Miss Fournier, won't you sing for us?" Mrs. De Forêt asked later in the evening, when Cécile was back in the parlor near the piano.

"Oh no, I don't want to interrupt everyone's good time," Cécile demurred.

"Oh, please! We would be delighted if you could entertain us with a song."

"Yes, please sing for us, Miss Fournier," Pierre De Forêt seconded. It was the first time Cécile had seen the host and hostess together the entire evening.

Cécile nodded. "Who will play for me?" she asked, looking to the piano.

A young man volunteered, and sat on the piano bench. He looked to her with an eager smile. "What shall we play?"

A crowd began to gather in the parlor as word spread among the guests that she was about to sing. They soon filled the room, and the entrance from the dining room.

"Unfortunately, I am not permitted to sing one of my own standards outside of the club, it would violate my contract," she said with an apologetic shrug, palms up. "So I will sing something by an American composer—we still like Americans, don't we?"

The room filled with laughter.

"I had the pleasure of meeting Mr. Cole Porter at Bricktop's in Montmartre a few years ago, the last time he was in Paris. He sang for us this song, which I'm sure you all know."

She whispered in the ear of the young man at the piano, and he grinned and began to play. Her rich alto voice joined in after the opening bars.

"I get no kick from champagne…"

Enthusiastic applause greeted the end of "I Get a Kick Out of You," along with shouts of "Encore please!"

She bowed and smiled. "Alright, one more song. I'd like to sing you something new—brand new, in fact, so I'm afraid I'll have to sing it *a cappella*." She gave her accompanist an apologetic look, and he got up from the bench. "It was written for me by a dear young man, an unknown composer—for now, at least—an American living in Paris, named Oliver Carmichael. Enjoy."

She saw the stunned expression that passed across the face of Jean-Louis DuBois' companion, and wondered. She sang the lyrics that Oliver had given her a week ago, in the soft jazz rhythm she had suggested for them.

When she finished, the room applauded, and she bowed again and thanked them.

*

Lisette stood in the entrance from the dining room into the parlor when Cécile began her performance. When she announced that the second song had been written by Oliver, *her* Oliver, Lisette couldn't believe her ears.

She held her position as the crowd filed out of the parlor after the performance, until Cécile passed.

"Miss Fournier!" she said, reaching out to touch the performer's shoulder.

"Yes? Miss Rousseau, isn't it?"

"That's right. Thank you for remembering. I enjoyed your songs."

"Thank you."

"I was surprised to hear the name of the composer of your second song, though—Oliver Carmichael. I didn't realize you knew him."

Cécile didn't look surprised. "Yes, I know him. He plays at a jazz club called *Le Chien Errant*, not far from my home. A most talented musician."

Lisette felt suddenly irritated. "Yes, I know. We used to be…" she let her voice trail off, not sure what word to use.

"I understand," Cécile said with a gracious smile, letting Lisette off the hook. "What a nice coincidence. The next time I meet with him, I will mention that I met you."

"I didn't realize that he was writing music now," Lisette said.

"He has only recently begun. He approached me with a song—the one I sang a moment ago—and I liked it very much. I plan to add it to my performances."

"That's wonderful," Lisette said, though not feeling it.

"I hope that he and I can collaborate again," Cécile said. "If you see him, tell him that I'm looking forward to working with him much more. Good evening."

Lisette watched her go, tall and elegant and beautiful, and felt a sudden pang of jealousy.

*

Cécile found Jean-Louis alone in the hallway, coming out of the restroom.

His face lit up when he saw her. "Ah, Miss Fournier—Cécile. A pleasure to run into you again."

"The pleasure is all mine, Jean-Louis."

"It's a shame that we have not had more opportunity to renew our acquaintance," he said, looking at his watch. "It's nearly ten-thirty, and our time here draws rapidly to a close."

"Indeed, I wish we could have spoken more as well. You seem a most charming and intelligent man, Jean-Louis."

"Perhaps I could take you to dinner one evening?" Jean-Louis suggested. "When is your night off?"

"I am always off on Sundays and Tuesdays—but alas, I have an obligation tomorrow night, and this Tuesday is Christmas Eve.

Perhaps next Sunday? That is, if you don't mind going out on a Sunday."

"For you, not at all. Shall we meet at La Tour d'Argent, at eight o'clock?"

"That would be lovely, Jean-Louis. Thank you."

He gave her a polite bow and kissed her hand. "Until next week, then."

**

She did not see his car on her street, but she knew he was waiting for her. These days, it would be imprudent for his diplomatic license plate to spend time in her neighborhood.

She heard his footsteps in the snow as she turned her key in the building's front door. She entered the building without looking back, and he caught the door before it closed.

"*Bon soir, Monsieur*," she said, in case anyone was listening.

Frank Dryden smiled, then made a polite bow. "*Bon soir, mademoiselle.*"

She started up the stairs, and as he followed he placed his hand on her right buttock and goosed her.

She squealed in spite of herself, and he chased her up the stairs.

30

Monday, December 23

The insistent knock at the door startled Collette that morning. She was in the middle of packing a suitcase, and wasn't expecting anyone.

Karl had left for Salzburg that morning. It had been a tearful goodbye for her, and even his eyes had welled up before he looked away and strode out the door. Perhaps it was the hormones, but the thought of being away from him for a week made her emotional.

She'd sat on their bed and cried for the better part of an hour before deciding that this would be a good time to pay a visit to her parents in Picardy. She called the Gare du Nord and got the schedule for the trains to Ailly-sur Somme via Amiens, and began packing.

She had no idea who could be at the door. She hadn't called for a car. As she walked to the door, she wondered fleetingly if she was able to use the car service without Karl. Probably not.

The man at the door was short, balding, and wore a black suit. He carried a leather attaché case.

"Miss Lefevre, I am Captain Hochman, with the *Geheime Staatspolizei*," he said with a thick German accent. "*Sprechen sie Deutsch?*"

Collette shook her head. Her heart began to race. What did the Gestapo want with her?

"Have I done something wrong?"

"There is no need for alarm, Miss Lefevre. We just need to ask you some questions. May I come inside?"

Collette nodded and stepped aside. She allowed Captain Hochman to close the door behind himself. He strode to the table and set his attaché case down, opened it, and removed a stack of papers.

He motioned toward the chair across from him. "Please, take a seat."

She moved to the table without a word, and sat where directed. He took the seat across from her and began sorting papers into stacks. After a moment he looked up, folded his hands on the table, and stared at her with an intensity that made her recoil.

"We are aware of the nature of your relationship with Captain Gruder. You are no doubt aware that your intimate relations are in violation of the morality laws in effect here in France, and in Germany."

She gave him a tiny nod as her only acquiescence.

He leaned forward, his pale eyes taking on the look of the hunter. "I wonder, Miss LeFevre, if you are aware that Captain Gruder is a married man?"

She nodded and looked down. "Yes, I am aware."

"Another law violated." Then Hochman leaned back and smiled, a leering sort of smile that made her insides crawl. "But we are not inhuman, Miss LeFevre; we can understand how you might be drawn to a man such as Captain Gruder—and it is obvious why a man such as Captain Gruder would be drawn to a beautiful young woman such as you." He glanced down at her large bust and let his eyes linger there before looking back at her face.

She shifted in her seat, uncomfortable.

"We are also aware that you now carry his unborn child."

The words seemed to hang in the air over the table, and Collette's breath caught in her throat.

Hochman must have seen the look in her eyes, for he chuckled. "Doctors in France must now report such things to the proper authorities. We have been aware of your condition for some time."

A scowl crossed her face before she could stop it. *That damned doctor!*

Hochman held up a hand. "Do not blame the doctor, Miss LeFevre. He was only doing his duty. And besides, your condition is beginning to make itself obvious—or haven't you noticed? Soon, there would be no way for you to hide it."

"I would never dream of hiding it," Collette said, raising her chin. "I have done nothing wrong."

Hochman's eyes narrowed. "You French women really are immoral hedonists, just as it is said, if you think you have done nothing wrong."

They stared at each other in silence for several seconds.

Hochman was the one to break the ice. He smiled again—a cold smile, which gave her chills—and leaned forward to fold his hands on the table again.

"We in the Gestapo can see the big picture, Miss LeFevre. Your indiscretions are nothing compared to the future Europe that we Germans are building. It has not escaped our notice that your looks are most Aryan—you are blonde, blue-eyed, fair, and quite voluptuous if I may say—the ideal feminine archetype for the new world order. Captain Gruder is also blond, blue-eyed, and fair; so naturally your children are exactly the physical types that the Fuhrer hopes to see more of."

Collette noticed his use of the plural.

"Therefore, we have no intentions of keeping you and Captain Gruder from continuing your intimate relationship. Besides, it is good for our men stationed here in France—so far from the Fatherland and their families—to have distractions to keep them occupied. And happy." He added the last as a sort of after-thought.

Collette looked at him in some confusion. "Then, why are you here?"

"To ensure your cooperation, Miss LeFevre."

"My cooperation?"

"Yes."

"I don't understand."

Hochman chuckled again. "It is within our power to have Captain Gruder reassigned, should we ever feel the need…" he let his voice trail off and stared at her.

She felt her gut tighten. "What do you want me to do?"

"Tell me about the people you knew before you came here to the Hotel Lutetia. Tell me about those *bohemians*." He said the word with obvious distaste, his nose crinkling.

She hesitated, unsure what to say. "I don't know what you mean," she said at length.

"Come now, Miss LeFevre. We have a complete dossier on you." He removed a pair of glasses from his coat pocket, placed them on his nose, and consulted the papers in front of him.

"Collette Marie Louise LeFevre, born 17th April, 1918 in Ailly-sur-Somme, France. Your father Pierre was a wounded veteran of the last war, shot in the right arm. Your mother Josée works as a seamstress. You came to Paris in July 1935, where you worked as an actress in various theaters, taking small roles. For five years you lived in a garret on the 5th floor at number 13 Rue de Lagrange, in the 5th Arrondissement. You were frequently seen in the company of other actors, writers, and artists. Then in September, Captain Gruder moved you into his hotel suite—" Hochman set down the papers and removed his glasses, looking back at her—"where we now sit, having a conversation about your cooperation with us."

Collette stared at her hands.

Hochman leaned forward over the table. "So then, Miss LeFevre—what can you tell me about the bohemian rats you consorted with on the Rue de Lagrange in the 5th Arrondissement?"

**

The club was closed on Tuesday, the 24th of December, and Oliver took a trip on the Metro to the 7th Arrondissement to go shopping at Le Bon Marché, the famous department store.

He'd struggled for weeks trying to think of something to buy Lisette for Christmas. When they were together it had been so easy picking out something she would like; then last year they were not together, so it hadn't been an issue. This year, they were friends again, so he felt he needed to buy something for her.

She was certainly more stylish these days than she'd been when they were together, so he decided Le Bon Marché was the perfect place to find her something.

The store was full of holiday shoppers—French civilians as well as the occasional group of German soldiers. Oliver browsed for more than an hour, but nothing caught his attention.

She didn't need anything, and he wasn't about to buy her anything expensive like jewelry. Besides, that might open him up for rejection, if she misread his intentions. Just what did one buy for a former fiancée who was now a friend?

He briefly considered chocolates, but there were none to be found anywhere. He saw a small display of real coffee and hurried over, only to pull his hand back in horror at the price.

In the end, he left the store feeling dejected and moped back to the Metro.

Getting off at the Sorbonne station, he decided to stop at Shakespeare and Company to see if he could find a book Lisette would like. He walked to the Rue de l'Odeon, and was pleased to see the store open, though empty.

He greeted Miss Beach in French, and then switched to English. "I'm looking for a Christmas gift for a friend—a female friend—well, she's a friend now. And I don't know what to get her."

"I see." Miss Beach gave him a knowing smile. "Yes, such situations can be difficult."

"Do you remember Lisette Rousseau? She came here a few times. Mostly she bought French books at La Maison des Amis des Livres, across the street."

"I believe I remember her, Mr. Carmichael," Miss Beach said. "She does read English, though, doesn't she?"

"Yes, she can read English."

"Well then, let's see what we can find for her, shall we?"

They browsed for a while, with Sylvia Beach asking him questions about the French books Lisette read. He could only say what she used to read, and assume that she still read the same things.

Miss Beach suggested several titles, and in the end he selected *The Years* by Virginia Woolf. Miss Beach wrapped it in heavy brown paper and tied it with string, making a big bow. "All festive for Christmas," she said with a smile as she handed it to him.

On the way home, Oliver stopped at the phone booth a block from his building. He inserted a franc coin, and asked the operator to dial the number for Lisette Rousseau in the 8th.

He listened to the line ringing, before the operator came back on the line and told him that there was no answer. *As if I couldn't figure that out myself.* He thanked her, and retrieved his franc from the coin return.

She might have already gone to her parents' house for the holiday. He briefly considered calling her there, but he wasn't sure how her father would react to his call. He dismissed the idea and trudged home in the snow.

**

Captain Allard was wrapping up a day's work at the prefecture, and looking forward to a peaceful night with his family. The arrival of a directive from the Gestapo was not the way he had envisioned the end of the work day.

A Captain Auguste Hochman of the Gestapo sent him a directive by courier shortly before five o'clock, as darkness was falling. The directive gave a list of names to investigate in the coming days.

The Gestapo were interested in their "potential for seditious and criminal activity." Captain Hochman expected Allard's full cooperation, and a complete report by Friday.

By Friday! How could he possibly complete an investigation of more than a dozen people by Friday?

Robert Allard knew that it would not be good for a policeman's career to disappoint the Gestapo. And so he stayed past the end of his shift on Christmas Eve to scrutinize the list.

At least two of the individuals listed had been held at this prefecture within the last few months. One of them—Serge Faucheux—was a suspected agitator. The other, an American named Oliver Carmichael, had been picked up one evening for being out past curfew.

The others on the list Allard did not know off-hand. He looked at his watch and cursed under his breath. His parents would have already arrived at his house, bearing gifts for the children, and Claudette would be holding dinner.

The German Occupation authorities had graciously extended tonight's curfew to three AM, allowing Parisians to attend midnight Mass, followed by the traditional *Reveillon* feast, for which many restaurants would be open late.

265

He set Captain Hochman's list inside a desk drawer, on top where he could pick it up first thing on Thursday, and locked it.

31

Lisette's mother got on her nerves before the end of dinner.

It started with a natural lull in the conversation, which her grandmother filled by asking if she were still single.

"Yes, Grandmother."

"That's a shame, dear. You are such a pretty girl; you should have no trouble finding a man to marry you."

Lisette just smiled.

"Whatever happened to that nice young man from America that you were going to marry?" her grandmother asked when she didn't get a response to her previous statement.

Her father cast Lisette a knowing glance.

"We broke off our engagement more than a year ago, Grandmother."

"Yes, I remember. I thought perhaps that might be temporary."

"No, not temporary, Grandmother."

That was when her mother jumped into the fray. "Aren't there any other nice young men you've met, dear? Customers at the store, perhaps?"

Lisette silently cursed her mother for not only continuing the conversation, but also taking it dangerously close to an even more uncomfortable topic.

"I live well enough on my own, Maman."

"But surely you must meet nice men?" her mother pressed.

Lisette took a deep breath. "Yes, I do. I am actually seeing someone—a customer at the store—but it's not serious."

Her insides clinched when she saw the cool look her mother gave her.

The conversation moved on to happenings at her father's office, and Lisette listened in silence.

After dinner she helped her grandmother wash the dishes. The moment she finished and walked toward the bathroom, her mother cornered her in the hallway.

"Lisette, are you seeing a married man?" she asked in a sharp whisper.

"Maman, please!"

"Is that why you haven't mentioned anyone in over a year? Because he's married?"

Lisette raised her chin and stared at her mother. "Alright, yes, he's married."

"Oh Lisette, really! There is no future in such a relationship. You will always be second to his wife and family. And he will probably leave you before long anyway. You are wasting your time, when you should be trying to find a husband."

"Why do I have to find a husband?"

"Lisette, you are twenty-five years old. Time keeps ticking."

"I am happy with my life the way it is."

Her mother glanced toward the kitchen, leaned closer, and whispered more quietly. "If all that you want is a part-time lover, you should get a husband first, and then take a lover."

Lisette's mouth hung open. "Maman!"

Her mother waved her hand in the air dismissively. "Don't think I don't know that such things go on. I am not naïve, Lisette. And I am not a fool."

"I know you are not a fool, Maman."

"Do you? Is that why you never listen to a thing I tell you? Is that why you have always rebelled against me, and everything I have ever wanted for you? I have never understood why you would want to hurt me as you do."

Lisette stiffened. "I have never wanted to hurt you, Maman. But it is *my* life, and I decide how to live it. I am not a child for you to order around."

Her mother's eyes began to well up. "Oh my daughter, all I have ever wanted for you was that you be happy. *That* is why I want you to find a good husband. There is little happiness for old maids in this world."

"I know several women who are happy without husbands."

Her mother looked at her for a moment. "You aren't one of *those* women, are you Lisette?" she whispered, even more quietly.

"What do you mean?"

"Don't pretend you don't know what I'm talking about. I've met your friend Adrienne, the masculine one. Don't tell me she isn't that kind of woman. I may not know everything, but I can see that."

"Maman, I prefer men." Lisette left it at that.

Her mother continued to regard her for several seconds. "Whatever happened to Oliver?" she asked, no longer whispering.

"He is the same. I still see him from time to time."

"What is he doing for Christmas Eve?"

Lisette shrugged. "I don't know. Probably nothing."

"Why don't you invite him to come here? It must be lonely, spending Christmas far away from family."

"He doesn't have a telephone, Maman."

"Then send him a telegram." Her mother smiled, gave her shoulder an affectionate squeeze, and walked away.

**

Robert Allard bowed his head with the rest of his family around the table. "Heavenly Father, on this most holy of nights, bless this house and all who dwell in it. Bless our beloved France, and bring her peace. Bless this meal that we eat on the night that your Son was born to us, the most holy Lamb of God. Give us the strength to always follow Your will. In the name of the Father, and the Son, and the Holy Spirit, Amen."

He and everyone at the table made the sign of the cross before raising their heads and opening their eyes.

Meat was terribly expensive these days, but his wife Claudette had managed to secure a lamb roast. He took the carving knife and cut it into slices.

The room was lit only by candles, but there were several of them, and the room glowed with their warm light. Two three-pronged candelabras stood on the table, and several lit candles sat in front of the statue of the Virgin on a nearby shelf.

Allard wore a heavy wool sweater over his shirt and tie, under his suit coat. Given that he'd lost six pounds since September, this was not as tight-fitting as it might have been. The other men at the table were similarly dressed, and his wife and mother wore heavy shawls around their shoulders.

Allard chose to use his small coal ration sparingly, and as a result his furnace never got very hot. But he preferred to spread a little heat over the entire day rather than enjoying a couple of hours of warmth followed by twenty-two hours of cold, as most Parisians experienced.

Around the table sat his parents, both in their sixties now and gray-haired; his three sons, ages sixteen, fourteen, and eleven; and his wife Claudette. He smiled at her as he finished carving the lamb, and crinkles formed at the corners of his green eyes.

"The roast is lovely, my dear. Perfectly done."

Quiet conversation filled the room as they ate. There had been no school that day, so the boys spoke of playing in the snow with the other children in their middle-class neighborhood in the 6th Arrondissement. He smiled at their story, and asked if they had also spent time on their studies.

The boys' smiles faded, and they looked at their father with dutiful expressions. "Yes, Papa," they said in turn.

"Good. France does not need idle minds—even on a holiday."

Claudette asked him about work.

"Mostly routine," he said. "Though I did get a directive from a captain in the Gestapo this afternoon. Most unusual. That is the reason I was late this evening, my dear."

"What sort of directive?" Claudette asked, a wariness coming to her eyes.

Allard finished chewing a bite of meat and dabbed at his mouth with his cloth napkin. "A list of names we are to look into. The Gestapo suspect they might be agitators. They have asked us to investigate."

"I did not know you worked for the *Boche*, Papa," said sixteen-year-old Georges.

Allard shot him a stern look, and Georges looked down.

"I work for the Paris Prefect of Police, and he works for the Minister of Justice in Vichy—you know this, boy. The Germans have made few demands of us—only that we keep order. As long as we maintain order, they leave us to do it. When they have suspicions that French citizens are committing seditious acts, they ask for our cooperation in restoring order. That is our duty. Our duty to France."

His wife and younger sons looked at him with dutiful expressions. His parents stared straight ahead.

"The Germans shot Jacques Bonsergent yesterday," Georges said quietly, staring at his plate. "Firing squad."

Allard's expression tightened. "Yes, that is true." He supposed the boy must have read the newspaper this morning. "He was convicted of an act of violence against the German army, and sentenced to death by firing squad."

"He got into a fist fight with German soldiers. He fought with fists, and they shot him for it." Georges' voice was still quiet, and he continued to stare at his plate.

Allard scowled. "He was tried and convicted, and legally sentenced."

Georges looked up at his father. He had his mother's pale blue eyes, but there was a hint of defiance in his.

"He was tried by a military tribunal of Germans, not by a jury." His voice was hard now.

Allard's fist banged against the table, and rattled the dishes. "Silence, boy! You don't know what you are saying. Yes, it was a military tribunal. The crime was against the Germans, and they tried him for it under their laws. In times of emergency, jury trials are a luxury. Military tribunals are a necessary evil."

The room was silent. Allard took a drink of wine and cut another bite of lamb. After he finished chewing he spoke again. "It is my hope, my sons, that if we cooperate with the Occupation authorities and maintain order, they will return to their Fatherland and leave us in charge of France. In the meantime, we do our duty. Marshall Pétain is counting on us all."

"Marshall Pétain is a great man," Allard's father said, quietly.

"Indeed he is, Papa. And a great patriot."

Claudette's parents arrived as everyone was finishing the meal. Claudette rose to kiss them on the cheeks. "You are just in time for the *Buche de Noel.*"

Surprised Ah's rose from the table as she carried over the long log-shaped chocolate cake with chestnuts. She had saved for weeks to buy the chocolate for the traditional dessert.

"It is beautiful, my dear," Allard said with a smile.

His brother Michel arrived with his family after they finished dessert.

"Wonderful of you to come tonight, Michel," Allard said, shaking his brother's hand. "It is good of you to make the journey. It is always special for Papa and Maman when we all go to Mass together."

The children gathered in the main room of the house, and Allard and his brother distributed the gifts, wrapped in bright green and red paper. The children laughed and tore the paper in a rush to get to the toys inside.

Allard poured a small measure of brandy for himself, his brother, his father, and father-in-law. They lounged on the couch while he relaxed in his armchair, sipping the brandy and watching the children play.

"On our way here this evening, we saw that the clubs in Montparnasse were doing much business," Michel said. "Not like the Christmas Eves we knew once, eh? People drinking to excess—French and Germans—and behaving in the bawdiest manner. Not like it used to be."

"Those clubs have always catered to a sinful crowd," their father said. "We raised you boys to be good, moral men. We thank the Blessed Virgin Mother every night that you are. The evil ways of our neighbors have brought down the judgment of God upon our city."

Allard didn't immediately respond, and watched the children play on the floor nearby. He did not consider the Germans to be the hand of God, and was uncomfortable at the suggestion; but he also knew better than to argue with his father.

"It's good that the new regime has taken steps to restore moral order to France," he said at length. "We can thank Marshall Pétain for the restoration of our traditional values." *We do not need the Germans for that.*

"Absolutely," his father said with a firm nod.

Allard was pleased at his father's agreement.

"And yet, I hear that the regime has not closed down the night clubs and brothels because both are full of Germans every night," Michel said.

Allard tensed. "That is true," he said, keeping his words measured. "Unfortunate, but true. Hopefully the war will end soon, the British will surrender, and the Germans can return to their Fatherland—and then the good men at Vichy can return the government to Paris and restore the moral order more fully."

The clock on the mantle chimed half-past-eleven.

"It is nearly time to leave," he said. He finished his brandy, then rose from his chair and collected the glasses. "Come children, it is time to put away the toys and get ready to walk to the church."

He helped his wife into her coat before putting on his overcoat. He held the door as his family stepped out one-by-one into the snowy night.

**

Oliver waited in the falling snow outside the church of Sainte-Marguerite on the Rue Jean Macé, in the 11th Arrondissement. It was one AM, and he stamped his feet against the cold and couldn't stop shivering. His hands were shoved in his pockets, and he clenched his arms to his side.

Lisette's family weren't really religious, he knew. They only attended Mass a few times a year. But as long as he'd known Lisette, they always went to Midnight Mass on Christmas. He always declined their invitations to join them, preferring instead to meet them after Mass for the *Reveillon* meal.

This felt a bit like déjà vu, only he didn't remember it being this cold.

The bells in the tower began to peal, and a moment later well-dressed Parisians streamed out the front doors, smiling and wishing each other a joyous Christmas.

He saw Lisette's mother first, followed by her father and younger brother Gaston, and finally by Lisette herself with her grandmother. He raised a hand and waved until she saw him.

She approached a moment later, with her mother at her side. She smiled and kissed his cheek. "Joyous Christmas."

"Joyous Christmas to you also," he said.

Mrs. Rousseau extended her hand, and Oliver shook it. "Hello Oliver, so nice to see you. Joyous Christmas."

Mr. Rousseau walked up, and also extended his hand. "Hello Oliver. Joyous Christmas." His tone was polite, whereas his wife's had been warm.

"Thank you for inviting me to join you," Oliver said.

"Our pleasure," Mr. Rousseau said.

"I told Maman that you would be alone, and she insisted," Lisette said, giving her mother a teasing smile.

"I am glad to see you," he said quietly.

Mrs. Rousseau smiled at her daughter.

"Shall we go eat, then?" Mr. Rousseau asked, leading the way down the street and around the corner toward the Boulevard Voltaire. "The restaurant closes at two-thirty."

Lisette put her arm through Oliver's and leaned close to him. He could smell her perfume.

"I learned something about you the other night," Lisette said quietly as they walked.

"Yeah?"

"I met Cécile Fournier at a party on Saturday. I didn't realize that you knew her. And you never told me that you write music."

His face flushed, and he smiled sheepishly. "I've only recently begun. I'm afraid my songs aren't very good."

"She seemed to think otherwise."

Oliver wasn't sure if Lisette's tone was teasing or jealous.

It took ten minutes to walk to the restaurant, and the maître'd had their table ready. Oliver sat between Lisette and her mother.

"I'm afraid we cannot get the oysters and escargot before dinner this year," Mr. Rousseau told them. "We don't have enough ration coupons."

"I brought ration coupons," Oliver said, reaching into his pocket.

Mr. Rousseau scowled. His wife put her hand on Oliver's arm. "We wouldn't dream of it. You are our guest."

Oliver glanced at Lisette and saw a pained look in her eyes. He cursed himself for violating their French sense of hospitality. Even after nearly five years in Paris, he still sometimes used Midwestern manners.

He tried again, addressing himself to Lisette's mother. "Perhaps I could buy the oysters, as my Christmas gift to you."

She smiled and shook her head. "You are very thoughtful, Oliver. But it is not necessary."

"*No one* is getting hors d'oeuvres this year," Lisette whispered. "Not since the rations were reduced."

Oliver nodded and dropped the subject.

"That is a very nice suit you are wearing, Oliver," Mrs. Rousseau said. "Doesn't he look handsome in it, Lisette?"

Lisette sighed. "Yes, Maman."

"You look nice this evening," Oliver said to Lisette.

"Thank you."

Mrs. Rousseau beamed.

The waiter came, and Mr. Rousseau ordered two bottles of red wine, and the family portion of *coq au vin*.

After the waiter departed, he looked across the table at Oliver and put on a polite smile. "So, Oliver, are you still playing music at that club near Montmartre? Or have you found another line of work?"

Oliver knew where this line of questioning would lead, but he nodded politely. "Yes, I'm still playing at *Le Chien Errant*. I have not changed professions."

"Ah, good. How is business there these days?"

"Better now that the Germans have changed the curfew from nine to eleven. All through the summer and early autumn, the Germans were almost all of the customers we had."

"Things are returning to normal, then?"

"Nearly," Oliver said. "We still close early—eleven-thirty on Friday and Saturday nights—but at least our regular customers have returned."

Mr. Rousseau chuckled. "I never understood how you could stay up past four AM! I couldn't imagine. It would be easier if I were still young and unattached, I suppose—but very difficult for family life, wouldn't you say?"

Oliver felt himself tensing, and worked hard to keep his expression and voice calm. "Yes, I suppose it would."

"Have you been to the club recently to hear him play, Lisette?" Mrs. Rousseau asked.

"Not recently, Maman."

"I remember you used to go there from time to time," her mother said. "It would be nice to hear Oliver play again, wouldn't it dear?"

Lisette cast a glance at Oliver, and he saw the corner of her mouth curled up in a slight smile. "Yes, it would be nice Maman. I'll have to do that more often in the new year."

The bottles of wine arrived, and Mr. Rousseau ordered a glass poured for everyone. As soon as the glasses were filled, he raised his and proposed a toast. "To family, and to a most joyous Christmas together."

*

The restaurant was closing as they left.

"You are coming back with us, are you not Oliver?" Mrs. Rousseau said. "I have made up the spare bed in Gaston's room."

"Thank you, but I don't want to intrude upon your holiday."

"Nonsense! Please come home with us. We would be delighted to have you with us for Christmas."

He glanced at Lisette, who nodded. He smiled and acquiesced.

"Good!" Mrs. Rousseau said, and beamed at him.

After her mother had turned away, Lisette gave him a knowing smile, slipped her arm through his, and leaned close to him again as they walked back to her parents' house.

**

Collette sat awake for much of the night. She was irritated. And she was hungry.

After a sparse dinner at her parents' home in Ailly-sur-Somme, her stomach felt like it would gnaw at itself all night. How quickly she'd forgotten what it was like to be hungry.

For more than three months she'd been able to eat as much as she wanted. As the live-in mistress of a German officer, she wasn't limited by the rationing. That was a blessing as the child grew inside of her.

But the hunger was the least of her irritations. She wasn't sure what kind of reception she'd expected, but she hadn't been prepared for the one she got.

The stunned look on her mother's face when she opened the door was one thing, but it had not changed over to joy as Collette might have hoped. She'd smiled anyway, and said "Joyous Christmas, Maman."

Then she handed her mother the box of *macarons* she had picked up at the Amiens train station. She had been delighted to see them, having forgotten how much she loved Picardy's traditional Christmas almond cookies. She hadn't been back since she left for Paris at age seventeen.

"We had no idea you were coming, Collette," her mother said. "You could have called, or written us." Her hair, more gray now than blond, was pulled back in a bun, and her face was lined. Her cheeks, once plump, now sagged. She wore a dirty apron over a gingham dress.

"Aren't you happy to see me, Maman?"

Her mother gave her a weak smile. "Yes, of course dear. We just weren't prepared for your visit."

"I didn't realize until this weekend that I would be alone for Christmas," she said. She slipped off her coat, and her mother's gaze dropped to her belly.

Collette saw the deep scowl that creased her mother's brow. She forced a smile. "Yes Maman, I have news."

Her mother looked up. "Let's go talk to your father."

Collette followed her mother into the living room. "Frederic, we have a visitor. Collette has come for Christmas this year."

"Yeah?" he replied, his eyebrows arching. "After five years with no visit, she comes home unannounced?"

"Hello Papa," Collette said. "Joyous Christmas."

He sat in his wooden chair, facing the fire. His light brown hair, a bit disheveled, had streaked with gray since the last time she'd seen him. His eyes also immediately dropped to her belly; but rather than a scowl, a look of sadness came to his eyes. Collette felt as if someone had tightened a vice around her heart.

"I see why you have come this year," he said at length, his voice quiet.

"Yes Papa, I have come to tell you and Maman my wonderful news. I am going to have a baby, and I'm very happy."

There was a momentary silence.

"I don't know how anyone would be happy to bring a baby into the world these days," her father said.

He stood, pushing himself up from his chair with his left hand. He wore a dark gray sweater vest over his blue shirt and tie, and his right sleeve was empty, pinned up at the shoulder. He walked past her into the kitchen.

"Collette brought *macarons*," his wife said as he passed. He ignored her.

"There is no wedding ring on your finger," he said from the kitchen. "Is that because he is too poor to buy you one? I would guess not, since you don't look as if you have lost weight like everyone else in France. You must be eating well."

Collette turned around to face her father's back. She didn't address his observation.

"I'm nearly four months," she said, her voice rising in hope that she could excite him. "The baby will be here in early June. The weather will be lovely that time of year, and I can put the baby in a stroller and go for long walks through the *Jardin de Luxembourg*. I live near there now, in a nice suite."

Her father said nothing, but she noticed he'd opened the box of *macarons*.

"Karl and I are really quite happy about it. I wish you would be happy, too."

He turned around then, slowly, and stared at her with his mouth open for a moment.

"*Karl*? You are seeing a German?"

Collette forced a smile again. "He's Austrian actually, but yes. I didn't plan to, but he's quite wonderful."

"If he is so wonderful, why are you not with him in Paris for Christmas?"

Collette steeled herself. "He's in Salzburg for Christmas with his family."

"Oh, I see." Her father walked around her, a couple of cookies in his hand, and sat back down in his chair. He ate them in silence, staring across the room at the logs burning in the hearth.

"Has he promised to marry you?" her mother asked.

Collette shook her head. "No, Maman."

"A good man would marry you, Collette."

She took a deep breath. "He cannot marry me, Maman—he is already married."

A little squeaking gasp escaped her mother's mouth, and she covered it with her hand.

From his chair, her father's voice came hard and biting. "The word 'actress' was once a euphemism for whore—and I can see why."

Collette's face flushed. "I am not a whore, Papa! I have found a nice man who loves me and treats me well, and we are going to be a family."

"And he buys you nice clothes, I'm sure, and takes you to fancy dinners—does he not?" Her father twisted around in his chair to stare her down.

"Yes, of course. He makes a good living, and we share life together."

A smirk came to her father's lips, and his voice carried a bitter edge. "You give him what he wants, probably as often as he wants, and in return he gives you the nice things that you covet. It may not be cash, but it is still payment for services rendered."

Collette trembled with suppressed rage. "It is not like that at all, Papa! We are in love. He loves me, and I love him."

"You foolish girl," he said, shaking his head. "Such a man as that would say anything to get what he wants from a pretty girl. He is not in love with you, Collette. He is using you, and when his tour of duty in France is finished, you will be forgotten like yesterday's lunch."

Angry tears poured from Collette's eyes, and her hands fisted at her sides. "You don't know him, Papa. You shouldn't say such things about someone you have never met."

"I don't have to meet him to know what sort he is."

Her rage exploded then. "You hate all the Germans because you lost your arm! You blame all of them. He wasn't there, you know. It wasn't him. And the one who *did* shoot your arm could have been maimed or killed himself, and maybe he or his family blames all the French. Wars are so stupid! They make men hate each other when they've never met."

Anger flushed her father's face for a moment, but then he looked down at his feet in silence for several seconds.

"That is the most intelligent thing you have said all evening, Collette." His voice was quiet and sad again. "Yes, wars are stupid. Men are stupid, and kill each other for stupid reasons, all because someone ordered them to. Why anyone would want to bring a child into such a world as this is beyond my ability to understand."

Collette's body slowly relaxed, and she took a couple of deep breaths. "You did not always feel that way, Papa. You brought me into the world after you lost your arm."

A look of such sadness came to her father's eyes, such as Collette had never seen.

"Yes. A foolish hope, I suppose. A foolish hope indeed. We gave you all of our love, and all your life you have caused us pain."

Collette's tears flowed freely, and she hurried from the room.

Her older brothers arrived with their families later in the evening. Collette was told that her sisters would be with their in-laws this evening, and would come by tomorrow. "I'll see them all at Mass tonight, of course," her mother said. "You'll stay home with your father, won't you dear?"

Dinner had been tense. Her brothers and sisters-in-law didn't say much to her. Her nieces and nephews asked her about her belly, but were quickly silenced by their parents.

Sometime after eleven-thirty, they left for church—all except Collette and her father. He had lost his faith in God during the Great War. "Any God that would allow the things I saw in the trenches for four years isn't worth worshipping," she'd often heard him say.

She sat in a chair next to his, and stared at the fire with him.

"Your mother is afraid I'm going to Hell, you know," he said after they were alone. "I keep telling her that I've already been to Hell. There is nothing worse that God can show me than that."

Collette often wondered what he had seen. He was never specific.

Her father was silent for a bit before continuing. "There are lots of folks in town who say that Marshall Pétain is a hero for saving France from enduring all of that again." He shrugged. "I think he's a tired old man, who's seen enough war."

Collette looked at him for several seconds. He seemed so resigned, so stoic.

She thought of her old friends in the 5th Arrondissement, Serge and Sébastien mostly, saying the old Marshal was a traitor for giving up too soon. And then she thought of Karl, and she couldn't help wondering if he would have been killed if the fighting had continued. The thought brought tears to her eyes.

They sat in silence for a long time, each staring at the fire in the hearth as it slowly reduced to embers.

"Tell me, daughter, how do you know that this German of yours is the one you want? You have never known what you wanted, all your life chasing something else."

She looked at him. "I don't know what you mean, Papa."

"As a child, you tired of all of your toys, had to play with everyone else's. You could never have just one boyfriend at school. Then when you were seventeen you had to run off to the city because Ailly-sur-Somme wasn't enough for you. And you couldn't go to Amiens, seven kilometers away, even though it is a big city. It wasn't enough for you, either. Or too close to us, perhaps? No, you had to have Paris. From Paris you would send us letters, not often, and there were always different people you talked about in each letter. A new group of wonderful new friends each time. You always chased something you didn't have. So tell me, daughter—how do you know that this man, this German, is the one for you?"

She had begun to cry again. "You don't have to be mean, Papa."

He fell silent, and stared at the embers.

Neither spoke again until after the rest of the family returned from Mass. Then Collette kissed her parents on the cheeks and went to bed.

And she lay up all night, unable to sleep, stewing over what her father had said.

32

Thursday, December 26

Marcel was always grateful for a few extra francs, and working with Madeleine was always fun. She reclined against Marcel's leg, her hand seeming carelessly laid across his abdomen. The flimsy shapeless dress she wore was translucent. A large red maple leaf was placed conveniently over Marcel's penis; otherwise, both were naked. She gazed upward, while he looked down upon her face. A white sheet hung on the wall behind them.

A few feet away stood an iron wood-burning stove, and the glow of a fire shown through the grate. Even so, the room was chilly, and their nipples stood hard and pointy from their flat chests.

Aside from her tiny breasts, their pale androgynous bodies appeared nearly identical. Her bright red hair contrasted with his dark curls. Her face was made up to give the appearance of slanted eyes and arched eyebrows; and dark lipstick on only part of her lips gave her the appearance of a small, tight mouth. Each of them wore a crown of woven twigs sprinkled with bright red holly berries.

On the other side of the room, a middle-aged man with a thick black beard peered around the side of his canvas, while his hand furiously painted.

"Marcel, I need to see more longing in your gaze. You are a prince of the wood nymphs; you are used to having your way, and want to seduce this beautiful creature in front of you."

He saw Madeleine almost burst out laughing. She kept her gaze up at the ceiling, and he struggled to keep a straight face. He pictured Oliver in her place, imagined how he would look clad only in the translucent fabric, and hoped his expression looked longing.

The painter made a grunt, and mumbled "Good, good."

They continued to hold their positions for the next hour, until finally the artist announced they were finished.

"Your pay is on the table, you may leave when you are dressed."

They stood and stretched, then walked stiffly across the cluttered room toward the dressing screen in the corner. Marcel wasn't a bit ashamed to walk naked with Madeleine, and she pulled off the flimsy see-through dress before they reached the screen.

Their clothes sat in piles on the divan, and they chatted as they dressed. As usual, Madeleine did most of the talking. Marcel was an excellent listener, but he was never chatty. That was part of the reason the two of them got on so well.

"Thank you for taking that job with me," she said when they exited the building, bundled up in their coats and scarves.

"You're welcome."

"I've worked for him before. He pays well, and he doesn't get abusive. Some painters do, you know. If you have your hand a centimeter off from where they think it should be, they scream at you about how stupid and blind you are to not see how much better it would be if your fingers were over here instead of right there."

"Artists are temperamental," Marcel said.

"At least his apartment was heated," she said.

It was a long walk from the artist's apartment in the 6th Arrondissement to their neighborhood in the 5th, and they walked briskly to keep warm. It was the middle of the afternoon, and the sidewalks were not full; everyone was back to work. The store windows were still decorated for Christmas, but the shoppers were gone.

They turned up the Rue des Anglais as the light was fading, casting the entire street in deep shadow. They reached the door to her building first, just past Chez Marius. His was the next building. He thanked her again for the work, they bid each other "*A bien tot*" and kissed cheeks.

**

Captain Allard stood in the middle of the apartment, facing Adrienne Charbonneau and Marie-France Lavelle. Their roommate, Madeleine Racicot, was not in; a minor irritation. He had ordered them to sit—Miss Charbonneau on a chair by the window, and Miss Lavelle on a threadbare couch—so that he could tower over them, but it had not inspired the compliance he had hoped. All they would admit to was that they had known Serge Faucheaux since their days at the Sorbonne.

The door to the apartment stood open, and when he paused to collect his thoughts, he heard the floor creak in the hallway. He saw Marie-France Lavelle looking at the doorway, and make a subtle shake of her head.

Allard spun on his heel and marched to the door. A red-haired young woman hurried back toward the stairs, and he called to her, "Miss Racicot?"

She turned back toward the door. "Yes, I am Madeleine Racicot."

"I am Captain Allard, of the prefecture of police. I would like a word, please."

"Of course, sir." She came inside.

She nodded to Miss Lavelle sitting on the threadbare couch, and then glanced first at Miss Charbonneau, then at a gendarme standing in the corner.

"Have a seat please, Miss Racicot."

She took a seat on the couch.

The commanding approach had not worked, so Allard opted to try a friendlier tactic. He sat in one of the wooden chairs he moved over from the table. "We have been conversing for a little while, your roommates and I, so let me go back a little bit and ask you a few of the same questions, if I may."

"Alright."

"How old are you, Miss Racicot?"

"Twenty-one years."

A few years younger than the other two. "And how long have you lived in this apartment?"

"For three years." She glanced at Miss Charbonneau, and Allard followed-suit; her face seemed calm, but he could see her body was tensed like the spring on a mouse trap.

He nodded as he scribbled notes. "Where did you live before then?"

"In Angers."

"You came to Paris when you were eighteen, from your parents' home?"

"Yes, that's right."

"And what do you do for a living, Miss Racicot?"

"I am a model."

He looked up from his notebook and stared at her for a moment, evaluating her. "A fashion model?"

"When I can get the work, yes. But mostly I model for artists—painters and sculptors."

"I see," he said and he looked back down at his notebook, scribbling. *A dancer, an actress, and an artists' model.* Not a respectable profession among the three of them. He allowed a note of condescension when he asked, "What sort of painters? Abstract? Cubist?"

"Sometimes."

He narrowed his eyes. "Nude paintings?"

"Sometimes."

He grunted and scribbled. *Another bohemian tramp.* His brow furrowed in disapproval. "Did you know anyone in Paris when you came here?"

"No."

"And how did you come to live with these young ladies?" he motioned toward the other two.

"I answered an advertisement on the board at the fine arts building at the Sorbonne, for a female to share an apartment with two others."

"Where did you stay before then?"

"In a hostel off of the Rue des Écoles, near the Sorbonne. I went there directly from the station when I arrived in Paris. Why do you need to know this?"

"I am asking the questions, Miss Racicot. I expect your cooperation."

She nodded, sufficiently cowed. "Yes, of course."

"Do your parents still live in Angers?"

"Yes."

"What does your father do?"

"He is a butcher."

Allard continued to scribble notes. What would the butcher Racicot think of his daughter's 'work' in Paris? Perhaps Allard could use that. "And your mother, she is at home?"

"Yes, and she works in the shop with my father. They live in the rooms upstairs."

"Naturally. How many siblings do you have, Miss Racicot?"

"One younger sister, Charlotte. She's seventeen."

Allard scowled. "Just one sibling?"

"That's right."

"Your parents are not Catholic, then?" His lip curled in distaste.

She tensed. "No. My parents are Reformed."

Allard grunted and scribbled furiously. "Protestants," he said with disdain. "Your family, they are all Protestant?"

"Yes."

"I'm sure they are disestablishmentarian, then, the lot of them?" The religious minorities the Radicals tried to 'protect' from the established church.

She gave him a blank look and a shrug.

"Have they said anything against the changes in the French State? Against the re-establishment of the Catholic Church in France?"

"I have no idea."

"No matter. When was the last time you saw them?"

"In June, before I came back to Paris."

"You went home to Angers before the Occupation?"

"That's right."

Allard scribbled in his notebook for several more seconds, and then looked up. "I think that is all on that, Miss Racicot. Just one more question that I've already asked the others—how well do you know Serge Faucheux?"

He saw her glance at Adrienne Charbonneau. Then she looked back at Allard.

"I've known him since I moved here, three years."

"That did not answer my question."

"We are friends, he and I." She didn't elaborate.

No more forthcoming than the other two. "Do you know him well enough to comment on his politics?"

"I know he is a Socialist," she said. "He is for the workers."

Allard regarded her carefully. Her vague answer didn't contradict the other two. "Is that all you know of his politics, Miss Racicot?"

She just nodded.

"Very well," he said, standing, and snapped his notepad closed. "I had hoped you would be more cooperative, all of you. The prefecture will look favorably in the future on those who cooperate with us."

*

The tension inside Adrienne had been building since the police barged in, but the threat made something snap.

"What are you trying to say, Captain? That the Paris police will resort to bullying young women into giving false testimony against someone whose only crime is that he is a Socialist? Is that what the police do these days?" She stared at Allard in open defiance.

Allard's expression was cold. "I would be very careful, Miss Charbonneau. There are severe penalties for slandering the police."

"Are you going to arrest me, then?"

Allard stared at her for a long moment. "Not today."

He nodded to the gendarme, and they left. He turned as he went through the door. "If you change your minds and wish to tell us anything, I can be found at the local prefecture every day from eight o'clock in the morning until six in the evening. Good day."

Adrienne shook with fury as she closed the door. "How dare they?" she whispered, her voice trembling with anger.

Madeleine looked from Adrienne to Marie-France, and back again. "What was that? Why are they after Serge? What has he done?"

Both girls looked to Adrienne. Adrienne stood in stony silence.

"Adrienne, what do you know?" Marie-France asked.

"The war is not over in France," Adrienne said, her voice quiet. "But it is not only the Germans who are the enemy. The war is now between those who love liberty, and those who would make France a fascist police state, like Italy or Germany. Soon we will all be asked to choose a side. But for now, it is best if you don't know everything."

33

Sunday, December 29

Cécile arrived at La Tour d'Argent on the Champs Elysees a few minutes after eight PM.

Jean-Louis DuBois sat waiting at a table for two, fidgeting, and he stood with a smile as she approached. Cécile noted that the table was back in a corner of the candle-lit restaurant, for a semi-private ambiance.

He kissed her hand when she reached the table, and held her chair.

"Cécile, what a pleasure to see you again at last."

"Thank you. I apologize that I was not able to meet you before tonight. I am terribly sorry."

"Please say no more, I understand perfectly," Jean-Louis said with an eager smile. "I am happy that we were able to meet. I have taken the liberty of ordering a bottle of wine, I hope you don't mind."

"Not at all."

"I ordered a '31 St. Emillion, one of my favorites. You know it?"

"I haven't had it in many years," Cécile said.

"Then I hope you enjoy it." Jean-Louis signaled for the waiter, who brought the bottle and poured Cécile a glass.

Jean-Louis raised his glass. "To the beginning of a beautiful new friendship."

Cécile smiled, nodded and raised her glass toward him. She looked at her menu and pretended to peruse it. "I have not been to the La Tour d'Argent in many years."

"Really?" Jean-Louis replied, arching an eyebrow in surprise. "A sophisticated, elegant woman such as yourself? I would have thought this would be one of your regular restaurants."

She flashed him a dazzling smile. "You are most kind, Jean-Louis."

"I have dined here many times," Jean-Louis said, taking on the tone of an expert.

What a boor. A stuck-up, self-important boor. But she smiled and asked him for a recommendation from the menu.

"Well, of course *everything* here is excellent," he proclaimed, his chest puffing out as he looked down at the menu.

She knew he was buying time as he picked out something.

"I am partial to the duckling," he said, but continued to look over the menu. "Of course, the fois gras is second to none. And the escargot here is different—it is served in a red wine sauce instead of garlic butter."

"Let's try the escargot," Cécile said. "Followed by the roast duckling, as you suggest."

"You have excellent taste, Cécile," he said, and motioned for the waiter. He ordered the escargot first, followed by the fois gras, and then the roast duckling, followed by salad and cheese. "Then we'll decide later if we want dessert."

Cécile suppressed an amused smile. He was trying hard to impress her. She played along.

"That is quite expensive, Jean-Louis. I apologize for my manners, but I must ask—how can we have so much with the rationing?"

He waved a hand in the air. "*Bof*! I don't allow rationing to limit me, my dear Cécile."

She played dumb, putting on a confused look. "But how can that be?"

He gave her a smug smile. "My dear lady, there are always ways around any obstacle for those with the will to find them—and the means to take advantage of them."

She gasped, put her hand to her throat, and smiled at the same time, pretending to be both scandalized and thrilled at once.

It worked. His chest puffed out even more.

"Of course you must mean the black market," she whispered, continuing with the act.

"Of course."

The look on Jean-Louis's face was so smug, she wanted to smack it off. Instead, she acted impressed.

She leaned close and continued to whisper. "I hear you can buy anything on the black market—coffee, tea, chocolate, even bananas—but it is quite expensive."

He shrugged. "Expensive, yes—but some of us cannot endure the little meat that the rationing allows us. And if one can afford it, then why not?"

"Business must be good for you."

"Yes it is. My company has many contracts with the Wehrmacht. They find it more cost-effective to buy parts for their garrison here from French manufacturers, rather than shipping from Germany. And less likely that it will get bombed by the RAF on the way."

The escargot arrived, and he motioned for her to take the first one. "Please."

She gave him another dazzling smile and helped herself.

"Does it surprise you that we do business with the Germans?" he asked between bites.

"Not at all. Most of the people who pay to hear me sing these days are Germans. Or their guests. We all do what we must."

"Naturally. One must make a living, mustn't one?"

"Yes."

"And the Germans pay quite well," he added.

"And you are far from the only one, I am sure," she said.

"Not at all," he said, finishing off the escargot. "There are a great many of us who manufacture parts for the Occupation forces. The orders are quite large, and it takes many factories to supply their needs."

"Do you work in cooperation with other French firms, then?"

"Naturally."

She let the silence prompt him to continue on his own. As she suspected, he launched right into a list of acquaintances, and what they were manufacturing for the Wehrmacht or the Luftwaffe. It was another Who's Who of the former French-German Friendship Committee.

She recognized almost all of the names. And she was only mildly surprised at how easily he quoted numbers and other specifics. Her adept mind filed away every detail.

When they had finished dinner, he motioned for the waiter, who began clearing the plates.

"The duckling was excellent," Cécile said to the waiter. He acknowledged with a nod.

"And we would like to order dessert," Jean-Louis said. "We'll share a piece of the pound cake with chocolate sauce."

The waiter nodded and hurried away.

"I don't think I can eat another bite," Cécile said, putting her hand over her stomach.

"Oh you must. Chocolate is so hard to get nowadays."

They chatted for a few minutes until the dessert arrived. A dark chocolate sauce was drizzled over a piece of dense pound cake. The waiter cut it in half, and placed one half on a clean plate in front of Cécile. She thanked him, and he bowed before backing away.

Cécile ate a couple of bites—one to be polite, and a second because the chocolate sauce tasted divine—and then pushed the plate back.

"A refined woman such as you should have chocolate more often," Jean-Louis remarked between bites.

"I'm afraid that's a luxury I can ill afford on a regular basis."

"I would see to it that you ate chocolate regularly," he said.

She'd wondered how long it would take for him to proposition her. She was mildly surprised that he wasn't more direct, given his typically blunt manner. His *haute-bourgeois* manners held sway, apparently.

"And why should you buy me chocolate?"

He stared intently into her eyes. There was no mistaking his intentions. "Because you are a most beautiful woman, one who needs to be treated well by a man who knows how to treat a lady."

She gave him a coy smile. "But sir, you already have a lover, do you not? Or am I mistaken about your relationship with that adorable young woman who accompanied you to the party at the De Forêts'?"

Jean-Louis chuckled. "You are not mistaken, Miss. But I am capable of keeping two lovers, and not neglecting either."

She felt her stomach clench; she ignored it. "But then, won't you neglect your wife?"

His face broke into a grin. "Not at all. Jean-Louis DuBois can take care of his wife and two lovers quite well. You'll see, Cécile—if you give me the chance to show you."

He reached his hand across the table and set it atop hers. She let it stay there a few seconds before pulling her hand back and hiding it beneath the table in her lap.

"I am afraid, sir, that I already have a lover myself."

"And yet you are here with me now."

"That is true."

"Can he buy you fine meals, and chocolate, this lover?"

She resisted the urge to roll her eyes. She just shook her head, saying nothing.

"But I can."

He was staring at her quite intently again. He would not be easy to dissuade. And she had to do it in a gentle and open-ended manner, to keep him trying.

"He is a most capable lover," she said, throwing discretion to the wind. "Young and vigorous. Very pleasurable."

A hint of a scowl crossed Jean-Louis face for a second, but he recovered quickly. His eyes said that he would meet that challenge. "Let me assure you, dear lady, that this lover of yours—while he may be young and vigorous—surely has much to learn about how to pleasure a woman. For that, you need a man with age and experience."

"I understand your point, Jean-Louis—but I can assure you, in spite of his youth, he is most wonderful in bed. The best I've ever had, actually." She added that last as an after-thought, and she hoped that would close the conversation.

This time, the scowl stayed in place. "Well, if you don't find me attractive—"

"Oh no, it's not that," she lied. "It is only that, we women, we need time to consider an intriguing offer such as yours—as a man of your considerable experience must surely know—and I will consider your kind offer quite carefully."

His expression softened, and he bowed his head graciously. "I apologize if I was over-eager, Cécile. It is just that when a man is presented with a woman as beautiful as you, his instincts tell him to act quickly, before another man steals her away."

"Perfectly understandable, such instinct," she said. "And without a doubt, that is why you are such a successful businessman."

He smiled at the praise, and his chest puffed out a bit again.

Outside on the sidewalk ten minutes later, he hailed a cab. There weren't many motorized cabs operating in Paris these days, but a few electric cars had not been sidelined by the lack of gasoline, and these trolled for wealthy patrons on the Champs Elysees.

"To Montmartre," she said as she slipped into the back seat, and gave the address. Through the window, Jean-Louis handed the driver a bundle of franc notes, and told him to not dawdle.

The driver nodded and said, "Of course, sir." After he drove away, Cécile heard him mumble something under his breath. She laughed, and the driver looked at her in the rearview mirror and began to chuckle.

**

"What an intolerable, self-important boor!" Cécile said, flopping onto her bed twenty minutes later.

Frank Dryden sat down next to her and patted her hand. He felt a touch relieved that she hadn't enjoyed the evening. "No one ever said this job would always be enjoyable, my dear." He kept his voice soothing and calm. "Was dinner good, at least?"

She sat up, removed the pins from her hair and shook it loose, running her fingers through the long brown tresses.

"Yes, the meal was quite good. It almost made up for the company."

"And the information?" Frank asked. "Did he sing like a bird?"

She gave him a bemused look, and he realized that his literal translation of an American idiom hadn't worked. "Did he reveal many secrets?"

Her eyes grew a touch wider as she nodded. "Oh yes. Many secrets, and many details." She told him what she'd learned.

He was impressed. "Excellent work, my dear! That paints the picture nicely." He placed a hand on her knee.

She let her head drop back a little and let out a small groan. "I don't know how long I can keep him on the hook, though. He will be a persistent one, without a doubt. He won't keep accepting 'no' as an answer to his advances."

Frank felt his chest tighten around his heart. It was rumored the Soviet intelligence services used women in that way, but he would not. "Then I will find another way to keep tabs on him. Don't worry, my love—you will not have to endure him for long." He slowly slid his hand beneath the hem of her dress and up her thigh.

She let her neck go limp as his fingers found their way inside her panties. And she gasped and fell back onto the bed as they found their way inside of her.

Monday, December 30

Oliver mounted the steps to the American Library of Paris the next day. Butterflies seemed to flutter in his stomach.

He had no idea what this meeting was about, but he'd deduced that it was urgent. The message from Frank Dryden had been delivered by a courier from the American Consulate on the Place de la Concorde (too sensitive for a telegram?), and it had only given him three hours' notice.

He took the Metro to the Saint-Lazare station in the 8th Arrondissement, and took the steps two at a time up to the street. He walked at a brisk pace, hurried across intersections, and reached the imposing four-story limestone edifice at exactly two o'clock. Walking through the large double doors into the open atrium, he took a moment to get his bearings.

He'd been here once before, soon after arriving in Paris. He'd quickly discovered for himself what Miss Beach later told him at

Shakespeare and Company—that the blue-stockinged matrons at the American Library played moral censor, and refused to carry books they deemed objectionable. And their moral code obviously pre-dated the 1920s. Among the works they found objectionable was anything by F. Scott Fitzgerald, and most things by Ernest Hemingway—two of Oliver's favorites. Miss Beach once gleefully recounted how Ezra Pound had called them "The Right Bank Pigs."

He found Frank Dryden "browsing" through the European History section. There was no one else in their aisle, and the only person Oliver saw in the next aisle was at the opposite end.

"Found anything interesting?" Oliver whispered, and he also began looking at the book titles in front of them.

"I think so," Dryden said. "They have a considerable selection. I learned a great deal from the book I just returned, and it whet my appetite."

"Anything I could recommend?" Oliver asked, pleased with himself for falling easily into the code.

Dryden glanced up and down the aisle. "I have a job for you," he whispered.

"What kind of job?"

"Lisette Rousseau, your former fiancée, is currently seeing a man that we're interested in keeping tabs on," Dryden said.

Oliver's stomach clenched at the mention of Lisette's lover.

Dryden continued. "Jean-Louis DuBois is a director at a factory in Aubervilliers, a suburb north of Paris. That factory produces items for the German army. We want to know how much and how often."

Oliver felt confused. "How am I supposed to find that out?"

"Get close to Lisette again, and recruit her to spy on DuBois and his business."

Oliver stared at him in shock for a moment. "How am I supposed to convince her to spy on her lover for me?"

"I'll leave that up to you. I'm sure you can think of some way. You two were going to be married once—I'm sure you know her weaknesses."

Oliver's face tightened with irritation. The last thing he wanted to do was to strong-arm Lisette. "And how is she supposed to get the information you want? I doubt he tells her about his business." His irritation was obvious in his tone.

"My suggestion is to have her ask him for a job. If the factory is busy with orders from the Wehrmacht, I'm sure they need plenty of clerical help. Ask her to quit her job and go to work for DuBois. If she asks to work for him directly, she can get access to sensitive information—the kind of information we want."

Oliver's mouth hung open for several seconds. He couldn't believe what he was hearing. "How in the hell am I supposed to convince her to do that?"

"Shh!" Dryden scowled.

Oliver hadn't realized his voice had risen above a whisper. "She'll never agree."

Dryden looked him hard in the eye. "That is where your government is counting on you to find a way. You know her better than anyone, I'd wager. If you think hard enough, you'll figure out a way." He started to walk away, but turned back after a couple of steps. "And if all else fails, offer her a lot of money."

Oliver's eyes narrowed. "How much money?"

Dryden chuckled. "Let's just say that if the information is good, she'll get more than a year's salary working a clerical job, or selling wine."

Oliver stared at Dryden. "You must really want this bad. Why?"

"Because it's important."

"Tell me why."

Dryden stared back for a moment. "Alright. It's not really a secret that the United States favors Great Britain in this war. Everyone knows that. What is not publicly known—and this is classified, Oliver—is that the War Department has been preparing for the eventuality that we'll be forced to enter this war. When we go to war against Germany, our military will need to be prepared with what they are facing.

"Our military and naval attachés in Berlin have kept pretty good tabs on what the Germans are producing at home. What is much less clear is what they're producing in the occupied countries. This could make a significant difference. And this is where your country is counting on you, Oliver."

Oliver's mind raced. There could be dozens, even hundreds, of factories in France producing weapons for the German military. And countless others in Belgium, the Netherlands, Denmark, Poland, and Czechoslovakia. How could his part possibly make a difference?

He voiced that concern.

Dryden put a hand on his shoulder. "Just worry about your piece of the puzzle. I'll worry about the pieces around it. And others will worry about the rest of the puzzle. Just do your part, do it well, and you could return home a *much* wealthier man than when you left."

With those words, Dryden spun around and walked away.

304

34

Tuesday, December 31

Oliver walked into Les Deux Magots at noon the next day, and rubbed his hands together to warm them up. The popular place was full—half of the patrons were German soldiers—and Oliver's heart sank at the thought that they might not get a table.

Then he saw Lisette sitting at a small table on the far side of the room, next to the window. She was looking out at the Boulevard Saint-Germain, watching the bicycle taxis going by with their German passengers, while the civilians either walked or bicycled themselves.

She looked up as he reached the table. He grinned at her.

"Happy New Year," he said, taking a seat. "Thanks for meeting me."

She returned his New Year's greeting. "My mother will be pleased to hear I'm having lunch with you. She's asked about you several times this week."

Oliver laughed. "Really? I wonder why."

Lisette shook her head and waved a hand in the air. "*Bof*! She's got the idea that we should get back together."

"I see." This pleased him.

He rubbed his hands together again. The restaurant was warm enough—whether it was the cumulative body heat of all of the patrons, or the heat from the ovens in the kitchen, he didn't care—but he could feel a draft coming off the window. At least it was warmer than his apartment.

He ordered a sausage sandwich, and she ordered a paté sandwich. Oliver ordered a beer, even though he knew it would be watered down, a recent consequence of grain rationing.

When the waiter departed, Lisette looked back at Oliver. "I've nearly finished the book you gave me for Christmas."

"Already? It must be good, then."

"Yes, I'm enjoying it. It took me a couple of days to get used to reading in English again, I was out of practice, but now it is going well. It was a thoughtful gift, thank you. I am sorry that I didn't get you a gift."

"No apology necessary."

"I spoke with Adrienne yesterday. She said you all are having a little holiday tonight in Sébastien's apartment."

"Yes, we are. You should join us."

She smiled and shook her head. "I have plans this evening with some of the other girls from the shop."

"Ours will be more fun."

She laughed. "I don't doubt that. Knowing everyone as I do, I know there will be much gaiety." She leaned back in her chair, looked around the full restaurant, and sighed. "I do miss everyone. Adrienne keeps me informed of everyone's news, but it is not the same."

"You did sort of cut yourself off from everyone."

Lisette shrugged and didn't look at him.

"I didn't mean that the way it sounded," he said. "I only meant that you could come back around any time you want. Your friends will still be your friends."

"Yes, I suppose." She looked back at him, and he couldn't read the look in her eyes.

"Well, if you change your mind, you know where to find us."

A slight smile crossed her lips. "Yes, I do. Thank you for the invitation. Please tell everyone hello from me, and wish them a happy New Year on my behalf."

He agreed. An awkward silence fell over them. He wasn't sure how they'd managed in such a short amount of time to hit on the uncomfortable subject of her self-exile from the 5th Arrondissement, but it had happened. He didn't know what to say next.

He had plenty he needed to say, but he didn't know how to bring up the subject. And he was afraid to discuss it.

She broke the silence by asking if he'd spoken to his parents on Christmas.

"Yes, I called them in the evening. It was afternoon there, and they were about to have Christmas dinner. My brother and his wife were there. My mother commented on how much the call echoed." He laughed. "I told her it was a German censor listening in, and she thought I was joking! She scolded me for teasing her."

Lisette laughed with him. "Did you convince her that you were telling the truth?"

"I don't know. I tried. I told her they started listening the moment I asked for an international line to the United States. I'm not really sure if she ever believed me."

She looked away again, watching the people at the other tables. "I can't imagine being so far away from my parents."

"You get used to it," he said. "I lived in New York for a couple of years before I came to Paris. It's not really much different, except that we spoke on the phone more often while I was in New York."

She continued to stare off at another table.

He turned his head and followed her gaze. She was looking at a table of four German soldiers, all of them young, probably eighteen or nineteen years old. They were laughing and joking in their language, downing glasses of the watered-down lager.

"I bet none of them have ever been away from home on the holidays," Lisette mused. Her sad tone surprised him.

"Probably not," he agreed.

Their sandwiches arrived a moment later, served on sliced baguette. Oliver noticed that the restaurant had grown stingy with the lettuce. The shortages had begun to affect everyone.

They ate mostly in silence, chatting from time to time about nothing in particular. Oliver drank his beer, trying to ignore how nearly tasteless it was.

"I bet the beer in Germany isn't watered down to make it stretch," he said after he'd taken the last drink.

She shrugged.

"I can't remember the last time I had a real cup of coffee," he continued. "September perhaps? Maybe it was August."

Her expression grew stony. "I've gotten used to the taste of chicory," she said, referencing the main ingredient in the ersatz coffee served everywhere these days.

"I wish I had." He hesitated a few seconds before going on in a lower voice. "I hear you can buy real coffee on the black market. They say you can find it at certain stalls on market days over in the Marais. Real tea, too."

She looked at him. "I have heard that too."

"I don't know how they get it through the blockade," he said.

She gave him a quizzical look for several seconds. "From the colonies in Africa, I'm sure; then across the Sahara to Algiers or Oran. From there they could ship it to Marseille."

Oliver nodded. "I bet you're right. The hard part would be smuggling it across the line of demarcation into the Occupied Zone."

She continued to give him that quizzical look. "It is pointless for you. You cannot afford to buy their coffee, Oliver. For the risk they take, they charge a premium. That is why only rich people buy from the black market."

That was the opening. He took a breath before taking the plunge. "Has your friend Jean-Louis bought real coffee off the black market?"

A veil fell over her eyes, and her posture stiffened. "I do not know. If he does, he has not given any to me."

Oliver leaned across the table and lowered his voice. "I'm sure the Germans pay well for their orders."

She scowled. "What do you mean by that?"

"Well, only that if he was rich before, he must be even richer now. The war must be very profitable to men in his position."

She crossed her arms. "I think we should talk about something else."

Oliver ignored her. "The Germans aren't the only ones who pay well," he whispered.

She stared hard at him, not speaking, her eyes asking the question.

Oliver knew he was teetering on the precipice. "The American government would pay very well for information about what his factory is producing for the Germans—what, how much, and when."

Anger flashed across her eyes, but only for a second, and then was replaced by fear.

"Oliver, what have you gotten yourself into?" she whispered.

He didn't answer. He straightened back up and spoke in a normal volume. "Have you ever asked Jean-Louis for a job? You could probably make more money as a secretary in his office than working as a shop girl."

She stared at him, her mouth open. He waited for her to say something.

"No, I have not ever considered it," she said at length, sounding flustered.

"You should consider it. It would offer you better opportunities."

She looked out the window, her mouth still open in shock. She stared out at the Boulevard Saint-Germain for several minutes.

Oliver sat in silence, watching her, waiting for her to respond.

Finally she looked back at him. "I don't understand what is happening, Oliver. Why would you ever want to get yourself involved? That is not like you."

He shrugged. "Weren't you the one who told me I should be more ambitious? Do more than just play trumpet in someone's band?"

She looked flabbergasted. "This is not what I meant!"

"Obviously."

"You know what I mean."

He nodded. "Yes. You wanted me to work in an office for your father. It didn't matter that being stuck in an office would make me miserable. So I found something else."

The waiter picked that moment to deliver the check.

Oliver pulled out a bundle of cash, counted out the amount for the bill, and laid it on the table. Then he counted out enough ration coupons for the bread and meat, plus his beer, and laid those next to the cash. The waiter appeared instantly and took the money and coupons.

"Let's walk," Oliver said, rising from his chair. "I'll escort you back to the shop."

"I'm off work today."

"Then I'll escort you home."

"It's a long walk."

"I know." He took her elbow and followed her out of the restaurant.

**

It was nearly a mile along the Boulevard Saint-Germain to the Quai d'Orsay on the left bank of the Seine. The sidewalks were crowded with people returning to work from their lunch breaks, and the boulevard was full of bicycles and the occasional automobile. Oliver and Lisette barely spoke.

The bicycle traffic remained heavy across the Pont de la Concorde. The large open space of the Place de la Concorde seemed to be filled by German military vehicles, and countless clusters of German soldiers.

Oliver considered detouring onto one of the more deserted side streets, but he wasn't familiar enough with this part of Paris to trust his navigation.

The large *Jardins des Tuileries* were nearby, to their right, but he thought of what Frank Dryden had said about the Gestapo having eyes around all of the large parks. They would be in Lisette's quiet neighborhood before long. The conversation could wait until then.

She seemed to sense his frustration. "If we're not going to talk about it, we could have taken the Metro."

"It's good that we get to see all of the Germans here," he said quietly. "It lets you see what your friend is helping to perpetuate."

She pulled her arm from his grasp. "That is not what he is doing."

"Yes, it is."

"Are you trying to hurt me, Oliver?"

"No, of course not." Her accusation stung.

"Then stop making Jean-Louis sound like an ogre."

He didn't respond.

A squad of German soldiers on patrol marched past them as they walked north on the Rue Royale, the staccato beat of their jackboots echoing. Everyone else went about their business, ignoring the patrol; but Oliver noticed Lisette couldn't help but watch them pass.

They reached the Rue de l'Arcade a few minutes later, and it was as quiet as Oliver had predicted. "France is not free anymore, Lisette," Oliver said as they approached her building, his voice low. "Several of our friends have been arrested—beaten even—for things that we were free to do before the Occupation."

"Yes, Adrienne has told me," Lisette said, her words clipped. "You cannot blame Jean-Louis for that. He does not control such things. And to my knowledge, he knows no one at Vichy."

"But he is helping to perpetuate it," Oliver insisted as they reached the door of her building. He stopped speaking as they entered, aware that the concierge's door was open. They climbed the stairs in silence.

"Thank you for escorting me home," she said when they reached her door. She hardly sounded grateful.

"I think you should ask me inside," Oliver said.

"I don't think that would be a good idea."

"I think it would be an excellent idea." Oliver took hold of her elbow again.

She grimaced, and he realized he'd gripped her arm tighter than he intended. He loosened his grip, but ordered her to open the door.

She flashed him a look of pure fury as she unlocked the door and opened it.

"Oliver Carmichael!" She nearly shouted his name after he'd closed the door. "What is the meaning of this? You have *never* gotten physical with me before. How dare you?"

His heart filled with remorse, and her fury stung. He hated every part of this. "I'm sorry, Lisette. I have no choice. We *have* to talk about this. You have to see reason."

"I don't know you."

"Oh yes you do," he said, taking her by the shoulder and looking down into her face. "You used to be idealistic, too. You are the one who has changed."

Her expression calmed, but her eyes remained distant. "Say what you need to say. Then leave."

"What I need to say you already know. You need to get your head out of your ass and listen."

Her sharp intake of breath and the sudden flash in her eyes told him that was a mistake; he was making her too angry to listen.

He put his hands on her arms, and was conscious not to grip them too hard. He deliberately softened his expression and stared into her eyes.

"Lisette, please. You have a chance to make a difference in this war—for France, for your friends, for your family. None of us will be free until after the Germans leave. You know this. And you know that the Germans won't leave until they are forced to. If they stay armed, they might defeat the British, and then they will never leave. Ever."

She pulled away from his grasp and took a step back. Her expression was cool. "I don't want to get involved. I told Sébastien that already."

He looked at her, stunned. He could see instantly that she regretted saying that.

"You saw Sébastien? When?"

She hesitated, seeming to wrestle with what to say. Then her chin came up in that familiar look of defiance. "Yes, I saw Sébastien. He came here, several weeks ago, with another young man. He had been hurt—the other—and Sébastien asked me to help. I helped him, but I also told him that I didn't want to be involved. And I still don't."

"When was that exactly?"

She shrugged. "Six weeks ago, perhaps." She thought a moment, and added. "It was November eleventh. It would have been Armistice Day. I heard that night that there was a protest. I assume Sébastien and the other one were part of it."

Oliver shook his head. "Sébastien wasn't, but he wanted to help. He's not afraid, our friend. People like him will save us all. And he asked you to help, too." He could see the guilt working behind her eyes. "It's not too late to help."

She stared into his eyes, and he saw the skepticism before she spoke it. "How will me spying on Jean-Louis help? It won't stop what his factory is doing. Or will this information get to the British so that their RAF can bomb it? If that is what they plan to do, I want no part of it."

Oliver shook his head. "It is not for the British," he said, though in truth he couldn't be certain.

"You said it was for the American government. You said they would pay well, even. Why do they want this?"

He wasn't sure he was supposed to say anything, but he also figured at this point he didn't have much choice. "The United States is probably going to enter the war in the future, on the side of the British. If we go to war against Germany, we need to know how the Germans are getting their arms."

"So that they can bomb Jean-Louis' factory?"

Oliver's shoulders slumped. "I don't know," he admitted, his voice quiet.

"How is that helping France? By helping other countries to bomb her factories?"

He could feel this getting away from him. He was losing confidence in his ability to pull it off. He played his last card.

"The United States is interested in helping the resistance. Any information you provide will be used to help fellow Frenchmen in the struggle against the German occupiers."

He paused and watched her wavering. He added the *coup de grace*. "You know people who are in the resistance, Lisette. Old friends of yours."

She turned away from him, but not before he saw the conflict waging behind her eyes. "I need time to think," she said, facing the wall.

"Alright. How much time?"

She shrugged.

"Then I'll stop by tomorrow afternoon. Will you be home?"

She shrugged again, not turning around.

"I'll see you tomorrow," he said, and let himself out.

**

Her phone rang that evening as she was putting in her earrings. She smiled, thinking it might be Jean-Louis, calling to wish her a happy New Year before he went to a party with his wife.

"Lisette, this is Adrienne," her friend's familiar voice said.

"Oh, hello," Lisette said, surprised. "I thought it was someone else."

"Your married man?"

Lisette suppressed a heavy sigh. "His name is Jean-Louis. And yes, I thought it might be him calling."

"To wish you happy New Year? To tell you how much he'd rather be with you tonight than with his wife? To tell you he misses you and cares deeply for you?"

"Adrienne, I'm not in the mood to fight with you. I know how you feel about my relationship with Jean-Louis, and I don't want to hear it again. Not tonight."

"Alright, fine. But you will not be happy."

"Adrienne—"

"Alright, I've said all I need to say on that. I was calling to ask you to reconsider coming to our holiday this evening. Your friends care about you—truthfully, not just telling you they care like some other I won't mention again—and we would like to see you."

315

"Oliver tried to convince me to reconsider earlier, when we had lunch," Lisette said.

"You should listen to him. He cares deeply for you." There was a pause on the line, and then Adrienne added, "You know that he is still in love with you, do you not?"

Lisette's heart seemed to skip a beat. "Adrienne, really—I think that was long ago. He doesn't feel that way anymore."

"Of course he does. You would have to be blind not to see it."

"Well, then it would complicate matters if I came to your holiday this evening." *Things have become complicated enough.*

"Nonsense."

Lisette was disturbed at her own indecision. She took a deep breath. "I have plans with a couple of friends from work, but let's have lunch next week. Monday?"

"Yes, lunch on Monday. Les Deux Magots? And if you change your mind about tonight, you know where to find us. We will be in Sébastien's apartment until midnight. Happy New Year."

The line clicked off.

**

The party was lively, with swing music playing on the Victrola and much frivolous conversation and laughter; but Lisette wasn't in the mood for frivolity.

She was shocked to discover that she was the oldest one there. The young men in whose apartment the party was held were only twenty-one years old. One was the boyfriend of one of the girls who worked with her at the shop, and they seemed to have a lot of friends. There were about thirty people there, boys and girls, and a substantial amount of wine was being consumed. Trade school educated, they seemed to all work in offices on or near the Champs Elysee as low-level clerks or receptionists.

Lisette felt out of place.

Unable to interest herself in any of the conversations going on around her, she found herself watching the clock. It was only ten-thirty.

She found her coworkers sitting on the couch, kissing their boyfriends. She cleared her throat, but they didn't notice. She touched her coworker Vivienne on the shoulder and apologized. "I'm a lot more tired than I thought. I should go home and get some sleep."

"You'll miss the new year," Vivienne said.

Lisette shrugged. "It will be here when I wake up."

Vivienne got up and kissed her cheeks. "Good night."

Lisette thanked her and left, a little surprised at how easily they had let her leave, without much argument.

It was obvious even to them that she didn't fit in with this group.

So then, where did she fit in? With Jean-Louis and his crowd? Hardly, she realized. Those *haute-bourgeois* women at the Christmas party had looked down their noses at her, condescending through their false politesse.

She thought of what Adrienne had said, and what Oliver had said at lunch. Yes, she had fit in there, once. Would she still?

She made up her mind, and as she exited the building she headed not toward her own building a couple of blocks away, but toward the Metro station.

It had started snowing again, not heavily, but there was already considerable accumulation on the ground since before Christmas. She wrapped her scarf around her head and hurried toward the station.

**

Oliver was standing closest to the door when he heard the knock. It surprised him, given that it was almost eleven o'clock and everyone they were expecting was already there.

He caught Sébastien's attention across the room. "Someone else is knocking."

Sébastien shrugged. "See who it is."

There was another knock as Oliver reached the door and opened it. "Lisette," he said, stunned. "I didn't think you'd come."

"Good evening, Oliver." She stepped inside and kissed his cheek, then removed the scarf from her head. "It's snowing again."

Adrienne came from across the room, and kissed Lisette on both cheeks. "I'm so happy you changed your mind. Come." She took Lisette by the hand and led her into the middle of the room. "Look everyone! Our dear old friend Lisette is here!"

One by one their friends stepped forward to greet her with smiles and kisses—Marie-France first, then Madeleine, followed by Sébastien, Serge, and finally Marcel. Marcel was the least exuberant, but he still kissed her cheeks.

From his place by the door, Oliver watched the interactions with an odd mix of emotions. Lisette's expression was surprised and increasingly happy at the warm reception from her old friends, and he felt warmth emanating from his heart at the sight. It was as if nothing had changed.

And yet, everything had changed. Every one of them had changed.

Lisette looked around the room at the eight or nine strangers. "Who are all of these?"

"Students from the Sorbonne, friends of Xavier who came with him to join our holiday." Sébastien motioned to one of them.

Oliver saw recognition dawn in Lisette's eyes. "Oh, hello," she said to the boy who approached her. "Nice to see you again."

Curious, Oliver watched. The boy had been introduced to him earlier as Xavier, a student at the Sorbonne, with no explanation.

Xavier nodded to Lisette. "I did not think we would meet again."

"You were not properly introduced," Sébastien said. "Under the circumstances, well…" he shrugged. "Lisette Rousseau, this is Xavier Benoit."

Oliver watched them shake hands, and saw the wariness in Xavier's eyes.

Of course! He was the student from the Armistice Day protest, Oliver realized. Lisette had declined to help, and Xavier remembered.

"And these are his friends," Sébastien said to Lisette, and proceeded to introduce the five young men and three young women who had come with Xavier. She shook hands with each of them.

A while later, Oliver managed to corner Sébastien alone in the kitchen. "The students, they are all involved, aren't they?" he asked in a low voice.

Sébastien looked Oliver in the eye, silent for a moment. "They have all agreed to help, when called upon."

Oliver nodded, pleased at his deductive ability. "It's quite the network you all have set up," he said in genuine admiration.

He thought he saw a glimmer of a smile cross Sébastien's lips. "Thank you. We may need them."

"If you need any additional man-power, you can call on me as well. I mean that, my friend."

Sébastien stared deep into his eyes. "Yes, I know. Thank you."

**

Oliver found Lisette alone in the kitchen a few minutes before midnight, refilling her wine glass. "Would you?" he asked, handing her his glass.

She gave him a faint smile and shook her head, refilling his glass.

"Lisette, I'm sorry about the way things went this afternoon," he said. "I really hate putting pressure on you like that."

"Don't be sorry, it's alright," she said. "I've thought about it a lot this evening. You are right—I can help my friends. I *should* help my friends. The day after tomorrow, I am going to ask Jean-Louis for a job."

A thrill ran through Oliver. "You're sure?"

"Yes."

"Oh Lisette, thank you!" he said. "We can't tell anyone why you're doing this, not yet anyway. But eventually you can, and your friends will thank you."

"We'll see."

He held out his glass. "To 1941—may it be a better year than 1940 was."

She raised her glass, and they drank.

In the other room, bells began to ring. Oliver looked at the clock. It was midnight.

"Happy New Year," he said, and kissed her cheek.

"Happy New Year, Oliver."

321

Part III

35

Thursday, March 6, 1941

"Finish typing those orders for Mr. Dubois' signature, and you may leave, Miss Rousseau," said the office manager, Mrs. Orand. She was a fifty-ish widow with a long, severe face, and hair more gray than black, pulled back in a tight bun. "We will need twenty copies made for the rest of the Directors, but you can do that on the mimeograph in the morning."

"I don't mind staying late to finish," Lisette said.

Mrs. Orand glanced at the clock on the wall. It was already quarter past six. All of the other office girls had already packed up and left.

"You don't have to stay late every night," Mrs. Orand said. "A young woman such as you should go home and enjoy the evening."

"My boyfriend works nights, so I really don't mind staying a bit longer," Lisette said. She had taken to referring to Oliver as her 'boyfriend,' mostly to deflect suspicion that she was sleeping with the boss—which of course she was.

And working late, after the rest of the office staff left, gave her the best opportunity to make additional copies on the mimeograph machine of anything she'd seen earlier in the day. She might be able to get away with it during the day, but she didn't like to take the risk.

"Very well," Mrs. Orand said. "Good night."

Lisette finished typing the order a few minutes later, and set it in Jean-Louis' in-box for his signature. Then she went to the back room where the mimeograph machine was.

She took the stencils that she wanted, and set them in the machine. There were two today that Oliver's contact might want to see. She wrapped the first one around the drum of the double-roll machine, set the paper, and turned the crank. She made only one copy, and then repeated the process on the second stencil.

As soon as the ink had dried, she folded both copies into small squares, and took them back into the main office. She paused to look around, making sure she was alone.

She had sewn a pocket into the side of her purse. A careful inspection would have found it, but a cursory glance would overlook it. Security guards conducted random searches on a few people leaving the factory each day, but in two months she had never once been selected for a search.

She wondered if Jean-Louis had put her on some secret "do not disturb" list. Upper management certainly never got searched.

She put the cover on her typewriter, locked her desk drawers, and took her purse. She retrieved her coat from the coat room, and walked toward the exit.

"Good evening, Miss Rousseau," the security guard said as she approached. "Working late again this evening."

Her pulse quickened. "Yes, Martin. There were a lot of orders to type up today."

"Good, business must be booming," the guard said, and waved her through.

It was a few blocks to the Courneuve Aubervilliers metro station, but a cold wind at her face with a light drizzle made the walk seem far longer. She was relieved to descend the stairs and feel the heat of the station.

A pair of Aubervilliers police gendarmes patrolled the station while she waited for the train into Paris, but she ignored them and they walked past her without a word.

She relaxed once she got on the train, and it pulled away from the station.

It was a long ride into the city, and she had to change lines once to get to her neighborhood in the 8th Arrondissement. Several Paris police gendarmes patrolled the station while she waited for her connection, and her breath came short and quick as she stood there. She tried to look calm and ignore them.

No matter how many times she did this, it still terrified her whenever a gendarme walked by.

Her train arrived and she hurried on board, exhaling in relief when it pulled away.

As she exited the metro at the Place de la Madeleine, a squad of Wehrmacht soldiers marched by in front of the Church de la Madeleine, their leather jackboots smacking loudly on the pavement, and she had to stop to let them pass.

Like everyone else in Paris, she had gotten used to the constant patrols on the main thoroughfares and squares, seeing them as more of a nuisance than anything else, but she had not completely gotten used to the staccato sound of their boots.

The drizzle had stopped, but the cold north wind still whistled through the streets. The fading light shined on the wet pavement as she hurried down the Rue de l'Arcade to her building.

It felt warmer the moment she stepped inside, though she knew it wasn't actually warmer. It felt good to be out of the wind, and she unwrapped her scarf from her head.

She locked the door behind her as soon as she was in her apartment. She didn't bother taking off her coat—she could see her breath. She opened her purse and removed the two folded squares from their secret pocket, and unlocked a drawer in her bureau.

Sitting inside the drawer she had two other mimeographed copies from earlier this week. That was a larger than normal take, and for the second week in a row. New business had increased recently. She should get paid well for these.

She walked into the kitchen, uncorked a half-full bottle of wine, and poured a glass. She sank into her couch, put her feet up on the ottoman, and took a long drink.

She sat and relaxed for several minutes, taking a few more sips. Then she got up and walked to the bureau, picked up the telephone receiver, and dialed a phone number.

"*Le Chien Errant*, good evening," the voice on the other end said.

"Good evening. Would you please give a message to Oliver for me? This is his fiancée."

Friday, March 7

Oliver met Frank Dryden backstage at Cécile's club the next afternoon. They stood in a narrow hallway leading to Cécile's dressing room.

"You got a delivery last night?" Dryden asked.

"Yes, four documents this week," Oliver said, removing the folded squares of paper from his inside coat pocket.

"Same as last week," Dryden murmured. He opened the papers one by one and read them carefully, occasionally saying "Hmm, interesting...hmm, very interesting."

"What is it?"

Dryden smiled. "Nothing to worry about."

Oliver gave him a dubious look. "Something's going on. Lisette and I have been doing this for two months, and I can tell that something is going on. Can't you tell me anything?"

Dryden shook his head. "Not really. I will tell you that the Germans have stepped up production recently. That's obvious from all these new orders—big ones, too. You've seen them, that's not a secret to you. The mystery, of course, is why. My guess, they're gearing up for some sort of spring offensive."

"Where?"

Dryden smiled again. "You let us worry about that. Just keep the information coming."

"Alright." Oliver didn't bother hiding his disappointment.

Dryden refolded the papers and put them inside his coat pocket. At the same time he removed two envelopes and handed them to Oliver.

"The usual amount," he said. "Given the amount of information delivered this week, it's not quite enough. Here's a little extra for both of you." He gave Oliver two twenty dollar bills.

Oliver slipped them into his pocket.

"Any other news for me?" Dryden asked.

"Not this week," Oliver said.

"There was another execution last night," Dryden said. "It's not public knowledge. A *résistant* was arrested a couple of days ago after a failed attack on a Wehrmacht colonel outside the Hotel Majestic. He was tried by military tribunal yesterday, and shot by firing squad last night. It's the second one so far this month. Tell your friends to be careful."

"Thank you, I will."

All winter, small groups had ambushed and beaten lone Germans exiting the *Soldatenheimes*—soldiers clubs—scattered around the city. Oliver had little doubt that Serge and Sébastien were among the attackers who prowled the alleys near the *Soldatenheime* at 53 Boulevard Saint Michel, just south of the Place de la Sorbonne; he'd said as much to Dryden.

"How are they holding up this winter?" Dryden asked, sounding genuinely curious.

Perhaps he was; Oliver gave him the benefit of the doubt. "Everyone's cold and hungry, of course. It seems everyone's got short tempers these days, lots of squabbles, you know? I've never looked forward to spring so much in my life."

Dryden chuckled without humor. "Of all the lousy luck, the Germans would restrict coal rations right before the coldest winter on record." He shook his head. "It serves them right, the increase in attacks."

"Thanks for the warning. I'll let you know if I learn anything more," Oliver said. "I've got to get back to the club now. You know, Friday night and all."

Dryden nodded and turned toward Cécile's dressing room.

Saturday, March 8

Sébastien didn't hesitate for a second. The moment Xavier told him what was happening, he agreed to join.

Now he hurried with the young student through the narrow streets of the *Quartier Latin* between university buildings, to the Place de la Sorbonne. A loud, angry mob of students had gathered at the far end, on the corner of the Boulevard Saint Michel and the square, hurling stones at the bookstore on the corner.

A small contingent of outnumbered police gendarmes tried in vain to hold the mob back, but found themselves beaten with boards of wood from dormitory shelves, and other make-shift clubs.

Xavier dove headlong into the fracas, throwing a punch at the side of a gendarme's head, and Sébastien had to admire the eighteen-year-old's courage.

Sébastien picked up a large rock that had been dropped by one of the other students, and hurled it at the plate glass windows of the shop, some ten meters away. Several had already been smashed, and his rock shattered another pane.

Collaborationist writers Henri Jamet and Robert Brasillach had opened a bookstore at number 47 Boulevard Saint Michel, selling leather-bound German translations of French classics to German soldiers—in the very shadow of the most venerable institution of intellectualism in all of France. The students were outraged.

So was Sébastien, ever a loyal alumnus of the Sorbonne.

The gendarme a short distance away had fallen to the ground, and was shielding his face with his arms. The mob ignored him, but also began to trample him.

Sébastien swooped down to snatch his baton.

Whistles screeched from the direction of the Boulevard Saint Michel, and more gendarmes rushed around the corner, wielding their clubs against the students at the edges of the mob.

Sébastien grabbed Xavier by the shirt. "We need barricades," he shouted.

"Come with me." Xavier gathered a couple of his friends, and they ran to the nearest university building.

They sprinted up the stairs to the first floor classrooms, threw open the windows, and grabbed the nearest desks. "Look out below!" they shouted, and began heaving desks out the windows. Others on the ground who were running toward the growing melee stopped to grab the desks and carry them in teams toward the corner.

Sébastien, Xavier and the others went from classroom to classroom, throwing all of the desks and chairs out the windows. After they had denuded four classrooms, Sébastien looked toward the corner and saw with great satisfaction that a sizeable barricade was going up. He looked around the square, and saw desks and chairs flying from windows of other buildings, and he laughed.

"We're missing the fight," Xavier said.

Sébastien smacked the stolen police baton against his palm. "Alright, let's go fight the fascists."

Significant numbers of gendarmes had arrived by the time they made it back to the square, and formed a wall between the barricaded students and the damaged bookstore. As Sébastien and Xavier dashed into the mob, more gendarmes formed a wedge from the boulevard into the square.

"They're trying to encircle us!" Sébastien shouted. "We need to pull this end of the barricade back, or they'll flank us."

They tugged a mass of tangled desks and chairs backwards, but they were so cumbersome that they only budged a short distance, and threatened to topple.

The police moved fast. Almost before he knew what was happening, Sébastien found himself and his friends surrounded by baton-wielding policemen.

Sébastien saw a club flying toward the back of Xavier's head, and without thinking he raised his own stolen baton and blocked the blow.

The force pushed Sébastien's baton into the back of Xavier's head, but not hard. The boy looked up and saw what was happening, and managed to get a short punch into the gendarme's gut.

The gendarme doubled over, and in that second that he was immobilized, Xavier scrambled away. Sébastien struck a quick blow to the gendarme's shoulder, enough to knock him to the ground, and he turned and ran after Xavier.

Xavier was crouching down to pick up a large rock when Sébastien grabbed his shirt collar.

"We need to get out of here, now," he said, staring his young friend in the eyes.

"I am not a coward," Xavier said, and hurled the rock at the line of gendarmes standing in front of the bookstore.

Sébastien tugged at Xavier's collar, turning his shoulder. "No, you are not a coward. Now don't be a fool. Come with me."

"My friends," Xavier started to say, but Sébastien cut him off.

"There is no time. Come with me now, or you will be arrested."

Xavier hesitated only a second, and then ran with Sébastien toward the back of the square, and on to the safety of the narrow streets through the university.

**

Allard was furious.

Paris Prefect of Police Bousquet had screamed at him over the telephone for ten minutes, demanding to know how the prefecture for the northern 5th Arrondissement could allow such a riot to happen in its jurisdiction, and to allow him—Bousquet—to be so grievously embarrassed in front of the Germans.

Allard apologized and groveled beyond the point of humiliation. And still Prefect Bousquet screamed over the telephone line.

"What have you done about it, Allard?"

Allard kept his voice calm. "We arrested seventy-nine rioters, Mr. Prefect. They will be thoroughly interrogated. I have also posted a guard in front of the Rive Gauche bookstore to prevent further incident."

"You will find those responsible, Allard—find them and punish them severely—or you will be relieved of your post."

Allard stiffened. "Understood, Mr. Prefect."

The line clicked off.

Allard set his telephone receiver back in its cradle, hands trembling with rage. His face had flushed, and he paced furiously around his small office with his hands behind his back for several minutes.

When he felt that he'd recovered his wits sufficiently, he threw open his door and shouted down the hall for the shift sergeant.

"Yes Captain?" the sergeant said, hurrying in and giving Allard a quick salute.

"Prefect Bousquet has ordered us to find and punish those criminals responsible for inciting this riot. The men will use every means at our disposal to glean this information from the prisoners. I want no excuses, sergeant."

"Yes, Captain!"

After the sergeant left, Allard thought for a moment, walked to his desk and opened a drawer. He rifled through papers until he found the list of names from Captain Hochman of the Gestapo. Though his investigation in December had uncovered nothing damning, he was convinced they were all agitators.

His eyes rested on one name in particular—Serge Faucheux.

Every instinct told him that this young man, this socialist writer, this scruffy degenerate *bohemian*, was one of the most dangerous figures in the northern 5th Arrondissement.

Allard would not allow him to disrupt the peace, the order, in his prefecture.

He looked back over the list of names, and he knew what to do.

36

Sunday, March 9

Oliver knew something was wrong.

He'd awoken in an amorous mood, so he'd gone upstairs to see Marcel, and was surprised to get no response to his knocks. Then an hour later he knocked on Sébastien's door to see if his friend wanted to go to lunch, and again received no response. He walked to Chez Marius expecting to see at least some of his friends there, but saw none of them.

He sat for a few minutes, and wondered at first if no one was working. Then the owner himself came out to take his order. Oliver asked why no one was working, and the owner complained gruffly that "the queer one, Marcel, he was supposed to work today, but he never came."

Oliver ate alone, trying to fathom some logical reason that his friends weren't around, and why Marcel wouldn't show up for work. He grew worried.

After lunch he walked upstairs and knocked at the apartment Adrienne, Marie-France, and Madeleine shared. He suspected from the first knock that there would be no response—it seemed strangely quiet—and after a few more knocks he was certain that something was amiss.

He ran down the stairs, across the street, and up the five flights to Serge's garret. By now he didn't expect an answer, and got none, but he'd felt the need to check.

333

His mind raced, trying to think of any place he might find them.

He hurried to the corner phone booth, and gave the operator Lisette's phone number.

"Hello?"

He breathed a sigh of relief that she answered.

"Lisette, it's Oliver. Have you heard from Adrienne today? Or Sébastien?"

"No, I have not spoken to them today. Why?"

"I can't find anyone," Oliver said. "When did you last talk to Adrienne?"

"Tuesday, I believe." She paused, and when she spoke next her voice sounded concerned. "Oliver, you think something is wrong? Why?"

"I don't know. But something has happened—I can't find *anyone.*"

There was silence on the line for a few seconds.

"Oliver, what can we do?"

Oliver sighed, and rubbed his temples. "I don't know. I was hoping you had an idea."

The line was silent again for a few seconds. When Lisette spoke, she sounded frightened. "What do you think has happened?"

"I don't know." After a second's pause, he put voice to his concerns. "I'm worried they went on a mission, and something went wrong."

"But *all* of them?" Lisette sounded doubtful.

"I don't know." Oliver was getting tired of saying those words. The uncertainty gnawed at him.

"Do you suppose they've been killed?" her voice was little more than a whisper.

It dawned on him that they were being far too careless speaking this way over the phone lines. The Gestapo only had the capability to listen in on a tiny fraction of local calls, but you never knew when they might be listening.

"Are you free? Can you meet me in twenty minutes at the bar of the Hotel Bristol? That's the one with the big American flag on the Rue du Faubourg Saint-Honoré. It's not far from you."

"Alright," she sounded unsure.

"We'll be able to talk there. See you in twenty minutes."

**

Oliver saw Dryden in the bar, talking with a couple of reporters. At least, Oliver surmised they must be reporters from their outfits and their notepads. He noticed, however, that neither of them was writing anything down.

Dryden made eye contact with him and waved, but turned his attention back to the reporters.

Oliver didn't see Lisette anywhere, so he went to the bar and ordered a gin and tonic. A few minutes later, he saw Dryden shake hands with the two reporters, and wondered if there were any money slipped through those handshakes.

Dryden walked over with a smile. "Hello Oliver. Didn't expect to see you here today."

"I'm meeting someone."

"Mind if I keep you company while you wait?"

"Not at all."

Dryden took a seat on the stool next to Oliver. "Sounds like it was an eventful day in your neck of the woods yesterday."

Oliver had no idea what he meant. "Oh?"

"I see they've kept a good lid on it, then," Dryden said.

"Who?"

"The police. There was a riot yesterday, by the Sorbonne. A new bookstore for the Germans opened at the corner of Boulevard Saint Michel and the Place de la Sorbonne; the students didn't take too well to it, and they threw stones through the windows. When the police came, the students fought back. Put up barricades and everything, so I hear. Just like the Paris of old."

"I hadn't heard," Oliver said. He thought of the Sorbonne students who had come to Sébastien's apartment on New Year's Eve.

"Apparently the police arrested most of the rioters, though some escaped. Then yesterday evening there was a roundup in the area."

That had to be it. "How big was the roundup, Mr. Dryden?"

"I don't really know. Why?"

"I haven't been able to find any of my friends today," Oliver said. "Not Sébastien, Serge, Marcel, Adrienne, Marie-France, or Madeleine. It's strange that I haven't seen any of them all day."

Dryden put his elbow on the bar, and leaned his head back. "Interesting." He had a strange look in his eyes.

"What?"

"I'm not sure why the police would want to round up all of your friends, when the rioters were students," Dryden said. "None of your friends are students."

"Most of them graduated from the Sorbonne," Oliver offered.

Dryden shook his head. "So did tens of thousands of other people in Paris."

"Could this have something to do with Sébastien helping that student after the Armistice Day protest?"

Dryden looked doubtful. "I don't see how it could—unless he did the same thing yesterday. Even so, only he would have been arrested, not your other friends."

"Is there any way to find out?"

"Not without inquiring at the police prefecture—and that would only raise more questions for the police. It's probably best to wait."

Oliver didn't like that answer.

Over Dryden's shoulder, he saw Lisette enter the bar. He raised his hand and waved to her. When she reached him, he made the introductions.

"Ah, so you're Miss Rousseau," Dryden said, shaking Lisette's hand. "I have heard much about you. I will leave you two to your business. Good day." He gave them a nod and left.

"Is that your contact at the American Embassy?" Lisette asked quietly, slipping onto the seat Dryden had vacated.

"Yes, that's him."

"I didn't know we were coming here to meet with him."

"We weren't. I saw him when I arrived, and we talked while I waited for you. He gave me some interesting information."

Lisette looked surprised. "He knows something about our friends?"

Oliver shook his head. "No, not really. But he told me there was a riot yesterday by the Sorbonne. Some students attacked a bookstore for Germans on the Boulevard Saint Michel." He leaned closer and lowered his voice. "Mr. Dryden said the police rounded up a lot of people last night. I think our friends might have been caught in the round up."

Lisette gave him an incredulous look. "*All* of them? That hardly seems possible."

"Do you have a better explanation?"

She looked at him for a few seconds, then shook her head.

"The trouble is, we don't have any way to find out for certain," Oliver said. "Mr. Dryden said we have to just wait."

She looked away into the distance for several seconds. Then she asked without looking at him, "None of them know about my role, do they?"

"No, of course not. They have no idea."

She looked back at him. "Are you in any danger, Oliver? They know that you're working with someone at the American Embassy."

Oliver considered that. "I don't see how the police can arrest me for that. As far as our friends know, I haven't done anything illegal."

"You and I have," she whispered.

"But our friends don't know anything about that."

"That's good." She picked up her purse and stood, kissing him on the cheek. "I will see you next week."

"You don't want to stay for a drink?"

She shook her head. "Not today."

He watched her walk away, concerned about the sad look in her eyes.

**

Adrienne was furious. She knew her temper would get her in trouble, but she couldn't help herself.

"You have no right to keep me here!" she shouted, smacking her palm on the table in the interrogation room, and gave Captain Allard a challenging stare. "You have not charged me with any crime, so you must let me go."

"I'm afraid not, Miss Charbonneau," Allard said.

"This is an outrage!"

Allard's eyes narrowed. "The outrage, Miss Charbonneau, is the willful disruption of order and destruction of private property that hooligans perpetrated on the Rive Gauche bookstore yesterday. Those hooligans were acting under someone's direction, and I intend to find out whose."

"I have told you, I was not involved in that. I know nothing. How many times do I have to tell you?"

Allard stared at her across the table, his hands folded in front of him. "I believe that you were not involved. What I don't believe is that you know nothing about it."

"I'm telling the truth."

Allard took a deep breath. "Please, Miss Charbonneau—we both know that you have dedicated agitators among your friends, and yet you pretend to be ignorant. We have them all in our custody, it is only a matter of time before we learn the full story. Things will go much better for you if you are the one to tell us."

"What if I can't tell you anything?" Adrienne leaned back in the chair, raised her chin and stared at Allard defiantly.

"Then I'm afraid I will be unable to let you go." Allard stood and walked to the door.

"You have already held me here for more than twenty-four hours!" Adrienne shouted. "This could have *never* happened in the old France."

Allard turned to face her from the doorway. "The French State is no longer encumbered with the liberal technicalities that crippled order and justice during the Republic. You will be held until you cooperate."

He left the room, leaving her to scream at the closed door. "Tyrant!"

**

"How can none of them have cracked?" Allard pounded his fist on his desk. "Have you leaned on them hard enough? Have you kept them isolated? Hungry? Thirsty?"

"Yes, Captain," the sergeant said. "They all maintain that they know nothing."

Allard rubbed his forehead. He had a headache. He'd wanted to be home for dinner, and these bohemians had ruined that.

He'd participated personally in their arrests yesterday afternoon, and ordered them held apart from one another overnight. Then he came into work today—sometimes it was necessary for a police captain to work on Sundays—and took part in at least one interrogation of each of them. He'd been there all day.

And yet he still had nothing to show for it.

"Why are they still stonewalling me?" he muttered.

The sergeant shifted his feet. "Captain, I believe them."

Allard dropped his hand from his forehead and glared at him.

The sergeant shifted his feet even more. "We have done everything you suggested, and none of them have changed their stories, Captain. I think they are telling the truth."

Allard secretly felt the same way about most of them—except for that Serge Faucheux; and also Sébastien Bonnet—Allard had suspected from the beginning of his interrogation that Mr. Bonnet knew something he wasn't saying. He hardly spoke at all.

"Take me to Serge Faucheux."

A few moments later he sat across from Serge, whose face was black and purple from the multiple beatings Allard had ordered.

"We find ourselves in the same place again, Mr. Faucheux. Why won't you cooperate?"

"I've answered all of your questions," Serge mumbled between swollen and cracked lips.

"But you have not told us what we want to hear, have you?" Allard stood up and walked behind Serge. He put his hands on the table on either side of his captive, and leaned close to his ear. "You know that we have your friends in custody also. We won't release any of them until you tell me what I want to know. Think about them, Mr. Faucheux."

Serge's head drooped. "What do you want to hear?" he mumbled.

"How you and your accomplices organized this riot."

"I've told you, I didn't know anything about it until you came to my door yesterday."

Allard smacked him hard across the back of the head. "Stop lying! You know that I have the power to send you to Drancy, don't you?"

Allard hoped the name of the feared prison camp would affect more cooperation.

Serge lifted his head. "I have the right as a French citizen to a trial by a jury of my peers. You cannot send me to Drancy without trial."

Allard chuckled. "Oh, but yes, I can. The National Assembly voted emergency powers to the Prime Minister last summer. There is no constitution, Mr. Faucheux. There are no jury trials. And I can lock you up in Drancy on suspicion of inciting violence. How would you like to spend three months laboring at Drancy, Mr. Faucheux?"

"You are a traitor to France," Serge said.

Allard's face contorted in rage, and he threw Serge's head downward into the desk. Blood splattered on the walls from Serge's newly-broken nose.

As Serge's head came back up, Allard put his face inches away. "The traitors to France are those who weakened her with excessive 'liberties,'" he hissed. "I will not allow the likes of you to take us backward."

Allard marched from the room, and motioned the sergeant to follow him. "Release the women—Miss Charbonneau, Miss Lavelle, and Miss Racicot. Keep leaning on Mr. Bonnet and Mr. Thibault."

"What about Serge Faucheux?"

"I am sending him to Drancy."

**

Oliver sat at Chez Marius all evening, watching the street. It was after eight o'clock when he saw Adrienne, Marie-France, and Madeleine pass by, and he ran to the door and called to them.

"I've been worried," he said. "Where have you been?"

Adrienne's lips pursed tightly. "The police held us for more than a day," she said, the words spitting forth like venom. "They finally let us go a few minutes ago."

"What about Sébastien? And Marcel? And Serge?"

The girls shook their heads. "We have no idea," Marie-France said.

"We were all arrested at the same time yesterday, and taken in together" Adrienne said. "But from the start they kept us separate. I did not see anyone until they released the three of us just a bit ago."

"I haven't seen any of them," Oliver said. "They must still be with the police." He looked at the girls' haggard faces. "Have you eaten?"

They shook their heads, and he motioned them inside the bistro. He ordered sausage and cheese for everyone.

The girls sat and ate, and no one said anything. After a while they stood, thanked him for the food, and said they needed to go home and rest.

Oliver stayed at the table alone. He ordered another carafe of wine.

Marcel shuffled past an hour later, limping.

Oliver rushed out to him. "Marcel, are you alright?"

Marcel shook his head, almost imperceptibly. He didn't say anything.

"Come, let me get you something to eat."

"No." Marcel didn't look at Oliver. "I want to go home."

"Wait, let me take you." Oliver hurried back to his table, downed the last of the wine in his glass, and laid out a stack of franc notes and ration coupons. He came back to Marcel and took his hand. "Come on, I'll take you to my place."

Marcel started to protest, but Oliver insisted.

The interior of Oliver's apartment was freezing, and he hurried to turn on every lamp and light every candle. Like most Parisians, he hoarded candles that winter for the miniscule amount of heat their flames emitted.

He sat Marcel on his couch, then went to the kitchen and filled his kettle and set it on the stove to heat. While he waited on the water, he brought Marcel a half baguette from his cabinet and a glass of red wine. "What happened?"

Marcel shrugged. "They asked lots of questions. I had no answers. They didn't like that."

"What did they do to you?"

Marcel didn't answer.

The kettle began to whistle, and Oliver mixed a small amount of hot water with cold from the tap in his washbowl. He brought the lukewarm water and a wash cloth.

"Take your shirt off."

Marcel took off his shirt without a word.

Oliver had expected to see cuts and bruises all over him, but there were none. He ran his hands over Marcel's back, but felt nothing out of place.

"Where are you hurt?" he asked.

Marcel didn't say anything. After a few seconds he stood, unfastened his belt, and dropped his pants and underwear. His buttocks and upper thighs were black with bruises.

"Why?" Oliver asked.

Marcel gave him a half-hearted shrug.

Beat the queer on the ass, Oliver suspected. "Lay on your stomach."

Marcel stretched out on the couch, and Oliver put his washcloth into the rapidly cooling water. He laid it on his friend's bruised back side and left it there, thankful he wasn't seeing any cuts.

He went into the bedroom and brought out his towel, and carefully dried Marcel off. "You're staying here tonight. I'll take care of you."

Marcel turned over and sat up, grimacing as he did. "Why?"

Oliver was taken aback by the question. "Why? What do you mean?"

"Why do you want to take care of me?" Marcel asked. When Oliver didn't answer right away, he continued, "You don't want me most of the time. Why would you want to take care of me now?"

"Marcel..." Oliver started, but stopped, not sure what to say.

"Every week you go to see a married woman, when I am right upstairs," Marcel said. "Yes, I know about her. She only makes time for you when her husband isn't around. I would always make time for you."

Oliver became acutely aware that Marcel was sitting there naked, and he turned slightly away without thinking.

Marcel noticed; his eyes cast down at Oliver's knees as they shifted.

"Marcel, you know I'm not like that," Oliver said.

"But you come to see me from time to time, to use me in that way. And you can say you are not like that?"

"You don't understand," Oliver said. He struggled with how to explain it. "You know I enjoy doing that. Of course I do. But it's just a little fun, not my normal thing. I'm not like you—I'd rather make love to a woman."

Marcel's eyes began to well up. He looked away.

Marcel never showed emotion. Oliver didn't know how to react to this. He wondered how long Marcel had felt this way, and how he'd failed to see it.

"Marcel?"

Marcel looked back at him, and Oliver saw the tracks of tears on his cheeks.

"It is just a little fun to you, then?"

"Yes," Oliver said, as if it were obvious. "For you as well."

Marcel shook his head. "No, not for me. Perhaps at first that is all it was, but when you kept coming to see me, I thought perhaps…" his voice trailed off, and his eyes welled up again. He looked away, and Oliver heard him sniff.

Oliver looked at his hands, and felt his stomach drop. "Marcel, I had no idea. I thought—well, I mean—I know you've gone to bed with others besides me."

"Not in a long time," Marcel said, his voice quiet.

"I didn't realize that."

They sat in silence for several minutes.

"I think you are afraid," Marcel said, turning back to face Oliver. His brown eyes stared at Oliver with an intensity he had rarely seen.

"Afraid?"

"Yes, afraid. You are afraid of many things. You don't come to see me too often because you are afraid people will think you are like me. You keep me at a distance because you're afraid you'll start to care for me, and that your heart will be broken again. That is why you go to see your married woman—you can keep it part-time, casual, and that way you know she won't break your heart."

Oliver stiffened. "You don't know me very well."

"Yes, I do. I have watched you for three years, I see how you hide what you don't want people to see. I know you."

"Do you? Have we ever had a long conversation, Marcel, just you and me? No, we haven't. You don't talk much."

"No. But I listen."

Oliver didn't have an argument for that. "So what do you want from me?"

Marcel didn't answer.

"I think you're the one who is afraid," Oliver said. "You've known me for almost three years, you've watched me and listened to me, and yet you've never told me any of this before. Why?"

Marcel shrugged. "It was pointless while you were with Lisette. After you broke up, I made my intentions known to you."

"But you let me think you felt the same way I did."

Marcel's eyes filled with sadness. "I hoped you would notice."

Oliver suddenly wondered if anyone else had noticed. "Does anyone know how you feel?"

Marcel nodded. "Everyone does."

Oliver gave him a skeptical look. "How do you know *everyone* does?"

"I know."

Oliver stiffened again. "In other words, I'm the only one who's oblivious, is that it?"

Marcel didn't answer.

Oliver sighed. He knew it was true. He *had* been oblivious. Now that he knew, it seemed obvious in hindsight. He thought he'd learned to be so observant, and yet he had missed one of the most obvious things, right in front of his face. Why was that?

He looked at Marcel now, saw the hurt and sadness in his eyes, and it broke his heart. He reached out and rubbed Marcel's back. "What now?"

Marcel turned his back toward Oliver, and lay back against his chest. He took Oliver's arms and placed them around himself. He turned his head to rest his cheek against Oliver's throat.

Oliver kissed Marcel's forehead, and hugged the boy tight to him. "What is it that you want?"

"I want to be with you. We could be together."

"How is that possible?"

Marcel turned his face up to look at Oliver. "Anything is possible, if you want it badly enough. You have just been looking in the wrong places." He placed his lips gently against Oliver's and held them there.

Oliver couldn't understand all of the feelings sweeping through him—affection, fear, longing—but he knew that kissing Marcel felt like the right thing to do. He ignored everything else.

The thought crossed his mind that hopeless love affairs might be his lot in life, but he pushed it away and focused on what he was doing.

He would worry about that some other time.

348

37

Sébastien was released moments before eleven o'clock. He hurried home, reaching his building as the police sirens announced curfew. He hobbled up the stairs, his legs stiff from thirty hours sitting alone in a small interrogation room. He wondered who among his friends had also been released, but first he needed to get something to eat.

He walked into his apartment, stopped. His belongings were strewn everywhere. He walked into the bedroom; all of the drawers were open, and their contents scattered.

He sighed. He knew there was nothing for the police to find. Their search had been pointless, but he was left to clean it up.

It could wait. He walked to the kitchen and went straight for the ice box. He ate some bread and cheese, taking huge bites and washing it down with gulps of red wine from the bottle.

Once he'd finished eating, he washed and changed shirts. Then he crossed the hall and knocked on Oliver's door. There was no answer. He saw no light under the door, which was unusual at this hour— Oliver was almost always still awake. He needed to know if anyone else had been released, so he knocked a second time.

This time he heard the sound of footsteps on the floor. "Who is it?" Oliver's voice asked.

"Sébastien. Open the door."

Oliver opened the door less than half-way and poked his head out. He wore his bathrobe. "Sébastien! Did they just let you go?"

Sébastien nodded. "Yes. Have you seen any of the others? Serge? Adrienne?"

"I saw the girls around eight o'clock, all three of them," Oliver said. "I saw Marcel about an hour later. I haven't seen Serge."

"You have not been watching for him?"

"Not since shortly after nine."

"Get dressed, come with me to his place."

Oliver looked uncertain. "I can't. I'm—um—I'm not alone."

Sébastien stared at him, annoyed. "You said you wanted to help us, Oliver—so help. Get dressed and come with me. I'll wait by the stairs."

Oliver appeared a few minutes later, fully dressed and wearing his coat and scarf. "Alright, let's go."

"I apologize for interrupting your visit," Sébastien said as they started down the stairs.

"It's alright. We had a good talk earlier, and we'd finished what we were doing."

Sébastien opened the door and poked his head out, looking up and down the street several times before he was convinced the street was empty. He motioned for Oliver to follow him, and dashed across to Serge's building.

They climbed to the top floor, and walked down the hall to Serge's door. Sébastien produced a key from his pocket and unlocked it.

The little garret was dark. Sébastien walked to the middle of the room, nearly tripping over something on the floor, and pulled the chord of the naked light bulb in the center of the ceiling.

The room had been ransacked. Clothes and papers covered the floor, the desk, and the narrow bed.

"What happened here?" Oliver asked, staring at the mess, his mouth hanging open.

"The police. They were looking for evidence that Serge was involved in the riot at the Sorbonne yesterday. He wasn't."

Oliver's eyes widened. "Would they have found anything incriminating?"

Sébastien shook his head. "There was only one thing, and they would not be able to find it." He made his way to the chimney in the corner of the room, stepping carefully over piles of clothes and papers.

The bed was pushed against the side of the chimney. Sébastien kneeled in the corner, reached his hand into the narrow space under the bed, and removed a loose brick. Then he reached his fingers into the open space it had left, and grasped the paper inside.

He pulled out the folded square of paper, and took it back to the center of the room, under the light bulb. He opened it, and there were two pieces of paper folded together.

*

Looking over Sébastien's shoulder, Oliver saw Serge's picture on both of them, but the names and details were different—false identity papers.

Sébastien refolded them and shoved them into his coat pocket. He looked at Oliver and nodded toward the door. "Come on." He turned out the light and locked the door.

"Why did you want me to come with you?" Oliver whispered as they walked back down the hall.

"In case Serge was there," Sébastien said quietly, starting down the stairs. "Or in case we saw the police watching the building."

Oliver wondered if Sébastien would have sent him across if the police were watching. It wasn't yet midnight.

They continued in silence to the front door, where Sébastien again looked up and down the street several times before trusting that there was no one watching. They ran back to their own building.

Only when they reached their floor did Oliver speak. "Why did you take those?"

"Serge may need them."

"Why?"

Sébastien looked up and down the hall, then motioned for Oliver to join him inside his apartment.

Oliver looked around at the mess. "Yours too?"

"Yes. The police were very thorough."

"Was there anything they might have found here?"

"No, nothing." Sébastien motioned for Oliver to come close, and spoke just above a whisper. "Serge may need false papers because the police suspect him of something. He has not been released, but the rest of us have—and I was the only one involved in the riot yesterday, not Serge. Remember how the police beat him several months ago? They suspect him, and they will not leave him alone."

Oliver looked confused. "So why not leave those for him at his garret?"

"Because he may not go there, if the police are watching him. He may need to flee right away, and if so, we have arranged a rendezvous."

Oliver's face was grim. "When will you know to go there?"

"I'll go tomorrow at noon. Then again at six. I'll go back until I see him." He patted Oliver on the shoulder. "Don't worry. We will take care of him when the time comes. Now go back to Marcel."

Oliver's eyes widened in surprise, and Sébastien chuckled. "Good night, my friend."

38

Monday, March 17

Cécile strutted down the Avenue Foch with her head high, wearing her best dress and fur wrap, elbow-length white gloves, her most stylish hat with a feather in the side, and four-inch heels that clicked on the sidewalk.

If she had to appear before the Gestapo, she was going to make a grand entrance.

The notice had been slipped under her dressing room door on Saturday night, and it ordered her—in both German and French—to appear at Gestapo headquarters at 43 Avenue Foch in the 16th Arrondissement on Monday at nine AM. No reason was given.

After a moment of panic, she'd placed a call to Frank Dryden at his suite in the Hotel Bristol. He told her to meet him in the hotel bar. She arrived at midnight, and Frank was waiting for her with a glass of Cointreau. He took her elbow and guided her to a corner table.

After reading and rereading the notice, Frank set it aside and sighed. "Well, I don't think there's anything that can be done to get you out of it. You'll have to go."

"But what should I say?"

He put his hand on hers. "As little as possible, my dear. I really don't think they have much on you, or they would have come for you themselves."

She had relaxed a little bit then. "Then, what could it be?"

He shrugged. "They've probably received a tip from someone that you've been spending a lot of time with me. If so, don't deny it—that will only make them more aggressive." He put a slight emphasis on that last word, and she caught his meaning. "But say as little as possible. Make it seem perfectly natural—we met at one of your performances a couple of years ago, and we became lovers. That much is true, after all."

"And if they ask me about your work?"

"I'm some sort of diplomat, but that's all you know. We never talk about work."

She nodded and took a drink of the Cointreau.

He smiled and patted her hand. "Don't worry, darling. You are a great performer, I know you'll put on a premier performance on Monday. Act like you have nothing to hide, and then say almost nothing. That's very Parisian, is it not?"

She had to smile at his teasing. "Yes, it is."

And so this morning she had 'dressed to the nines' as Frank always said—the American expression mystified her—and she took the Metro to the Place de l'Étoile. Ascending into the daylight, she took a good look at the massive Arc de Triumph, and took some strength from it.

It was two and a half blocks down the grand tree-lined Avenue Foch, with its wide sidewalks bordered by a central park-like esplanade. She took a walkway across the green space a half-block up from number 43, and walked the remainder of the way on the small sidewalk in front of the buildings.

She hardly noticed the grand facades of the magnificent 18th century mansions, only counting down the addresses until she stood in front of number 43. It was a few minutes before nine o'clock. She looked up at the six-story limestone façade, took a deep breath, and marched through the gate to the front door.

She approached the reception desk, with a pretty young brunette sitting behind it in a dark dress, and wondered if the Gestapo employed French girls like all of the other Occupation ministries, or if they only trusted Germans.

She got her answer soon enough. She gave her name to the receptionist, who showed no signs of recognition and asked her in a German accent to have a seat and wait.

Cécile sat for more than forty minutes, watching the minute hand on the wall clock. Occasionally men in black suits entered the front, conversing in German. She pretended not to understand them. They showed badges to the receptionist, who nodded them through.

Finally a young man came down the stairs and approached her. He clicked his heels and nodded crisply in a very Prussian way, and asked her in good French to come with him.

She followed him up two flights of stairs to the second floor, then down the hall to an office door. He stood aside and motioned her in.

The name on the glass was *Hauptsturmfuhrer Auguste Hochman*.

Hauptsturmfuhrer—Head Storm Leader. A silly grandiose Nazi title. Even so, a shiver ran down her spine.

The young man who brought her up clicked his heels and nodded again, then closed the door behind her.

The man on the other side of the desk was shorter than she, round in the middle, balding with his thin hair slicked back. He wore a crisp black suit and white collared shirt with a narrow black necktie.

He greeted her in German. "Miss Fournier, I am Captain Hochman of the Gestapo. Please take a seat."

She feigned incomprehension, giving him a questioning look and a slight shrug. "Pardon?" she said in French.

Captain Hochman chuckled. "Let us not pretend that you do not understand German, Miss Fournier," he said in French. Then he switched back to German. "We are not fools, Miss. We know that your mother was from Alsace, and that you speak German fluently. Let us be polite and respectful to one another, and speak only the truth, yes?"

Her face felt tight in spite of her best efforts to look unperturbed. She had not expected that. She nodded and replied in crisp German. "Yes, my mother is Alsatian, and I speak German." She took a seat in the chair in front of Hochman's desk.

Hochman smiled, a cold smile that didn't reach his eyes. "Thank you for your honesty, Miss Fournier." He retook his seat.

"Why am I here, Captain?"

"We have some questions for you, Miss. We are most curious about you. Why, for example, have you hidden your fluency in our language? You have met a great many German officers and soldiers at your performances, and yet you always speak to them in French, and pretend not to understand German. Why is that?"

A loaded question. How best to answer?

It took only a second to settle on Parisian arrogance. She raised her chin, allowing a touch of defiance to come into her voice. "I prefer to speak in my mother tongue. I am *Parisienne*, Captain, and my father was Parisian, as were his parents. German is my second language."

Hochman's smile hardened. "I am not asking your preferences, Miss. I am asking why you pretend *not* to speak German to our officers, some of whom do not speak French as fluently as you speak our language."

"You are the ones in my country, Captain, not the other way around." Her heart pounded, and she hoped she wasn't overplaying the Parisian attitude.

Hochman's fake smile vanished. "So you are saying that if we sent you to Germany, then you would speak German? Is that it, Miss Fournier?"

She felt her insides go cold. "That would be good manners, yes." She hid the trembling of her hands by folding them in her lap, under the lip of Hochman's desk.

The fake smile returned to Hochman's lips. "Indeed. But we'll come back to that subject. First, I want to ask about your relationship with an American diplomat named Frank Dryden."

She widened her eyes in feigned surprise. "Frank? Yes?"

"We have been told that you and Mr. Dryden are, shall we say, friends." Hochman's smile turned leering.

She allowed the corners of her mouth to turn up in fake amusement. "Yes, you could say that we are friends."

"We have received a tip that you are more than friends, Miss Fournier."

"Oh, from whom?"

Hochman chuckled. "Denunciations to the Gestapo are anonymous, Miss—as you well know. Now, tell me about your relationship with Mr. Dryden."

She shrugged, tried her best to appear relaxed. "We met a couple of years ago. He came to one of my performances, and he approached me at the bar during intermission. We chatted, and I found him charming; and very handsome."

Hochman chuckled again. "Of course. Go on."

She shrugged again. "There is not much more to tell. He asked me to dinner, we had a lovely time, and then he took me to bed." Ordinarily a Parisian would be more modest about that subject, but she counted on the Gestapo officer expecting her to be frank.

"You are aware, of course, that Mr. Dryden works at the American embassy."

It wasn't a question. Cécile nodded. "Yes."

"What do you know of the work that Mr. Dryden does there?"

Cécile released a short puff of air. "I have no idea. I know that he is some sort of diplomat, but I really don't know more than that."

"How can that be, Miss Fournier? You have been lovers for two years."

"We don't talk about our jobs, Captain."

Hochman's stiff smile and narrowed eyes told her that he didn't believe that. "How often do you see Mr. Dryden?"

"A couple of times a week, usually."

"And he spends the night with you, at your apartment?"

"Sometimes."

"Do you ever stay with him, at the Hotel Bristol?"

She shrugged. "Rarely."

"But you have, then?"

"Yes, once or twice."

Hochman leaned back in his chair, and folded his hands across his belly. "Do you talk to the other Americans there?"

"Of course."

"What do you talk about?"

"Many things—music, films, books, the weather. Americans love to talk about the weather."

"And do you ever discuss world events? International relations?"

She puffed out air between pursed lips, that typical French response to an impossibly vague question. "I suppose so, on rare occasions."

"Such as?"

"When the Wehrmacht invaded Czechoslovakia, for example," she said. "*Everyone* was talking about that, of course. The Americans were not immune to the topic."

Hochman looked impatient. He sat up and leaned forward across his desk. "Let's talk about what happened after we marched into Paris last June. Did you stay in the city, Miss Fournier?"

"Yes, I did."

"And did you meet with Mr. Dryden during that time?"

She became wary, and answered slowly. "No—he was far too busy. But we spoke on the phone once. He told me not to leave the city, because of what was happening to the refugees on the road south. I agreed to stay."

The look of irritation that crossed Hochman's face at the reference to the dive bombing and strafing of refugees brought her a bit of satisfaction.

His voice grew impatient, irritated. "And after the Occupation began, when did you first see Mr. Dryden?"

"A few days later."

"And what did he say about the events that had taken place?"

She shrugged. "Very little. *No one* spoke of it, Captain."

"Have you discussed it with him since then?"

"Not really. There are much more pleasant topics of conversation."

Hochman turned his attention to a file on his desk. He opened it and perused its contents.

"We know that you have many relatives in Alsace, Miss Fournier," he said, not looking up from the file. "And we know also that you and your family visited them on at least two occasions when you were a child. We have customs records from August 1909 and July 1912, attesting that you and your family crossed the border into the German Reich at Saales, and listed your destination as Riquewihr in Alsace."

Cécile nodded. "Yes, that is correct."

Hochman looked up and stared at her, his eyes cold. "Of course, after the French Army marched into Alsace in November 1918, we no longer have official records of who crossed the Alsatian frontier from France."

She gave him a haughty smile. "That's because, after 1919, Alsace *was* France again. There was no border to cross."

Hochman scowled. "That situation has been rectified, Miss. Alsace-Lorraine has been brought home to the Reich."

Cécile leaned back, cocked her head, and looked at Hochman from the sides of her eyes. "Is your intention to engage me in a political argument, Captain? I hardly see the point of that."

Hochman ignored her. "When was the last time you saw your Alsatian cousins, Miss Fournier?"

She puffed out her breath again, and looked up in thought. "About four years ago, I believe. My cousin Eva came to Paris with her family, and my parents and I met them for dinner one night."

"What language did you speak?"

"French, of course."

"When was the last time you saw them in Alsace?"

"That would have been 1920, Captain. I was nineteen years old, and it was the last summer vacation I took with my parents."

Hochman closed the file, folded his hands over it, and gave her a menacing smile. "Then you are overdue for a visit, Miss. I hope your passport is in good order."

She nodded, but stayed silent.

"Good. We are sending you to Riquewihr. A member of my staff will accompany you as far as the border. I will write your *Ausweis*, there will be no trouble with the border guard. Your cooperation is expected." He emphasized that last word.

Cécile felt her heart drop into the pit of her stomach.

Hochman seemed to enjoy her discomfort. His humorless grin widened.

"Now, this is what we want you to do."

39

Dryden's face went white when she told him.

"Shit!"

She knew he was upset; he rarely cursed in English. She could only imagine how it would look in the newsreels—the popular Paris *chanteuse* Cécile Fournier singing an Alsatian song at a rally of the province's Hitler Youth troops; a rally at which she would pin an award on the uniform of her cousin's son.

"What should I do?"

"We can't let you go to Alsace, that's certain." Dryden's face was drawn. "Forget the PR implications—the moment they get you inside their Reich, they probably won't let you leave."

Cécile sucked in her breath, stunned. "Why would they do that?"

Dryden was quiet for a moment. "Did they say when they received the denunciation?"

"No."

He pondered another moment. "They've probably known about our arrangement for some time now, or at least suspected. They'll want you far away from me. They obviously had time to look into your past, and they might have even dug up something about your work for French Intelligence. The Gestapo could have talked to someone who knew some little thing about your involvement—some intelligence officer turned collaborator or double-agent."

He must have seen the terrified look on her face, for he softened his expression and put his hands on her shoulders. "I'm sure the records were all burned before the French government left Paris. The British Embassy burned absolutely everything, and I'm sure the French were as thorough. You remember all of that black smoke billowing over the Champs Elysee for two days, don't you? Besides, if they had any hard evidence they would have arrested you."

"If they've suspected for a while, then why are they doing this now?"

"Because they're angry that the United States Congress repealed our Neutrality Act last week," Dryden said. "Congress authorized President Roosevelt to lend or lease war materiel to the British and Chinese if he determines that it's in the interest of national security. The Germans now see us as a hostile country, and our informants as fair game."

She grabbed his hand and held it tightly. "Frank, I'm scared."

He squeezed her hand, brought it up to his lips and kissed it. "I know, darling. I'll think of some way to get you out of this."

"If I could get to the Unoccupied Zone," she suggested. "I'm sure you know someone who could get me over the Line of Demarcation. Or maybe to Switzerland." She knew he had clandestine connections, and surely someone could help.

He shook his head. "I already thought about that, my darling. They'll be watching you. I'm sure they know you're here now, talking with me. The moment you make a move to flee, they'll arrest you."

She knew he was right, and it terrified her.

He looked up in thought, and his expression gradually changed—his eyebrows rose and his eyes widened, and his mouth opened slightly as the corners turned up. He wagged a finger in the air for a few seconds in growing excitement, and then suddenly snapped his fingers.

His excitement was contagious, and she felt a tingle run up her spine. "What is it?"

His face lit up with a full grin, he took hold of both of her hands, and looked directly in her eyes. "Marry me."

**

"This is unorthodox," *Chargé d'affaires* Robert Murphy told Dryden a short while later.

"Yes, it is, sir. But I have verified that you have the legal authority to marry U.S. citizens in France—as long as we qualify under French law to be married."

"And do you?"

Dryden grinned. "We will shortly. It took a fair amount of my petty cash for this month, but the mayor of the 18th Arrondissement—where Cécile lives—is willing to forge the date on the wedding banns to the 7th. That will fulfill the ten-day requirement under French law. He said he is a fan of Miss Fournier's, and he will swear an oath that he posted those wedding banns on the 7th."

"Just because he tells you he'll swear an oath, doesn't mean that his fortitude will hold up under Gestapo interrogation. You're as aware as I am of their reputation."

"We can get around that," Dryden said. "You can send me to Vichy for the week. I have things I can follow up on there, anyway. I'll take my new wife with me. My diplomatic passport plus the signed marriage license will extend my diplomatic immunity to her, and they will be powerless to detain her or prevent her from crossing the Line of Demarcation."

"And then?"

"I'll return to Paris alone at the end of the week."

Murphy looked Dryden hard in the eyes. "This could cause friction with the Occupation authority. Is her safety worth that to the U.S. Government?"

Dryden nodded his head firmly. "Absolutely. We cannot let the Germans learn all of the information that she's provided me. There are many things we know because of the intelligence she provided, things that the Germans don't know that we know. And with the recent chilling of relations…"

Murphy nodded. "You think that's what prompted the timing of their inquiry, don't you?"

"Yes, sir."

"I do, too." Murphy stood and shook Dryden's hand. "Then I guess congratulations are in order."

"Thank you, sir."

"How soon will you and your bride be ready?"

"In an hour. I just need to round up a couple of witnesses."

**

Oliver always felt apprehensive whenever he received a message from Mr. Dryden sent by embassy courier, and it instructed him to come immediately. This time he was instructed to go to the embassy, dressed in his best suit. He wondered whom he would be meeting.

Dryden beamed when Oliver entered his office, and Oliver thought that might have been the first time he had seen a truly genuine smile on the man.

Dryden shook his hand and clapped him on the shoulder at the same time. "Oliver! Thank you so much for coming. I can't tell you how much I appreciate this."

"Sure," Oliver said. "What's this about?"

"I'm getting married," Dryden said, almost laughing. "I need a witness, and I thought you might be available for the job. I'm marrying Cécile Fournier."

Oliver grinned. "Congratulations, Mr. Dryden." He shook Dryden's hand again. "But why me?"

"Because I like you, Oliver. And Cécile likes you." He paused and shrugged. "And besides, it will look less suspicious if the witnesses aren't embassy employees."

"Suspicious?"

Dryden chuckled. "Let's just say Cécile needs to get out of the Occupied Zone in a hurry."

Oliver felt a shiver go up his spine. "Should I be worried?"

Dryden shook his head and patted him on the shoulder. "Not at all, Oliver. The Germans have no reason to suspect you of anything."

Oliver wasn't convinced. "But will they start suspecting me when they see my signature on your marriage license?"

Dryden gave him a reassuring smile and squeezed his shoulder. "Relax, my good man. You're an American citizen. The Germans have no desire to provoke an international incident by arresting an American citizen without solid proof. Suspicion is enough to arrest a French citizen, but not an American."

Oliver felt only slightly reassured. "And if they do find proof?"

"Relax! We'll know if they start poking around. One thing we've learned in the last nine months is that the Gestapo are far from subtle. And if worse comes to worst, we'll get you out of the Occupied Zone."

Oliver forced a smile. "Alright."

The ceremony began twenty minutes later. Cécile wore an ivory dress with a corsage of lilies. The other witness was someone Oliver had never seen before, a short, dark-haired Frenchman who spoke English; Oliver wondered if he was another of Mr. Dryden's informants. He wondered if Mr. Dryden had any actual friends in Paris. *Probably not.*

A red-haired man in a dark suit officiated. The ceremony only took five minutes, and then the officiant pronounced them husband and wife, and they kissed.

The whole thing had a whirlwind air to Oliver.

After congratulatory handshakes all around, Dryden took Oliver by the arm and told him he wanted to introduce him to someone important. He led him to the officiant.

"Oliver Carmichael, this is Mr. Robert Murphy—formerly First Secretary of the U.S. Embassy in Paris, but since July the acting *chargé d'affaires* of the embassy, since the ambassador is in residence in Vichy."

Murphy gave Oliver a firm handshake. "It's a pleasure to meet you, Mr. Carmichael. I'm familiar with your work for Mr. Dryden. We could use more men like you doing what you do."

Oliver was taken aback. "Thank you, sir."

Murphy nodded to acknowledge the thanks, then turned and walked away without another word.

"He's an important man to know, Oliver," Dryden whispered. "If things continue to escalate—well, let's just say I'm certain you'll encounter Mr. Murphy again." Dryden patted Oliver's shoulder and walked toward his bride.

Not for the first time, Oliver wondered how involved he had become.

40

Tuesday, March 18

Sébastien had studied medieval French literature under Professor Trusnik four years ago, and he was surprised that the bearded Russian recognized him.

"I am a friend of Serge Faucheux," Sébastien said after re-introducing himself.

Trusnik smiled. "Ah yes, Serge Faucheux took many of my classes. I remember him well. He's a talented writer, if I recall."

"Serge told me to come see you if he ever disappeared."

"Did he?" Trusnik's expression didn't change.

"Yes. He told me to bring you these," Sébastien removed the false identity papers from his pocket, and unfolded them on Trusnik's desk.

Trusnik picked up the papers and scrutinized them for a moment, his expression deadly serious. "These are very good," he said at length. He set them down and regarded Sébastien over the rim of his reading glasses. "How long ago did he disappear?"

"One week. We were arrested a few hours after the riot at the Rive Gauche bookstore, several friends with us. All of us were released the next evening, except for Serge. He has not been seen since. An American friend went to the police a few days ago, but they won't say anything."

Trusnik took the false identities and put them in a drawer. "Leave everything to me."

Sébastien knew better than to ask questions.

Sunday, April 6

On the morning when the German Army invaded Yugoslavia and Greece, and the world was distracted, Serge walked out through the gates of the American Hospital of Paris, in the suburb of Neuilly. He was clean-shaven, wore a clean white shirt, brown slacks and sport coat, pressed and in good condition, and a brown fedora.

Ten minutes later, a Mr. Michel Lagrange passed through the German checkpoint at the Paris city limit, with identity papers indicating that he was an editor for Le Figaro.

He made his way across the city on foot, not taking the Metro, crossed the Seine and walked along the Boulevard Saint Germain into the 5th Arrondissement. He reached number 13 Rue de Lagrange and knocked on the door of the concierge.

Gireaux, the concierge, took him to the cellar, to a back room with a cot all made up.

"Sébastien brought your things a week ago," Gireaux said, nodding toward three boxes in the corner. "You know the back exit, from the cellar into the alley."

"Yes, I remember."

"Do be careful, Mr. Lagrange." Gireaux gave him a wink and an amused smile as he left.

**

Two days later, the American Hospital of Paris reported that patient Serge Faucheux had died overnight from pneumonia contracted at the prison camp of Drancy. The death certificate was signed by none other than Dr. Sumner Jackson himself, the medical director of the hospital.

The hospital recorded that Mr. Faucheux was buried in an unmarked grave in the hospital cemetery.

41

May 7, 1941

Oliver went to see Frank Dryden at the bar of the Hotel Bristol for lunch. An unusual cold snap had struck that week, and he wore his heavy wool coat. They sat in a corner booth, and Oliver slipped him some folded mimeographs from Lisette. Dryden slid him two envelopes of cash.

Oliver had gotten quite good at these exchanges over the months.

"I have news for you," Dryden said, looking uncomfortable. "The Germans have ordered us to close the embassy here in Paris. *Chargé d'affaires* Murphy is shuttering the building as we speak. My office has been moved to the embassy in Vichy."

Oliver was stunned. "Why?"

"The Germans are still angry about Lend-Lease," Dryden said. "They're punishing us for supplying the British by ordering us out of the Occupied Zone. Of course, Washington sees that as further provocation; and the downward spiral continues."

"How will we continue to…" Oliver left the rest unspoken.

Dryden nodded. "I still have an *Ausweis* to cross the Line of Demarcation whenever I need to. I'm keeping my suite here at the Bristol. I still have diplomatic immunity—but I'm not going to abuse that privilege too often. I'll come back every two weeks or so, for a day at a time. I'll send you a message, and we can meet like this. We'll need to be cautious, as I'm sure the Gestapo will be watching."

Oliver wondered what would happen to the American community in Paris now, with no diplomatic mission to call on for assistance. He asked about that.

Dryden's expression was grim. "I don't think the Germans will get aggressive with Americans, at least not in the near term. Still, we'll have little means to assist if they do—if we even find out. By closing our diplomatic mission in Occupied France, the Germans are also eliminating our oversight."

A cold fear crept into Oliver's belly. Butterflies began to flip inside his stomach. "Should I think about leaving?" He couldn't believe he had to ask that.

Dryden didn't answer at first. He stared at his hands for a moment. Then when he spoke, his words came slowly, carefully.

"The official State Department answer is 'Yes,' American citizens should leave the Occupied Zone. My recommendation is to stay and continue working—but you understand why I'm saying that. The choice is yours, Oliver. I'll understand either way."

Oliver considered this carefully for a moment. "If I stay now, will it be impossible to leave later on—if I have to?"

Dryden looked him in the eye. "I can't say, Oliver. It's a risk."

Oliver felt his gut clench. "Thank you for your honesty."

"What will you do?"

Oliver shrugged. "I'll stay, I suppose. Where else would I go?"

"Keep in mind, Oliver—the United States will end up in this war sooner or later, and when we do the Germans will lock up Americans as enemy aliens, just as they locked up the British and Canadians last year. I don't know how much warning there will be; you may have to leave in a hurry."

"I understand."

Dryden lowered his voice. "What I'm saying is, have an escape plan all worked out, ready to go at a moment's notice."

**

At rehearsal that afternoon at *Le Chien Errant,* Jerry the alto saxophonist announced to everyone that he was leaving that weekend. "I only stayed this long because of Mirabel," he said, mentioning his French wife. "But I can't stay with no protection. Terrance, brother—you better think about gettin' out, too."

Terrance shook his head. "Man, how am I gonna leave? I own this place, brother! I can't walk away from that."

"Won't do you no good owning nothin' if you end up dead," Jerry said. "Everybody always talk about how damn *polite* them Germans are—but they ain't so polite to Jews and Negroes, now is they? You think they gonna be any better behaved when we ain't got no embassy to run to?"

Terrance sighed. "I got lots of experience with that type. I grew up in North Carolina. I know how to keep my head down. I survived Jim Crow, I can survive *Mein Kampf.*"

"Where will you go?" Oliver asked Jerry.

"Lisbon," Jerry said. "We can take a train that far. Then I'll see if we can book a cabin on a steamship to New York. They got clubs in Lisbon where I can play while we wait."

Oliver shook his hand. "Best of luck, Jerry."

"You too, brother."

June 22, 1941

It was on a Sunday when the Germans invaded the Soviet Union.

Oliver actually breathed a little easier—if the Germans were at war with the Soviets, that made it less likely for the U.S. to enter the war, in his thinking. Communists were as hated and feared back home as Nazis. And the Germans would have their hands full.

He felt some of the tension of the last six weeks ease away.

371

"The communists in France won't sit quietly any longer," Sébastien said that afternoon over lunch at Chez Marius. "The *Boche* will rue this day."

"Do you know any communists?" Oliver asked.

"No," Sébastien said. He glanced around, then leaned in and whispered, "But Serge does."

"What will they do?" Oliver asked.

Sébastien shrugged. "Who can say? But I would not want to be the *Boche*."

Monday, June 30

Oliver met Collette at the corner of the Boulevard Raspail and the Rue de Babylone, a half-block from the Hotel Lutetia. An expensive-looking frilly blue stroller stood next to her. Her face lit up when she saw him.

"Hello, my dear friend!" she gushed, and they kissed cheeks. "It has been far too long."

"I was surprised to get your message," Oliver said. In spite of their mutual promise to have lunch from time to time at Les Deux Magots, they had done so exactly once—last fall, two weeks after Collette moved away. He looked down at the tiny newborn asleep in the stroller. "And I was really surprised to hear your news."

She reached down and picked up the infant, waking him in the process. He began to fuss, and she laid him on her shoulder and began to bounce, shielding his face from the bright sun with her other hand.

"This is Max," she said with a big smile. "Maximilian Fabian—a name that works in both French and German."

Oliver looked at the nine-day-old boy's round pink cheeks, and the dusting of fair hair on his head, and said that he was beautiful.

Collette kissed the baby's head, and laid him back in the stroller.

They began strolling west along the Rue de Babylone, toward the Eiffel Tower that loomed above the buildings in front of them, a mile away. They walked slowly, and Collette was animated and excited as she peppered him with questions about their friends. He answered her questions, not going into too much detail.

"I'm sure they all still hate me," she said at one point, not sounding too concerned.

"Will you do any more films now?" he asked, changing the subject.

She grew excited again, and told him about a script she had been sent that morning, for a picture that would begin filming at the beginning of August. She went on about it all the way to the *Champ de Mars*, the large park in front of the Eiffel Tower.

"It will be nice to work again," she said as they strolled toward the tower, its massive frame contrasting with the blue sky. "There were no roles while I was pregnant."

The park was busy. Several mothers sat on blankets on the grass, reading books in the sunshine or chatting with other mothers, occasionally calling out to children who ran around laughing and squealing.

Oliver wondered at the innocence of the children, who seemed so unaware of the conflict and hardships of the past year; or perhaps they just more easily forgot them in the wonder of a beautiful summer day.

Collette was talking about the studio, but Oliver barely listened. His eyes were riveted by the sight of Hélène standing in the shadow under the tower with two teenage boys. He recognized her son from the family photos in their home, and assumed the other was a friend of his.

"Oliver? Are you listening?"

"Sorry," he said, flushing. "I thought I saw someone I know."

Or used to know. He hadn't seen Hélène in almost two months. Their rendezvous had grown sporadic as winter melted into spring, and the last time she'd summoned him had been at the beginning of May. He'd sent her a discreet telegram a couple of weeks later, but received no reply.

"Excuse me," he said to Collette.

Hélène saw him when he was only a few steps away, and her lips parted in a cool smile that didn't reach her eyes. She extended her hand before he reached her, perhaps to preempt him from kissing her cheeks.

He shook her hand.

"Good day, Mr. Carmichael," she said in the polite bourgeois way. "What a surprise to see you."

He felt stung by the false politesse. His lips were tight as he replied, "Yes, it's been too long. I hoped we'd see each other more often."

Something flashed across her eyes, and she turned to her son. "Bernard, go and buy three tickets. I will join you boys in a moment." She handed him some money.

Bernard looked relieved to take his leave of the adults as he turned away, but his friend—a strikingly handsome boy with clear pale complexion, blue eyes, and luxuriously wavy black hair—gave Oliver an appraising look for a couple of seconds before a slight smile of satisfaction crossed his lips. Then he followed his friend, a smug look in his eyes as he turned away.

Oliver knew in a flash that Hélène had replaced him with her son's seventeen-year-old best friend. He couldn't hide the shock in his eyes when he looked back at her.

She seemed not to notice it—or pretended not to notice, he figured.

"Is there anything you wished to discuss, Mr. Carmichael?"

Her formal and polite manner infuriated him. "Keeping up appearances?" he asked, his tone bitter.

He saw her stiffen, and then the polite smile returned. "I should return to my son and his friend," she said, beginning to turn.

He put his hand on her shoulder, and she stopped. "Why didn't you just tell me?" he asked.

She gave him a bewildered look. "What?"

He lowered his voice. "You could have told me you didn't want to see me anymore."

She cocked her head and regarded him with a strange expression. "But why?"

Her incomprehension took him aback. "Why? Because that's the decent thing to do when you want to end a romantic liaison."

She stiffened again, and anger flashed across her dark brown eyes. When she spoke, her voice was low, but biting. "Decent? What do Americans know of decency? One should not be so indiscreet. When a Parisian love affair is over, it simply ends. It is *unseemly* to make a fuss."

She took a step backward, straightened her shoulders and raised her chin. She extended her hand. "Very nice to see you, Mr. Carmichael. Good bye."

He shook her hand grudgingly, and watched her walk toward her son Bernard and his handsome friend, who stood at the end of the line for the elevator. She stood between them, and the handsome boy discreetly put his hand on her waist, letting his little finger rest on the top of her buttock. He cast a glance at Oliver, saw him watching, and gave him a triumphant grin.

Oliver tugged the brim of his fedora lower over his face as he spun away and marched back toward Collette.

Thursday, August 21, 1941

On a hot morning, German naval cadet Alfons Moser became the first German assassinated in occupied Paris, shot by Communist Pierre Fabien while boarding a train.

In retaliation, the Germans rounded up random prisoners from nearby police prefectures and shot them.

Moscow had unleashed the French comrades. The war had come to the streets of Paris.

From his hiding place in the cellar, Serge took note.

42

Friday, September 26, 1941

Serge stood in the shadow at the corner of a building on the Rue Saint-Honoré, leaning against the stone wall. He smoked a cigarette while watching the door of the restaurant half a block away. From time to time he caught a glimpse of Sébastien waiting in the shows a half-block the other direction.

He tossed away the butt of the cigarette and shoved his hands back in his coat pockets. It was a damp night. He had the bill of his cap pulled low over his face for anonymity, but it also served to keep the drizzle off.

There was movement at the door, and Serge straightened. His fingers found the trigger of the Colt .45 hidden in his right coat pocket.

The group that exited were dressed in civilian clothes, and he relaxed back against the wall.

A moment later the door opened again, and this time a large number of men in gray Wehrmacht uniforms filed out, talking loudly in German. He saw the target, surrounded by several other officers.

Too many of them. Serge cursed the luck.

Three black Citroëns pulled up to the curb a few moments later, and the officers began to file into the back seats.

Serge watched with contempt. The Ritz Hotel, where these officers all lived, was only two blocks away. It was just like the *Boche* to take a car such a short distance.

A shiver ran up Serge's spine as he realized that the target was one of the last ones waiting. Time to see if he was man enough for this. He squared his shoulders and took a bold step onto the sidewalk.

He took long, fast strides, keeping his face down so that his cap would hide his features, and also giving the appearance of not watching in front of him.

The last three Germans were taking a slow stroll toward the last Citroën, conversing in their language, of which Serge understood nothing. He glanced up a few times to make sure he was aimed properly, and then propelled himself into the side of his target, a portly colonel.

He made a show of almost losing his balance and stumbling, and with his left hand grabbed the colonel's shoulder for stability. "Oh! Pardon me, I'm so sorry," he said loudly as he deftly spun the colonel away from his companions.

With the colonel's wide frame blocking his companions' view, Serge whipped the pistol from his pocket and shoved it hard into the colonel's gut. He fired two quick shots and spun away, running at full tilt.

"*Halt!*" several voices shouted after him in German.

He 'crashed' headlong into Sébastien, who had stepped onto the sidewalk the moment Serge ran into the colonel. He slipped the pistol into Sébastien's hand while turned away from the Germans, as they had practiced hundreds of times in the past few weeks, and he took off running down the alley.

If they did catch him, he wouldn't have a gun on him.

"Hey! Watch where you are going!" Sébastien yelled after him, sounding suitably incensed. He still had his back to the Germans as they ran past, and he slipped the pistol into his trousers and walked across the street.

Running down the alley, Serge couldn't be sure if he were outrunning his pursuers. "Never look backward," M. Beauxdoin had instructed.

As he reached the end of the alley, he saw his boss waiting on the opposite corner with a newspaper. Their eyes met, and Serge saw the printer fold up the newspaper and step off the sidewalk when Serge sprinted past. Serge flew forward with all the speed his legs could muster, and didn't look back.

**

Beauxdoin began to walk toward the alley. As the first two Germans rounded the corner, they crashed into him and fell to the ground. He allowed himself to fall backward, careful not to strike his head on the pavement, and sprawled his legs and arms in every direction, tripping up the third and fourth Germans who rounded the corner.

The others who came after them skidded to a stop to avoid running into the mass of bodies on the ground.

"Get out of our way, you fool!" one of the first Germans shouted at him as he scrambled back to his feet.

Beauxdoin took his time getting up, making his shoes slip on the wet pavement.

As he climbed to his feet, the Germans flowing around him like a stream around a rock, he overheard one of them shouting, "Where did he go? Where did he go?"

"How should I know, I was on the ground," another replied, angry. "I lost sight of him when I almost landed on my face."

"Shit! Shit! Shit!"

Beauxdoin, who understood German, smiled to himself. He mumbled an apology in French, and walked down the alley toward the Rue Saint-Honoré.

**

Sébastien's heart thumped against his chest as he walked down the street, away from the restaurant. A crowd of people had gathered after the gunshots, and it was easy to hide amongst them.

Just as they'd planned.

When he reached the end of the block, he glanced back. With the size of the crowd, he couldn't see their target on the ground, no doubt bleeding all over the sidewalk.

He turned right at the corner and hurried toward the river.

**

For two weeks Serge had walked the alleys of the 1st Arrondissement around the Ritz Hotel, and by now he knew them as well as his own neighborhood. He took as many turns as he could manage, until he was certain that he had lost his pursuers long ago.

He found his bicycle where he had stashed it behind some trash cans a couple of blocks north of the Ritz. He straddled it and began to pedal, moving away from the scene of the attack.

He stayed in back alleys for a while, until he reached the Avenue de l'Opera. It was a busy thoroughfare, and he blended in with the other French civilians bicycling home. He crossed the Seine at the Pont du Carrousel, and headed down the Quai toward the 5th Arrondissement.

He wondered if Sébastien had gotten away. Certainly there was less danger for him than for the shooter, but it was possible their transfer of the gun had not gone unnoticed. Serge worried about his friend.

He reached his apartment building a short while later, and dismounted the bike. He stood next to it at the corner of the alley by the building, and waited, watching down the street for Sébastien.

His friend rounded the corner from the Rue Domat a few minutes later.

Serge walked his bicycle out to meet him. "Did you take the Metro?"

"Yes, of course."

Serge breathed a sigh of relief, and a nervous smile came to his lips. Sébastien was the picture of calm, and Serge began to laugh. "We did it!" he whispered, and clapped Sébastien on the shoulder.

Sébastien seemed a little less enthused, but he smiled and nodded in agreement.

"This calls for a drink!" Serge said, putting his arm around Sébastien. "Come, let's share a pastis." Back home among the simple folk in Languedoc, pastis was the drink for celebrations.

"Yes, I think I need a drink," Sébastien said.

They walked into Chez Marius. Marcel was working that night, and he gave them a table in the back. Serge ordered two glasses of pastis, and Marcel's eyebrow rose before he nodded and turned away.

When Marcel brought the glasses, Serge lifted his. He almost toasted "to success," but at the last second he thought that might sound suspicious to anyone listening. So instead he toasted "To France."

Sébastien raised his glass and echoed, "To France."

They drank. Serge took a long gulp of the anise-flavored liqueur, while Sébastien sipped his. "Ah," Serge sighed in appreciation as the warmth spread through his belly, and he leaned back in his seat and put his hands behind his head.

"When will we know what happened?" Sébastien asked.

"What do you mean?"

"Well..." Sébastien glanced around, leaned in, and whispered. "When will we know if he died?"

Serge laughed. He picked up his glass and took another big drink before answering. "Oh, he will. Perhaps not tonight, but definitely by tomorrow."

Sébastien looked unconvinced. "How will we know for certain?"

Serge whispered, "Listen, I got off two shots, point blank range, right into his belly. It is not possible that neither bullet hit vital organs. He will bleed internally."

Sébastien still looked troubled. "But a doctor could—"

Serge shook his head emphatically. "No! No surgeon can save him. It probably blew away half of his back." He grinned and clapped Sébastien on the shoulder again. "Relax, my friend. It was a success."

Sébastien returned the smile, and his shoulders seemed to relax. He took a drink.

Serge downed the last of his pastis, and raised his hand for Marcel. "Another please, Marcel. And another for Sébastien as well."

Marcel cast a glance at Sébastien's half-full glass, but bowed his head and backed away. He returned a moment later with two more glasses, and set them on the table as Sébastien took another sip from his first one.

Adrienne walked through the door a few minutes later, with Marie-France and Madeleine behind her. They took the table next to Serge and Sébastien, who stood and greeted them with kisses to the cheeks.

"What is all of this for?" Adrienne asked, motioning toward the four glasses on the table, three with dark liquid. "A Friday night holiday without us?"

Serge grinned and didn't answer. He raised his glass in Adrienne's direction and drank.

The girls ordered a cheap bottle of red wine, a *vin de pays*. Adrienne sat at the end of the table, next to Sébastien. She leaned toward their table and asked, "Well boys, are we dining tonight, or just drinking?"

Sébastien looked hard at Serge. "We should eat."

Serge shrugged. "Alright."

Adrienne looked at him warily. "You should eat before you lose your head," she whispered.

Sébastien raised his hand for Marcel, and ordered a baguette and a cheese and sausage plate. The girls ordered the same for their table.

**

After they had all eaten, and Serge had drunk a third glass of pastis, they got up from their tables and left together. Adrienne walked between Serge and Sébastien, and when they had passed through the door she asked for a word.

The trio walked down the alley toward Serge's cellar door.

"Are you going to tell me what happened tonight?" she asked in a low voice.

Serge grinned. "A certain Colonel Rasmussen was relieved of his duties at the Stadtkommissar's office."

"Oh? For what reason?"

"He can no longer fulfill his duties on account of his death this evening." Serge began to laugh.

By now they had reached the cellar door, and stopped. Adrienne looked at Sébastien. "See that he gets to his room without talking to anyone." She turned to Serge. "And you see that you do not drink too much and lose your head and begin blabbing to everyone about what you've done."

Her stern voice brought a cowed look to Serge's face, and he nodded in exaggerated fashion.

"Now go, before anyone notices us loitering and denounces us to the police," Adrienne said, giving Serge a little push toward his door. She hurried back up the alley to her own building.

"Come." Sébastien took Serge by the arm and led him inside.

**

The next morning, September 27, Colonel Rasmussen died in the hospital. That afternoon, German troops seized thirty prisoners from

French police precincts—thieves and pick-pockets, mostly—and shot them at dusk in the Place de la Bastille.

When the news reached Serge in his cellar, he shook with rage. More Germans would die in retribution, he vowed.

43

Wednesday, October 22

Captain Allard was in a foul mood that afternoon as he walked back to the police prefecture from lunch.

He had met his son Georges—now a first-year student at the Sorbonne—at a café on the Boulevard Saint Michel. It had started as a pleasant lunch, until Georges brought up politics.

His son had become quite a radical since starting at university, and Allard was not pleased. Today Georges brought up the retaliatory execution of fifty prisoners by the Germans two days before. After each fatal attack on a German officer, the Occupation authorities had begun summarily executing dozens of random prisoners by firing squad.

Allard's patience broke when his son called the condemned men "martyrs."

"Do not dare utter such sacrilege! A martyr is someone who died for the faith at the hands of heathens, not a criminal."

"Some of the men who were shot had been arrested only for being out past curfew," Georges said. "They were unlucky to be in jail the night a Lt. Colonel was killed. The Germans didn't care who they shot for it. The people will not put up with this kind of violation."

Allard's temples pulsed. "The people should turn their anger against the Communists who are bringing down this kind of retaliation. If it weren't for their murder spree, the Germans would not need to make examples."

Georges stared back at his father. "At least they are willing to fight for France."

Allard barely spoke to his son the rest of the meal, and left in a huff.

He stomped up the Boulevard Saint Michel, but rather than going straight back to the prefecture, he detoured at the Place de la Sorbonne, and decided to burn off steam by walking through the narrow streets of the *Quartier Latin*.

He walked up the Rue de la Sorbonne toward the Rue des Écoles, and half-way up the block he stopped dead in his tracks. He thought he'd seen a ghost.

He had, in a way. A few meters ahead of him, exiting one of the arts buildings, was Serge Faucheux.

Serge Faucheux is supposed to be dead! Allard wondered for a second if his eyes were playing tricks on him, but then their eyes met and he knew. He saw the moment of fright in his adversary's eyes before he turned and sprinted away.

"You! Stop!" Allard shouted, pointing. He ran after him. "Police! Stop that man!" he shouted to the crowds of curious young faces gathering along the edges of the street, watching the chase. None of them made a move to stop the fugitive.

Rounding the corner onto the Rue des Écoles, Allard saw that Serge was outrunning him. He removed his pistol from his hip, though doing so slowed him down. He raised the gun and shouted, "Stop, Mr. Faucheux, or I will shoot!"

He saw Serge glance backward, but not break his stride. The crowds on the side of the street began to disappear.

Allard seethed. *What arrogance*! He stopped running, aimed his pistol, and fired.

He saw Serge clasp his hand over his right ear, but he barely faltered. Allard watched him look at his fingers, red with blood, and sprint even faster toward the entrance of an alley.

He disappeared just as Allard was ready to fire a second shot.

"Damn!" Allard rarely cursed.

He holstered his pistol and hurried back to the prefecture.

**

Oliver arrived home from rehearsal to see police gendarmes exiting Sébastien's apartment. He paused to look inside, but was ordered away. He unlocked his door, and the gendarme who had ordered him away from Sébastien's door called to him.

"You live there, sir?"

No, I'm breaking in with a God damn key. "Yes."

The gendarme raised his hand. "Please wait there, sir."

Oliver waited beside the unopened door. A moment later, a man in a brown suit emerged from Sébastien's apartment, holding a brown derby hat in his hand.

"You are Mr. Carmichael."

"Yes." Oliver wondered how they knew who he was.

"I am Captain Allard, Police. Please open your door."

"What is this about?"

Allard's eyes narrowed. "Please open your door, Mr. Carmichael."

Oliver struggled to think of the French word for 'search warrant.' Not coming up with one, he asked, "Do you have an order from a court to enter my apartment?"

Allard's eyes narrowed further, and he stepped to within two feet of Oliver. He was shorter, but stared up at Oliver with an air of almost parental authority.

"This is not the United States of America, Mr. Carmichael. I do not need such an order. Now open your door, before I have you arrested for obstructing a police search."

Oliver took the threat seriously. He opened the door and entered, then stepped aside as Allard and two gendarmes marched in behind him.

They spent only a few minutes. They opened his coat closet and pushed aside the two coats he had hanging inside. They looked briefly inside his water closet, checking behind the door. They snooped around his kitchen for less than a minute, looked behind his curtains at the living room window, and moved on to his bedroom.

He watched them look under his bed, behind his door, and inside his little closet.

"What is inside this chest?" Allard asked, pointing to the cedar chest in the corner.

"My sweaters," Oliver answered.

"Open it, please."

Oliver retrieved the key from the top drawer of his dresser, and opened the chest.

Allard pushed aside the stack of sweaters, proving that there was nothing else in the chest. "When was the last time you saw Serge Faucheux?"

Oliver faked a shocked look. "Serge? He died several months ago."

Allard gave him a hard look. "We were meant to think so."

Oliver let his mouth drop open. He hoped it looked convincing. "Serge is alive?"

Allard stared at him for several seconds; then he handed Oliver a card with his name, and the address and phone number of the local prefecture. "He has been seen in the area. If you should see Serge Faucheux anywhere, call the police at this number immediately."

Oliver nodded and took the card.

He followed Allard and the gendarmes to the door. As he started to close the door behind them, he saw Sébastien standing against the wall in the hallway, between two gendarmes; his hands were behind his back.

"Sébastien? What's going on?"

Allard spun around and gave Oliver a hostile stare. "This is police business, Mr. Carmichael. I suggest you go back inside your apartment."

Oliver didn't back down. "What has Sébastien done?"

Allard marched to him and stood close, glaring up at him. "That is none of your concern. Go back inside now."

Oliver felt his anger getting out of control. "No. Tell me why you are holding him."

Allard's eyes narrowed to mere slits. Then in one swift move he punched Oliver hard in the gut.

Oliver wasn't prepared for the blow, and he doubled over, feeling the wind knocked out of him. As he bent over, Allard's elbow struck him on the crown of the head, and he fell backwards.

Before he knew what was happening, he was on his back with Allard standing over him, his foot on Oliver's chest, pressing down.

"Do not defy the police, Mr. Carmichael. Just because you are American does not mean you can defy our orders. Let us be very clear—when I tell you what to do, in the future you will do it without question. If you do not, the penalties will be severe."

Oliver had still not caught his breath enough to respond when Allard spun and marched into the hall, slamming the door behind him.

Oliver sat up with effort, and took a few minutes to catch his breath. With each inhale his gut hurt. He felt a touch dizzy.

The dizziness subsided before the pain. He climbed to his feet and peeked into the hall. The gendarmes were searching the neighbor's apartment. Sébastien was nowhere in sight.

He locked his door and slipped down the stairs. He wondered if Serge were still hiding out in the cellar. He considered asking Gireaux, but thought better of it and went out the front door.

He immediately noticed police gendarmes standing guard—one beside their building door, one across the street in front of Serge's old building, and one each at both ends of the street.

He walked next door and climbed the stairs to the first floor. Marie-France and Madeleine were home, but Adrienne was not.

"The police were here a half-hour ago," Marie-France said, not disguising her anger. "They said they were looking for Serge. We told them nothing."

"They've arrested Sébastien."

"What for?" Madeleine asked, eyes wide.

"They wouldn't say. They got brutal when I kept asking."

Marie-France's face flushed. "This is no longer France, the land of the Rights of Man."

"We need to find Serge," Oliver said.

Marie-France shook her head. "Wait until Adrienne returns. Perhaps the police will be gone by then."

"Is she dancing tonight?"

"Yes, but she will be home before eleven."

"We can't wait that long." Oliver went to the window and peeked through the curtains. The police guards still stood at their posts. He turned back to the girls. "Do you know if Marcel is working tonight?"

Madeleine shook her head. "No, not tonight. Why?"

"I wonder if the police searched his room, too."

"They have searched everywhere," Marie-France said with contempt. "After they finished here, they went to our neighbors' apartment, and then onto the next apartment. They searched everywhere in this building."

A chill ran up Oliver's spine. "I have to go talk to our concierge," he said, and bolted from their apartment.

It was already too late. When he walked through the front door of his building a moment later, he saw Captain Allard talking with Gireaux and Simone in the hall while gendarmes searched their apartment. Oliver caught Gireaux's eye as he passed.

He climbed all the way to the top floor and knocked on Marcel's door.

"Have the police been here?" Oliver asked when Marcel answered.

"Yes, twenty minutes ago. They asked if I had seen Serge."

"What did you tell them?"

"I said that Serge is dead, of course."

"Anything else?"

Marcel gave him a curious look. "No. What else would I say?"

Oliver took him by the arm. "Come down to my apartment. We'll wait for the police to leave, then go look for Serge."

Marcel followed him without a word.

Oliver went to the window the moment he was inside his apartment. The police guards still stood at their posts. "Damn!" he muttered in English.

He looked at the clock; it was just after six.

**

The printer Beauxdoin stood in silence while the police searched his workshop. When Captain Allard told him they were looking for Serge Faucheux, he acted baffled. Allard suspected he only pretended to be baffled.

"He has not worked here in several months. I heard he was sent to Drancy. Then I heard he had died. I do not know what is true and what is rumor, but he does not work here."

The gendarmes searched the storeroom, and Allard asked him to open all of the crates.

After they had gone through the crates, leaving the packing straw strewn across the floor, they searched closets, water closets, and even the cabinets. A pair of gendarmes rummaged through the trash cans in the alley, but found no evidence of Serge's presence.

As the gendarmes conducted their search, Allard turned to Beauxdoin. "We would like to see your books, please."

Beauxdoin seemed stunned. "My books?"

"Yes, particularly your equipment ledgers."

"They're in my office. Come with me." He led Allard to his office, removed the ledgers from a shelf, and opened them on the desk.

Allard turned the pages slowly for several minutes, looking over each entry.

"This shows that you ordered a small press in July of last year for forty francs, and that it was sold a few days later for the same price. Does that seem strange to you, sir?"

Beauxdoin shrugged and puffed air out his lips. "I discovered that I did not need it after all, so I sold it for cost."

"To whom, sir?"

"I sold it in the store."

"You sold it to Serge Faucheux." Allard stared at him. "You ordered it for him, so that he could print the seditious garbage that has been found all over the 5th arrondissement."

Beauxdoin acted offended. "That is not true, sir!"

"But it is," Allard said. "We know that you are a socialist, like Serge Faucheux."

Beauxdoin nodded once. "I was a member of the Socialist Party, before Vichy outlawed opposition parties. But that hardly—"

"You can save your explanation for the Gestapo, Mr. Beauxdoin." Allard enjoyed the brief look of terror that flashed across Beauxdoin's eyes. "I'm sure they will call on you soon."

**

After the police left, Beauxdoin went to his office and opened the closet door. He reached up and pried loose the false ceiling. He stepped on a box and peered into the crawl space above his office.

"You can come down, it is safe."

Serge clamored down. "I heard what he said."

Beauxdoin's eyes were heavy with worry. "I can't have the Gestapo snooping around here. We were lucky that there were no gun shipments with the print supplies this week. And I have heard that the Gestapo arrest whole families now, not just the suspects."

Serge was silent for a moment. "Then we will take a lesson from them."

**

Oliver looked out his window frequently, and always saw the police guards standing watch over the dark street. In between, he paced. Marcel sat on his couch, but neither of them said much.

It was after seven-thirty when he heard a knock at his door, and he opened it to see Serge standing in the hallway.

"How did you get in the building?" Oliver asked.

"Through the cellar. Have you seen Sébastien?"

"He's been arrested."

"Shit!" Serge stared down the hall for a moment. "And the others?"

"Only Sébastien," Oliver said. "I've seen Marie-France and Madeleine; Adrienne is doing a show until eleven."

393

Serge lowered his voice. "Take Marcel and get the girls, then meet me at the cellar door in ten minutes. Everyone wear a scarf." He hurried toward the back stairs.

"I'll get my scarf," Marcel said.

Ten minutes later they all stood by the cellar door in the alley behind the building. Oliver was surprised to see Adrienne standing with Marie-France and Madeleine.

"The police came to the Theatre and took me to the prefecture," she said, her brows knit in irritation. "The understudy had to go on in my place. I wouldn't tell them anything. That Captain Allard told me to go home and stay there."

Serge handed each of them a Colt .45 pistol. "Hide these inside your coats."

"What are these for?" Oliver demanded.

"We're going to get Sébastien freed," Serge said.

"How? By storming the police station? You must be crazy!"

"No. Captain Allard's house."

Oliver stared at him, speechless.

"I don't know how to shoot," Madeleine said.

Serge looked at Marie-France. "Do you?"

"Yes, I can show her."

"Good. Everyone come with me."

They walked in silence, across the Boulevard Saint Germain and through the streets of the *Quartier Latin*. They crossed the Boulevard Saint Michel south of the Sorbonne, and through the *Jardin de Luxembourg* into the neighborhoods beyond.

They stopped in front of a row of low two-story brick townhouses. Serge told them to put their scarves over their faces. He pulled out his gun.

"How do you know this is Captain Allard's house?" Oliver asked.

"The telephone directory."

Serge mounted the front steps and motioned for the others to follow him. "Get out your guns. Marcel, you stand guard outside—if anyone comes toward the door, whistle twice."

**

Allard answered the knock, annoyed at the interruption when they were about to start dinner.

He was stunned to find himself staring into the barrel of a pistol.

"Good evening, Captain," he heard Serge Faucheux say. "We would like a word."

44

They corralled Allard, his wife, and two sons into the front room. Adrienne, Madeleine, and Marie-France stood over the family, guns drawn. Oliver stood by the front window, peeking out the curtains. Mrs. Allard trembled, and held her sons on either side of her on the couch.

Serge kept his gun pointed at Allard's head. "Captain, you will come with me. Your cooperation will ensure that your family is not harmed."

Allard stared at Serge with pure hatred. "I will see you guillotined for this."

Serge motioned with his gun toward the front door.

Allard kissed his wife on the cheek, retrieved his hat and coat from the stand by the door, and walked out without a word.

Serge stopped in the doorway and told the girls to stand watch. "Do not let them answer the telephone. If something goes wrong, I will call and let it ring once, then I will call back and let it ring twice. If that happens, shoot the wife, cut the telephone wire and go to the rendezvous point."

He motioned for Oliver to come with him. They stashed their pistols inside their coats as they walked out the door.

"You can't let them kill Allard's wife," Oliver whispered as they went down the front steps behind Allard. "She's done nothing."

"This is war." Serge took Allard's shoulder and pushed him. "Do not attempt to raise an alarm, Captain. If you do, we will shoot you dead, and go back and shoot your family. We are going to the prefecture. You will have our friend Sébastien Bonnet. If you do not cooperate, I will call my compatriots and instruct them to shoot your wife."

"You will not get away with it," Allard said, keeping his gaze forward.

"We shall see," Serge said.

**

They walked in silence the rest of the way. A cold drizzle began to fall.

It didn't distract Oliver from the questions rolling around his head. Would Serge kill Allard anyway after Sébastien was freed? He'd been wondering that since the beginning. How else could Serge hope to get away with it? Allard knew who they all were, in spite of the scarves they wore over their faces. Oliver supposed that had been so Allard's wife and sons wouldn't see them.

He also wondered what would happen if anything went wrong. Marching into a police prefecture, any number of things could go wrong. Fear crept through him, and a trickle of sweat ran down the back of his neck.

They crossed the Boulevard Saint Germain at the Rue Saint-Jacques. As they neared the prefecture on Rue Domat, Serge leaned close to Oliver's ear and whispered, "Let me do all of the talking."

Entering the building a moment later, Serge dropped his scarf from his face. Oliver followed suit. They approached the front desk, Oliver and Serge walking a step behind Allard. Allard told the sergeant on duty to bring out Sébastien Bonnet.

"Yes, Captain," the sergeant said. He looked at Oliver and Serge. "If you are here to visit the prisoner, you need to sign the book."

Serge reached into his coat and held up some sort of badge that Oliver didn't recognize. *"Deuxieme Bureau,"* he said in a commanding voice. "You understand why we cannot provide our names, of course."

Oliver recognized the colloquial name of French Intelligence. He wondered how Serge had faked one of their badges.

"Of course, sir. My apologies," the sergeant said, instantly deferential.

"Bring the prisoner to Captain Allard's office," Serge said.

"Yes, sir."

"I will sign the transfer papers, Sergeant," Allard said.

"Yes Captain."

Oliver and Serge followed Allard to his office. Allard took a seat behind his desk; they stood. A few moments later, the sergeant entered with Sébastien. If Sébastien were surprised to see them with Allard, he didn't give it away.

The sergeant handed papers to Allard. "To transfer the prisoner to the *Deuxieme Bureau*, sir."

Allard glanced over the paperwork and signed. "Thank you, Sergeant."

"Close the door," Serge instructed.

The sergeant bowed his head and backed out of the room, closing the door behind him.

"I have done as you asked," Allard said, glaring at Serge. "I demand that you release my family at once."

Serge shook his head. "You are not in a position to make demands, Captain. Now let's talk about your report to the Gestapo."

"It has already been sent," Allard said, a bit too quickly and gruffly.

He's bluffing, Oliver thought.

"Let me see it," Serge said, cool as the October weather. "Surely you keep a copy of such things."

Allard stared at Serge for a moment, a calculating expression on his face. "Let us not pretend that you are not going to try to kill me. That's what you intend to do, so let's be honest. You know that there is no other way for you to escape."

He folded his hands on the desk and leaned forward, a cat-like glint in his eye. "But what if Captain Hochman at the Gestapo already knows you are alive? They will come for you, whether I am dead or not. They will hunt down all who are involved in the Resistance, sooner or later. They are relentless, the Gestapo. You cannot hope to escape for long, even if you kill me. But suppose we came to an agreement, you and I."

Serge's expression gave away nothing. "What sort of agreement?"

"You release me unharmed, and I will arrange for an *Ausweis* for each of you, in whatever names you desire. You cross the Line of Demarcation, make your way to Marseille, and book passage on a ship to anywhere. I give you 48 hours to leave France, and then I report your escape to the Gestapo, and to Vichy."

Oliver looked at Serge, wondering if he would agree. His friend voiced the question that was on Oliver's mind as well. "How do we know you will keep your word?"

"I swear on my honor as a policeman."

"How can you arrange an *Ausweis* for anyone?" Sébastien asked. "Those are issued by the *Boche*."

Allard's expression remained cool. "I will attest that you and Mr. Faucheux—whatever names you choose—are needed in Vichy on an assignment for Minister of Police Benoist-Mechin. Once you are in the Unoccupied Zone you can make your way to Marseille. Mr. Carmichael can travel under his own name, saying that he has chosen to return to the United States."

Oliver had to admire Allard's thinking, even if he didn't trust a word of it.

"What collateral will you provide?" Serge asked.

Allard looked offended. "You have my word."

"Not good enough."

Allard's eyes narrowed. "I will not negotiate with terrorists. I have made you an offer, and that is all I will offer. Do you accept my terms?"

Oliver watched Serge, who stared at Allard in silence. What would he say?

"Your word is nothing. We are leaving, Captain. Come with us."

Oliver watched Allard, who continued to sit.

Serge scowled. "Captain, you are coming with us, now."

Allard leaned back in his chair. "No."

Serge's scowl deepened. "Then your family is dead."

Oliver continued to watch Allard, who smirked.

"How will that be? Your compatriots at my house are waiting for a signal from you, by telephone. How will you do it? One word from me now, and you will all be locked up; then I will go home and arrest your friends."

Oliver felt his stomach drop. His palms and his forehead began to sweat.

"Ha!" came Serge's defiant laugh. "Your gendarmes will not obey your order to arrest agents of the *Deuxieme Bureau*!"

Oliver thought Serge sounded less certain than he intended. He also noticed the rapid movement of Serge's eyes. He was scared.

Allard chuckled. He reached for the telephone.

Serge pulled out his pistol.

Oliver noticed that Allard had lifted the telephone receiver with his left hand—though he had signed the release papers with his right.

Oliver bolted from his chair in time to see Allard's right hand opening a desk drawer.

"He's got a gun!" he shouted as Allard's hand whipped out the pistol.

Serge fired first, but his bullet missed, and buried itself in the wall behind Allard.

Sébastien lunged at Allard, and struck his right shoulder as he fired, sending his shot into the ceiling. Plaster rained down over them.

Oliver had his pistol in his hand, and brought the butt down on Allard's wrist. Allard's hand opened involuntarily, and the pistol dropped onto the desk. Oliver smacked it away, and it clattered to the floor. He pointed his gun at Allard's head.

"Go!" he shouted to Serge and Sébastien.

Serge opened the door. Several gendarmes were running down the hall toward Allard's office.

Oliver shouted a random string of German words he'd picked up over the last year, praying none of the gendarmes spoke German and could tell that he was shouting gibberish.

The gendarmes stopped in their tracks and stared at him wide-eyed. Oliver made his voice harsher. *"Nicht! Nicht!"* he shouted, motioning them away impatiently.

The gendarmes hurried away.

"Go!" he repeated to his friends, quieter.

Serge bolted from the office. Sébastien paused at the door and looked Oliver in the eye. He gave him a quiet nod before he disappeared.

Oliver looked back at Allard, who regarded him with an even expression. "Very good, Mr. Carmichael. But while your ruse may have temporarily fooled the gendarmes, you cannot pull it off for long."

Oliver knew it was true. His odds of escape were slim, but he played the only card he had. "Unlike my friends, I don't want to see your family harmed," he said, entirely sincere. "Serge and Sébastien will find a public telephone within minutes, and give the signal to shoot your family. I can stop them."

Allard's eyes narrowed in suspicion. "How?"

Oliver wasn't really sure. "Give me a car."

**

Allard considered his options quickly. He was furious at this meddling American, but he also knew not to let his rage distract him from his real targets—the *résistants* Serge Faucheux and Sébastien Bonnet.

And whatever he did, he had to do it now. He thought of Claudette and his sons, held at gun-point in their own home, and his blood boiled. He would make them all pay for that violation—but first, he had to save his family.

"Come with me," he said to Oliver, and marched out of the office and down the hall.

**

At Allard's house, the telephone rang once. The girls jumped at the sound, as did their prisoners. Adrienne, Marie-France, and Madeleine looked at each other, breathless, waiting to see if it would ring again.

The house was silent for several seconds, and the girls remained tense.

The phone rang again, and this time it rang twice. Then it fell silent again.

Claudette Allard squeezed her eyes shut, and tears escaped and streamed down her cheeks. She bowed her head, and her lips began to move silently.

Adrienne, Marie-France, and Madeleine continued to stare at one another for several seconds, their hands trembling.

Marie-France broke the silence. She looked down at Claudette Allard's bowed head, and whispered, "I don't think we should do it."

Madeleine's face had drained of the little color it had. "I don't think I can," she said, shaking her head and taking a step back.

Adrienne scowled. She gripped the handle of her pistol more tightly and raised it to the back of Mrs. Allard's head. "I can."

The two boys on either side of their mother looked at her in wide-mouthed horror, but she focused on the back of Mrs. Allard's head. "This is for France." She cocked the hammer.

They heard Marcel's voice from the sidewalk, shouting frantically. "Police! Run! Run!"

Adrienne hesitated, unsure if she should do the deed before fleeing.

Marie-France made her decision for her, grabbing her forearm and pleading, "Let's go!"

Adrienne's courage broke. She turned and fled out the kitchen door behind Madeleine and Marie-France, into the dark alley behind the house.

**

It had been a long time since Oliver had driven a car, and he killed the engine twice while shifting from first gear. But he got the hang of the clutch and gear-shift after a few minutes, and sped off toward Allard's house.

Allard sat next to him, staring forward in stony silence. Oliver didn't look at him.

The car was clearly marked as a police vehicle, and as he turned onto Allard's street, he saw Marcel emerge from the shadows of the corner and shout a warning toward the house, then bolt away.

Oliver slammed the brakes, opened the door and leaned out. "Marcel, wait! It's me."

Marcel skidded to a stop, and turned back. His face broke into a huge grin when he saw Oliver, and he jogged back.

Allard started to get out of the car, but Oliver pulled the pistol from inside his coat and aimed it at his midsection. "Get back in the car, Captain."

The unarmed police prefect obeyed. Oliver motioned for Marcel to get in the back seat.

"What are you going to do with me, Mr. Carmichael?" Allard demanded.

"Don't worry, Captain, you're safe as long as you cooperate. We're just going to give everyone time to get away."

"Can I see my family?"

"Later."

"How do I know they're safe?"

Oliver nodded toward Marcel. "If they had already been killed, my friend would not have still been standing guard."

He sped away. Oliver's mind raced as he drove. Where could they drop Allard where it would take him a long time to find a telephone? Then he realized that Allard's wife had probably already called the police. He cursed himself for not thinking to cut the telephone line before they left.

He glanced back at Marcel. "Did they see your faces?"

"I don't know, I never went inside."

At least if she did call the police, Mrs. Allard couldn't really tell them anything, Oliver reasoned. "Keep your gun on him," he told Marcel.

He kept to side streets, winding his way in a generally eastward direction until he came to the Boulevard Saint Michel and crossed into the 5th. As he drove he came to the sinking realization that there was nowhere isolated enough where he could drop off Allard and hope to have enough time for everyone to escape.

He slammed on the brakes and the car jolted to a stop. He pulled his gun from his coat and pointed it at Allard. "Get out."

As Allard opened his door, Oliver killed the engine. He looked back at Marcel and motioned for him to exit as well, and whispered, "Cover me."

They all stepped out into the cold damp night, and Oliver opened the trunk. "Get in," he ordered Allard, waving his gun at the open trunk.

Allard raised his chin and gave him a haughty look. "And if I do not?"

Oliver cocked the hammer.

Allard chuckled, and his mouth turned in a sneer. "You will not shoot me, Mr. Carmichael."

Oliver stared at him a moment, then lowered his pistol toward Allard's foot. He squeezed the trigger, and the crack was nearly deafening. Chunks of concrete flew from the sidewalk where the bullet hit inches from Allard's foot.

Allard jumped back, his face draining of color.

Oliver's hand hurt. He hadn't fired a gun since a camping trip with the Boy Scouts when he was fourteen. But he kept his gaze and his voice steady as he told Allard, "Next time, I won't miss. Get in the trunk."

Allard stared back at Oliver for a second, swallowed hard, and climbed into the trunk. Oliver closed it, and looked around at the grimy tenement buildings. He saw the movement of a few blackout curtains falling into place as the occupants stepped back from the windows.

He looked at the police emblem emblazoned across the sides of the car, and realized none of them would report the gunshot. He chuckled as he got back in the car.

Marcel got in the front next to him, Oliver restarted the car, and drove toward the rendezvous point.

**

No one was in sight when Oliver pulled up to the curb next to the botanical gardens, and he realized they were hiding from the police car. As he and Marcel got out and walked into the deep shadows of the trees, he whistled.

A moment later, he heard Serge in a loud whisper several yards to his left. "Where is Allard?"

"We have him, locked in the trunk."

"You should have killed him." Sébastien's voice was a few feet behind Oliver, and it made him jump. His heart pounded.

"Jesus! You scared the shit out of me!" Oliver's breath came hard and fast. "Why didn't you tell me you were right behind me?"

"We had to make sure it wasn't a trap," Sébastien's voice said in the darkness.

Oliver had to concede that. He exhaled slowly, trying to calm his startled nerves. "Are the girls here?"

"Yes, we are here," Adrienne's voice came from his right. "Was it you when Marcel yelled that the police were there?"

Oliver nodded, then realized they probably couldn't see that in the dark. "Yes, it was me. I took Allard's car. I wanted you to have time to get away."

"That explains why they didn't kill Allard's wife." Serge's tone was bitter, biting, perhaps even accusing.

"It's better this way," Oliver said. "Allard's wife doesn't know who any of us are, and I've got Allard himself. We can take our time, think this through."

Serge's voice grew harsher. "Do you think the police have not reported Allard's car stolen?"

Oliver felt himself growing defensive. "Why would they have? Allard was with me when we took it from the prefecture. They won't report it until at least the start of Allard's shift tomorrow morning. We have hours."

There was silence in the darkness for several seconds.

"We should have never gotten you involved," Serge said.

Oliver felt his blood rise to his face. "Why? I saved you from being murderers tonight."

Serge's reply came to him as a whisper, but with a sharp tone. "We should never shrink from killing the enemies of France."

Oliver gave up trying to convince them. The French could be so damned exasperating. "At least now you have time to decide what you want to do next, how you want to make your escapes." Oliver realized with a start that he hadn't planned his own escape.

"Contingencies have been in place for some time," he heard Serge say. "Sébastien and I will go to a safe house in Montmartre. Adrienne is going to her parents' home in Tours. Marie-France will take Madeleine to her family's farm for a while, until it is safe for them to return." There was a pause. "You and Marcel must decide where you will go—and what you will do with Allard if you won't kill him."

Oliver's heart sank. For more than a year he had fought all attempts by his parents to convince him to leave Paris. Now, he had no choice.

The thought that his father may have been right all along stabbed pain through his gut. He forced that thought from his head. *Idiot.* The idea of having to tell his parents he'd left Paris made his heart feel as if it were being squeezed by a vice.

But there could be no other outcome.

He briefly wondered if death might be more welcome, but just as quickly dismissed the thought. He had to get out of Paris.

His thoughts raced. And then an image of Lisette blotted out all other thoughts, and the realization that he might not see her again felt like a knife plunging into his chest.

"I will go where ever you go," Marcel whispered close to his ear. "Even to America."

A wave of sadness rushed over Oliver, so intense he had to fight back tears. Poor, loyal Marcel, who felt about him the way he felt about Lisette. He stayed silent for a moment, afraid his voice would crack.

"We'll go to the Unoccupied Zone," he said at last.

"*You* can cross the Line of Demarcation," Adrienne's harsh whisper said. "You are American. You have only to say that you wish to return to America, and they will wave you through. But what of Marcel? How is he to get into the Unoccupied Zone without an *Ausweis*?"

Oliver remembered their conversation last December, when Serge and Sébastien had finally told him about their clandestine activities. "Sébastien has connections to underground escape routes."

There was silence for a moment.

"We should not risk the network when the danger to Marcel is not certain," Sébastien said, his voice quiet.

"Allard saw Marcel's face," Oliver said.

"Then kill Allard," Sébastien replied.

Oliver cursed to himself that it kept coming back to that. "Perhaps we wouldn't have to use your entire network," he suggested. "Marcel could come with me as far as the Cher, and then use your connections to smuggle him across the river into the Unoccupied Zone."

"I do not know the operators who ferry the escapees across the river," Sébastien said. "I only know the ones who get them out of Paris. Others take them from there, and I do not need to know."

"But can you send a message ahead? Find out where we should contact them?"

"No." Sébastien's answer was flat, but final.

"Surely there are entrepreneurs who will ferry people across the river for money," Oliver mused. "I have money. What I don't have is a way to find out who runs that kind of business."

There was silence for several seconds, and Oliver held his breath.

"Do you know the nave doors to Saint Sulpice?" Sébastien asked.

"Yes." Of course Oliver knew the nave doors; Saint Sulpice was mere blocks from their building.

"Meet me there at four o'clock. I will see what I can find out for you."

Oliver thanked him.

"Clear out your apartment now," Serge said. "We don't know when the police will come. Or the Gestapo."

"I will. Come on, Marcel."

They returned to the car without looking back, and got in without a word. Oliver restarted the engine and sped toward home.

**

"Pack what you want, and be back down here in five minutes," Oliver told Marcel as they parted on the stairs ten minutes later. He hurried to his apartment, went to his bedroom closet, and pulled out the steamer trunk he'd brought from New York five years before.

He opened it and began throwing clothes into it, followed by a few photographs. There was a photograph of him with Lisette in the summer of 1939, smiling and looking happy together. He stared at it for a few seconds and touched her face, then tossed it into the trunk with the others.

He ran to his desk, and quickly went through the drawers, taking out important papers he wanted to keep, and the savings book from Chase Bank; followed by the box where he hid the cash Frank Dryden gave him.

He counted out two thousand dollars and stuffed it in his pocket, then put the box with the rest of the cash into his trunk. He stripped the blankets off the bed and put them on top of everything in the trunk, then had to sit on it to get the straps fastened.

There was nothing else in the apartment that he needed, so he dragged the trunk to the door. He saw Marcel in the hall, holding a bundle of spare clothes under his arm.

"Is that all you want to bring?" Oliver said before he thought better of it.

Marcel shrugged and said nothing.

"Come on, let's get going. Help me carry this."

Once outside, they put the trunk in the backseat, and Oliver started the engine. He drove to the Boulevard Saint Germain, and took it west toward the Seine. He crossed the river at the Pont de la Concorde and headed north.

"You're going the wrong direction," Marcel said as they passed through the Place de la Concorde. "We need to go south."

"We need to make a stop first," Oliver said, and turned into Lisette's neighborhood.

45

The curfew siren began to wail as Oliver parked in front of Lisette's building. It was louder here, he noticed, killing the engine. German military headquarters was only a few blocks away, at the Place de la Concorde.

"Wait here," he told Marcel.

"What if a German patrol comes by?" Marcel asked before Oliver closed the door.

Oliver considered that, but then shrugged. "Duck down on the floor. I won't be long."

As he walked around the back of the car, he could hear the muffled sound of pounding coming from within the trunk. It was hard to hear through the thick steel, and he smiled at the thought that no one would hear it after curfew.

He ran up to Lisette's floor, taking the steps two at a time.

Her eyes widened with surprise when she answered the door. "Oliver! What are you doing here at this hour?"

"Were you expecting someone else?" Oliver replied, a bit more sharply than he intended. He stepped around her. "Our friend Jean-Louis, perhaps?"

She regarded him with a questioning expression. "No, he doesn't come here anymore."

It was Oliver's turn to look surprised. "No?"

She shook her head. "Not for many weeks."

He was dying to know more about that, but there wasn't time. "Lisette, I have to leave. I have to get out of Paris, tonight."

"Tonight?" She looked startled. "Why? What's going on?"

"There's been trouble. I can't tell you much more than that, but the Gestapo will probably be looking for me by morning."

"The Gestapo?" her voice sounded horrified. "Will they come here?"

He shook his head. "The trouble has nothing to do with you, or our business."

She began to pace, agitated, her hands moving as she spoke. "Oliver, the Gestapo will find out that I know you, and they will come asking about you. They are very thorough, and people will talk. If they ask me when was the last time I saw you, and what we spoke about, I won't know what to say."

He took her hands between his, stopping her pacing. He stood close to her and looked into her eyes. "Come with me."

Her mouth dropped open, and she was silent for several seconds. Then she pulled her hands away and turned. "I can't leave Paris, Oliver. My family, all my things—"

"You can pack a trunk with anything you need. Everything else you can do without. And your family will understand." He thought of Frank Dryden and Cécile Fournier. "Marry me."

He thought he saw a trace of a smile at the corners of her mouth, but then she shook her head and looked away.

"You're crazy," she said.

He put his hand on her chin and turned her face back towards him. "I know you still love me. You won't admit it, you're as stubborn as an old mule, but you do. I know I'm not exactly the way you want a husband to be, but tell me you don't imagine me being the one you spend the rest of your life with. When you picture that perfect future, with that perfect husband, it's my face you picture, isn't it Lisette? Tell me it's not."

She scowled, pulled away and folded her arms. "Oh Oliver!"

A tingle ran through him, and he couldn't help but smile. "It is, isn't it?"

She made a sound of exasperation and turned away. She trounced to her desk and yanked open the drawer. She took out a few sheets of paper and thrust them at him. "Here! The copies I made a few days ago, of the latest orders."

Oliver stared at the papers for a second. It hadn't crossed his mind that she had reports she hadn't given him yet. He reached for them—and then it dawned on him that if he were caught while trying to cross into the Unoccupied Zone, and they found those papers on him, he'd be shot as a spy.

"Burn them."

"What?"

"I said burn them. You can't keep them here, in case the Gestapo come calling, and I can't have them on me."

"Oh," she said, so quietly he barely heard her. Her eyes had a vacant stare, but she walked to the kitchen and got a match.

"Do you want to see them first?" she asked.

He nodded, wishing he'd thought of that. He took the papers, and read through them three times, trying to commit the details to memory. Then he handed them back to her, and she struck the match. Once they were aflame, she threw them in the sink.

"I need to use your phone," he said. That was one of the reasons he'd come here, actually.

When the operator answered he asked for a line to Vichy, to the *Hotel des Ambassadeurs.*

The line was scratchy when it rang through, and there was an echo when the desk clerk answered. Oliver knew a German censor was listening. He asked for Frank Dryden's room.

"Hello?" Dryden's voice answered a moment later.

"Mr. Dryden, this is Oliver Carmichael." He figured his name wasn't on the wanted list yet.

If Dryden was surprised to hear from him, his voice didn't reveal it. "Oliver, good to hear from you. How are things in Paris?"

"I've had a very exciting night out with my friends. I'll have to tell you all about it when I see you in Vichy. I'm hoping to catch the train tomorrow. I do hope we'll get to spend some time together."

"I shall keep my evening free," Dryden said. "We can have dinner when you arrive. Will you be vacationing alone?"

Oliver didn't want to mention Lisette's name, lest the censor write it down. Besides, he hadn't convinced her to come yet. "Most likely."

"What a shame. Mrs. Dryden sends you her regards."

"Thank you. Please tell her I look forward to seeing her again. Goodnight."

He placed the receiver in its cradle and looked back to Lisette. "Please come with me."

She looked as though she were wavering. Then a somber look came to her face, and she looked down at the floor. "I can't, Oliver. I wish I could, I wish I were as brave as you, but…" she let her voice trail off.

He stepped close to her, put his arm around her, and held her tight. "I won't let anything happen to you."

She remained stiff in his arms, and after a moment he stepped back. Her eyes were wet, but her face wore that determined look he knew so well. It was pointless to argue.

He nodded in resignation, and started to turn away, but stopped and put his finger on her chin, lifting it up and leaning it to kiss her. His lips lingered on hers for several seconds, barely touching. When he finally pulled away a few inches, he stared into her brown eyes.

Neither said anything for a moment. Then he whispered, "I love you very much," and walked away.

**

He was halfway down the stairs when he heard the gunshots.

46

Serge crept through the darkness, glancing around constantly for any sign of the police or a German patrol. He wore all black, but he took few chances when he had to cross streets, staring deep into the shadows for any signs of a hidden sentinel.

It took a long time being that careful, but he arrived at the Rue de l'Arcade to find Oliver's police car parked near the north end of the street. He could faintly see Marcel's silhouette in the passenger seat.

He had told Sébastien when they parted that he was going to the safe house in Montmartre, but he had already decided to make one stop along the way. There was a loose end that needed to be eliminated.

It hadn't been hard to guess where Oliver might go. He removed his gun from his coat as he approached the car.

Marcel jumped when Serge tapped the gun against the window. He exhaled visibly when he saw Serge, and rolled down the window. "What are you doing here?"

"Give me the keys," Serge said.

"Why?"

Serge didn't have time to explain. He cocked the hammer. "Give me the keys, Marcel."

After a few seconds' hesitation, Marcel took the keys from the ignition, and handed them over.

Serge opened the trunk while Marcel stood next to the car. "Get out, Allard."

The police captain crawled out, his movement stiff.

"Stand up, face me like a man," Serge said.

Allard straightened with difficulty, and looked at Serge with undisguised hatred. "I should have killed you instead of sending you to Drancy."

Serge extended his arm and pointed the gun at Allard's chest. "Captain, I give you the opportunity to face death like a man. I find you guilty of treason against France, and sentence you to death by firing squad. Would you like to make your peace with God?"

Allard glared at him, but then bowed his head, made the sign of the cross, and folded his hands.

Then in a flash he leapt at Serge, knocking him to the ground before he could react.

Serge's gun clattered onto the cobblestones.

From his place beside the car, Marcel moved toward the fallen gun, but Allard was quicker. He grabbed it up while Marcel was still a few feet away.

Serge scrambled to his feet, but he was too slow. Allard got off his first shot before Serge could stand all the way up, and his shoulder wrenched backward from the blow. Then a second shot hit Serge in the gut, and he collapsed.

**

Marcel stared in open-mouthed horror as bloody fabric and flesh flew from the back of Serge's shoulder, and then from the center of his back. His throat constricted when he saw Serge fall, and no sound would come out.

His insides clenched in terror as he saw Allard point the gun at him. He froze in place.

Allard kept the gun aimed at him as he backed up several steps, and then turned and sprinted down the street toward the Hotel de l'Arcade.

Marcel began to shake horribly, and he fell to his knees on the pavement.

**

Oliver bolted out the door, then stopped in his tracks when he saw Serge lying on the ground in a giant pool of blood, and Marcel on his knees a few feet away.

It took a second to process the scene, and then Oliver rushed to Serge's side, crouching down next to him.

Serge's eyes were open, but his breath came shallow and very fast. Oliver's eyes filled with tears, and he knew he should have something comforting to say, but he struggled to think of anything. His father was a fucking minister for God's sake, and he couldn't think of a damn thing to say to his dying friend.

All he could manage was to croak out Serge's name.

"Allard…my gun…" Serge whispered, his voice hoarse. His eyes struggled to focus.

"Shh." Oliver looked up and saw Lisette standing at the door of her building, her hand over her mouth. When he looked back at Serge, his eyes were glassy and still.

Oliver put his hand over Serge's mouth, and felt no breath. He closed the eyelids. He sat still for a moment, and sighed heavily before getting to his feet and walking toward Lisette.

They put their arms around each other.

Marcel turned away from them and stared at the car.

"Oh Oliver!" she said, voice trembling. "I am so sorry. And I do love you, I always have."

He kissed her head and stroked her hair. "Please come with me."

"I…I don't know."

He didn't press it. He pulled away and said to Marcel, "Which way did Allard go?"

Marcel motioned down the street toward the Hotel de l'Arcade.

"I have to go, before the captain finds a telephone," Oliver told Lisette. "If you change your mind, meet me at the nave door at Saint Sulpice at four AM."

He hurried to the car and got in. Marcel didn't look at Lisette as he got into the passenger seat, and the car sped away.

47

Allard found the desk unattended after running across the lobby of the Hotel de l'Arcade. He waited a moment, seeing no public telephone booths in sight, and strummed his fingers on the desk. Then he rang the bell. A few seconds later he rang it again. After a few more seconds he began to bang on it continuously.

He heard frantic whispering behind the office door, and then a maid emerged, smoothing her uniform dress. She hurried away. A desk clerk followed, his shirt hastily and incompletely retucked in the waist of his trousers.

"May I help you, sir?"

"I am Captain Allard of the Paris Police. I need to use your telephone at once."

The young man gave Allard a quick bow of the head. "Certainly, Captain. May I see some identification?"

Allard flashed his police badge with a scowl, and the clerk produced a telephone from beneath the desk. Allard asked the operator for the Hotel Lutetia.

"This is Captain Robert Allard, Paris Police," he told the clerk who answered at the Hotel Lutetia. "I must speak with Captain Auguste Hochman at once. It is quite urgent."

**

Oliver knew he had to ditch the police car as soon as possible. But he also knew he needed a vehicle—he didn't want to carry his trunk, let alone sneak around after curfew—and so he needed another vehicle with the *Service Publique* license plate.

The solution leapt to mind, and he sped off to the 16th Arrondissement.

**

Sébastien went to the window at the first sound of sirens. He parted the blackout curtains a crack and peeked out.

There was a commotion in front of the Hotel Lutetia down the street, with several black Citroën sedans pulling away from the curb, tires squealing, while dozens of men in black overcoats streamed out of the doors and into waiting cars. Frantic shouts in German echoed down the street.

"The Gestapo have been alerted." Sébastien turned away from the window and let the curtain close.

The light from a single candle danced on the far wall, and cast the rest of the room in deep shifting shadow. The dim light at the end of a cigarette briefly glowed brighter as his friend François took a drag.

Sébastien heard him exhale hard.

"Then you were right," François said. His figure was mostly shadow as he sat on the couch in his white boxer shorts, elbows on his knees, and smoked. His wife Isabelle paced the kitchen floor, her robe tied snug around her and her arms crossed.

Sébastien had known François since they were five years old. They had grown up on the same street in an affluent bourgeois neighborhood in the 7th Arrondissement, the top of the Eiffel Tower visible from their bedroom windows above the roofline. They were both raised in liberal families, with fathers who were active in the *Parti Radical* and mothers who worked together in the family planning movement. They had gone to school together, and went to the Sorbonne together, each disappointing their parents with their choice of "impractical" courses of study—art for Sébastien, culinary arts at the *Cordon Bleu* for François.

And now they worked together on the underground escape route.

"It's almost midnight," Sébastien muttered. "I'll need to stay here at least three more hours."

François exhaled and stubbed out the cigarette. "Stay as long as you need."

"I need to step out for a moment to make a phone call, as soon as they have all gone."

François struck a match and lit another cigarette. "You know where it is."

Sébastien peeked out the window again. A Citroën was disappearing around the corner at the far end of the street, and there seemed to be only a couple of men still standing in front of the Hotel Lutetia. They appeared to be talking, not looking around, but he couldn't hear them.

He'd wait a few more minutes. He took a seat next to François.

"How long will you stay out of sight?"

Sébastien shrugged. "Not long. A couple of weeks perhaps, just until the heat has died down."

"You'll contact us with your new identity?"

"When I can."

Isabelle came around behind the couch and put a hand on Sébastien's shoulder. "Please don't keep us waiting any longer than you have to. We'll worry until we hear from you."

Sébastien patted her hand. "I'll be fine, don't worry."

He waited a few moments before checking the window again. Seeing the street deserted, he nodded to François and went to the door without a word. He crept down the stairs, careful not to make a sound.

There was a public telephone less than half a block from the entrance of the building, but that was far enough to be seen if he weren't careful. He was still wearing all black, and the street was dark, but that was no guarantee. He barely cracked the door and looked up and down the street several times, peering into the shadows for any sign of loitering informants. He eventually took a deep breath and darted out, keeping close to the wall as he hurried toward the phone booth.

Once inside he crouched down in front of the seat, hidden from any gendarme or drunken German who might wander by. He slipped a franc coin into the phone and asked the operator for the Hotel Lutetia.

He gave a name to the desk clerk, and waited as the call rang through to the room.

"*Ja?*" the sleepy voice answered. At this hour he doubtless assumed his caller was a fellow German.

"Good evening, Captain," Sébastien said. "You know who this is. It is time for you to keep your bargain."

There was a moment's silence. "What do you want?"

"Meet me at the nave doors of Saint Sulpice at three-thirty. Come alone. I'll be watching; if you aren't alone, I'll shoot you."

"And if I don't come?"

"Then your wife will be handed the photographs of you with Collette tomorrow."

"Very well then." Captain Gruder's voice was clipped.

Sébastien heard a loud click as Gruder slammed down the phone.

Sébastien was bluffing. It was true that he had photographs of Gruder with Collette, and in some of them they were being quite affectionate—but nothing as salacious as he had implied weeks ago, when he first called Gruder.

The whole thing had been Franz's idea. He said he'd made use of the technique to great advantage; and while he gave no specifics, he said there was a certain SS officer who was beholden to him for not revealing real photographs of his indiscretions to the Gestapo. And in exchange for his silence, Franz on occasion had the officer chauffeur him around southwestern Germany.

Sébastien poked his head up to the glass and glanced around quickly before putting a precious five-franc coin into the phone and ducking down again. He asked the operator for a line to Lyon, waited while it connected, then gave the Lyon operator a number.

"Oliver has broken his trumpet," he said when the phone was answered.

There was a moment of static-filled silence, and then the voice at the other end replied. "We'll see if we can get him another one. I have a favorite store. It can be delivered in three days."

The line clicked off.

Sébastien glanced around again, and dashed for the shadows along the wall. He hurried toward the door and slipped inside. He crept up the stairs to François and Isabelle's apartment, and knocked their sequence of two, one, three as quietly as possible. He watched the neighbors' doors nervously until François cracked his, and he slipped inside.

Thursday, October 23
Oliver tried to sleep, but couldn't. His eyes were heavy, but he sat awake in the driver's seat of Jacques Chastain's 1939 Citroën, staring straight ahead as if he could will his eyes to see anything in the darkness of the garage. Marcel slept with his head on Oliver's shoulder, and his even breathing was the only sound.

Oliver had no idea how long it had been since he'd heard a distant church bell chime two o'clock. Surely it had been at least an hour. But he'd heard it every hour since midnight, and knew it wouldn't skip three.

They'd arrived in the alley behind the Chastains' townhouse in the 16th shortly before midnight, and Oliver had stood for several minutes staring at the door on the side of the garage, wondering how on earth he was going to break in. He hadn't planned that far ahead. Marcel rooted around in the trunk of the police car and found a hammer and tire iron, and together they busted the door frame around the latch.

Once their belongings had been transferred to the Chastains' car, Oliver left Marcel there, took the police car and parked it several blocks away. He snuck back to the alley as fast as he could, grateful that there were few patrols in this wealthy bourgeois part of Paris. He resolved to wait as long as possible before stealing the car, to minimize the risk that Jacques Chastain would hear something and report the theft.

And so they sat in the dark in the front seat and waited. It seemed endless.

In the silence his mind had plenty of time to wander around every angle of their predicament. German military checkpoints guarded every avenue and boulevard crossing the Paris city limits—were there also checkpoints at little side streets? How would they know? And if they had to cross a checkpoint, what would they do? They'd never be able to talk their way through. He imagined running at full tilt, German soldiers chasing them, and bullets ricocheting off the cobblestones all around them.

He realized that he pictured three of them running—him, Marcel, and Lisette. And in his imagination Lisette was running right beside him.

Would she be there, at the nave door at Saint Sulpice? If she didn't come, would he ever see her again?

The church bells chimed three o'clock, and he felt Marcel stir, groaning softly. He shifted his arm around the boy's shoulder, and Marcel nestled his head in the crook below his collar bone.

**

Lisette didn't sleep, either. She paced around her apartment, agitated and indecisive.

If she stayed, she would probably never see Oliver again. The thought tore at her heart, more than she could have imagined. But if she left with him, it could be years before she saw her family again, if ever.

She was furious that she had to choose, and hot tears burned her eyes. She wiped them away with hard swipes of her fingers.

If she stayed, the Gestapo would surely come knocking, asking questions about Oliver; if she left, would they decide to harass her family, or arrest her father? They had that reputation, and she had no way to know if it were true.

Still, she couldn't force herself to dismiss the notion of running away with Oliver.

She looked around her apartment, knowing she would have to leave almost everything behind. It wasn't the furniture or dishes that concerned her, or her wardrobe of nice clothes—it was all of her books, three long shelves full of them, and the thirty-plus notebooks full of the poems she'd written over the years. She'd never be able to take all of them. And the thought of the Gestapo throwing them into a fire made her blood boil.

And how could she possibly get across the Seine unseen to meet Oliver at Saint Sulpice at four AM? The idea was ludicrous. That was it, that was the decision. She nodded her head in a show of finality to herself, and marched into her bedroom to get undressed.

But as she undressed and lay down, she didn't feel nearly as convinced as she knew she should be. She tossed and turned, stared at the ceiling, tried to count sheep.

When the bells at the Church de la Madeleine chimed three o'clock, her heart began to pound. In her mind she saw Oliver driving away in that police car he'd stolen, and she began to cry. A moment later she was sobbing uncontrollably into her pillow.

48

Sébastien waited in the shelter of the nave door as Gruder approached at three-thirty, not revealing himself until he was certain the captain was alone. When Gruder was five meters away, Sébastien stepped out of the shadow with his pistol drawn.

"Stop right there, captain."

Gruder stopped.

"Raise your shirt, and turn around slowly."

Gruder hesitated, and Sébastien cocked the hammer and repeated his order. Gruder untucked his shirt, but barely raised it above his navel as he began to turn.

Suspicious, Sébastien ran to him as his back was turned, pressed the pistol against the back of his head, and reached his left hand up his shirt. He cursed when he found the small wiretap nestled in the divot of Gruder's sternum, and ripped it out.

Gruder began to turn, but Sébastien brought the butt of his Colt .45 down hard on the side of his head. Gruder crumpled to the ground. Sébastien kneeled where the wiretap lay and smashed it with the butt of the pistol.

**

The idea came to Lisette quite suddenly, in the midst of her despair, and she stopped sobbing and sat up, wide-eyed. Would it work? Did she have any alternative? Nothing came to mind, and this just might work.

She looked at the clock. It was quarter to four. It was now or never.

She was still sniffling when she picked up the telephone and asked the operator to ring a number for her. She mused that it was fortunate she was still only a hair's breath away from weeping again.

There was an echo on the line as it began ringing. She had company, she realized, but knew she couldn't worry about that now. *Let the bastards listen.*

Jean-Louis' voice sounded both sleepy and irritated when he answered. "*Allo?*"

She imagined Oliver driving away from her while she desperately ran after him, and the tears came as if on command. "Oh Jean-Louis!" she croaked. "Oh Jean-Louis, please!"

There was silence on the line for several seconds, and she heard a murmured female voice asking something she couldn't make out.

Jean-Louis' voice had taken on a commanding tone when he finally spoke. "Yes, this is Mr. DuBois. What do you mean by calling my home at this hour? It's nearly—yes—what's wrong?"

She smiled at his theatrics, and thanked God he was playing along. She forced herself to sniffle. "Oh Jean-Louis! It's my friend Adrienne—she is dying."

"What?" his shock sounded genuine.

"There has been an accident," Lisette improvised. "I don't know what happened, she wouldn't say. But she told me she is dying, and she asked me to bring the priest from Saint Sulpice." She paused to cry for a moment. "Oh Jean-Louis! How am I going to fetch the priest? I can't be seen outside, I'll be arrested!"

"Yes, yes, that is terrible," Jean-Louis said, sounding distracted. Lisette pictured his wife standing nearby, listening to his every word and trying to decipher them.

"Jean-Louis you must help me!"

"How?"

"You have a car, Jean-Louis, and your *Service Publique* plates allow you to drive after curfew. Please, Jean-Louis! Please come help me fetch the priest, please."

It was the best lie she could think up, one that Jean-Louis wouldn't likely question, even if he surmised that Adrienne hadn't stepped foot inside a church in more than ten years. Though less than half of all Frenchmen ever attended Mass these days, even on Easter, they all called for the priest when it was time for last rites.

There was a long pause, and she forced herself to keep sniffing instead of holding her breath. She had done her best.

Finally an overly-exasperated sigh came over the line. "Fine, if I must come in, then I will come in. Let it never be said that I am not dedicated to this company." The line clicked off.

Lisette smiled as she ran to her closet to fetch her valise. She had little time to pack.

**

Jacques and Hélène Chastain were awakened by incessant pounding at the front door. Even two stories up, it was enough to rouse them.

Jacques turned on the lamp beside their bed, and glanced in irritation at the clock on the wall. Ten minutes before four in the morning.

The pounding on the door continued as he stepped into the hall, tying the belt of his robe.

"What's going on, Papa?" he heard his son's sleepy voice ask.

"Go back to sleep," he ordered, and marched down the stairs.

The maid was hurrying across the front hall in her robe and slippers as he descended the last flight, her hair in a loose ponytail with stray wisps dangling around her face; he motioned her back with an irritated wave.

"What is the meaning of this?" he demanded of the men in black overcoats who stood on his front stoop. He noticed a pair of police gendarmes behind them on the sidewalk, looking apologetic.

"We are sorry to wake you, sir," one of the men in black said in German-accented French. "A stolen police car was found around the corner, and we are searching the neighborhood for the thieves. They are known terrorists. Have you seen anything out of the ordinary tonight, sir?"

"Of course not," Jacques said. "I would have reported it immediately. Do you know who I am?"

The man's eyes narrowed. "Yes sir, I know exactly who you are. And I am Captain Hochman, of the *Geheime Staatspolizei*, so now you know who I am. I am sure you will not object to us looking around."

Jacques fumed, but stepped aside and allowed the Gestapo men inside. They were followed by the two gendarmes, who posted themselves at his front door and stood staring straight ahead with their hands behind their backs.

"How many people are in the house, sir?" Hochman asked.

"Just my family—my wife, our daughter, our two sons—and the maid."

"No one else?"

"No, the cook has her own home." Jacques' haughtiness didn't fail, even in the face of this armed invasion.

"You will gather them here immediately," Hochman said, and then barked orders in German to his men.

Jacques gathered them into the parlor, and poured himself two fingers of brandy. He downed it, and stood behind the couch with his arms crossed. Hélène sat on the couch with her legs crossed at the ankles, the picture of calm. Whenever one of the children fidgeted, she placed a hand on their arm and they sat still. The maid sat in the rocking chair in the corner, her arms hugging her shoulders, rocking back and forth.

Captain Hochman strode into the parlor several minutes later, mouth pinched but eyes shining with triumph.

"The door of your garage has been broken open, sir," he said.

Jacques' eyes widened. "Oh?"

"What were the contents of the garage?"

Jacques shrugged and exhaled a puff of air in that Parisian manner. "Mostly supplies for the car—wax, towels, a scrub brush for the tires, motor oil—plus tools, a tire iron, things of that nature. There is not much to steal—the bin in the corner is full of charcoal, but aside from that and the tools, there is nothing any thief would want to take."

"And your car, sir? Owing to your position, you were not required to surrender it last summer."

Jacques lifted his chin, and the corners of his mouth rose. "No, we still have our car. A Citroën Traction Avant, 1939."

"It is not there."

Jacques' jaw dropped.

A satisfied smile spread across Hochman's mouth. "Tell me, sir—the stolen police car was found three blocks away, and there are many garages between here and there. At least two of them also still have automobiles that are permitted for *Service Publique*—so why would the thieves, the wanted terrorists, steal your car in particular?"

"I have no idea!" Jacques stammered. Then he found his voice and repeated, "Absolutely no idea."

On the couch, Hélène uncrossed and recrossed her legs, and began unconsciously wringing her hands.

Hochman glanced at her, then back at her husband. "Are you certain?"

Jacques had regained his composure, and raised his chin. "Absolutely certain."

Hochman stared at him for a moment, then reached inside his coat and took out a business card. He handed it to Jacques.

"Call me if your memory decides to come back, Mr. Chastain." He motioned his men toward the door, and marched out with a curt nod.

**

Oliver arrived ten minutes early, and parked in an alley a block from Saint Sulpice. He and Marcel waited in the car in silence.

Only when the church's bells began to chime four o'clock did he nod to Marcel, and the two of them exited the car, closing the doors as quietly as possible.

The sky had cleared, and the street was partially bathed in the pale light of the moon. Oliver looked around carefully before motioning to Marcel. They hurried across the street to the long shadow cast by the tall Gothic spire, and crept around the side of the church to the nave door.

At first he saw no one, but then a shadow moved in the doorway, and he heard Sébastien say, "We have a problem."

The shadow's hand gestured toward the stone path that led along the side of the church, and in the moonlight Oliver saw a man's figure, dressed in the gray uniform of a Wehrmacht officer, sprawled. A dark spot on the side of the man's head contrasted with the light blond of his hair, and Oliver's stomach seemed to drop.

"Is he dead?" he whispered.

"No, he still breathes." Sébastien's tone sounded almost disappointed.

Marcel looked at the man with an odd expression. "Who is that?"

"Collette's German," Sébastien said, the words clipped.

"I thought so."

Then Oliver noticed several pieces of twisted metal inches from the man's side. "What is that?"

"A listening device," Sébastien said. "He was wired."

Oliver stared at Sébastien. "What have you done?"

**

Sébastien explained how he used blackmail to lure Gruder there, and how he'd planned to have the captain drive Oliver and Marcel to Vierzon on the River Cher, so that they would pass through German check-points unquestioned. At Vierzon they could locate a *passeur* who could ferry them across the river to the Unoccupied Zone.

"How could you have trusted him?" Oliver asked, incredulous.

Sébastien stiffened, and felt his face flush. "A similar arrangement has worked well for a friend."

"Please tell us you have a Plan Two!" Oliver said.

"That was only an insurance policy on Plan One. Come with me."

Sébastien reached behind the shrubbery along the church wall and fished out a large brass key. He had specifically waited until Oliver and Marcel arrived to remove it from its hiding spot. He unlocked the nave door and beckoned them into the darkness.

**

Lisette drummed her fingers on the top of her valise as she watched out the door for Jean-Louis' car. Then when the bells of the Church de la Madeleine chimed four o'clock, her heart began to race. *I won't make it in time.*

By the time his maroon Citroën pulled up a few minutes later, her forehead and upper lip were beaded with perspiration. All the better to look upset, she realized.

Jean-Louis's eyes widened in surprise when he saw her lugging her valise, then narrowed in suspicion. "You packed a bag to fetch a priest?"

"In case I have to stay with Adrienne for a day or two."

Jean-Louis seemed to accept this explanation, and took the valise from her. His shoulder dropped, unprepared for the weight of it. "You didn't pack for only a day or two," he said with a scowl as he hefted the valise into the backseat of the car.

Lisette shrugged and waited for him to open her door.

"Thank you, Jean-Louis," She said quietly as he pulled away from the building. "I know we haven't been lovers for several weeks now, but I didn't know who else to call." Then she played it up with false emotion. "Oh Jean-Louis—you do still care!"

"Of course I care," he grunted, not sounding very caring. His eyes stayed on the road, and his foot was heavy on the accelerator. The tires squealed as he rounded a corner out of the Place de la Madeleine. "Detour," he explained. "I'm not driving through the Place de la Concorde, no matter how much more direct it is. We'd be stopped by a German patrol for certain."

"But you have permission to drive," she said.

"I'd rather not have to explain that," he muttered. "It's a hassle." He veered onto the Avenue de l'Opéra and sped toward the Seine.

Lisette glanced at his watch as they crossed at the Pont du Carrousel. It was already ten minutes past four. She took a deep breath to calm her nerves. It was only a short distance now.

He parked across from the front doors of the church a few minutes later, and kept the motor running. "I'll wait here."

"Thank you, Jean-Louis," Lisette said as she exited the car, then hurried around the side of the church toward the nave door, praying that Oliver hadn't left yet.

**

Hochman returned to the Hotel Lutetia at quarter past four o'clock in an irritable mood. Not only had they failed to find the American who had stolen that police captain's car, but there had also been no news over the wireless from that Culture ministry officer, Captain Gruder, who had gone to meet with a *résistant*.

As soon as he stomped through the hotel's door, he marched across the lobby toward the listening office in the back. He didn't bother to knock.

The three Gestapo men looked up from their wireless sets as he stood in the door, dropped their pencils and removed their headsets.

"What news from Gruder?" Hochman demanded without preamble.

"Nothing, captain," the man in the middle said. "There has been some sort of trouble with his wire—there has been only static on that frequency for the last forty minutes."

Hochman's temples pulsed, and his rage exploded. "Why didn't you think to notify me half an hour ago?" He backhanded the man, drawing blood from his lip.

The other two seemed to shrink in their chairs.

Hochman stared them down. "You should have sent someone to Saint Sulpice."

One man's eyes widened in apparent realization, and he managed to speak in a cracked voice. "Captain Hochman, sir? I monitored a telephone call thirty minutes ago, from a young woman in the 8th Arrondissement to a residence in the 10th, asking someone with a *Service Publique* license to drive her to Saint Sulpice. She said she needed to fetch the priest for a dying friend."

Hochman couldn't speak, he was so stunned at their incompetence. His right hand fisted, and he shook it at them.

"Imbeciles!" he shouted as he turned and stormed out of the room.

He shouted to his men resting in the lobby chairs to return to their cars, and they all sped toward the famous medieval church.

**

Soft candlelight danced across the limestone walls of the chapel in patterns of yellow and red from the wicks of dozens of votive candles in red glass in front of a four-foot statue of the Virgin, her arms outstretched and her sympathetic eyes cast down at anyone who knelt before her.

"How did you get a key to Saint Sulpice?" Oliver asked.

Serge looked past the illuminated Virgin toward the red-draped altar on the dais in the sanctuary. "There are many escape routes out of Paris, not just the one I am part of. One starts right here." He looked back at Oliver and Marcel. "Do you know the Way of Saint James?"

Marcel nodded, but Oliver shook his head.

"The Way of Saint James is the old pilgrim route from Paris to the Pyrenees, and on to Santiago de Compostella in Spain. It was the most travelled pilgrimage of the Middle Ages, and the paths can still be followed. Best of all, these paths do not follow modern roads."

Oliver nodded slowly. "So they are out of reach of the Gestapo's cars."

"Exactly. Come with me." Sébastien led them down a corridor behind the altar to a heavy wooden door. Oliver and Marcel followed him inside. It was pitch dark and musty.

Oliver heard the sound of a pull chain, and electric light illuminated a long narrow closet. Along one wall hung many dozens of black shirts with white clerical collars and matching black pants, in every size imaginable.

"Father Bernard's donations to the poor fugitives," Sébastien said. His expression grew philosophic. "War brings out the best in some, and the worst in others; it shows us that good men can be found everywhere—even in the Catholic Church."

"You want us to dress as priests?" Oliver asked, an amused smile slowly spreading across his lips.

Sébastien shrugged. "No one will question a pair of priests walking the pilgrim path."

Marcel's expression had grown stony. He marched to the nearest hook on the wall and began tugging down the clerical garb. "Priests can never be trusted!" He pulled furiously at garments.

Oliver grabbed him by the shoulders and tugged him back. "What are you doing? This is our way out."

Then he saw the look in Marcel's eyes, the tears welling up. He grew embarrassed. He knew Marcel came from a small market town with an old castle an hour's drive east of Paris; and he knew Marcel had left when he was seventeen, that he'd lived on the streets of Paris for weeks before he found a job at Chez Marius and had enough to rent a tiny garret room—as it happened, the garret that Oliver had only just vacated after a year to move into a larger apartment. Beyond that, Marcel had always been reticent.

He pulled Marcel to him and hugged him tightly. "It will be alright. This is our best hope."

After they found clothes in the correct sizes and dressed, Sébastien showed them boxes filled with rosaries, vials of oil and holy water, and purple vestments. "Best to look the part."

When they had finished their outfits, Sébastien handed Oliver a small printed set of instructions for following the pilgrim trail. "Take this as far as Orléans; from there the path veers west toward Tours. Instead, you should head south toward Vierzon. Once there, go to the bar at the inn on the main square on Saturday evening, and someone you know will meet you there."

"Who?" Oliver asked.

"Safest if I don't tell you," Sébastien said. "But you will know him when you see him. He will find a *passeur*, and someone else you know will be waiting for you on the other side of the river."

As they walked back to the chapel in the nave, Oliver asked Sébastien what they should do about Gruder.

"We can prop him up by the nave door. When the priests arrive at seven o'clock, they will care for him—they care for anyone, even a *Boche*."

Loud knocks from the nave door echoed off the limestone walls, and they froze in place.

Then a familiar voice, muffled by the heavy door, sounded in Oliver's ear.

"Oliver! Oliver, are you there?"

A grin spread across Oliver's face as he hurried to the door and yanked it open.

"Oh Oliver, thank God! I saw the soldier lying there and I thought—" Lisette stopped and her mouth dropped open at the sight of his outfit.

Then she began to laugh. She covered her mouth with both hands, but the laughter wouldn't be contained.

"I'm not *that* funny-looking," Oliver said, scowling.

"No, no—it's just, how could you have known? You *couldn't* have, and that's what's so funny." Her laughter broke out again, hard enough that she doubled over and clutched at her stomach.

**

After propping Gruder by the nave door, still unconscious, Sébastien wished them luck and kissed their cheeks, then hurried around the back of the church and disappeared.

They crept along the side of the church and around the front. Jean-Louis' car appeared, and he opened the door and stepped out as they began to hurry across the street.

Suddenly the street was illuminated bright as midday. Oliver turned toward it involuntarily, and was blinded by the spotlight.

"Halt!" a sharp German voice demanded.

They all froze.

The sound of tense conversation in German reached Oliver's ears, two voices that sounded increasingly argumentative.

**

"It's the girl from the phone call," the lieutenant argued. "And she has fetched two priests, just as she said she would."

Hochman wasn't convinced. He stared at the four figures in the street—the young woman with the terrified expression, the two priests staring ahead blankly with their arms raised, and the stocky man in a three-piece suit next to the open door of a Citroën sedan. This certainly didn't match the fugitives he was tracking, but something about the scene didn't fit.

"Everyone keep your hands up," he shouted in French. "One of my men will search you for weapons." He motioned to one of his lieutenants, who hurried forward.

"Now see here," Jean-Louis said, reaching into his jacket. "I have a per—"

He never finished the sentence. The Gestapo man walking toward them whipped out a semi-automatic and fired. Several cracks in the span of two seconds echoed through the narrow street. Five bullets struck Jean-Louis in the shoulder, chest, and abdomen. His body crumpled to the ground, shuddered for a few seconds, and fell still.

Blood spread across the cobblestones like a river in a flood.

49

Lisette screamed. Oliver stared in open-mouthed horror.

Marcel walked calmly to the body, knelt down, and put on the purple vestment. He removed a vial of oil and a rosary, dabbed oil onto Jean-Louis' forehead in the shape of a cross, and began reciting Latin phrases.

Oliver watched him in wonder. When had he learned all of this?

*

Hochman shouted in French to the young priest to stop and stand up. When he did not, Hochman turned to the lieutenant with the semi-automatic and ordered him to shoot.

The lieutenant shook his head and took a step back.

"Shoot him!"

"No sir," the lieutenant replied, still shaking his head and stepping back. "I can't shoot a priest giving last rites! I won't go to Hell."

"Fucking Bavarian," Hochman muttered, and unholstered his pistol. He wouldn't be restrained by superstition. He cocked the hammer and raised it to fire.

A loud crack reverberated from above them, and the side of Hochman's head exploded in a gush of red and gray.

*

It took a couple of seconds for Oliver to comprehend what he saw as he watched Hochman fall, and the other Gestapo men turn toward the church and look toward its roof, guns drawn. When they began to fire aimlessly in the direction the fatal shot had seemed to originate, Oliver's wits came back to him and his thoughts began to move at lightning speed.

He grabbed Lisette by the shoulder. "Quickly!" he said, shoving her into the open car door. As she scooted across the seat he turned toward Marcel, only to see him already on his feet and hurrying to the back door.

In front of them one of the Gestapo men cried out as a fountain of blood erupted from the back of his right shoulder, and his firing arm dangled uselessly. He dropped to his knees, clutching at his shattered shoulder with his left hand.

Oliver wasted no more time getting behind the wheel and grabbing the gear shift. "Get down!" he shouted to Lisette and Marcel, then realized they were both already curled up low on the seats.

The Citroën flew forward with a burst of speed as Oliver slammed on the accelerator, and he plowed into a Gestapo man who tried to hold up his hand and shout "Halt!" The black-suited figure crumpled in half as he flew over the hood of the car, crashed into the windshield, and landed on the cobblestones behind them.

Oliver remembered the first few lines of directions for the Way of Saint James; he turned down the Rue Servandoni and sped away from the church.

**

From a rooftop across the Rue Palatine from the church, Sébastien watched the Citroën speed away with his friends inside.

The three remaining Gestapo men in the street had scattered as the car bore down on them, and Sébastien took this opportunity to slip away from the spot where he'd hidden behind an eave and used the sniper skills he learned during his stint in the French Army. He hurried down the stairs and out a back door. After looking around to make sure that none of the Gestapo men had come this way, he ran off and disappeared into the night.

**

The pilgrim path from Saint Sulpice followed some of the most ancient streets of Paris, some barely wide enough for the car to pass through without breaking off its side mirrors, and beset with sudden changes of direction at random angles. These streets had been built for ox-carts, not automobiles. The slitted blackout covers dimmed the headlights, and sudden turns sprang up as if from nowhere. Oliver drove as fast as he dared, which was only about thirty kilometers per hour.

"Read me the rest of the directions," Oliver instructed Marcel.

"Where are we going?" Lisette asked.

"The pilgrim trail south," Oliver said.

On three occasions the trail crossed one of the wide boulevards that Napoleon III had ordered torn through the labyrinthine streets in an effort to prevent the riots for which the Paris mobs were notorious. Oliver hesitated only briefly at each crossing to glance around, and sped across at no sign of German patrols, losing themselves once more in the maze of ancient streets.

A blue sign on the side of a grimy building read "GENTILLY" in white letters; it was the only announcement that they were crossing into the suburbs, and with no other fanfare they found themselves outside of Paris.

Oliver breathed an audible sigh of relief that there was no German checkpoint at the city limit, and thanked God that the pilgrim trail didn't follow major streets.

The streets widened slightly through gritty working-class neighborhoods, and Oliver pushed on the accelerator to put distance between them and the city. The engine roared, and he prayed that anyone looking out their window at the noise would see a dark

Citroën sedan and assume they were Germans. Everyone knew the Gestapo drove black Citroëns, and with any luck Jean-Louis' maroon sedan would look black in the darkness.

They'd been in the car an hour when they reached the place some thirty kilometers south of Saint Sulpice where the suburbs faded into country fields, and the trail became a dirt path across a barley field, identified by a wooden post with a scallop shell carved at the top.

They abandoned the car without a word and hiked across the fields.

**

Two gendarmes had been lounging against the wall of a building on Rue Bonaparte at four-thirty that morning, smoking cigarettes, bored on the night patrol, when they heard gunshots from the direction of Saint Sulpice. They cursed and stubbed out their cigarettes, then ran toward the sound.

Shouts in German echoed in the narrow streets, but the little square in front of the church was empty save for three bodies lying on the ground. They crept cautiously around the square. They found a fancy Citroën Avant sedan with a *Service Publique* license plate in the shadows beyond the church, the keys still in the ignition; it took only a moment's discussion for them to decide not to call for the Germans, and instead drive the car to their precinct.

It took little investigation to learn that the car was registered to a high-ranking government official in the 16th, and that it had been reported stolen an hour before. Their captain accompanied them as they drove it to his house.

**

Jacques Chastain looked through the contents of the traveler's trunk that had been found in the back of his car. He looked at the photographs, and the young man smiling beside a pretty young woman looked familiar. It took him a few moments to place him—he was a musician at one of those jazz clubs in Montmartre that he and Hélène had visited on occasion.

It wasn't difficult to figure out that he must have been Hélène's lover. Why else would he have come here to steal this car?

"Does this belong to anyone in your family, sir?" the police captain asked.

"Not exactly," Jacques said. "It belongs to my daughter's boyfriend. He knows where I keep the keys, and he must have taken it joy-riding with his friends. I will take care of this. I will tell him how lucky he was not to get arrested."

There was a stack of money in the trunk, U.S. dollars. Jacques was certain the police had already thinned the stack on their own, but he handed them each a twenty-dollar bill. "Thank you for your trouble. I appreciate your discretion."

After they left, Jacques pocketed the rest of the money. These were lean times, after all. Like any French bureaucrat worth his salt, he'd always skimmed off the top—until the last year, when German auditors had made that impossible.

Jacques surmised that this young musician was probably fleeing south, to the Unoccupied Zone. He would keep the trunk for now, and hide it in the garage. There were men he knew in Vichy who could help him locate this young musician, if he were still alive.

Then Jacques might have a use for him.

**

Robert Allard entered his prefecture in the 5th shortly after seven AM, while the night shift was still on duty.

He'd slept little, and was irritated to learn that there was no news concerning any of the *résistants* he had battled last night. The body of Serge Faucheux had been taken to the morgue, but everyone else had disappeared, including the American Oliver Carmichael. Allard seethed, replaying in his mind every moment of his abduction. He would get revenge somehow.

The one moment of pleasure came when he opened the newspaper and saw the story on the second page. He had written the release himself at one AM, and the editor had changed little:

> Captain Robert Allard, Paris Police, tracked down and attempted to arrest a suspected *résistant* about midnight who had earlier attempted to extort police and abduct law-abiding citizens. The *résistant*, identified as Serge Faucheux of the Fifth Arrondissement, was killed in an exchange of gunfire with police. Captain Allard's bravery has been praised by the Prefect of Police.

50

Friday, October 24

It took a day and a half of walking to reach Orléans.

The fields through which the path passed provided little cover this time of year, with the winter wheat still young and green and the barley already harvested. Every few kilometers they passed a hamlet of ten or twelve stone houses with slate roofs clustered around a little stone church. Oliver's chest tightened and his breath grew shallow each time, until they'd left the village well behind.

They had stopped for a few hours late on Thursday to eat and rest at a church in the tiny village of Ste. Therese sur Loir, one of several identified in Father Bernard's instructions as "available to assist pilgrims." The priest there asked no questions, but ushered them quickly inside and gave them a little bread and cheese, then allowed them to sleep in the pews. He woke them a few hours later and sent them on their way.

Oliver's feet ached, and blisters on his heel burned with each step. He noticed Lisette beginning to limp, and he put his arm around her to help steady her.

Marcel said nothing and wouldn't look at them.

Oliver's nerves tensed when they reached Orléans, and he noticed Lisette's posture stiffen. Orléans was a sizable city, and after a while it seemed they were as anonymous here as they were on the streets of Paris. German patrols goose-stepped along the major streets, but the citizens paid them no attention; they attempted to do the same.

From Orléans, the Way of Saint James shifted southwest along the banks of the broad green Loire toward Tours, and reluctantly they abandoned the pilgrim trail with its country paths and instead crossed a bridge over the Loire and took a dirt road south.

Oliver hadn't thought of an explanation for their travels once they'd left the pilgrim path, and he prayed they wouldn't be asked.

They passed sturdy farmers driving horse-drawn carts toward the city, or peasant women carrying baskets on their heads. These would eye the strangers warily, nod and say "Bonjour" as they passed.

Oliver hoped the sight of two priests walking along the road with a young woman didn't seem too strange. But then, these people wouldn't be the type to gossip to strangers, so there was probably little reason to worry.

There was little motorized traffic, a few produce trucks driving north, engines rumbling and belching charcoal smoke. Just once they heard the hum of good engines behind them, and they stepped off the road into the weeds and watched as two black Citroën sedans roared past, Nazi flags flying from the front fenders, the unmistakable uniforms and hats of SS officers inside.

Oliver's gut tightened, and he whispered a little prayer that these men weren't searching for them.

Oliver began to worry they wouldn't reach Vierzon by the next evening. It was ninety kilometers—sixty miles—south of Orléans, and their pace had been steadily slowing. What would happen if they missed their rendezvous?

Then around midafternoon an empty livestock truck driving south stopped ahead of them, and the driver waved his arm out the window. They hurried forward, and the stench of pig manure hit them like a wall.

"Need a ride, Fathers?" the driver asked.

"Yes, thank you," Oliver said, trying hard to imitate a French accent. He could do alright if he only said a few words at a time.

The driver eyed Lisette's legs as she climbed into the cab and slid onto the seat beside him. Oliver slid in beside her, and Marcel scowled as he pressed himself into the tiny remaining space.

"Where to?"

"Vierzon," Oliver replied.

"Me too," the driver said. "I just delivered twenty pigs to some general in Orléans. The *Boche* like their pork." He grumbled the words, and they nodded in agreement.

They rode in silence for an hour, and then a few kilometers outside of Vierzon the driver asked where they wanted to stop. "The Church of Notre Dame," Oliver said, recalling the name from Father Bernard's list.

They drove into the town, and the truck stopped at a corner in the old quarter. "The church is that way, Fathers," he said. They thanked him and got out.

"We're early," Marcel said after the truck drove away.

"We'll get a full night's sleep, and stay out of sight until tomorrow evening when we go to the hotel bar," Oliver said, and motioned for them to follow him into the church.

**

The white-haired priest gave them some bread and cheese and a few raw vegetables. They thanked him quietly and ate in silence. He nodded and said he would come back with bedding.

After they'd eaten, Oliver wandered toward the back of the sanctuary and sat in the farthest pew. He stared up at the crucifix hanging above the altar, brooding.

He'd killed a man. He was almost certain of that, and he couldn't put it from his mind. Sure, the man was going to kill him and those he loved, but still…

He heard his father's voice in his head, telling him that it was justified, that God did not disapprove. Oliver exhaled hard and shook his head. His father always saw things in stark moral contrasts of black and white—the Gestapo were all Nazis, vicious and deadly, and therefore he'd see killing one as a moral thing to do. Oliver himself had never liked the rigid right and wrong, had never been comfortable with its absolutism.

And it brought him no comfort now.

Lisette followed a few moments later and sat beside him. She put her hand on his knee. "You've been awfully quiet." Her voice was not much more than a whisper.

"Yeah," he agreed with a shrug. His body tensed, and she seemed to sense it, pulling her hand back from his knee. She folded her hands in her lap and stared down at them.

Shit! Don't do this again, he scolded himself. *Talk to her, for Christ's sake! Let her in. Don't be an idiot.* "I'm sorry. I just—I just can't get the image out of my head of that man I hit with the car."

She regarded at him for a moment, and he looked away from the intensity of her gaze.

"You did what you had to do, Oliver," she said quietly. "You saved us."

"I know." He leaned forward to put his elbows on his knees, staring at his hands. "But that man had a family in Germany, just like I have a family back in Indiana. He probably had a mother who's inconsolable right now because her baby boy is dead. Maybe he had children, and I left them without a father."

He felt Lisette's hand on his shoulder, felt it rub his back. He looked up at her, and her brown eyes were wet. "I hate this war," she said. "I hate it so much. But you mustn't blame yourself, Oliver."

He nodded. "I know. Thank you."

She kissed him on the cheek, and let her lips linger for a few seconds. "I love you," she whispered in his ear, and then slipped away and left him to sit alone.

**

After they'd bedded down, Oliver found he couldn't sleep. He climbed the stairs of the bell tower, and sat looking out at the roofs of the town. Just to the south, less than a kilometer away, lay the south bank of the River Cher and freedom. He sat there with his elbows on his knees and his chin in his hands, staring.

This was how Marcel found him an hour later.

Oliver smiled, and patted the stone next to him. "Come sit with me. It's a nice view."

Marcel sat, and they stared out in silence for a moment.

"What are your intentions after we get to the Unoccupied Zone?" Marcel finally asked.

"I have to go to Vichy to meet someone. But after that, I'm not sure. Lyon or Marseille, probably."

"I meant, what are your intentions with Lisette? With me?"

"Oh," Oliver said. He'd avoided giving the matter too much thought.

"Well?"

"I'm in love with Lisette. She loves me too. I want to marry her." Oliver felt relieved to say those words out-loud.

Marcel was silent for a moment. "You cannot have us both," he finally said, his voice quiet.

"Yes, I know." Oliver was surprised at how sad that made him, and yet he was glad to have made that decision. He wasn't sure he'd ever be able to explain it.

He heard Marcel take a deep breath and exhale it slowly.

"When we get across the river, I will leave you. I will go with our guides—the ones Sébastien said we would recognize—to Lyon. I can make a new life there. Perhaps I will see you there someday."

"I hope so," Oliver said, as Marcel rose from the step. He watched Marcel's shadow descend the spiral stairs and disappear.

His heart felt heavy.

Saturday, October 25, 1941

Oliver's stomach fluttered while opening the door to the hotel on the square. He saw the open door to the bar on his left, and motioned for Lisette and Marcel to follow him.

The bartender nodded to them as they entered, and said, "Good evening, Fathers."

A short, broad-shouldered figure at the far corner of the bar turned toward them, and Oliver recognized the scruffy tan face immediately.

Franz Lemiel's cheeks dimpled in a broad grin as he took in their clerical garb, and his eyes twinkled. "Greetings, Fathers!" he said in a mischievous tone. "Come, let me buy you a glass of non-sacramental wine."

**

The sun was setting when they left the bar an hour later. The dusk deepened into twilight as they walked east along the river road out of town.

Franz had a noticeable limp, and once they left Vierzon's houses behind, Oliver asked him about it. He saw Franz shrug in the deepening darkness. "I had some trouble getting out of Germany a couple of weeks ago. I don't think I'll go back anymore."

They turned off the road at a narrow path through the meadow, barely visible in the dim light. The path descended gradually, and Franz whispered for them to tread quietly.

Oliver took Lisette's hand.

A line of trees, shadows looming ahead of them, marked the edge of the river. As they approached, Franz held out his arm for them to stop, and made a sound like a quail call. A few seconds later there was an identical response, and Franz motioned them forward.

When they had stepped down over exposed roots to the sandy bank of the river, the light of a kerosene lamp, muted by a thin cloth, showed a boat at the water's edge. When they reached the boat, Oliver noticed that the lamp was held by a skinny youth who didn't look much older than fifteen.

"I was about to give up," an adolescent voice said.

Oliver heard the clinking sound of coins being exchanged, and Franz saying, "We're glad you didn't."

Oliver helped Lisette into the boat, then followed behind. He turned to offer his hand to Marcel, but the young man ignored it and held the side of the boat as he stepped in.

Once Franz had joined them, their unknown *passeur* reached over the side and pulled a rope out of the water. He tugged on it, leaning back with all of his weight, and the boat began to move across the water.

It took two minutes for the boat to cross the river, and Oliver's heart pounded so hard in his ears that he wouldn't have been shocked if the German garrison in Vierzon had heard it from there.

As they entered the shadows cast by the tree-line on the south shore, a gruff older man's voice called out. "Stop pulling Pierre, I've got the boat."

Oliver heard hands grasping the prow and felt a tug as the boat was pulled onto the sand.

"Welcome to the Unoccupied Zone, friends," the gruff voice said, and a hand helped Lisette onto the shore. The men were left to help themselves out.

"Good luck!" the adolescent voice said, and the pair tugged the boat out of the water and into the darkness of the trees.

"Come, this way," Franz's voice said, and Oliver strained to see his shadow as it moved up the bank and between the trees. He reached for Lisette, found her shoulder, and fumbled for her hand.

"We made it!" he whispered in her ear, a shiver going up his spine at the thought.

She squeezed his hand.

They reached an open field, and the faint light of the stars lit their way up a path toward a road. There, a small car waited, a tall figure with light hair lounging against its side. He stood and hurried toward them, his arms outstretched.

"My friends, my old friends, it's so good to see you at long last!" The big figure took them all in a big, warm embrace.

Oliver recognized the voice and the German accent.

"Dolph!"

Thank you for reading Gray Paree! If you enjoyed this book, please tell a friend, update your social media, and/or write a review on Amazon, Goodreads, or other forum.

Questions or comments? Feel free to contact me or sign up for my newsletter at www.garretthutson.com

Also by Garrett Hutson:

In A Safe Town

The Jade Dragon (Death in Shanghai, Book 1)

Assassin's Hood (Death in Shanghai, Book 2)

No Accidental Death (Death in Shanghai, Book 3)

Hidden Among Us (Martin Schuller Spy Catcher, Book 1)

Spy Tango (Martin Schuller Spy Catcher, Book 2)

The Swiss Conspiracy (Martin Schuller Spy Catcher, Book 3)

About the Author

Garrett Hutson writes upmarket mysteries and historical spy fiction. He lives in Indianapolis with his husband, four adorable dogs, two oddball cats, and more fish that you can count. He has one grown daughter. You may contact him at his website, www.garretthutson.com.

Historical Note

This is a work of fiction. All characters, with the exception of a few historical figures noted below, are fictional.

Among the historical figures included in reference only are President Franklin Roosevelt; German chancellor Adolf Hitler; song-writer Cole Porter; singer Edith Piaf; film stars Danielle Darrieux and Louis Jourdan; artist Pablo Picasso; novelist Robert Brasillach; and General Charles De Gaulle.

I try to avoid casting real people as characters, but on occasion it is necessary for the story—some historical figures that appear *briefly* in the narrative include Sylvia Beach (owner of Shakespeare & Company); Ambassador William Bullitt; First Secretary (later *Chargé d'affaires*) Robert Murphy; Alfred Greven, head of Continental Films; film director Christian-Jaque; Dr. Sumner Jackson (American Hospital of Paris); Colonel Horace Fuller, U.S. Military Attaché to France; and Commander Roscoe Hillenkoetter, U.S. Naval Attaché to France.

Most of the events I've written are fictional, products of my imagination—however, I have included some real historical events for context. The invasion and fall of France happened as described here. The Armistice Day protest in November 1940 was a real event, the first overt act of resistance in France, and it was violently suppressed by French police, as described. The student attack on the Rive Gauche bookstore in March 1941 was also a real event, and I have attempted to describe it as it actually happened.

The execution of Jacques Bonsergent in December 1940 for fighting with German soldiers was real, and he was the first French national executed by German occupation authorities. Alfons Moser was the first German assassinated in occupied Paris in August 1941— a surprising fourteen months into the occupation, and he was shot by

Pierre Fabien. After this, the French Communist underground began a terror campaign against Germans in the Occupied Zone.

The period from 1939 to 1941 was an interesting time for American intelligence gathering. Aside from domestic counterintelligence, no formal intelligence organization existed outside of the narrow purview of the Army and Navy. With war now a reality in Europe—albeit a distant reality to most Americans—the U.S. government saw the need to step up its political intelligence gathering, but without any concrete plans. As a result, American embassy and consular staff around the world were given little direction and had to make things up as they went along.

This has left me plenty of room to use my imagination in regards to Frank Dryden's activities in Paris in 1940 and '41. Oliver's assignments are entirely a creation of my imagination, and to my knowledge do not resemble any real events or people. I tried to stay consistent with the general track of U.S. involvement in Europe during the early war years, though, which focused on quietly supporting the Allies against Germany and Italy.

I've endeavored to be as accurate as possible in describing the political and social environment of the story, and the complicated interlocking games of diplomacy and espionage in the first years of World War Two. I have taken only a few liberties, such as when Serge, Sébastien, and Beauxdoin assassinate a German colonel in September 1941. I have found no documentation of any assassinations conducted by non-communist French *résistants*. In writing this scene, I felt that this change was in keeping with the overall spirit of the French Resistance.

I have also taken liberty with the timeline of French film production after the invasion, which in reality was on hiatus until Continental Films began production at the end of 1940. The

Charlemagne film in which Collette is cast in August 1940 is a figment of my imagination, but it fits with the type of propaganda that the German occupation's Office of Culture favored.

The bohemian subculture of Paris is well-documented, though many writers have straight-washed out the prevalent gay and bisexual nature of many Parisian bohemians. While it's no secret that bohemian subcultures around the world challenge established mores, little fiction has focused on the well-documented bisexual subculture of Paris's *Quartier Latin*. While perhaps not as visible to the world at-large as the more routine bohemian flouting of social conventions, the literary and artistic community centered around the *Quartier Latin* was home to many gay and bisexual men and women who were relatively open about their orientation—at least, among themselves. I have attempted to depict them as they would have been in 1940. Throughout the 19th and 20th centuries, Bohemian subcultures tended to accept alternatives to heteronormative sexuality regardless of the attitude of the larger culture, a fact which is not often well-known among cishet people.

That said, French mores in general—and Parisian mores especially—might seem shockingly scandalous to many Anglophone readers. This is especially so with a certain, shall we say, ambivalence to marital fidelity. The Paris love affair has become legendary in literature, and for good reason. When a French politician dies, often the most vexing protocol question is where to seat his mistress. No, I'm not making that up! This is why I felt comfortable writing Oliver's and Lisette's relationships with Hélène and Jean-Louis, respectively.

As always, I have done my best to be as historically accurate as possible, except where noted above. Any errors are mine alone.

Acknowledgements

Contrary to appearances, writing and publishing a novel is never a solitary endeavor. I've worked on this book for eight years, and so I have many people to thank for their contributions.

First, as always, my thanks go to the talented writers in the IndyScribes critique group—Laura VanArondonk Baugh, Stephanie Cain, Stephanie Ferguson, Marcia Kelly, Jim Meeks-Johnson, and Jim Thompson—who patiently read and critiqued many sections of the first and second drafts, and provided excellent feedback. They've had a hand in improving every book I've published, and the stories are better for it. You all are the best!

My friends Jessi Rauh, Anna Langford, and Katie Spina reviewed the first 100 pages of the manuscript when I was first thinking of publishing it, all the way back in 2014. They also recommended Sione Aeschliman, who provided professional editing services for Act I. Her guidance helped me hone the book's message.

My sincere thanks to my beta readers—Brenda Havens, Marcia Kelly, and Hawthorn Mineart—who took the time to read the entire manuscript at various stages, and provided valuable insights and feedback. You all helped to bring out the best in this story, and I can't thank you enough.

Many thanks to Stuart Bache for the incredible cover. It really captures the essence of the story.

And last, but never least, my deepest gratitude, love, and devotion to my husband David Lee. I can't say how much your support means to me. You put up with countless hours during which I immerse myself in my stories. You give me the freedom to live this amazing and sometimes infuriating life of a fiction writer, and you're always supportive through all of its ups and downs. I am incredibly lucky, and I know it. I love you more than words can express.

-Garrett B. Hutson, September 2020